ELDERS AMONG THE ELDERS

As he strode between the tables crowded with neatly dressed youths and hard-eyed gals wearing powder and paint, Longarm's eyes swept across four older gents at one table, all dressed cow, and hence standing out in a sea of Mormon faces. Anywhere else, he'd have breezed on by. Idly wondering if they were Gentiles who knew the local action better than he did, he paused to smile down at them and say, "Evening, gents."

That was when all hell broke loose.

Longarm was already on his feet as the swarthy one on the far side rose to his feet with his .36 Navy Colt Conversion riding low and side-draw. College boys and whores scattered like spattered grease at the report of Longarm's .44-40. He held his fire when he saw his man going down with three more non-Mormons left.

One of the cowboys was sobbing, "Don't shoot me! I'm too young to die and I don't know what the hell got into old Sandy just now!"

Covering the three of them, Longarm fished out his federal badge as he said, "Save it for the Provo P.D. I know who he was. It just came to me as I was shooting the son of a bitch!"

DON'T MISS THESE
ALL-ACTION WESTERN SERIES
FROM THE BERKLEY PUBLISHING GROUP

THE GUNSMITH by J. R. Roberts

Clint Adams was a legend among lawmen, outlaws, and ladies. They called him . . . the Gunsmith.

LONGARM by Tabor Evans

The popular long-running series about Deputy U.S. Marshal Long—his life, his loves, his fight for justice.

SLOCUM by Jake Logan

Today's longest-running action Western. John Slocum rides a deadly trail of hot blood and cold steel.

BUSHWHACKERS by B. J. Lanagan

An action-packed series by the creators of Longarm! The rousing adventures of the most brutal gang of cutthroats ever assembled—Quantrill's Raiders.

DIAMONDBACK by Guy Brewer

Dex Yancey is Diamondback, a Southern gentleman turned con man when his brother cheats him out of the family fortune. Ladies love him. Gamblers hate him. But nobody pulls one over on Dex . . .

WILDGUN by Jack Hanson

The blazing adventures of mountain man Will Barlow—from the creators of Longarm!

TEXAS TRACKER by Tom Calhoun

Meet J. T. Law: the most relentless—and dangerous—manhunter in all Texas. Where sheriffs and posses fail, he's the best man to bring in the most vicious outlaws—for a price.

TABOR EVANS

LONGARM

AND THE BARTERED BRIDES

JOVE BOOKS, NEW YORK

THE BERKLEY PUBLISHING GROUP
Published by the Penguin Group
Penguin Group (USA) Inc.
375 Hudson Street, New York, New York 10014, U.S.A.
Penguin Group (Canada), 10 Alcorn Avenue, Toronto, Ontario, Canada M4V 3B2
(a division of Pearson Penguin Canada Inc.)
Penguin Books Ltd., 80 Strand, London WC2R 0RL, England
Penguin Group Ireland, 25 St. Stephen's Green, Dublin 2, Ireland (a division of Penguin Books, Ltd.)
Penguin Group (Australia), 250 Camberwell Road, Camberwell, Victoria 3124, Australia
(a division of Pearson Australia Group Pty., Ltd.)
Penguin Books India Pvt. Ltd., 11 Community Centre, Panchsheel Park, New Delhi—110 017, India
Penguin Group (NZ), Cnr. Airborne and Rosedale Roads, Albany, Auckland, New Zealand
(a division of Pearson New Zealand, Ltd.)
Penguin Books (South Africa) (pty.) Ltd., 24 Sturdee Avenue, Rosebank Johannesburg, 2196, South
Africa

Penguin Books Ltd., Registered Offices: 80 Strand, London, WC2R 0RL, England

This is a work of fiction. Names, characters, places, and incidents either are the product of the author's imagination or are used fictitiously, and any resemblance to actual persons, living or dead, business establishments, events, or locales is entirely coincidental.

LONGARM AND THE BARTERED BRIDES

A Jove Book / published by arrangement with the author

PRINTING HISTORY
Jove edition / October 2004

Copyright © 2004 by The Berkley Publishing Group.

ISBN: 0-515-13834-7

JOVE®
Jove Books are published by The Berkley Publishing Group,
a division of Penguin Group (USA) Inc.
375 Hudson Street, New York, New York 10014.
JOVE is a registered trademark of Penguin Group (USA) Inc. The "J" design is a trademark belonging to Penguin Group (USA) Inc.

PRINTED IN THE UNITED STATES OF AMERICA

10 9 8 7 6 5 4 3 2 1

Chapter 1

April Fool's Day in and about the usually high and dry city of Denver was, in a word, wet.

The more often tawny open range all around rolled golf-course green to meet the skyline everywhere but due west, where the looming snowcaps of the Front Range were surrendering to the spring thaw to raise usually piddling prairie creeks dangerously high.

One such watercourse wound through Denver to divide the rich from the poor in a fashion one could most often hopscotch across, dry-shod, from sand bar to sand bar. But that morning Cherry Creek had risen as a raging torrent of overcreamed coffee, and so Deputy U.S. Marshal Custis Long of the Denver District Court was on his way to work at the federal building by way of the Larimer Street Bridge, and this in turn was fortunate for Miss Radiant Kinderhook, on her way to her own new job at the bakery on Curtis Street.

For out near the middle of the crowded wrought-iron span, a barefoot boy with cheeks of tan in bib overalls snatched Miss Kinderhook's purse to run like hell as the petite brunette turned in mute horror and tried in vain to let fly the screams she felt inside.

The fleeing purse snatcher bulled his way between two other ladies on their way to work and then all of a sudden his bare feet were sort of waving like the tail fins of two trout on the same hook as one big fist held their owner clear of the sun-silvered planking by the stout bib of his running costume.

Barely lowering the startled youth's bare feet to tiptoe purchase on the splinters, Longarm, as they called him more often west of, say, longitude 100°, took the once-more-

1

fashionable time-worn purse in his free fist as its owner ran back to them, pleading, "That's my purse, good sir! That ruffian you are holding just snatched it from my very grasp!"

Longarm said, "I noticed, ma'am."

As he handed the worn article of black kid leather back to its rightful owner, Longarm asked, "What do you want done with this poor excuse for Jesse James, ma'am?"

The neatly but inexpensively dressed young thing with a hint of something Spanish in her eyes became aware of others all around as she confessed, "I don't know. I'm new here. Out in the Mother Lode country where I grew up, I fear the vigilance committee would hang him from a live oak tree. But he's so young, and there wasn't but two dollars and forty-eight cents in this purse if he'd gotten away with it!"

A voice in the crowd suggested, "Toss him over the rail and let the Lord and the floodwaters decide. No rat who steals from a young gal who counts her money that tight deserves to hang like a man!"

Ignoring the unasked-for advice, Longarm ticked the brim of his coffee-black Stetson to introduce himelf and add that while a purse snatching was hardly a federal offense, he'd be proud to frog march her assailant to the nearest Denver P.D. precint house if she'd care to tag along and press charges.

She said in that case she was Radiant Kinderhook just in from the Mother Lode country by way of the Pueblo de Los Angeles and added in a worried tone, "I dasn't be late for work where they only hired me five mornings ago! Isn't there something else we can do with him, ah, Custis?"

Longarm said he'd try. He shook the purse snatcher the way a rat terrier shakes its prey and growled, "The drought and the great depression of the seventies have run their courses, and things ain't as bad as they were. Are you listening to me, squirt?"

The kid gasped he surely was.

Longarm said, "I know for a fact the Dawson Livery near the freight yards have been looking to hire a strong back and a weak mind to swamp out the stalls and mangers. On my way home from work this evening, if you ain't working there at an honest job, you had best not be anywhere else we might

2

meet in these parts, and my boss sends me off in every fool direction serving writs or executing arrest warrants. Do we understand one another, squirt?"

When the hopefully reformed purse snatcher agreed they did, Longarm let go, and the kid lit out running as most everyone else on the bridge laughed at him.

The petite brunette he'd tried to rob dimpled up at Longarm to ask, "Do you really think he'll apply for that honest job, Custis?"

To which Longarm could only reply, "Not hardly. But we won't see him on this bridge for a spell, and one can only eat an apple or save the world a bite at a time. I'd be proud to see you safely to your place of employment, now, Miss Radiant."

The California girl who'd only been in Colorado a few weeks was about to say she had no need of an armed escort on the streets of downtown Denver. Then she wondered why a girl who'd been in a new town longer would want to say a dumb thing like that to a sober man who strode tall, dark, and handsome in army boots under a tobacco tweed suit with his six-gun discreetly riding his left hip in a cross-draw holster under the tail of his frock coat.

So the end result was Miss Kinderhook arriving for work just a few minutes late after a sit-down ice-cream soda, while Longarm, having to walk much farther, got there just plain late, albeit with a new name and place of work tucked away. He wasn't sure he needed her rooming house address just yet.

As he entered the offices of Marshal William Vail on the second floor of the federal building, old Henry, the young squirt they had playing the typewriter out front, favored Longarm with one of his now-you're-going-to-get-it smirks and simpered, "Marshal Vail said to send you right in as soon as you got in, if you ever got in, and he's got a visiting lawman from out-of-state waiting on you, too!"

Longarm muttered, "Shit!" and ambled on back, fishing out one of his own three-for-a-nickel cheroots in self-defense and lighting up before he opened the door of the smokehouse Billy Vail called his private office. But as he stepped inside, he saw the usually closed and shuttered windows had been

3

opened wide to the raw breezes of an overcast April Fools' Day, and old Billy Vail was seated like a pissed-off Buddha on the far side of his cluttered desk with something missing on or about his bullet head.

Vail snapped, "Get rid of that damn smoke! Toss it out yon window, and don't you dare sit down in that guest chair! He just went down the hall to take a leak. But he'll be right back, and he's not only a Mormon but the kind with an Abe Lincoln beard and an altitude."

Longarm realized what was missing from Billy Vail's face as he got rid of his own far less pungent brand, mildly asking, "Ain't *attitude* the word you were groping for, boss?"

Billy Vail said, "I never grope for words. Every Mormon I've yet to meet has an *attitude*. This one's a captain in the Utah Territorial Police, as they've taken to calling their former Nauvoo Legion. Worse yet, we just got orders from Washington to be *nice* to the stuck-up cuss in spite of his altitude!"

There being but the one forbidden leather chair on his side of the desk, Longarm moved over to rest his butt on the sill of an open window as he asked what a Utah lawman wanted from their Denver District Court.

Vail said, "You. How come you never put anything in an officious report about wangling free passes for Mormon elders and their multiple wives that time you escorted Miss Sarah Bernhardt through Utah for our state department, protecting a national treasure of France?"

Longarm shrugged and said, "Wasn't anything officious about it. I felt it was only common sense, and the divine Sarah agreed with me as soon as I suggested it. Most of the folk buying tickets to her touring show in the railroad towns across Utah Territory were naturally non-Mormon Gentiles, as they call us all. So some church ladies from a sect that forbids alcohol, caffeine, and nicotine were inclined to suspect a whole posse of French actresses of . . . smoking, until anyone with an open mind could see the divine Sarah advertised herself as an *artiste très dramatique* with no hootchy-kootchy spider dances or even dirty words in *French* as she read from this play about an unfortunate French lady. I wasn't able to follow what she was declaiming, but she

4

sure talked in an entertaining way and, anyhow, I invited the sheriff up in Ogden to bring his wives and family to the show, free, and once word got around, the divine Sarah had heaps of Saints, as they prefer to be called, smiling at her and her French actresses like they were from down home. Wasn't anything a lawman had call to report, officious."

Vail said, "I can see how the Salt Lake Temple should have been sort of pleased when you reported those fanatics you tangled with out on the Great Salt Desert were renegades acting crazy without the sanction of what you yourself put down as the Church of Jesus Christ of Latter-day Saints. Didn't your momma never tell you Brigham Young in the flesh organized those Danites or so-called Avenging Angels, for Pete's sake?"

Longarm said, "I doubt either of my parents knew much about Brigham Young and whatever he might or might not have done. He wasn't there to say how he might have felt about those bearded prophets running wild out on the salt flats long after he'd died from that mortified appendix a good many miles away."

Vail grimaced and asked, "You don't buy into the Book of Mormon, do you? Mr. Mark Twain, in spite of being such a humorous cuss, has dismissed the writings of Joseph Smith as the pathetic efforts of an illiterate plagiarist!"

Longarm shrugged and said, "I ain't as well read as Mr. Twain, and I've never managed to read the Book of Mormon all the way through. But the question before the house was whether those fanatics out on those salt flats was operating with the approval of the Salt Lake Temple, and the evidence read they were not. When you find the accused innocent, it ain't required that you attend the same church."

Vail shook his head wearily and said, "Well, don't blame me for the mission coming up, thanks to your uncanny ability to get along with everyone from fucking Apache to clannish Zuni and . . . hold the thought. I hear his high-and-mighty altitude approaching, and ain't it a wonder even a Saint has to take a leak now and again?"

The lean and hungry individual who strode loudly in aboard high-heeled Justins that made him look even taller than Longarm was a few years older and, sure enough, sport-

5

ing an Abe Lincoln beard of rusty barbed wire or mayhaps ginger streaked with gray under a broad-brimmed hat of floppy black felt. The rest of him was dressed as one might well imagine a poor but honest undertaker, save for the way his rusty black wool coat hung open to expose the staghorn grips of two .36-30 Navy Colt Conversions, carried cross-draw as most more-experienced gun toters on either side of the law preferred.

When Billy Vail introduced him as Captain Jubal Burbank, the tall, lean Utah lawman shook hands like a natural man with no expression either way on his craggy, bewhiskered face. Then he sat down in the only guest chair as if presiding over the meeting.

When Vail suggested Burbank fill Longarm in on what was about to transpire, weather permitting, the Mormon almost spat, "Everyone has always known that the *Salt Lake Tribune* is bitterly opposed to the Church of Jesus Christ of Latter-day Saints. Yet they will read the rag back in Washington as if there was any truth to that old saw about there having to be fire wherever some avowed Gentile enemy was smoking his own filthy tobacco!"

Longarm avoided his cigar-puffing superior's eye as he soberly asked what the *Tribune* was accusing its Mormon neighbors of, lately.

Burbank shook his head wearily and told perhaps that banjo clock on the oak-paneled wall, "Lord knows we've *tried* to meet the rest of the country more than halfway since President Young decreed, not long before he died, that the law of the land was the law to be followed on to statehood. The Danites have been disbanded. Multiple marriage has been discouraged by the elders, and there was never a time any woman was forced to marry any man against her own free will!"

Twisting in his seat to almost smile up at Longarm, Burbank went on, "Your interview regarding that so-called runaway bride of our poor old President Young was well recieved clean across Utah Territory when it was picked up by our own local papers!"

Billy Vail groaned. "Oh, Lord, you rescued a runaway bride, and this child never heard about it, old son?"

Longarm chuckled fondly and explained, "Reporter Crawford asked me what I thought of this vaudeville lecture offered down on Larimer by this actress who claims she was dragooned into marrying Brigham Young but escaped his vile embrace on foot across the salt flats the way Miss Eliza got away across the ice in *Uncle Tom's Cabin*. I pointed out the similarity along with the simple fact that the salt flats she was bragging about lie way off to the west, on the far side of the Great Salt Lake for any gal escaping east over the South Pass from Salt Lake City. She had some other holes in her tale of woe, and I had to conclude anybody giving such odd descriptions of the Mormon delta had simply never been paying attention if they'd ever passed through it at all."

Turning back to their visitor from the mysterious lands in question, Longarm asked, "Could we get to the here and now instead of what a swell cuss they think I am around the Salt Lake Temple, Captain?"

Burbank stiffly warned, "I'm not here as a missionary of my own particular faith. I'm here as an official of the territorial government of what you Gentiles persist in calling Utah!"

Longarm made a wry face and insisted, *"Bueno,* suppose you tell me as a paid-up lawman of the Utopia of Deseret, or one of its honeybees, for all I care, what in tarnation your *problem* might be!"

Captain Burbank heaved a vast sigh and said, "The *Salt Lake Tribune* made the accusation, and now other false witnesses have come forth with accusations of their own, may they never be saved!"

Longarm heaved another sigh and said, "Amen. So what have they been accusing your bunch of, this season?"

Burbank bitterly confided, "They say we've been kidnapping Gentile girls and forcing them to marry Mormon elders, of course."

To which Longarm could only reply, "Of course, and why didn't I ever think of that old chestnut?"

Chapter 2

Captain Burbank began, "No women of any sect seem to be missing in the delta or anywhere else in the territory occupied by Saints."

Possibly misunderstanding the thoughtful expression on Marshal Vail's face, the Mormon added rather smugly, "I refer not to one river delta such as that in Egypt but the ribbon of irrigated industry forty thousand Saints had carved from bleak, dry wilderness by the time of the Civil War. Over three hundred miles of irrigation canals watering nearly two hundred thousand acres of city and farm with bishop and apostle, male and female, working side by side like honeybees and—"

"I know what your Mormon delta is. I been out West a while," Billy Vail cut in, adding, "Where are all these women missing from if they ain't missing from your Utopian state of Deseret, and how many missing women are we talking about?"

The Mormon lawman grimaced, not a pretty sight, and said, "We have been asking those very same questions. The venomous *Salt Lake Tribune* has offered neither precise numbers nor proof that even one woman has been abducted at all. They claim in that mealymouthed way our enemies so often attack us that they're only reporting travelers' tales from the Old Spanish Trail.

He cocked a brow at Billy Vail.

The crusty older Gentile nodded his bullet head and said, "Desert wagon trace to Pueblo de Los Angeles you Mormons ran from Salt Lake by joining up with the Spanish trail headed the same ways from Santa Fe. I told you I been out here a spell. So we're jawing about women vanishing from pack or wagon trains going which way?"

Captain Burbank said, "We know for a fact no women bound for the West Coast by way of any Utah settlement have turned up missing, thanks to Western Union with all its uninvited telegraph poles."

Billy Vail said, "Hold on, the late Mr. Cornell cleared the right of way for every pole he ever erected across mostly federal land out our way!"

Burbank sniffed. "Whatever. My point was that no Mormon Bluebeard seems out to abduct Gentile brides as they're passing through parts settled and controlled by the Church of Jesus Christ of Latter-day Saints. If any have been abducted at all they've vanished farther west along the Old Spanish Trail, en route *from* the West Coast and hence outside our jurisdiction, but try and sell that to the venomous *Tribune!*"

Longarm asked, "En route from the West Coast to *where,* Captain?"

Burbank started to dismiss the question with a shrug. But being a lawman and hence following Longarm's drift, he suggested, "Over the Divide to Wyoming, Montana, or here in Colorado, I imagine. Not one female *convert* on her way to join *us* by way of California or Nevada has failed to arrive. The complaints, according to the *Tribune,* have originated from Gentile farmers, stockmen, and miners along the eastern slopes of the Rockies. Wives or wives to be they've sent for have never arrived and they've been writing to their congressmen about that, a lot. That's where you come in, Deputy Long."

Longarm asked how come.

Burbank said, "After the Army of the West insisted it was too busy with the Apache at the moment, a congressional fact-finding expedition was formed back East, consisting of congressional aides of both parties and newspaper reporters chosen for their impartiality. That's what they call a Gentile newspaper that's never confused the late Brigham Young with Hasan bin Sabah: impartial!"

Billy Vail asked, "Has been who?"

Longarm said, "Hasan bin Sabah was that old man of the mountains as led them assassins out of his Persian stronghold of Alamut."

Turning to their Mormon guest he added, not unkindly,

9

"No offense, but I can't follow such drift. Didn't the old man of the mountains lord it over exactly forty thousand followers in a fertile green Garden of Eden surrounded by bleak mountains and parched deserts?"

Burbank snapped, "If you ever get tired of this job, you might apply for a staff position on the *Salt Lake Tribune*! But we were speaking of that unwelcome fact-finding expedition. They've requested Western guides who know the Great Basin and specified an impartial even number of Saints and Gentiles."

The penny dropped. Longarm said, "I can promise you and your temple or, all right, impartial government, I'll call 'em as I see 'em with no ax of my own to grind. Where are we supposed to meet up with the rest of our fool expedition?"

Captain Burbank said, "Cheyenne. Day after tomorrow as their Ogden-bound U.P. Combination pauses there. We'll board their train and get to know them some, in comfort, along the set-down rails west or south to our jumping off point at Provo. The riding stock we'll need to ride on past Utah Lake will be waiting for us there, along with more Utah riders, red and white. Our . . . government has arranged for some of the white Utah riders to be resident Gentiles. Most of the Paiute desert guides probably pray to their Tobats and Shinob. They seem to have a time understanding they're one of the lost tribes of Israel."

Billy Vail muttered, "Must not have read the Book of Mormon, and who says illiteracy is all bad?"

Longarm shot the old fuss a warning look, but His Altitude ignored the thrust to explain, "As we've already assured Washington, our own riders have of course scouted for sign down the Old Spanish Trail beyond the site of that Fancher misunderstanding and outlying mission trading posts beyond. . . ."

Billy Vail dryly observed to Longarm, "That's what they call that Mountain Meadows Massacre, a misunderstanding."

Longarm said, "I wasn't there. But I understand the execution of Elder John D. Lee closed the books on that case as far as the U.S. government was concerned, and being Lee died in front of a firing squad and Brigham Young died natural in the same year of our Lord, 1877, it hardly matters, now, who gave the order to attack that wagon train on the South Smith Trail, earlier."

Turning to a now thinner-lipped Jubal Burbank, Longarm asked how far along the Old Spanish Trail he was prepared to ride.

Burbank grimly replied, "As far as it takes for those Washington dudes to resolve the issue or turn back. We'll cut some sign or we'll fail to cut sign, and if push comes to shove, I've always wanted to have a look at that Pacific Ocean, anyway."

Longarm shot his boss a dirty look but tried to sound like a sport as he said, "Traffic along that desert trail will already be commencing to taper off as another summer waits in the wings. Summers get serious everywhere in the Great Basin, and the Old Spanish Trail crosses some mighty serious parts of the same!"

Vail suggested, "If you cut no sign all the way to Californee, come on back by rail. For by that time it'll be too blamed hot to cross the desert wastes afoot or astride."

Longarm nodded and said, "Might as well go home and start packing, then."

But Billy Vail laughed and said, "Nice try. But didn't you just hear the man say you'll be meeting up with them dudes the day after tomorrow? Report down the hall to Judge Dickerson for courtroom duty, and we can talk some more tomorrow about the day after tomorrow, hear?"

Longarm replied, "Don't beat me, Mr. Simon! I's gwine fast as mah po' ol' foots can shuffle!"

Captain Burbank followed him out to the marble hallway. So Longarm held back the dreadful thing he'd been fixing to say about his boss and asked their visitor where he was staying in Denver, explaining, "I thought when and if I ever get off work here, you might want me to introduce you to this new gal in town."

Jebal Burbank prissed like the clerk typist they'd just passed on the way out as he stiffly replied, "Not hardly! I'm a happily married man, and none of my wives would ever forgive a thing like that!"

Longarm almost asked, "A thing like what?" but decided to content himeself with, "See you later, then," and turned

11

away as the long, lean Mormon headed for the nearby stairwell.

Longarm knew it wasn't fair to blame other Saints for the few who took being a Saint that seriously. There were some things in that Book of Mormon he found as hard to buy as talking snakes, pigs possessed by evil spirits, or the sun holding still in the sky. But old Brigham himself was said to have enjoyed dancing to good music or a good clean drawing room comedy from his own theater box, and Longarm had met up with men of all religious persuasions, including atheism, who worked so hard at being morally superior to everyone that their minds got as dirty as hands might, dredging out a cesspool. So he figured it would have been a waste of his own helpful nature and a needless shock to Miss Radiant Kinderhook, had he insisted on introducing a Utah lawman to a California gal who'd just negotiated his mysterious Old Spanish Trail unscathed.

When he reported to the stern but fair Judge Dickerson in chambers, he was told His Honor wanted six-guns on his own side covering all the ways in and out of the courtroom out front.

It seemed a mad-dog killer said to be a man of his word was on trial for his life while promising to take the judge and jury with him if they presumed to hold no more than four mail car robberies, with twice that many federal murder charges, against him.

So, having promised His Honor neither the soon-to-be-late Shanty O'Shay nor any would-be rescuers were likely to get past him without winning, Longarm found a stool to perch just inside the main front entrance, noting that while the soon-to-be-late defendant was sitting scared and subdued for all his earlier brags, the court stenographer taking any last words down was the blond, pneumatic, and aptly named Miss Bubbles he knew in the biblical sense, and His Honor was usually inclined to call a two-hour adjournment at noon.

But that morning Miss Bubbles seemed to be avoiding his eye, and no gal could manage that so well unless she knew he was sitting there like a big-ass bird, trying to catch either big blue eye, bless 'em both.

Then he caught that new young bailiff in that pretty-boy

12

blue outfit smiling across the courtroom at her, possessive, and had to laugh at the shitty little green-eyed monster popping up out of nowhere to demand both their deaths by slow torture.

He had to laugh because he'd long since learned the hard way how one of the few things wrong with an easy lay was that it was easy for other gents to lay them, too.

So he muttered, "Simmer down, my jealous heart. I know it hardly seems fair, but there's just no way this world could work the way most every man in it would like it to work. The human race would have died out had there ever been a time one man got to screw all the women in his world while no woman ever got to screw anybody else, and I fear Miss Bubbles has put on a few pounds where they don't help a bit. So let's study on something else!"

The soon-to-be-late Shanty O'Shay was turning out to be a letdown as well, just sitting there sweating bullets instead of making a hell-for-leather break for it. Because Longarm knew he'd never have to join that desert expedition down the Old Spanish Trail if he was stuck in Denver for a coroner's inquest, and it always took 'em a few days to clear you when you had to gun an escaping prisoner or better yet some pals out to rescue the same.

But the morning just ground down, interesting to watch as any other gristmill and then, sure enough, His Honor said they'd all get together after two P.M. to wind things up, and Miss Bubbles seemed to be going to have a bite with, or be eaten by, that handsome young bailiff.

So Longarm ambled on over to the nearby Parthenon Saloon, where the suds sold a little steep, but the free lunch counter didn't stint on the deviled eggs or pickled pigs' feet.

They provided thin-sliced but fairly fresh bread at the Parthenon as well. So having paid for his beer, Longarm was building a ham and cheese and deviled eggs on rye sandwich for himself when he was joined by a heftier figure in a derby hat and checkered suit.

Reporter Crawford of the *Denver Post* said, "You're going to dislocate your jaw trying to open wide enough for that invention, Longarm. What's this I hear about Mormons abducting young Christian girls for their already overflowing harems of love slaves?"

Longarm busted the heroic sandwich in two after trying in vain to crocodile it and said, "Mormons consider themselves Christians. That's how come they call themselves the Church of Jesus Christ of Latter-day Saints. Like Moslems, Mormons are allowed more than one wife, but most have enough trouble supporting one. I was told the notion started out when they noticed they had way more she-male converts than male, and the leftover gals were all for it."

He found he could wash some grub down after all and did so before he went on. "I ain't been invited to join such festivities, but since I have noticed they all wear one-piece union suits with strategic holes cut in 'em, and a housewife tends to look like a housewife the whole world over, I can't quite picture orgies as might shock a Roman, and a man who'd force a woman to join in, or senior wives who'd let him, is a stretch."

The reporter demanded, "Then how come we keep picking up such leads on the news wires?"

Longarm said, "Don't know. Aim to find out, Lord willing and it ain't another desert mirage. Have you gents ever followed up on that Spanish galleon prospectors keep reporting at full sail across that white sand sea down New Mexico way?"

Crawford insisted, "*Something* has been happening to the women, all young and pretty, setting out across the desert along the Old Spanish Trail and never making it out the other end!"

Longarm nodded and said, "I recently met a young and pretty woman who says she just got here by way of the Old Spanish Trail. I hadn't heard at the time I first talked to her about those other gals never making it. Now that I have I reckon it's my duty as an investigating peace officer to question her about such matters, in depth, provided that fool Judge Dickerson ever turns me loose this evening!"

14

Chapter 3

Longarm's original offer to introduce a worried Utah lawman to a gal who'd just traveled the Old Spanish Trail had been pure. But thanks to seeds of shocking suggestion planted by such a lofty cuss and the continued cruelty of Miss Bubbles as she sat there the rest of the day taking notes with that Mona Lisa expression of the recently well taken care of, Longarm showed up at that bakery on Curtis Street after work with a bunch of store-bought pussy willow and a bag of butterscotch.

As he'd hoped, her bakery stayed open way later than the federal courts, and he found Radiant Kinderhook waiting on an older woman way too fat already to be stocking up on glazed doughnuts, even if they were on sale. Radiant looked flustered when she saw Longarm standing there so tall, dark, and handsome. But the fat lady was too famished to notice, and as she left Radiant said, "Oh, no, you shouldn't have!" before she ever looked in the bag and, if her job *had* dulled her sweet tooth by that late in the day she was too good a sport to let it show as she told him butterscotch was one of her favorite sweets.

Longarm said, "Nothing else they had looked like as much a change from chocolate, vanilla, or cinnamon, and I didn't want to turn up empty-handed, ma'am."

She blushed and called him an old silly.

He said, "Reason I wanted to see you this evening involves what you said before about coming all the way from California by way of that Old Spanish Trail."

She looked both pained and puzzled until he gallantly assured her, "I might have wanted to take you to supper at Romano's in any case, you being new in town and all. I never meant to imply any natural man could only regard you as a possible material witness."

Another customer came in, this one a gawky teenaged boy who said he was in the market for a birthday cake to surprise his mom. So the puzzled bakery gal had all sorts of questions she couldn't ask piling up inside her pretty little brunette head as she waited on the kid, and Longarm wasn't sure whether that was her reason or whether she was just a nice gal when the kid allowed the cake he liked best cost a tad more than he could afford and Radiant dug out another, just like it, and allowed they could let him have it for less because it was a day old.

After she'd sent the happy squirt on his way with the birthday cake, Radiant asked what he'd meant by Romano's or material witnesses.

He said, "Romano's Restaurant, which ain't far, is one of them Eye-talian spaghetti joints. You've et spaghetti, right?"

She reminded him she was new in town.

He said, "Spaghetti is fancy noodles served under a spicy sauce with meatballs and this dry wine they call Dago red. We can speak of other matters as we dine. When were you fixing to close?"

She said, "Less than half an hour," then protested, "I could never sup in a real restaurant in the clothes I'm wearing right now! I have to put this sweet spray of pussy willow in a vase as well. So I fear I must insist you take me home to freshen up and put on some suitable evening wear before you take me to supper in a *restaurant!*"

Longarm said he understood, wishing he didn't. A new gal in town who didn't aim to show off her supper date at her rooming house was by definition not a new gal in town.

It got worse. An old geezer and his visiting grandson came in for some doughnuts, and when the old geezer recognized Longarm and wanted his snot-nosed grandson to shake hands with Denver's answer to Wild Bill and Buffalo Bill combined, Radiant's big blue eyes got even bigger as her supper date tried to be a modest sport about it.

A few minutes later, as he was walking her home in the gathering dusk, Radiant said she hadn't known he was *that* Deputy Long, great day in the morning.

Longarm tried to change the subject by questioning her earlier than planned about the close to six weeks she'd spent along the Old Spanish Trail that very spring.

To do so he had to fill her in on the complaints that fact-finding expedition out of Washington aimed to find out about. It took him to within sight of the Larimer Street Bridge, talking terse.

As they crossed the same, with Cherry Creek raging faster after a whole day of snowmelt up its ass, Radiant confided that her own long days aboard a Spanish riding mule, side-saddle, in the company of an organized wagon train, had been mostly pure tedium punctuated by stretches of more interesting scenery. She said her party had mostly made camp by wood and water where they could, bedded down cold and dry where they couldn't, and enjoyed more luxurious trail breaks at widely scattered trading posts or the few friendly pueblo Indian or Mex settlements to be found. She said they'd met up with shy Digger Indians who'd run off on foot through the low chaparral. But nobody they'd met along the way for such a considerable way had acted menacing.

She added, "There was this one sort of flash thing riding with us. Said her name was Ruby. Said she was one of those mail-order brides on her way to marry up with a mining man in Virginia City, Montana. Said she'd never yet laid eyes on her intended, but he'd writ kind letters and sent her a tintype of a not bad looking man of around forty. Ruby didn't want to talk to me anymore after I pointed out they haven't been taking studio tintypes for some years, now. Can you see yourself riding all that far to marry up with a man you've never met, even if he sent a recent photograph?"

Longarm said, "Not hardly. Not even if he was a she. But now we do have you, a proper-looking young lady, no offense, and a flashy gal advertising herself as available by mail order and . . . nobody along the way even got forward with you, Miss Radiant?"

She dimpled and didn't seem too upset as she confessed, "Oh, heavens, a girl wonders whether there's something nasty in her hair when a day goes by without any man getting forward with her. But you are speaking of men getting forward in a *spooky* way, right?"

Longarm said, "That's about the size of it. Setting aside the usual trailside flirting, might you or this Miss Ruby have met up with . . . let's say more insistent advances as you passed through Mormon country?"

They'd crossed the bridge, and he idly wondered where they were headed along an unlit, cinder-paved path on the unfashionable side of Cherry Creek as she confided after some thought, "As a matter of fact, Mormon men seem more standoffish than most, considering they're harem masters and big fibbers."

Longarm asked what made her say that.

She replied, "I read in the papers how the Utah Mormons claim to have outlawed having more than one wife. Yet we passed more than one homestead where more than one lady allowed quite openly they were married up with the same dirty old man!"

Longarm explained, "Let's be fair and study on that, Miss Radiant. Back in the thirties the Prophet Joesph, or some said it was Brigham Young, I wasn't there, had this revelation that it was jake with the Lord to have more than one wife as long as both ladies went along with the notion. Then, leaving aside whether the notion was more or less moral than say the Prince of Wales having one understanding wife and a corporal's squad of royal mistresses, the Mormon approach to such matters stirred up more trouble for them than any-thing in their Book of Mormon and, like all Good Books, there's heaps of other notions a skeptic might question. Where are we headed, ma'am? I don't recall any rooming houses for working girls down this lane."

She asked, "Who said I roomed with other girls? I've hired my very own 'dobe on the far side of those lights ahead. You were telling me why those two-faced Mormons weren't lying when they said they'd outlawed polygamy."

Longarm said, "They have and they haven't. Just before he died, old Brigham Young, having noticed how much trou-ble those earlier revelations had caused him and his follow-ers, had another revelation that since a good Mormon was a law-abiding man, the time had come to obey the law of the land and apply for full statehood."

He saw, now, the lights ahead were the crossroad bodega

18

and Mexican *herrería* or smithy he'd expected and continued, "The Church of Jesus Christ of Latter-day Saints no longer performs multiple marriages, or they don't in any of the main settlements of Utah Territory, leastways. But after that, things get more complexicated. After his own revelation, Brigham Young left seventeen widows to grieve for him. Other elders as ain't died yet have as many or more wives, some of them getting on in years, and whilst it's one thing for the Prince of Wales to just tell his butler not to show an aging mistress in, it would hardly be saintly to dismiss a lawfully wedded wife and her kids to fend for themselves. So what they have right now is a state of *discouraged* polygamy. Mormons who already have more than one wife get to keep 'em, but they're not to marry up with any more, see?"

Longarm was trying not to tense up as they approached the puddle of lamplight where half a dozen Mex males of all ages lounged as if with nowhere better to be at that hour. Longarm was known on both sides of Cherry Creek, locally, but the gal he was walking home through a tough Mex neck of the woods might not be the only one new in town.

The rules were simpler and engraved in stone to Spanish speakers of the working classes: When you saw a woman you weren't related to in the company of a man you didn't know, you didn't say one word unless you were looking for a serious fight.

But as he and Radiant got close enough to matter, as if she, too, could sense the tension in the air as the two of them passed, the petite brunette nodded graciously and murmured, *"Buenas noches, caballeros."*

At which point the tension evaporated in a shy, quiet, collective murmur of *"Buenas noches, Señorita Kinderhook,"* and Longarm waited until they'd passed on into the shadows again to ask, *"Como se va tu casa?"*

She laughed lightly and replied, *"Cerca de aqui,* and I told you I grew up in California. How else did you think I wangled my own place down this way at a price I could afford? Speaking a little Spanish was a help along that Old Spanish Trail as well. More people along it speak Spanish than English until you get well up the Virgin River."

19

Longarm didn't argue about that. He'd been down that way. But as if she misunderstood his silence, she sighed and said, "All right, one of my California grandmothers was a greaser, if you must know!"

Longarm replied in an easier tone, "Mine wasn't. Had to learn some Spanish the hard way, and I can't speak for any elders farther back than, say, a dozen generations, by which time we're bragging on over a thousand seperate and distinct ancestors and Lord only knows whether all of them or even most of them were white Anglo Saxons. So I don't worry about such brags. I figure if it matters, we'll just have to wait in hopes of our knowing more about it farther along, like that old church song goes."

She led him through a weathered picket fence to a 'dobe roofed with corrigated elephant iron. He saw she hadn't locked the door. It was a neighborhood where one didn't have to if they liked you, but no lock made by man was going to keep your shit safe if they didn't.

Radiant struck a match inside and lit a hurricane lamp on a chest of drawers near the door. The interior was plain but well dusted and swept, with the clean odor of a bakery worker who bathed regularly and didn't stint on the lilac water. There wasn't a hint of tobacco odor, and what the hell, they were going out to supper. So he took his hat off and let the cheroot in his vest pocket be.

Radiant waved him to a seat on the chesterfield against a wiped-down 'dobe wall and allowed she meant to serve him a glass of wine after all that walking.

He allowed that sounded swell. As she poured what turned out to be a not bad vintage of *rojo seco* from a Santa Fe winery, Radiant asked how he felt about some Mormon Bluebeard kidnapping girls for a harem *forbidden* by his Salt Lake temple.

Longarm sighed and replied, "I wish you hadn't suggested that. I met up with such free-thinking Mormons out on a sort of island sticking out of the impassible salt flats betwixt the Great Salt Lake and the craggy headwaters of the Humboldt, and you ain't met a religious fanatic until you meet one who considered Joseph and Hiram Smith backsliders!"

She said she was glad she hadn't run into any fanatics on

her way up the trail, wistully added, "Might have made for a more exciting trip if I'd been on the watch for sex fiends, though. Excuse me for a minute as I take a quick dip and change out of my work clothes."

Longarm told her to take her own sweet time and settled back to grit his teeth and just wait out the year or more it always took a woman to gussy up to go to town. Some took less time at it than others, but he had seldom met a woman who could fix her fool hair in the time it took most men to shave, shit, shower, and shine.

So he was pleasantly surprised when, less than twenty minutes later by his pocket watch, Radiant Kinderhook rejoined him, smelling mighty nice, to sit down beside him and confide, "I just don't feel up to such a long walk just to fill my tummy when I've plenty of perfectly good grub out in the kitchen, Custis. Would you mind terribly if I whipped something up for us . . . in a while? To tell the truth, I'm not feeling very hungry, for food, this early. We used to dine late, Spanish-style, where I grew up along the Stanislaus."

He figured that accounted for the way she'd joined him after her bath in that wine-dark kimono with pom-pom slippers on her otherwise bare feet and her long black hair let down. So he rose to peel off his frock coat and unbuckle his gun belt to get comfortable as he allowed he'd et Spanish as late as ten at night in his time.

So Radiant Kinderhook suggested he trim that one lamp as they both got more comfortable and, being a natural man, Longarm strode across the braided rag rug to heed the lady's request.

As the room was plunged into darkness, Longarm asked if that suited her fancy, turning back toward her as he said it.

Then she was in his arms, pressed tight against him from the vest down as she asked in a husky voice if he didn't think they might be even more comortable in the back room.

Not wanting a naked lady in the dark to consider him a sissy, Longarm said the back room sounded swell as he picked her up to carry her off to bed, with her kissing him, French, every step of the way.

21

Chapter 4

When Radiant Kinderhook said she hadn't had any loving since she'd last seen the Pacific Ocean, Longarm had to believe her. Any gal who kept such a trim figure by working hard enough to overcome the temptations of a bakery job had to be, in a word, powerful. And when she failed to break his spine with her petite, shapely legs, she got on top to literally jerk him off again with her whole bounding being until, seeing they were both only human, they'd run out of wind and perforce had to stop and just cuddle a spell.

Having spent enough time in her sweet mouth and between her scrubbed walls to know she didn't smoke or entertain many heavy smokers, Longarm contented himself with just puffing in her ear from time to time as she just had to explain why she'd been acting so wild just now. For all the blushing and shy giggles it sure beat all how tough the average woman found it to just let the man she was fucking at the moment figure out she must have been taught by an expert he didn't really need to know about, somewhere, sometime as didn't matter.

The few gals who'd learned to just smile sneaky when complimented on their screwing abilities were known and admired as Mystery Women with a Past.

Radiant Kinderhook's past had been a gambling man called Ace who'd taken her down the coast with him when he'd been run out of the Mother Lode on false charges, she still seemed to believe. She'd left him when he'd added her trim, sweet torso to the ante and lost it to a grizzled ranchero with uncounted sheep grazing the Santa Monica Range and groves of citrus and olive trees drilled in across the flatlands to the south.

She said the old dear, as she called him, had been a sport about her not wanting to go home with him. Longarm had to agree the old-timer had been more than a good sport when he'd staked his poker winnings to an escape to the northeast along the Old Spanish Trail. But when she got to how she'd started to wonder, by her second week alone in the saddle, whether she might have at least tried the old dear on for size, Longarm changed the subject to the details of her time alone in the saddle. He really wanted to know more about that.

The apparently impulsive brunette with a hint of something Spanish in her eyes said that while she'd heard it was possible to ride such a public right-of-way alone, nobody with a lick of sense tried it. She said that the old dear who'd been such a sport about winning her in a game of chance had introduced her to a wagon master, another older gent called Uncle Zeb Myers. They'd paid Uncle Zeb ten dollars, or just under two cents a mile, and in return she'd been given a place in the strung-out wagon party with mules to ride, assured space at the campfires, and more biscuits and beans washed down by strong joe than she ever wanted to think of again. She said the next time she'd go by rail.

She said that as she'd told him before, the trip had been long, hot, and dusty in spite of them saying that was as cool and damp as it ever got along some stretches of a now well-rutted trail. She said the first two weeks of the six on the trail were the worst. Jumping off from San Bernardino east of the Pueblo de Los Angeles, you followed the occasional Mojave River off across the desert of the same name until it swung off to your right at the dusty trail town of Barstow to die like an agonized earthworm under the hot sun in a bodacious maze of alkali flats. You could wind up in Death Valley if you strayed too far *north* of those alkali flats.

Radiant said some of her party had turned back or never gone on past Barstow. She repesssed a shudder and added, "I was sorry I'd gone on before we ever crossed that infernal Mojave Desert! It was mile after mile of dusty birdcage gravel with distant, cool-looking mountains or the inviting waters of mirage lakes ever retreating as you rode on toward them. Wherever stirrup-high sticky-pricky greasewood wasn't growing, the sticker brush was nastier, save for the harmless but spooky looking old joshua trees spread out to look more like tarred and feathered scarecrows than any natural trees, for heaven's sake!"

Longarm blew in her ear and said, "Mormon converts bound for Deseret by way of the desert after sailing 'round the horn named them sort of tall yuccas after the prophet Joshua, who'd led others, earlier, to a promised land. Things got cooler once you were hauling up that long grade of the Providence Range, though, right?"

She snuggled closer to say, "The desert was high and dry but not as hot. We laid over a weekend at the oasis of Las Vegas, and then we'd made it to the ever-handy water and afternoon shade of the Virgin River valley. The few Mormon sheepherders we met up with that far west were shy but friendly enough. The Shit-Wit Indians got to be a bother as they gathered 'round like begging squirrels at every trail break."

Longarm dryly observed, "I believe those particular Digger Indians call themselves *Shivwitz,* Miss Radiant. They're considered harmless, and you say neither you nor that mail-order bride, Miss Ruby, got any guff from any of the Mormons you met up with?"

She said, "The few we talked with seemed too shy to ask who or what we were. Uncle Zeb knew some wherever we stopped for fodder and water working our way to Provo through ever more settled country. He warned the rest of us not to trade with Mormons he didn't vouch for because a few such folk had been known to skin greenhorns. But he never said a thing about Mormons *kidnapping* anybody, Custis! Don't you think Uncle Zeb would have mentioned it if he'd heard about those missing girls?"

Longarm said, "I mean to ask him when and if we meet along the trail. Might you know if he was a Hebrew Myers or a Scotch Myers? That name is common to both persuasions."

She said she didn't know. She'd taken Uncle Zeb for plain American.

When she asked what difference it made, Longarm replied, "It ain't so important as to guilt or innocence, but my boss likes to ask questions like that. He calls it the process

24

of eliminating, and I do find it a wonder how sometimes you can surely misjudge a book by its cover. You find Irish folk can get downright surly when you mistake the Irish names Cohen or Costello for say Hebrew or Hispanic and, like I said, Myers can be Scotch and so can Mingis. I once witnessed an ugly scene when one fur trapper asked another if that name meant he was some sort of freckle-faced Indian."

He didn't feel it would be polite to add he'd taken her for a prim and proper Anglo shopgirl, likely rooming with others of her ilk. But, as ever, the pleasant surprises she'd sprung on him might help him keep an open mind in the days ahead as he scouted for ogres along that Old Spanish Trail.

So a good time was had by all as she finally got around to serving a late supper in bed with ring-dang-doo dessert and, better yet, when Longarm walked her to work the next morning, nobody snatched her purse on the Larimer Street Bridge, and when they got to her bakery, she didn't want him to kiss her out front and told him it might be best if nobody started walking her home past that bodega night after night as if they had some sort of understanding.

He agreed it might be best for a new gal in town to keep her options open, and they parted friendly, with him idly wondering whether he was supposed to be smiling with relief or feeling used and abused. There was just no way a mortal man could feel he had an exclusive franchise to a world of hot and horny virgins who would always be true to him and him alone.

After a morning on courtroom detail, with Miss Bubbles pouting when he didn't pester her during the breaks in spite of the bailiff on that occasion being fat and bald, Longarm met up with Captain Burbank in the marshal's office at noon.

It was a pain in the ass to hold a sit-down-eat-and-talk with anybody who couldn't even abide the smell of liquor, coffee, tea, or tobacco smoke. The visiting Mormon didn't cotton to Longarm's suggestion about the cafeteria up at that Papist parochial school on Capitol Hill. So in the end they bought hot tamales and soda pop off that old street vendor on the corner of Colfax and Broadway to picnic on the granite steps of the statehouse up the slope. Captain Burbank seemed pleased by the view of the mountains one had from there. Longarm felt no call to brag about the last out-of-towner he'd brought up there to show such sights. She'd said she *really* liked the view.

Burbank found his account of that bakery gal's uneventful ride the length of the Old Spanish Trail mighty interesting and warmed to the Gentile gal's observation that the natives had been friendly.

Longarm left the sassy details about Radiant Kinderhook out, but he did feel obliged to note, "She was not only young and pretty but small and helpless-looking enough to attract purse snatchers in a crowd. A flashier gal in the party called Ruby was known to be available to the highest bidder, and neither gal was traveling tight with an armed escort."

Burbank suggested, "They were traveling with a big party led by an experienced wagon master. I know Zeb Myers. He's all right, for a Jewish Gentile, but known from the Wasach Range to his spread by the wide Pacific as a tough old bird it's best not to trifle with. Killed a man along the Colorado for calling him a Christ killer without it sounding like a josh. Shot a Mojave mule thief another time and dared the entire Mojave Nation to do someting about that."

The grimly smiling Mormon washed down some ham and cheese with his orange soda pop and added, "What the Mojave Nation did about it was to present Uncle Zeb with some mules they'd stolen from somebody else. Would you raid one of *his* wagon trains if you were a white slaver?"

Longarm said, "Reckon I might think twice. Who says I'm a white slaver? I have it from the horse—or whore-monger's mouth that forcing a woman to whore against her will, in a world so filled with willing whores, is a lot of bother made up for the most part by whores who've found religion or religious gals who've always wondered what it might be like to be a whore, against their wills, of course."

Burbank stiffy replied, "I take it you prefer to assume the monster preying on unescorted women miles from civilization has to be a maniac waving his virile member in one hand and the Book of Mormon in the other?"

Longarm said, "I ain't saying what he might be, if he's not a she, until we have more evidence to go on. More than half the Old Spanish Trail, including some mighty wild canyon lands you could hide entire towns in, lie south of the Utah line. Your folk ain't too thick by the sides of said trail past, say, the Cedar Breaks southwest of your Indian mission at Panguitch, and Miss Kinderhook says her party met up with Saints nigh cheek by jowl once they got into . . . Saint-hood. So I'm having a tough time picturing anybody vanishing that close to civilization. I know you only ride for the territorial government, but we both know you'd know it if some elder right in the delta had come down with another revelation."

Burbank graciously conceded, "I wouldn't want this to get around. But we have our rare criminal cases now and again."

Longarm said, "Figured that might be why you needed your own police force. Correct me if I'm wrong, but whether they ordered it or or not, didn't your Salt Lake Temple know about Elder John Dee's massacre of that Fancher party almost as soon as it happened?"

The Mormon snapped, "The Salt Lake Temple never authorized that madness! John Dee offered a full confession clearing anyone higher in authority before he surrendered to the U.S. Army!"

Longarm wearily replied, "Like I told my boss yesterday, that's a literally dead issue. My point is that I doubt we'll find anything sinister along the heavily settled north end of the trail. Far be it from me to accuse you Saints of being angels, but if the mystery had been a sinister Mormon enterprise, it would have stopped as soon as the *Salt Lake Tribune* broke the story and made that accusation. You'd never know it from the way Pinkerton men keep lobbing bombs through windows, but if there is one part of these United States neither Frank nor Jesse might be found, it has to be Clay County, Missouri, where they grew up and haven't robbed or been seen by a soul for some time."

Burbank suddenly shot Longarm a surprisingly boyish grin and asked if he'd go on record with that.

Longarm said, "Not hardly. I'm saying we can likely eliminate any sane and sensible Saints from the game. But, no offense, there's a whole lot of mighty crazy folk out yonder. So I'm only suggesting somebody a whole heap of Mormons don't know must be up to . . . whatever."

They parted friendly. Longarm went back to the federal building, and as luck would have it, Billy Vail had a court order for Longarm to serve out Arvada way, closer to the mountains. So Longarm rode out yonder, had to search some for the cuss they wanted served, and then, seeing it was so close to quitting time and he was out that way, ambled over to the Arvada Orphan Asylum to see if they might need some riot control.

They didn't, but their young head matron, Miss Morgana Floyd, said she'd never meant to imply Longarm was *never* to darken her door again when she'd yelled at him like that. So Longarm gallantly agreed he'd stay for supper, alone in her quarters with her, served by the very same ten- or twelve-year-old Longarm had taken away from that pimp a spell back, speaking of how easy it was to hold any gal to whoredom against her will.

The young but worldy matron, having heard more stories of more wayward gals than most, agreed with Longarm, as he filled her in on stuff out Utah way, that one or more of those missing women would have shown up again had some Mormon elder been forcing them into marriage without chaining them up at night.

Then Morgana suggested, since he had to leave for Utah Territory the next day, she meant to slip into something more comfortable.

And it sure beat all how two petite brunettes who kept in shape with hard work could look so different, without either being ugly.

You could see how swell Morgana Floyd looked at the moment, all over, because her current notion of something more comfortable seemed to be French perfume over stark-ass naked.

Chapter 5

Longarm had started toting a badge under the rough-and-ready Grant administration, when showing up for work halfway sober with your shirt tucked in had been worth an A for effort. Since Rutherford B. Hayes, a lesser general but a way better president, had been elected on a reform platform, Longarm had been ordered to wear a suit and tie over his stovepipe cavalry boots and six-gun while on duty in or about those federal courts he served. But common sense prevailed on field missions, and so he'd packed his tobacco tweed outfit in one of his saddlebags to get on over to the Union Station in jeans and jacket of clean but weathered blue denim, along with the same boots, six-gun, and hat, worn cavalry square with its crown telescoped North Range or Colorado style. As Longarm stood out on the platform with his heavily laden McClellan saddle and Winchester '73 grounded at his booted feet, he saw Captain Burbank hadn't shown yet, with the northbound for Cheyenne and the U.P. Line fixing to back in and roll out most anytime, now.

Lighting a smoke while he had the chance, Longarm muttered as he shook out the waterproof match, "Mebbe the white slavers of the Old Spanish Trail have him, and I won't have to go with him and . . . Shit, how would I ever get out of that piano recital invite I declined this very day?"

A familiar figure with a smaller total stranger was moving his way as the platform crowded more. Neither looked like Captain Burbank.

Reporter Crawford of the *Post* introduced the younger and way, way lankier Miles Hovak as one of their cub reporters. As they shook hands, the older newspaperman explained, "We're sending Miles to join up and cover down that fact-finding expedition out of Washington. You mind if he rides up to Cheyenne with you, Longarm, seeing your objectives are the same?"

Longarm was too polite to point out that writing about missing gals and finding missing gals were hardly the same objectives. He nodded and said, "It's a free country." Then he asked the cub reporter where his own baggage might be.

Crawford explained, "The lucky young cuss is on an expense account, and you'd be doing us a favor we won't forget in your obituary if you see those Mormons don't take cruel advantage of him. Managing editor just decided on us sending someone we could spare to cover the lead that we just got over the wire."

"Is it a deep, dark secret?" asked Longarm.

Crawford said, "Leadville mine owner named Angus MacQueen pissing and moaning about his betrothed, a Miss Flora Davidson, missing somewheres, anywheres, along the Old Spanish Trail. Speaking as a fellow Scot, I feel for yon Angus indeed, for he's out the moving expenses of his betrothed as well as a bonny lassy indeed, according to our Leadville stringer who's seen her sepia-tone."

Longarm said, "Just talked to a gal who paid a wagon master no more than a week's salary for a fair rider, and she allows they treated her right and got her to her railroad ride out of Provo without incident. Did your Leadville stringer wire whereabout along said trail this Flora Davidson was last seen?"

It was the cub reporter, Miles, who piped up, "Barstow, California. Wired she was on her way once she made it that far. She said that was the last place she'd get to wire from before they got on up to Provo."

Longarm thought and decided, "Makes sense. Has her worried mining man checked since with anyone else to see if she even made it back to her traveling companions before they'd hauled on across the Mojave?"

The cub reporter looked confounded.

Longarm said, "Never mind. We'll be in telegraph contact with Denver and Leadville until we jump off from Provo into the same great unknown. Gives me time to consider other questions I might have for old Angus by the time I compose him a night letter."

Captain Burbank and his own baggage showed up, walking fast and just in time as their Burlington Combination backed in from the other way.

Longarm tossed his cheroot out on the tracks to let the train run over it before he introduced the bewhiskered Mormon to the newspapermen.

Burbank said, "Sorry I'm late. Got tied up at the Western Union. Do you know yet another young woman has vanished along that accursed Old Spanish Trail?"

Longarm said, "Flora Davidson. We were just talking about her. We better get aboard."

They did. Taking a Mormon back to the club car made less sense than taking one's maiden aunt to a Larimer Street saloon. For while one's maiden aunt might sip tea at a corner table, gents like Jubal Burbank couldn't. So, parting with Reporter Crawford in the vestibule, Longarm wangled a private compartment from his other pal, Conductor Gus, so the three of them could conduct a private meeting on the subject.

When Miles Hovak asked if they weren't being a tad dramatic, seeing as not one gal had vanished in Colorado, Longarm asked, "How do you know?"

Captain Burbank nodded and said, "That mining man waiting for the last one up in Leadville, Colorado, never said she'd vanished in California, in Nevada, in Utah, in Wyoming, or even in Colorado. Until such time as we find out where she was last seen, she could have been snatched off the streets of *Leadville* for all anyone can prove!"

The kid looked all around and out the grimy glass window as their train moved ever more certainly north through the Burlington Yards. He said, "Brrr! We'd never considered some vast conspiracy extending all the way from here to the Pacific Ocean, and our managing editor's an old hand at the game! He brags that when he was my age, he covered the trial and hangings of Mrs. Surat and those other Lincoln assassins! How come he never thought to ask . . . who are we supposed to ask next, about what?"

The Mormon lawman said, "We ask the Provo & Ogden Line. We question the Union Pacific Line out of Ogden and this Burlington Line out of Cheyenne. But don't get your hopes up, Mr. Hovak. We have already tried in vain to trace a railroad ticket bought by even one of those missing girls, speaking of the process of elimination, and so far we haven't eliminated a single thing!"

Longarm said, "No offense, Captain, but I have. I know Miss Flora Davidson got to Barstow before she vanished. I'm still working on which wagon train she vanished from. I've eliminated wagon trains led by Uncle Zeb Myers because you've told me he's a good old boy, and Uncle Zeb did deliver two unescorted single gals to their destinations safe and sound."

"You suspect some wagon master, rather than a fiendish band of our notorious Mormon Danites?" the Mormon lawman dryly asked with a sort of grudging smile.

Young Hovak asked, "Oh, wow, what's a Danite?"

Longarm shook his head at Burbank to mutter, "Some old boys just never know when to quit when they're ahead. It's too early to accuse anybody serious, but how would you go about abducting anybody riding with a professional wagon master across dangerous country without him being in on it or too careless by half to call himself a professional? Ain't they supposed to take a head count every time they haul on after a trail break?"

Burbank shrugged and said, "I was old enough to be paying attention when we came in by prairie schooner in the fifties and, yes, we did leave two kids and an old lady behind along the way. She said she'd been heeding a call to nature when our riders got back to her. We never found out what happened to the two missing boys. Bears, most likely, Shoshoni would have counted coup on the old woman as well."

Longarm said, "No offense, but you and your folk were greenhorns, and professional wagon masters ain't paid to leave playful kids or shitting adults behind. How many wagon trains might play that same trail in any given greenup, Captain?"

The Mormon lawman thought, shrugged, and decided, "One to, say, four may pass a given dooryard on a given day. So say a hundred to four hundred during the heavy traffic of the cooler hundred days of greenup time. So, good heavens, we've eliminated Uncle Zeb out of a possible four hundred wagon masters!"

Longarm said, "This Chinee sage I read about said the longest walk commences with a single step. But I follow your drift."

Miles Hovak asked, "What's a Danite?"

When the sardonic Mormon just looked pissed, Longarm told the cub reporter, "There ain't no more Danites, officious. Some Saints I know now assure me there never were any. But the story goes they worked a mite like the assassins of Hasan bin Sabah, the old man of the mountain, who had his own troubles with those who wouldn't buy his own version of A-rab scriptures."

"Are you mocking me?" demanded Captain Burbank.

Longarm said, "Calling things as I see 'em. Had more than one shoot-out with self-styled members of your Danites, Nauvoo Legion, Avenging Angels, or whatever they thought they were, well after your Salt Lake Temple declared Brigham Young dead as whatever he might have thought he was doing. I told your current leadership as I told the newspapers at the time that I was satisfied they were just dead lunatics if they were satisfied I hadn't had to gun any paid-up Saints."

"You *are* mocking me!" Captain Burbank declared, rising from his seat to storm out.

Miles Hovak asked, "Were you mocking him?"

Longarm said, "I'd have lit a cheroot to blow smoke in his face if I'd meant to rile him. They ain't all like that, no matter what you may have heard. The late Brigham Young was noted for his sly sense of humor. He could give and take with outsiders by cracking a joke that turned the thrust back on his critic. Gents short on humor and thin of skin think they're being mocked, no matter what you say to them, even if you belong to their congregation."

Then he leaned back and fished out a couple three-for-a-nickel smokes to add, "His misfortune and none of our own if he aims to sulk the rest of the way."

As they lit up, young Hovak observed, "You were going out of your way to avoid offending him with these cheroots, weren't you?"

Longarm shrugged and said, "We live and learn, and if people don't like me, they can leave me alone."

Having nothing of his own to offer about those missing women, and sensing the famous Longarm was too sure of himself to rawhide dudes, Miles Hovak felt less bashful about asking questions, now that they were alone.

Cheerfully confessing he'd been born and raised in the coal and steel country along the upper Ohio, with only a hazy notion which end of a cow pony the shit fell out of, the cub reporter proceeded to ask questions that would have gotten him hit alongside the head as a wiseass mockingbird in many a cow camp.

But Longarm had been back East, where wiseass mockingbirds had laughed at some of his questions. So he was content to pass the time assuring the kid there really was a hot spring called Old Faithful that gushed steaming hot water every now and again, if not on the hour, and there were no such things as hoop snakes, horned jack rabbits, or the infamous side hill runner. But, he warned, there were mousetraps set amid the tall tales. So one had to listen tight when invited to a snipe hunt.

He explained, "There is such a shorebird as a snipe, and to shoot such an elusive critter for the pot rates a shootist as one hell of a sniper, hence the military term. So a dude who sneers there's no such bird as a snipe is risking a serious bar bet."

He took a drag on his cheroot and added, "On the other hand, should a smirksome cuss invite you to hunt snipe with him in tanglewood or on open prairie, with gunny sacks, just tell him the last time you dined on roast snipe and mountain oysters it upset your stomach."

Hovak asked, "Are there really oysters in some mountain streams?"

Longarm said, "Not in the streams. Hanging from bull calves. Mountain oysters are a by-product of castrated steers. They ain't bad. Better than snipe, leastways."

Captain Burbank came back in, smiling sheepishly, and as he sat back down he said, "I was out of line, and I'm sorry, Longarm. I confess I'd forgotten that interview you gave defending President Young from the charges of that adventuress. But some of you people make me so mad . . ."

Longarm accepted the gracious concession but went on smoking without comment. They both understood he'd grown weary of walking on eggs as if they were in some Rome built by disapproving Saints instead of, when you thought about it, aboard a smoking car in Colorado.

The trouble with the run from Denver up to Cheyenne and the Union Pacific, or Uncle Pete as it was locally known, was that the trip took long enough to be tedious while it was short enough to make starting a romance in the club car or even opening a good book like, say, *Ben Hur*, hardly worth the effort.

Longarm refrained from lighting up a second cheroot after he smoked his first one all the way down. After that they talked in circles about how little they really knew yet, and then they finally rolled on into Cheyenne, where things turned out even more tedious than expected.

The plan had been for Longarm and Captain Burbank to beat that bunch from Washington in by half an hour, wait for them in the depot, and overnight with everybody at the Mountain Vista Hotel while they all got to know one another some before forging on over the divide by rail.

But there was a wire waiting for them in the care of Uncle Pete. It said the big pooh-bahs in charge of the fact-finding expedition had wangled a section of private cars, set up like a rolling hotel with its own kitchen and dining car, for God's sake, and they were supposed to wait for its arrival around the mighty awkward hour of ten P.M.

Longarm was too polite to leave anybody in the waiting room while he went over to Hoffmann's, and there was no sense pestering Beverly the waitress there in the depot if he'd only have to kiss her farewell before ten. So he toughed it out in the waiting room with Burbank and Hovak until that son of a bitching special section rolled in well after ten, dad blast it.

Then the three of them got aboard, and all was forgiven as their hotel on wheels rolled on west for the gangplank pass over the Laramies.

Chapter 6

They had to get aboard fast because the special combination of four private Pullman cars had been coupled to the caboose of a long, California-bound highball freight that only stopped at Cheyenne for steam water. The brakeman in the caboose ahead was in command of the whole shebang, of course. But the combination was presided over by a sort of combined butler and conductor known only by his last name, which was Merryweather, assisted by an even snootier old gent of the Ethiopian persuasion called Caligula, who appeared to have no last name. A younger, just plain colored porter called Mason took charge of Longarm's saddle and Captain Burbank's Gladstone bag to lead the way, cheerfully explaining as he did so how the baggage compartment and crew's quarters rode up front, followed by the sleeping car, then the lounge and meeting-holding car, followed by the dining car with its galley. Anyone could see the layout was convenient. Mason confided that when they were not traipsing fact-finding committees around, they were the sort of private land yacht for a New England rich kid with textile mills and senatorial ambitions. He'd loaned a toy he wasn't using to a congressional pal who wanted to know what those infernal Mormons were up to now.

Captain Burbank didn't let his feelings show. Longarm suspected he was getting used to the water away from his own froggy pond. That was likely the reason they said travel broadened a body's mind.

They were each dealt a small but posh private compartment. Mason said most of the others had turned in early after a swamping meal atop their long day of staring out at gently rolling or dead flat prairie. But he added that the expedition

36

leaders were sitting up late in the lounge car and wanted to talk to the two lawmen, once they settled in.

Alone for the moment in his mahogany-lined jewel box with the train already swaying some as it picked up speed, Longarm split the difference by hauling on the tweed pants and donning a fresh shirt and shoestring tie from his saddle-bags. Sensing a six-gun might seem needlessly dramatic and knowing his double derringer rode in its usual vest pocket as he put on the same, Longarm figured that was sissy enough for Washington dudes in for-Chrissake-Wyoming and hung his gun belt and Stetson near the head of his al-ready made-up berth, which served as plush seating in the daytime.

When he got back to the lounge car, he found the already besuited Burbank and Hovak had beaten him. Young Hovak was seated discreetly at the far end with a highball in his hand. The Mormon sat empty-handed, of course, trying to ignore the cigar smoke escaping like teakettle steam from Special Investigator Hudson Livermore as he introduced himself. He was a man of about thirty-five trying to dig an early grave for himself with self-indulgence and hence al-ready fixing to burst out of his right ridiculous outfit.

Longarm found the expedition leader's beaded and fringed white deerskin shirt ridiculous, not only for how silly it looked on a fat man, but because the Ojibwa beadwork clearly stated he was a virgin looking for men who could count coup. Their only hope was that few if any of the In-dians west of the Divide read Ojibwa beadwork.

A younger cuss in sensible broadcloth, looking more shy and greenhorn than Cub Reporter Hovak, yonder, was intro-duced as Livermore's *segundo,* Congressional Aide Brett Garwood. He wasn't blowing smoke at a Mormon guest and shook more manly than he looked.

The two women present, speaking of contrasting looks, were introduced as twenty-year-old Dawn Atwell, stenogra-pher to either the boss or his assistant, and a rough-and-ready newspaper gal Longarm had met and been interviewed by before, Miss Cassandra La Belle of the *New York Sun.* All three names were surely bullshit. She bylined her stories as no more than Cassandra, that Greek prophetess nobody ever

37

believed until it was too late. You had to take La Belle with a grain of salt, albeit she'd no doubt been younger and prettier, or younger, leastways, when she'd covered Sherman's army marching through Georgia and, some said, through Cassandra La Belle.

Others who liked her no more implied old Cass liked young gals more than old soldiers. The results, either way, were shooting for pleasingly plump of a certain age with more powder and paint than you usually saw off the wicked stage, and her upswept hair, whatever color it might have started out, touched up a lot with the help of a henna bottle.

Longarm had walked in as Captain Burbank was winding up about Flora Davidson wiring her beloved from Barstow. But Livermore wanted Longarm to track over the same ground.

Sitting down between young Garwood and the older reporter gal, he conceded he had nothing to add to the Mormon's account. He said he wouldn't know Angus MacQueen or his betrothed, Flora Davidson, if they walked in from the dining car and added, "Wasn't there when she wired him from Barstow. Can't say for certain she went on from there."

Miles Hovak piped up, "I can. She must have. I understand you could throw a snowball from one side of Barstow to the other if it ever snowed there, and there wasn't a San Bernardino—bound party she could have gone back with for a full forty-eight hours."

"Who says so?" asked Special Investigator Livermore.

The cub reporter replied, "One of the telegraphers at Barstow is a stringer."

He turned to the ladies to explain, "A stringer is a part-time freelance reporter who sends in news items in hopes of being paid space rates if the paper runs his lead or tip."

Cassandra La Belle said, "How fascinating! Have you been a newspaperman long, young man?"

Longarm said, "Long enough if he knows anything, no offense. Go on with what that stringer wired in, Miles."

The cub reporter said, "When the story broke, the *Post* naturally sent out an all-points invitation to all stringers anywhere in this land of opportunity. Before I left the press room this afternoon, I could have told you our man in Barstow asked all around town, such town as there is there, and no-body in Barstow had seen any strange women doing anything their side of the three-hundred-and-sixty-degree horizon. So unless she went on with her party, where was she?"

Captain Burbank said, "I told you earlier I'd been on the wire this afternoon myself. Everything Reporter Hovak just said accords with what I got from another source, a member of my church selling trail provisions in Barstow."

Noting some thoughtful exchanged glances, the Mormon explained, "For some time many of our mostly European converts have been arriving in California by sea to travel overland to Deseret, I mean Utah Territory, mostly from the southern ports of California. As I was saying, our own man in Barstow knows nothing about this missing Gentile bride but confirms what Reporter Hovak just said about her not being in town after her party went on. Better yet, he was able to furnish me the name of her own wagon master, a known quality called Buckskin Jacobs. He seems to be somewhere out along some desert trail at the moment, but like Uncle Zeb Myers, he is a long-established wagon master who's never lost any of *our* girls along the way!"

Longarm said, "That's two names I'll want to have a word with when and if we meet up. If Flora Davidson left Barstow with him, she must have gone missing farther along, like the old song says. She still had five or more weeks on the trail ahead of her when she wired from Barstow."

Cassandra La Belle asked, "Why was that the last place she could have wired from, if you can wire stringers in Barstow from Denver?"

Longarm said, "Modern wonders. The telegraph wires can run all over. So when her party got to the last chance water at Barstow, she'd reached the end of that branch of the Western Union network. Her wire to Leadville would have been routed back to San Bernardino and from there likely up the coast to Frisco and the cross-country long-line poles we've been whipping by a spell. Another branch line runs south along the mountains from Cheyenne to El Paso, with twigs to mountain towns all along its main trunk and—"

"I'm sorry I asked!" Cassandra cut in.

Longarm relentlessly explained, "There's naturally

another such north-south trunk branching off at Ogden to wind up south of Provo. But there ain't no direct telegraph connections across the heart of the shrinking but still considerable great American desert."

Chief Investigator Livermore yawned like a beached walrus and said, "There's nobody we can wire from this moving car tonight. How long do you think it should take us to get to Provo, Captain Burbank?"

The Mormon said simply, "I don't know. Based on past experience, this combination ought to drop us off in the Ogden Yards around eight in the morning. After that, it's anyone's guess how long this section may wait on a siding for a southbound engine. Once we're under way again, it should take no more than three hours to reach the end of the line."

"Then what?" asked Cassandra dubiously.

The Mormon favored her with a frosty smile and said, "We get out and walk, or actually, in point of fact, we'll spend some time preparing for some serious riding, and it will depend on when we get there when we move out. We'll be meeting experienced trail hands, red and white, as well as some other territorial police. We won't move out in the heat of the day, even at this time of the year, when we don't have to."

The ash-blond Dawn Atwell, who'd been silent up until then, asked in a pensive tone why they'd be riding with a police escort.

Burbank followed her drift. He read the *Salt Lake Tribune* to stay abreast of the rumors. He said, "They'll be riding with you to protect you, ma'am, not to keep you from escaping with your virtue intact. If I had anything to say about this, there'd be no ladies coming along with us. We *are* trying to find out what happened to at least nineteen other ladies, and we're still counting."

He let that sink in and grimly added, "We only have reports on those missing women who've been *reported* missing. There could have been others—any number of others—and you don't want anybody guarding you?"

She murmured, "Oh," and fell into pensive silence again.

The fat Livermore rose grandly, like an Indian chief in the market for a wife, and said, "We've commenced to talk in circles. People do that when they're overtired. I suggest we all turn in and sleep on the little we know for now."

Longarm got up when Burbank and Hovak did. Brett Garwood allowed he had some notes he wanted Miss Atwell to take down for him. Cassandra La Belle shot Longarm an amused look as she, too, rose rather grandly in her rust-red summer-weight frock.

His Fatness in white deerskin got to the sliding door to the next car first but didn't hold it open as he marched through like a monarch on his way to his chambers. So Longarm grabbed the brass latch as the deck lurched under them to swing it shut.

Once he had, of course, he was stuck with it while Burbank and Hovak passed through, albeit the kid earned a point by offering. Then, as Longarm waved Cassandra La Belle of the *New York Sun* on through, she stopped to murmur with a glance to their rear, "Got any dictation for me, sailor?"

Longarm smiled wistfully and tried in vain to console himself with the observation that Dawn Atwell seemed a tad young, and then he had to allow she was a fair actress, too, if that shorthand book she'd just produced meant toad squat.

Following the older and broader Cassandra along the swaying corridor of their sleeping car, she swayed nice for a gal who'd marched through Georgia with Sherman when he'd been a rookie who only shaved every other day. Longarm idly wondered if it was remotely possible young Garwood really had something other than Dawn Atwell's figure to figure out.

When he got to his own compartment, he naturally stopped and bade the big henna-rinsed newspaper gal good night. She paused and neither spoke nor turned as she watched the distant door of Miles Hovak slide shut. Then she turned and whispered, "Custis, we have to talk!"

Lest somebody else come along and catch him lollygagging like a moon calf with her in the swaying corridor, Longarm slid his compartment door to usher old Cassandra inside. It was light enough to see by without striking a light, thanks to the full moon outside. But since he'd left the door open, he felt it best to thumbnail a match head and set the wall sconce above the built-in sink aglow as the newspaper gal set her ample foundations on the made-up berth by the window.

Longarm remained standing, knowing if he made mention of the fifth of Maryland rye in his saddlebag there was no telling where things might go from there, and he hadn't seen half the other fact-finders in this very Pullman car yet.

He asked politely what she wanted to talk about. She told him to shut the door. So he did, remaining on his feet as she said, "This is all one big whitewash, arranged by friends of Brigham Young amongst Western members of Congress!"

Longarm soberly assured her, "Brigham Young, say what we may about him, died back in '77 and left his considerable legacy, say what we may about it, to younger and . . . let's say more diplomatic leadership. But after that, if the truth be known, Utah Territory rates no representation in Congress, and the powers that be in other Western states or territories regard the Latter-day Saints with the same warm regard the czar of all the Russians is said to hold toward his subjects of the Hebrew persuasion."

She demanded, "Then why is this expedition under the command of a fat buffoon who thinks he's Daniel Boone, if it's meant to find facts that are sure to embarrass those Mormon sex fiends?"

Longarm didn't answer as all hell seemed to cut loose outside. As the last of five gunshots echoed away above the rumble of their steel-on-steel wheels, Longarm snatched his gun belt from its hook and told her, "Stay right where you are, Miss Cassandra! That sounded like a .45 aboard this very train, and I'd best go see!"

Out in the corridor, he slid his door shut as, up forward, Captain Burbank was yelling, "All you people get back in your own quarters and stay there in the name of the law!"

Longarm caught up with Burbank and two others with drawn six-guns who identified themselves as deputies from Washington. Longarm asked if anyone there at the far end of the sleeping car had any notion what was going on.

One of the Washington deputies said he was sure the shots had been fired in the next car forward, adding, "Only way to find out for sure involves crossing those two open platforms and exposing one's flesh and bone to somebody with a gun on the far side of that next car's sliding door!"

Longarm sighed and said, "Well, we all got to go sometime. So I reckon I'll go first."

Chapter 7

Nobody on Longarm's side seemed about to argue. Before he made his move across the suddenly wider-than-ever field of fire, he reviewed an earlier and less tense inspection of a similar Pullman product.

He knew the third of the forward car meant for baggage and storage would be at the less-convenient forward end, with the crew quartered along a corridor similar if less posh to the car behind him and about a quarter of the car, the part he had to get through first, an open salon or lounge for off-duty help.

He took a deep breath, knowing your legs were a tad stronger as you were breathing out, and made it across the gap betwixt cars, and had the far door sliding open as he yelled, "Drop that gun and reach for the stars!" as he moved in low and crabbed to one side in the dimly lit interior.

Nobody shot him. There was nobody there, until the colored *segundo,* Caligula, appeared in the far archway in his pants and undershirt to gravely announce, "I'm not armed, sir. The shots you just heard were fired by our Mason, and he's run foreward to barricade himself in the baggage compartment."

Lowering the muzzle of his .44-40 to a more polite angle, Longarm asked what all the shooting had been about as he stepped inside, aware of the other lawmen following him as if walking on eggs.

Caligula gravely replied, "Mason just killed Mr. Merryweather. Follow me, gentlemen, and I'll show you."

Caligula did. Their majordomo, Merryweather, lay spread out naked as if in expectation of the autopsy he had coming at some handy county seat. His private compartment reeked of sloe gin. Longarm had wondered earlier, as they'd boarded, whether the older man had a head cold or a drinker's nose. Merrywheather had lost a lot of blood as well as even more dignity, thanks to the cluster of bullet holes in his pale, puffy torso. He had a full erection, indicating at least one spine shot, and what he had waving in the lamplight as the deck swayed under them was stained with shit.

There was no way the most determined sodomist could shove it up his own ass. So Longarm quietly asked Caligula, "How long had he been buggering the boy?"

Caligula replied, "That's not for me to say, sir. I was never consulted in the matter."

One of the Washington deputies marveled, "With any luck, the nigger will pay on a federal gallows instead of a streetlamp. For he murdered a white man *interstate!*"

Longarm quietly suggested, "We're supposed to be law-men, not a judge and jury." Then he asked, "You say he's up in the baggage compartment, now, Caligula?"

"Bare ass, save for Mr. Merrywheather's cavalry pistol, sir," the older man replied, adding, "As he ran off, he yelled he'd reloaded, and when he referred to our mothers, he never said 'Mother dear.' "

Longarm said, "I'd better go have a talk with him. Could you see if you could find his uniform jacket and, above all, his pants?"

Caligula said he'd try. Longarm moved on up the corridor, nodding reassuringly at brown faces peeking out at him through door slits as he passed. The sliding door to the baggage compartment was ajar. Longarm trimmed the corridor lamp on the bulkhead behind him and was crouching in a dark corner clear of the doorway in less time than it would take to yell, "Ready! Set! Go!"

Nothing happened. It was dark as the pit away from the flickering moonbeams streaming through the small square of glass in the side door. Longarm took a breath, let half of it go so's he'd sound calm, and softly called out, "Mason, I'd be Deputy Long, the one dressed more cow than the others when we came aboard. You showed me to my sleeping quarters, and I told you then I was much obliged."

There came no answer. Longarm suggested, "Why don't you tell me your side of the story, old son? I haven't been able to get much out of anybody else aboard this train, and when we stop to jerk water up ahead at at Rawlins, they are surely going to want to know."

No answer.

Then the far door slid open, and Longarm threw down but held his fire as the burly figure in the lamplit doorway bellowed in a thick brogue, "Jasus, Mary, and Joseph, I'll have no gunplay back here, Goddamn your eyes!"

Sensing that could hardly be young Mason, Longarm called back to the U.P. brakeman, "Deputy U.S. Marshal Custis Long, here, and we may have the shootist pinned down betwixt us. Have any bare-ass colored boys run through your caboose, lately?"

The brakeman laughed and said, "They have not, and is that who fired all thim shots? I'd be Sean O'Corrigan at your service, and what do we do nixt?"

Longarm said, "I'd be obliged if you set a lantern just inside that forward door and then slid it shut to cover from the other side. You do have your own six-gun, right?"

O'Corrigan replied, "I do not. It's a sawed-off ten-gauge Greener I'd be protecting this highball and its valuable cargo with. So if our dark desperado is listening, he'd be well advised not to mess with the Union Pacific Railroad!"

Within moments, a brakeman's lantern with clear glass was shedding a fair ammount of light the length of the swaying deck as it outlined the bags and boxes piled to either side. The door behind Longarm slid open a crack so Captain Burbank could ask what was going on in there.

Longarm called back, "Nothing. Shut the door so's me and old Mason, here, can decide what's best for a boy so far from home with another jerkwater stop in his future."

As the door slid shut to pinch off that unwelcome slit of light, Longarm called out in a conversational tone, "As you likely know, being a railroading man, steam locomotives don't bother with condensers like they have on steamships.

So they just let the spent steam suck fire through the boiler tubes as it escapes with the smoke. So that means they have to stop and jerk water for their tender every two hundred miles, meaning the next stop has to be five hours west of Cheyenne, and we left Cheyenne over an hour ago."

He let that sink in and said, "That gives us plenty of time to study on your fix, but not an *indefinite* time, Mason. So why don't I spell out some choices we have here?"

He waited, got no answer, and said, "If I wanted to be more famous as a gunfighter, there are two reporters I know of aboard this train, and they'd be proud to put it on the wire as a famous lawman winning a wild shoot-out aboard a speeding train with a deranged Negro. That's what they call a gentleman of color when he has to gun a white man, a deranged Negro. Why did you have to gun him, Mason?"

A small voice in the dark sobbed, "I told him and I told him I had more than one real gal for that kind of stuff! I told him and I told him a high-toned sport with a *railroad* job made out grand in most any darktown along the Eastern seaboard, and he didn't push it as long as we was back East where he could find his own sort of fun. But once we got west of Lake Erie, he kept calling me his brown sugar and begging to suck my chocolate bar ever' time he was drunk, and Mr. Merryweather drank a lot when we was off duty."

Longarm nodded in the dark and replied in that same conversational and nonjudgmental tone, "I have heard such tales before from younger convicts and even cowboys. This older gent got you to drink with him, and after a lot of sassy tales and rational suggestions about how pals could help each other out when there were no ladies present, you went along with the notion of letting him suck you off, once he'd promised that was all he wanted and, what the hell, you figured it would feel a whole lot better and not much sillier than beating your own meat?"

Mason sniffed. "He hurt me."

Longarm said, "He meant to. Some natural men like to hurt women with their old organ grinders too. Makes some born bullies feel more like the leader of the pack to fornicate with weaker folk who keep begging them not to hurt them no more."

He waited for an answer, got none, and said, "Speaking from the experience of others, he finally got you to let him go down on you, and of course that meant he got you to take off your pants. So the next few minutes felt like a hard-up kid's heaven and then, in those moments of limp heavy breathing just after he'd made you come in his mouth, he was atop you with his own exited cock up your ass, right?"

Jason said, "It hurt and, after it hurt it shamed me like fire. Mean old white man keep calling me his nigger whore and jeering in my ear I loves it and he aims to give me all I craves!"

Longarm said, "I told you I'd heard the tale before. Merryweather was a twisted bastard, not because he was a cock-sucker but because he liked to hurt and degrade his prey. Lynch mob got this one old boy in West by God Virginia for just fucking a gal. The part that had the mob het up was that the gal had been six years old."

"Oh, Lord have mercy, I don't want no lynch mob after me, Captain! I seen an old boy after the KKK took him out of his momma's cabin after he trifled with a white lady! They poured coal oil on him and set him on fire as they strung him up, and it smelled awful!"

Longarm had mentioned that possible outcome on purpose. He calmly told the terrified kid, "I doubt the Klan has a Klavern in Wyoming, and the late Mr. Merryweather may have been white, but he was hardly a woman. After that, he was on the payroll of a rich industrialist, and none of the government employees aboard this train are likely to want their names connected in any way, shape, or form to a ho-mosexual scandal. That's how I'm going to list what happend on my official report, unless they'd rather go along with us partway, Mason."

The unseen porter cautiously asked what Longarm was talking about.

Longarm said, "We can remove the corpse and report his death to the Wyoming authorities at the next stop, or we can leave him be, behind a locked door, 'til we get to Ogden, where I can report what happened to gents I know better."

"You means you can get me off scot-free?" the young porter gasped.

Longarm never lied when he had no dire need to. So he replied in that same conversational tone, "Let's not get silly, Mason. You were partly in the wrong as soon as you stripped for him. No federal prosecutor with a whole crew of witnesses would have trouble proving you ran out of a sodomite's compartment bare ass, waving his six-gun with your shit on his dick!"

"I never told him he could do that! He was bigger than me, and he up and raped me!"

Longarm said, "That's what we call extenuating circumstances, Mason. When I turn you over to the federal court in Ogden, seeing all this shit took place aboard a federal charter out of Washington, I'll see you have a good public defender, and he'll surely advise you to cut a plea bargain, saving you and all these other folk the embarrassment of of a public disclosure of a sticky lovers' quarrel."

Mason didn't understand. Longarm said, "A plea bargain is when your lawyer gets the prosecution to ask for a lighter sentence in exchange for a guilty plea, saving the expense and bother of a trial. You can go on trial as what the courthouse gang is sure to call a colored kid shooting an old white queer who'd been fucking him. On the other hand, your lawyer could say, 'It's a nasty can of worms, but what can my client shave off if we say, sure, he killed the cocksucker, and what's it to you?' "

Mason laughed weakly. Then asked, "You say this lawyer you know can speak for me? I don't have to say nothing? How much time in jail do I have to spend if I comes quiet, Captain?"

Longarm asked if he had a record.

Mason shyly confessed he might have cut that fool nigger in Boston that one time, but it hadn't been over any sort of fucking, and as a matter of fact, Mr. Merryweather had fixed it with the law.

Longarm said, "Oh boy. You're fixing to do some time, Mason. But it'll be in a federal prison, not on a chain gang, and you'll still be a young man when you get out."

He let that sink in before he said, "I know that sounds cruel. But if I have to take you the hard way, and you live

48

through it, they will surely hang you. So what's it going to be?"

There was a long silence. Then Mason said, "Shit, I ain't got no more bullets for this gun anyways. So don't go shooting me as I come out, now, Captain."

Longarm rose, covering the slender, dark form with upraised, empty hands as he slid open the nearby door and called out, "Caligula, might you have them duds I asked for?"

When the older colored man handed the jacket and pants in, Longarm tossed them at Mason's feet and said, "Put them on. You'll have to ride the rest of the way handcuffed as we take turns guarding you. Where's the empty gun?"

As the kid hunkered down to gather up the clothes, he replied he'd dropped the empty gun in the dark along the way. Then he shyly asked, "You knew all the time I couldn't shoot nobody, and yet you still let me surrender without you getting to carve another notch on your gun?"

Longarm said, "Gave that hobby up after I'd whittled the grips clean off my first six or eight guns. If it's any comfort, I wasn't sure you hadn't reloaded until that brakeman opened that other door within point-blank range, and you never fired."

Sliding the door all the way open, Longarm called the others in to explain the plan. Then, leaving Mason well-arrested indeed, Longarm ambled back to his own compartment to resume his conversation with Cassandra La Belle of the *New York Sun*.

He thought at first glance she'd ignored his warning to stay put, because the lamp was out, and he didn't see her sitting there, outlined by the moonlit passing scenery. Then a throaty voice purred, "Welcome aboard, sailor. What took you so long?"

Chapter 8

Since he was damned if he did and damned if he didn't, Longarm didn't order the naked newspaperwoman in his bed to get up and get dressed. He sensed it might be more diplomatic to shuck his own duds and get under the covers with her, and there was a lot to be said for all she had to offer above the rumble and the roar of a highballing combination on a downhill grade.

For old Ben Franklin had been on the money in that notorious letter of advice he'd written a younger diplomat posted to Paris, France, if he'd ever really written it.

The advice about older women had been true to life, whoever had said it was smarter for a Yankee skating on the thin ice of the fancy French court to stay out of duels over flirty young French gals when there were all those older flirty French gals who knew how to get away with a thing or two and felt flattered by the effort.

As he entered her, Longarm once again recalled old Ben's observation that, much like trees, women commenced to wither at the top long before their roots dried out, and in the kindly flickering moonlight winking in at them you could see old Cass had been a belle indeed in her younger days. So what the hell, as long as you were kissing a pal, you might as well kiss her passionate.

The sassy-talking newspaper gal kissed back like a cat in heat and gave him a hell of a ride in her love saddle before she moaned, "Oh, shit, I'm rally coming!"

So, seeing she wanted to talk romantic, Longarm laughed and whooped, "Powder River and let her buck!"

Then, as they lay still with the rolling trucks under them helping them tingle as he soaked it inside her, old Cass murmured, "Jesus H. Christ, that was *good!* The trouble with taking most nice young boys home to raise is that as one gets . . . more motherly, it gets tougher to decide whether you're fucking a baby or *having* one. You're good as they say you are, Custis. Am I good as they say I am?"

He muttered, "Better." As he blew some of her hair out of his face, sensing it might not be diplomatic to mention those stories to the effect of her reciting Sapphic poetry to younger gals.

The Pullman berth had been designed for one adult, sleeping alone, and neither of them were midgets. So Longarm swung his bare feet to the carpet to grope out and share a smoke with her. She smiled up at him as the moonlight played across his naked muscles and marveled, "You are built like a Greek god! How do you stay in such shape? You can't be that much younger than me, and as I'm sure you just noticed, I'm getting old and flabby."

Lighting the cheroot, which exposed her reclining figure in a way more clinical manner, Longarm soothed, "They work me hard for what they pay me, and I have to eat on the run a heap. But you ain't all that flabby, and gals are supposed to be softer than boys."

By way of illustration he told her about the lovers' quarrel up in the car ahead, adding, "I'd be obliged if we could tone it down for readers of the *New York Sun*. I told young Mason they might not hang him."

The worldly newspaperwoman replied, "We don't run queer killings. Let's talk about those fair white maidens being passed around by sex-mad Mormons. Anyone can see neither Washington nor Salt Lake really want to know. So tell me true, sailor, are we on a snipe hunt led by a fucking incompetent?"

Longarm let her have a drag as he honestly replied, "I can't speak for anyone in Washington. I suspect the Salt Lake Temple really wants to know."

She passed the smoke back, murmuring, "Mormons are creepy. Why do they want to act so creepy, Custis?"

He shrugged his bare shoulders and suggested, "We must make them as uneasy. Neither side is trying. Both are acting the way their Good Books tell them they ought to act. Some

51

ancient Greek I ain't about to try and pronounce wrote, in Ancient Greek, that one man's religion was another man's madness. Papists are supposed to eat fish on Friday, a Protestant or Jew can eat most anything but pork on a Friday, whilst a Navaho wouldn't eat a fish at the point of a gun. It's all in the way the folk around you act, I reckon."

He took a drag, put the cheroot to her lips again, and confided, "Met up with this right sinister Mormon gal a spell back, night-riding with a gang of killers, and when honest Mormon lawmen found out about her working both sides of the law, they were more shocked by her having rutted in her holy underwear with a man who *smoked cigars* than anything *else* she'd done."

"Do they really all wear those ridiculous union suits designed by Joesph Smith?" She laughed.

He said, "There's heaps of Saints I've yet to see in their underwear, and I can't say who first came up with the notion. Can't say who first said folk of the Hebrew persuasion could eat meat, or cheese, but not with the same meal. Wasn't consulted when some Pope said it was just fine with our Jewish Lord Jesus if you ate pork, but you'd best stick to fish on Friday. Did you know there's a church in the old South where it's all right to hand a baby a rattlesnake to play with as long as you never let his innocent hands touch playing cards?"

Cass sighed and said, "I've covered too many stories about innocent babies to believe anyone I'd like to talk to could possibly be running this confusion. But you have to admit those Mormons are more confused than most! Have you ever read that Book of Mormon, Custis?"

He said, "Not all the way through. Been meaning to finish *Ben Hur*. I took what I thought was *Ben Hur* home from the Denver library without noticing it came in two volumes. Both thicker than your average Good Book."

She reached languidly for his lap as she sniffed, "Magic spectacles allowing a New York State farm boy to read ancient Egyptian, for heaven's sake, and what was that about an angel named Macaroni appearing to Joseph Smith in a New York State apple orchard?"

"I think the mysterious visitor was called *Moroni*, Miss

Cass." He pointed out as she took the matter in hand.

Seeing she didn't really care, Longarm snuffed the cheroot out as he added, "I wasn't there. But to tell the truth, I have less trouble picturing anybody talking to an angel under an apple tree than I do a naked lady talking to a snake."

She didn't answer. She couldn't, with her mouth full. Longarm said, "Well, all right, but be advised I got to take my turn on guard duty up in the next car in a spell."

In point of fact, Cassandra La Belle had used him, abused him, and retreated discreetly to her own compartment before it came Longarm's turn to guard the handcuffed and dozing Mason up foreward. Alternating with Captain Burbank and Deputies Teller and Coyle out of Washington, they managed between them to turn the youth over to old Billy Vail's opposite number in Ogden, U.S. Deputy Abraham Dixler, within the hour of their private section being uncoupled in the Ogden Yards so's all those highball cars could continue along the tracks of the Central Pacific from there west. Marshal Dixler, a good old boy Longarm knew from earlier cases, agreed Mason would likely get off with less than ten at hard, which was a hell of an improvement on dead.

When they got back to the four cars parked on a siding, it only *felt* like they were stuck there all day. It beat all how unnatural and confining it felt aboard any railroad car that wasn't moving.

But at last a dinky 0-4-0 Baldwin was hauling them south as its own special chore, courtesy of the "territorial government," made up of mostly Gentile federal apointees and their Mormon "assistants," if they meant to get much done.

Longarm knew statehood, and hence their own elected governor, was being held up in Congress by gents of other persuasions who kept on harping about past quarrels, and he could see why Salt Lake was anxious to tidy things up along the Old Spanish Trail. Most every newspaper item on those more recently vanished fair white bodies made mention of that California-bound Fancher party running into a whole lot of Mormon trouble on that same Old Spanish Trail back in '57. Trying to blame the slaughter on Digger Indians had left a stink similar to one resulting from farting in the bunkhouse and trying to blame it on the new kid in the outfit. Having opened the windows to air that old stink away, Salt Lake wanted straight answers with no loose ends, and the infernal mystery stale news the next time Utah statehood was debated in Congress.

Having wired the owner of their private cars about the killing of their straw boss, Caligula had been wired to take over pro tem, and so the service improved as they sipped and munched their way south along the Mormon delta.

All the party being up by now, if not yet bright-eyed and bushy-tailed, Longarm got to meet others besides Deputies Teller and Coyle, their peerless leader Livermore, his assistant Garwood, and the two women he already knew, one in the biblical sense, albeit you'd never know from her prim, reserved expression.

There were five newspapermen aboard, counting Hovak of the *Post*. Livermore had twelve male disciples, counting Garwood, and the young ash-blond Dawn Atwell seemed in charge of four other young things who took dictation, if nothing more sassy, for the men appointed by various congressmen.

Cub Reporter Hovak got Longarm to one side to ask about that.

He said, "Colorado, Kansas, and Nebraska are states. Neither Utah, Wyoming, nor Montana rate congressmen. So what am I missing?"

Longarm said, "California and Nevada appointed two of the squirts. Grooms left waiting at the church along the Front Range no doubt wrote the congressmen from their home states. Hardly anybody old enough to vote yet has been born in Wyoming or Montana since Mr. Lo, the poor Indian, was evicted shortly after Little Big Horn. Never wipe out a squadron of cavalry or a wagon train if you don't want trouble with your landlord, Miles."

Hovak flustered, "Why didn't I think of that?"

It wouldn't have been kind to tell the squirt he had some thinking ahead of him if he didn't aim to wind up one of those newspaper hacks reporting Calamity Jane as young and beautiful.

The long-settled, irrigated farmland and mostly fenced-in pastures from Ogden down to Salt Lake City bespoke an awesome amount of hard work when you threw in such labor-saving inventions as the famous Mormon plow, a sort of backwards earth-moving blade pushed instead of pulled by mules or draft oxen. Cottonwood windbreaks and orchards of mostly apple, cherry, and pear had been planted far enough back for the apple and cherry, leastways, to rise impressive. You planted pears for your heirs, but the folk who'd worked like beavers with turpentine under their tails to literally make a desert bloom were more patient farm folk than most.

Prophets having less honor in their own country, the founders of the Church of Jesus Christ of Latter-day Saints had recruited more new converts from *old* England than *New* England, and farming had gotten way more scientific since Colonial days, resulting in progressive practice along with religious zeal. Jim Bridger had offered to bet Brigham Young a dollar for every ear of corn he and his followers would ever grow on the shores of the Great Salt Lake, and lived to be mighty glad Brigham Young hadn't held with wagering for money.

They only stopped at Salt Lake City long enough to pick up three more Mormon lawmen who followed Captain Burbank to his compartment to hold a secret meeting that made Cassandra and some of the others uneasy.

Longarm knew the isolated metropolis that travel writers had described as an emerald city in the great American desert. Most of the others had to content themselves with admiring it out the windows in passing.

You didn't see the lake the town was named for from the tracks but, like Denver on the far side of the Divide, Salt Lake City offered them a swell view of the nearby Wasatch Mountains, closer and higher than the Front Range looming above Denver. Some know't-all sniffed that the fairy-tale towers of the distant temple hadn't been fashioned in the true Gothic style. Most agreed with Longarm that they were impressive enough as soon as you studied on how many Goths lived out Utah way.

More of the same fertile farmland stretched south of Salt Lake City a ways, the leaves and blades of grass greened up like parsley that early in the year. But of course as they rolled farther south, the land was more recently and not as thickly settled, so they'd gone past open stretches of Great Basin sage flat in the raw, which wasn't half as inviting, and the increasingly smaller settlements they passed could have used more shade by half, because it took a spell for cottonwood windbreaks to sprout when you buried green cottonwood logs along your fence lines and watered them good, a summer or more, before anything much came up.

When they got to the end of the line in the purer and hence saloon- and coffee shop–free town of Provo, Captain Burbank came out, backed by his three armed-and-dangerous-looking prophets, to announce they had decided there was no sense going on before morning and suggesting they, the infernal Gentiles, spend the night aboard and coffee up some.

He said, "We've arranged to join a Califonia-bound wagon train led by a respectable Saint who won't, I fear, be serving coffee with your biscuits and gravy on the trail. As we haul out, we'll be joined south of Utah Lake by two trustworthy Paiute guides who grew up out in the desert and ranges we'll be crossing. I'll be leaving you all for the night because we'll all be more comfortable that way, and I have some last-minute wires to send and details to thrash out. Are there any questions before I bid you good afternoon?"

Cassandra La Belle said, "I have one. Will these cars be staying here, or heading back where they came from?"

Special Investigator Livermore said, "I can answer that, ma'am. As soon as we've moved on, these private cars will naturally be returning to their owner back East. There's no point in tying them up on this remote siding for as long as we're liable to be moving down the Old Spanish Trail and back. Why do you ask?"

The experienced newspaper reporter said, "Because you may go as far as you like down the Old Spanish Trail or the road to perdition, but this girl is going back to civilization, enjoying coffee and her after-supper smokes all the damned way!"

Chapter 9

Longarm and some of the others went into town to send wires of their own and stretch their legs as their shadows lengthened across the ground. The most important thing there was the Brigham Young Academy, which they didn't feel welcome to explore. Like the bigger briny Salt Lake to the north, the imposing-enough freshwater Utah Lake waxed and waned considerably within gently sloping shores. So Provo, like Salt Lake City, stood far enough from its lake to keep its skirts dry.

They got back to the parked private cars in plenty of time for the swell supper served by the dining car crew after old Caligula told them not to stint on what figured to be the last serious cooking they'd be up to for a spell.

By then Cassandra La Belle was in a serious snit because she hadn't talked anybody into turning back with her, even though she seemed to have scared a couple of the young stenographers skinny with her tales of twelve-foot desert diamondbacks and ferocious wild camels known to bite.

When Dawn Atwell asked Longarm about that, he could only reply he couldn't say for certain. He explained, "The U.S. Army experimented with a camel corps out this way just before the war. They imported a bunch of riding camels from the Ottoman Empire with some Moslem camel hands to show the U.S. Cav how you ride a camel."

"You're teasing me." Dawn protested.

Longarm shook his head and insisted, "You can look it up. The U.S. Cav and Turkish camels didn't take to one another well. It seems when you try to treat a camel like a mule, it bites you, serious as Miss Cassandra says, or, when that don't work, it just lays down and dies. So the U.S. Camel

Corps was disbanded in time for the War Betwixt the States. Most of the camels as hadn't died already were sold off to be circus freaks or dog meat. Some may have run loose across the desert. From time to time, desert rats claim they've seen one running wild. But I understand there's seven cities of gold, lemonade springs, and a range of big rock candy mountains out there, somewheres."

He let that sink in before he added, "I doubt any of us will be bit by twelve-foot diamondbacks, either."

Cassandra snapped, "I'm not as concerned about wild *critters* as I am about wild *Indians,* or Indians those sneaky Mormons classify as wild when they sic them on us outsiders! They don't *want* us looking for those girls they've kidnapped. Can't any of you see that?"

Longarm didn't ask her what she was talking about. They'd been over that same ground, in bed together, so he'd thought they'd thrashed it out. It was just as likely they had, and she'd still made up her mind she wasn't up to roughing it away from the comforts of these Pullman cars. It was a caution how some excused their being poor sports without admitting they just wanted to pick up their marbles and go home.

After coffee and dessert, old Cass murmured to Longarm she was going to her compartment, Compartment F, to write up her notes. If she thought he'd come bleating like a lamb back East with her, she only knew him in the biblical sense. He took some magazines from town to his own compartment, figuring she figured the one serving that night as the host of the orgy would feel empowered to call the tune.

So he got a good night's sleep, alone, after reading all four magazines, including the advertising and counting one hell of a heap of sheep just walking through a gap in the fence. There was no sense in counting anything *interesting* when you wanted to fall asleep.

When he woke up with a fuzzy fading memory of an ash blonde herding sheep aboard a camel, costumed like Miss Cleopatra if she'd had on any costume at all, the sun was bright outside, and there went that bullwhip again. So Longarm sat up and opened the window blinds to see, sure enough, a dozen prairie schooners, as the lighter Western version of the Conestoga freight wagon was called, had formed up alongside the tracks with others coming in.

Longarm's watch read six-twenty, so he knew the wagoners had been up and about nigh two and a half hours loading the wagons, stuffing their guts, and hitching up the teams. A tinny bugle blew out yonder, and a gruff voice called, "First call and listen up! All know we're moving on at seven sharp, and you can come along with us, run after us, or stay behind! For I am Captain Esau Skaggs, a hairy man on my way to Californee, and if you don't like my ways, it was never my notion to invite you lost souls to tag along!"

Longarm was dressed and out on the dusty wagon trace by six-thirty-four. He'd ridden the Old Chisholm Trail when the Kiowa-Comanche were out. But despite all his fuming and fussing, it was going on seven-forty-five before they were under way. One of the secretary gals and two more reporters never made it. It wasn't clear whether they'd had trouble believing they didn't have until eight or decided to go back with Cassandra La Belle.

Having been instructed the night before by Livermore, pontificating from a guide book that made some sense, everyone ready to go had on riding duds with their baggage neatly packed. Longarm was the only one with his own saddle. But Captain Burbank and those other Mormon lawmen, five of them all told, called everyone back to the remuda of saddled riding stock, with Venus Brand sidesaddles provided for the ladies, of course.

Some of them seemed bemused at the notion of riding Spanish saddle mules instead of ponies.

Longarm let the Mormons explain the advantages of mules over horseflesh on desert trails. They weren't out to win races of chase cows on the dry and dusty trail ahead. They were out to follow it aboard surefooted critters that tended to get you there at the cost of way less fodder and water. The perfect steed, in Longarm's opinion, would be a Morgan pony with the endurance and grit of a burro. Since such a paragon didn't exist, you rode what you could get.

Captain Burbank and his Gentiles rode up with the pilots ahead of the considerable dust of a wagon train in motion. Two half-naked Paiute dogtrotted out ahead of everybody.

The riding mules had to be reined in so's their canteen water and baggage could keep up on wheels.

Each wagon was drawn by a six-mule team, faster than oxen could have managed, to deliver the famous honey, beeswax, wheat flour, and smoked hams of Deseret to the growing, water-short Pueblo de Los Angeles in return for machine-made goods shipped around the Horn.

Men and boys, mostly boys, drove the considerable herd of relief or spare stock farther back. This was partly because stock drove easier trailing its own kind over obviously safe ground and partly so's the drag riders would spot anybody lagging behind. For all his crusty ways, Captain Skaggs took his responsibilities seriously and still suffered nightmares over that poor old drunk who'd apparently wandered off in the dark, back when they'd first elected him a wagon master.

They rolled south around three miles an hour, taking most of the morning to make the Spanish Fork emptying into that same bodacious Utah Lake. The lake was still there when they nooned an hour to grub, change teams, and sound the horn again at one P.M.

By the time the sun was low in the west, it was still bouncing at them off the waves of Utah Lake. After they made camp at sundown, with each wagon dropping its team in order to circle up in spite of the Mormon farm kids who came over from a nearby spread to gawk at them, Captain Burbank said they'd seen about the last of Utah Lake. So one of the reporters asked if anyone there wanted to go skinny-dipping with him, and a secretary said she felt faint.

Around the campfire after a tolerable supper, they got to die for tobacco while sipping sweet cider with Special Investigator Livermore questioning Mormons who didn't know about those missing Gentile gals none of them had ever laid eyes on.

Knowing Billy Vail expected him to question folk at such trail stops as they might have passed through, farther along, like the old song went, Longarm rose to stroll out through sagebrush to where sedge and cattails warned him to watch his step or take off his boots.

Somebody had abandoned a leaky rowboat in the lake shallows that had turned to dry land since the last high water.

Longarm sat on the sun-silvered stern to light a forbidden cheroot, alone in the dark with his own thoughts.

Or so he'd thought until the ash-blond Dawn Atwell joined him to chide, "Captain Burbank would never approve, ah . . . Custis."

It wouldn't have been polite to ask whether Brett Garwood or their peerless leader Livermore would approve as he calmly replied, "Old Jubal is a fellow lawman, not my momma. But don't tell on me, and I won't . . . What might I do for you, Miss Dawn?"

She said, "We were wondering, the other girls and me, whether it was true we've seen the last of any open water forever."

He suggested, "Forever is a long time, Miss Dawn. Two days at the most ought to see us on the Sevier River running north from higher canyon lands and wooded mesas to the south. You and the other ladies are likely to see more splishy splash than you ever wanted to by the time we leave the banks of the Sevier after a week or more beside her."

She said, "I was told the Sevier dies in the desert, Custis."

He nodded and said, "It does, in the Sevier salt flats off to the west. We ain't headed that way. We're fixing to join the still-fresh stream a couple of days' drive south of here, where it oxbows out to die, like you said, where we ain't going."

She said, "Oh. I guess I'll never understand how all these Utah rivers never make it down to the sea like natural streams are said to."

He said, "That's how come they call all this land betwixt the High Sierra and the Rocky Mountaints the Great Basin, Miss Dawn. It ain't one big washbasin. It's what the geology professors call a basin-and-range province, with mostly north-south ridges rising and sort of watering the sort of dried-up sea bottom between. Where the land lies lowest, it forms lakes, salt lakes, or salt flats, with some of those poison alkali, after collecting millions of years of runoff without, as you said, ever getting to drain on down to the seven seas."

Since she still seemed to be standing there, he shrugged and went on, "We'll follow the Sevier upstream to its headwaters, and then we'll go west beyond the Cedar Breaks to the headwaters of the south-flowing Virgin River, which winds up in the Grand Canyon if you don't watch out. So before that happens, we'll leave the Virgin and make for Las Vegas, meaning *the meadows,* on the Old Spanish Trail proper. The Old Spanish sure named things optimistic. But the high desert won't be so hot and dry before June."

She asked, "What about the *low* desert, the Mojave?"

"You're going to just hate it." He replied cheerfully enough and went on to explain, "The hottest couple of weeks of this expedition will be coming up in May as the wondrous desert blooms have died off and things are commencing to get serious. But not as serious as things are fixing to get after the Fourth of July. Anybody trying to cross the Mojave in high summer might as well set their hair afire and get it over with."

She protested, "Then how will we ever get *home* if we persist in this madness all the way to the Pacific Ocean?"

He said, "By way of the Pacific Ocean, of course. We'd be crazy to come back overland in high summer. So whether we've solved the mystery or not, we can catch a northbound coastal steamer up to Frisco Bay, take the Sacramento River boat up to Sacramento, and head on back by way of the Transcontinental Central and Union Pacific Lines, see?"

She said, "I do indeed! So why do you suppose those missing girls went by wagon train, a six-week trip, when they could have made it by steam in a matter of days?"

It was a smart question. He said so. Then he suggested, "Money may be the root of the evil. Wagon trains will allow you to tag along for next to nothing. The passage up to Frisco alone would set a lady on a budget back more than all those days on the Old Spanish Trail. Cattle on their way to market are driven slow and cheap, as much of the way as practical."

She insisted, "If I was an adventuress willing to marry a rich man I'd never met, I'd insist he send me enough money to take the faster steam route! Those rich old mining men sound mighty cheap, if you ask me!"

He said, "They well may be. Men starting out poor get in the habit of scrimping. They say Uncle John Chisum, the biggest cattle baron in New Mexico Territory, sleeps on the floor beside his feather bed. Seems he can't get to sleep unless he's stretched out on the grass or a fancy Persian rug. But you have given me some eliminating to do, and for that I thank you, Miss Dawn."

He snubbed out his smoke and sighed. "I wish we'd had this talk back in Provo. It's too late, now, to wire some questions for my home office to follow up on."

She demurely suggested, "You had a lot on your mind back in Provo." Then, when he wouldn't rise to the bait, she said, "That silly Cassandra La Belle said she was going to get you to go back to Cheyenne at least, and mayhaps beyond, if you must know!"

Longarm cautiously asked, "Must know, Miss Dawn? Did you notice me headed back with Miss Cass and those others?"

She laughed triumphantly and said, "I never believed half what she boasted, but I feared that where there was smoke there could be fire."

"You smelled a lot of smoke aboard that train?" he asked with a thin smile, adding, "Funny, I thought I was trying to cut down."

She said, "That's what the other girls and me were wondering about. Speaking as a maiden betrayed by a congressman who had a wife back in Indiana all the time, I told the other girls the old bawd was making it all up when she bragged on . . . all you'd done to her."

Longarm didn't answer. This one was bolder than Miss Bubbles back in Denver, and whether she'd been screwing Livermore, Garwood, or both all this time, Longarm figured he didn't really need to piss either of them off. So he said they'd best go back and join the party.

Chapter 10

The Mormons had provided extra sleeping ambulances for their guests, four berths to a wagon. Longarm, along with other seasoned travelers, prefered to spread his bedding upwind of the camp, out in the pungent but not unpleasant sage.

Falling asleep with tempting visions of ash-blond and henna-rinsed ring-dang-doo on his mind would have been tough enough. Other bugs the flirty Dawn Atwell had put in his ear made it tougher. So at four A.M. when first call was sounded, Longarm scouted Captain Burbank up to tell him, "I got to ride back to Provo and send me a mess of wires. If Easau can outfit me with a couple of good trail mules—"

"You'll wind up hopelessly behind!" the Mormon lawman cut in.

Longarm said, "No I won't. You'll be averaging less than twenty miles a day, while I can easily do thirty, changing mules on the hour and not stopping too often to pick flowers. I'll catch up well before you all get halfway up the Sevier, and I've taken your word all of those missing gals went missing the other side of yonder."

Burbank wanted to know what was so all-fired important to send out on the wire. Longarm told him, "Elimination. Or in this case mayhaps addition. It . . . occured to me last night we don't know toad squat about neither the missing brides to be nor their prospective husbands. So what if I ask Billy Vail and other marshals closer at the moment to both ends of the trail to canvass witnesses for us? They'll have more than enough time to probe in more depth and wire me in care of the telegraph office in Barstow next month, see?"

Likely grumbling from experience, the older Mormon lawman observed there was forever somebody holding up the picnic with last minutes back in the infernal house. But being a fair lawman as well as anxious to go on, he agreed more domestic detail on the missing women couldn't hurt.

They both knew Anglo pioneers had discovered the charms of California well before the gold rush of '49, so Radiant Kinderhook, with a hint of something Spanish in her eyes, was hardly the only born and bred gal of the golden West who might or might not have a record out yonder. When Burbank pointed out whores hardly ever used their right names, Longarm nodded but shot back, "More than one soiled dove has amassed a right impressibe yellow sheet under such given names. The former Catherine Fisher has been arrested more often as Big Nose Kate Elder than by any name her momma ever gave her. Were Big Nose Kate to respond to a more honorable proposition than usual by mail, she'd likely leave for Montana as Kate Elder and by any name she could have a pissed-off pimp or former owner anxious to get her back. So one of the things I mean to eliminate is a California cathouse getting mail from all over."

Burbank grimaced and asked, "Are you suggesting some madam could be operating a lonely hearts club?"

Longarm said, "Too early to suggest anything. But whores feeling overworked and starting their own mail-order operation seems way more likely than a madam or vice lord anxious to get shed of their whores."

Burbank brightened and said, "I like that notion! What if some vice ring is reclaiming runaway Cyprians on the sly, closer to, say, Barstow?"

Longarm said, "There's grimmer eliminating at the east end of the line. All I have on the complainants, so far, is that they sent for California gals that were never delivered, and who's to say not a one of 'em ever lost a wife down a well before or headed west in a hell of a hurry after some neighbor gal went missing?"

The Mormon whistled, shook his head, and said, "Hold on, would any man who'd disposed of a mail-order bride after she'd arrived report her missing if he was the only one who knew what had happened to her?"

Longarm said, "It happens. Firebugs often turn in the first alarm, and many a killer's been driven by a guilty conscience to hang around his precinct house. A man who knew kith and kin out California way could have love letters he'd sent in his own hand to show the law might well want it known the missing gal never turned up on *his* damn doorstep."

Gazing about in the confusion of an early morning shape-up, Longarm added with a sheepish smile, "On the third or fourth other hand, I may be playing chess when the name of this game is tic-tac-toe. Only way to make sure is by asking others for some eliminating, and there ain't any telegraph lines this far south."

Captain Easau Skaggs was proud of his Spanish saddle mules and soon had Longarm headed back to Provo, riding one and leading the other at a mile-eating trot.

The greenup was hanging cool, and Longarm knew he'd find homesteads and even settlements every few hours as far in the wake of the wagons as Saint George, where the late Brigham Young had built a winter home on the lower and hence warmer desert beyond the Cedar Breaks. So they were traveling light, trotting downgrade and walking up, at a pace a green cavalry trooper might have protested, but Longarm knew how to keep his balls out of the ventilation slit of the McClellan cavalry saddle, designed with the comfort of the mount in mind with the rider left on his own.

The trick was to stand in the stirrups when trotting. You could tell an experienced cavalryman or cowhand at a distance by whether he was riding his mount at a mile-eating trot or alternately walking it or loping it, both gaits being easier on potato sacks or sloppy riders.

Averaging thrice the speed of a wagon train, Longarm made it back to Provo just after noon. Knowing it was going to take some time for his home office to wire back a confirmation, Longarm rode first to a hotel he knew on Center Street that catered to enough cross-country traffic to allow a guest to smoke in his own hired room. But, first things coming first, he had to see his mules were rubbed down and cooled off with sensibly supplied water and fodder, *never* the other way 'round, before he stored his saddle and Winchester '73 upstairs, stuck one of his matchstick burglar alarms under the bottom hinge, and headed out to send those wires.

Provo being a college town, the acadamy Brigham Young

had dreamed of opening in '75 and named for him when he died in '77, the Western Union there was manned well enough to handle all the wires home for money sent from any college town.

Longarm sent his longest explanation collect to Billy Vail at day rates, and if he got hell, he got hell. But seeing he had to wire all those others out of his own pocket, he sent night letters, knowing they all needed more time to get going than he had there in Provo. He asked everybody to take such time as they needed and wire him whatever they turned up in care of the Western Union in Barstow, weeks on down the trail.

Then he went out on the string-straight streets of the tediously tidy Mormon Utopia to scout up a belated dinner or early supper. He was hungry either way. The town was laid out in a no-frills gridiron with each block exactly four square, centered on the intersection of Center and Academy. Then, lest strangers in town find it too easy, the north-south avenues were numbered 100 W, 100 E, 200 W, 200 E, and so on. Streets north and south of Center were as grandly described as 100 N, 100 S, 200 N on to 800 N, or eight whole blocks by the time you got to the bodacious campus of the academy. Nobody had ever accused the late Brigham Young of thinking small or lacking the self-confidence of a self-taught Augustus Caesar.

The townsfolk he passed on the streets of Provo were as inspiring to the imagination. A well-traveled history teaching gal in Denver had confided after some time in the Mormon delta that if ever the Know Nothing Party had its way, their pure America for Americans was in danger of winding up like the same. For not even New England had as many pure Anglo-Saxon faces hanging out, thanks to the Irish and French Canadians moving in to work New England's mills and factories since the Revolution and, having assured the local Utes and Paiutes they were long-lost Israelites and hence saved, as long as they stayed in their place, their scriptures had nothing to say about colored folk, Mexicans, or even Irishmen. So Mormons married up with their own kind, a lot, and by their second or third generation, their purity showed and in a manner neither Joseph Smith nor his angelic

67

mentors could have had in mind. The resulting blandness was about to save Longarm's life.

He ate a wholesome but bland supper in his hotel dining room and then, seeing it was early yet to go back and check with Western Union, he mosied west along Center Street toward the lake, where he'd heard there was a boathouse and band pavilion, possibly offering diversion if not hard cider. A similar establishment up in Salt Lake City catered to a mixed crowd of Saints and lost souls passing through.

As the danger of occasional flooding increased, the mostly frame structures to either side of Center went from less impressive to shabby.

Provo being a Mormon town, the gals lounging in doorways or perched on windowsills were sedately dressed and said nothing as he passed by.

Provo being a college town, it seemed doubtful they were expecting a circus parade to pass by. A Salt Lake City gal had once pouted about Brigham Young Academy not being coeducational. Young Saints away from home while suffering the pangs of male skin problems could well have noticed the same imbalance over on their campus. Some college boys he passed seemed mighty jovial for youths not allowed to drink anything stronger than soft cider. On the other hand, *cider* was a Hebrew word covering applejack hard or soft. So when Longarm came upon what sure looked like a Dutch beer garden, advertizing *Bier*, he decided, *This is the place,* and turned in.

He was never to find out whether they bent the rules with whatever they had on tap. As he strode between the tables crowded with neatly dressed youths and hard-eyed gals wearing powder and paint, his eyes swept casually across a quartet of somewhat older gents at one table, all dressed cow, and hence standing out in a sea of Mormon faces.

Anywhere else, he'd have breezed on by. Idly wondering if they were Gentiles who knew the local action better than he did, he paused to smile down at them and say, "Evening, gents."

That was all he got to say as all hell broke loose.

Longarm's edge was that he was already on his feet as the swarthy one on the far side rose to his feet, as he had to, with his .36 Navy Colt Conversion riding low and side-draw.

College boys and whores scattered like spattered grease as the report of Longarm's .44-40 proved that, while a side-draw was faster standing up, experienced gunslingers carried cross-draw with more likely positions in mind. He held his fire when he saw his man going down with three more left.

One of the cowboys was sobbing, "Don't shoot me! I'm too young to die, and I don't know what the fuck got into old Sandy just now!"

Covering the three of them, Longarm fished out his wallet with his federal badge as he said, "Save it for the Provo P.D. I know who he was. It just came to me as I was shooting the son of a bitch!"

Holding the badge in his teeth, Longarm put the wallet away before he pinned the badge to the breast of his denim jacket while another of the cowed riders protested, "We ain't outlaws, lawman! We didn't know Sandy was until he slapped leather on you just now!"

The last member of the trio, who seemed less scared, said, "That was dumb of old Sandy, whatever he was wanted for."

Seeing they seemed to have the emptied-out beer garden to themselves as they waited for the local law, Longarm asked the survivors who they might be. The amiable cuss who seemed most sure of himself allowed he was Mike Cassidy off the Parker spread near Circle City up the Sevier and a Mormon despite his rare Hibernian surname. The other two were Cassidy's associates in the horse trading business, both Gentiles new in the territory. Mike said the late Sandy Desmond, wanted for horse theft and murder in Colorado, had only approached them that very day about purchasing some riding stock, and so Longarm had just played hell with their business meeting.

Longarm figured their horse trading was the beeswax of the local law and felt no call to delve deeper, already being deeper in side-issue shit than he liked to think about.

He was glad he was wearing his badge when the local law showed up in the form of six neatly uniformed Provo patrolmen. When Longarm explained who he was and why he'd just had to shoot a wanted outlaw, they said they just worked there and suggested he expain it all to their desk sergeant over by the tabernacle.

Leaving two men to see the late Sandy Desmond didn't escape before a morgue wagon came for him, the Mormon officer in charge politely but firmy marched everyone east to the center of town.

Once there, the desk sergeant seemed ready enough to buy Longarm's story, backed willingly by fellow Mormon Mike Cassidy. No mention was made of posting bail. The desk sergeant felt certain their coroner's jury was going to find Longarm had only done what he'd had to.

Things got less friendly when Longarm protested, "Hold on, I can't stay here in Provo that long! I'm traveling with a special investigation with your own Captain Burbank and other territorial lawmen. I only came back to town to send some telegraph wires. Even as we speak the wagon train I'm with will have gained another twenty miles or more on me."

The Mormon lawmen exchanged glances. The desk sergeant sounded as if he meant it when he politely but firmly replied, "I don't know how they do things in Denver or Dodge City, Deputy Long, but here in Provo we do things by the letter of the law, and the law isn't written the way Mr. Ned Buntline seems to have it in those Wild West magazines. The law says when you shoot a man, for any reason, you have to explain it to the the county coroner and his panel before you go chasing after wagon trains or butterflies. So, do we understand one another, Deputy Long, or do we have to lock you up until the coroner can hold that proper inquest?"

Longarm sighed and said, "I'll be good. How long do you figure I'll be stuck here, Sarge?"

The desk sergeant shrugged and replied, "That's not for me to say. You'll be free to go when the coroner says you're free to go. Not one second earlier."

Chapter 11

Having told them where he could be found, Longarm went back to the Western Union to get a night letter off to his theater-loving pal, the sheriff up Ogden way. He didn't know any other elders of the LDS any better. He got another wire off to Billy Vail, hoping Billy might have more pull with the Salt Lake Temple.

Then, his taste for the nightlife of such a tidy town dulled considerably, Longarm stopped at a corner candy store to pick up some reading material—they didn't sell cheroots— and ambled back to his hotel.

As an experienced traveler he'd learned to pocket his hired room key, saving himself and the room clerk needless palaver every time he went in or out. Room clerks didn't care. They had special "French keys" to freeze the locks of guests who tried to stay with them for free. So the room clerk had to have been watching out for him, since he called Longarm over to say yonder lady under an elk head on the wall above her armchair had been asking for him.

Longarm joined the shapely but sort of hard-looking honey blonde in beige shantung in her chosen corner of the lobby, ticked his hat brim to her, and allowed he was at her service.

She said she was Theresa Mondale from San Pedro, California, but answered to Trixie and added, "I've been waiting for the next train up to Ogden and out of this land of lunatics. When I heard just now there was a regular Christian lawman staying here, I determined to ask if it would pay me to press charges or just quit whilst I was still ahead and just get the hell out of here! Isn't there anywhere around here a lady could order a damned *drink?* I'm so mad I could spit, and I

71

feel the need of something to steady my nerves!"

Longarm hesitated, then confessed, "I have some snake-bite remedy in my saddlebag, upstairs. You say you're rooming here as well, Miss Trixie?"

She offered her room number. Seeing they were almost neighbors, Longarm figured he'd let her decide, once they broke out that fifth of Maryland rye, where they ought to discuss whatever might be eating her.

They wound up with his bottle in her room, catty-corner across the hall, after she'd confessed that while she was far from a prude, they said bad things about girls who drank with a gent in his hotel room.

He didn't ask what they said about gals who invited gents to their own rooms after they'd been burning incense. She sat on the made-up bed as he mixed hotel tumbler highballs for the both of them at her corner washstand. As he joined her by the bed with them, Trixie told him to sit and patted the coverlet closer to the foot of her bed. So he sat down and repeated his question as to what she'd wanted to tell the law.

Trixie took a good swallow, hesitated, and confessed, "I feel so *low* as well as foolish. But a girl gets so weary of slinging hash in a waterfront beanery, and it's not as if I was a maiden pure when I answered that newspaper advertisement."

Longarm sipped more sedately and held his fire until, sure enough, she blurted, "All right, if you must know, I wrote a letter to this gent who said he had his own freight-hauling business out of Saint George, down south. Knowing it was in Utah Territory, I asked right out if he was one of them Mormon birds who expected a Christian girl to share her bed and board with his other wives. He wrote back saying he didn't hold with the preachings of Joseph Smith at all! So, like a fool, I took him for one of us, you know, *regular* Christians!"

Longarm quietly asked, "Hold on, Miss Trixie, are you saying some gent in that Mormon winter resort proposed marriage by mail, sight unseen?"

She sniffed, "Don't laugh at me. I'm going on thirty-five, and we did exchange pictures by mail. At least, I sent him a

72

picture of me. Lord knows whose tintype he sent me, and you understand there was this period of some months, writing back and forth, before I said I'd at least come on over to Saint George and meet up with him. I never in this world promised anything more. I was desperate, and it ain't as if I was above, well, getting to know old Ben. But I'll have you know I never agreed to marry up with any man before I'd ever met up with him!"

Longarm agreed that sounded reasonable. She said, "To make a long story short, Ben sent me some money and the name of a wagon master he said we could trust, even though he was a Mormon."

Did this wagon master have a name?" asked Longarm, fishing out his notebook and pencil stub.

She said, "Nugent. Caleb Nugent. He was all right. I should have guessed Ben wasn't when that Mormon wagon master didn't seem to know who we were talking about. He treated me right, and it only took me a million years to get to Saint George. I'm going back for certain by steam, all the way out of *here!*"

"Did your Ben ever explain why he wanted you coming to him such a slow way?" asked Longarm, adding, "By the way, might Ben have a last name, too?"

She said, "O'Mar, Ben O'Mar, or so he said, the big fibber. When we finally met in Saint George, he looked more like a fat Mexican than any O'Anything this girl has ever met. But I tried to be a sport about it. He confessed he'd sent that other picture because he'd been afraid I might not want to come to him, and that was the pure truth, until we got to talking about his freight-hauling business and all the horses and mules he breeds on his big rancho in Arizona Territory."

Longarm made a note to that effect and asked, "Then this Ben O'Mar don't haul from Saint George up this way, same as most?"

She finished the highball and held out the empty tumbler as she replied, "I don't think so. He said something about hauling up a South Smith Trail to Saint George out of Yuma. Did I say something wrong?"

Rising to freshen both their tumblers, Longarm told her, "I hope not. Jedediah Smith, no relation to Joseph and Hiram

Smith, albeit he hailed from New York State, too, was a mountain man of the Methodist persuasion and a caution for blazing trails until Kiowa or Comanche got him about the time Joseph Smith was having revelations back East. They never found Jed Smith's remains. Back around '26 or '27, old Jed blazed two trails across this Great Basin to northern and southern California. The north route's the one you'll be following aboard the Central Pacific, once you get up to Ogden. The South Smith Trail is also known as the robber's trail because it skirts the Mormon delta as it runs mostly down the Green and Colorado Rivers to cut west well above Yuma but . . . Yep, somebody hauling up the west bank of the Colorado would be on the South Smith Trail before it crossed the Virgin a ways downstream from Saint George. I'm sorry. You were saying . . . ?"

As he handed her tumbler back, Trixie sighed. "I don't know where his fool rancho is. I knew as soon as he kissed me I wasn't going no place with him, and that's all I let him do to me, one time!"

Longarm sat back down and sipped his own highball without appearing to pass judgment.

Her voice seemed a tad slurred as she said, "I might have let him kiss me twice if he hadn't slipped up. We were talking friendly like this, sipping some snake medicine I'd brought along, and the next thing I knew, he was all over me, groping and grunting and telling me both his wives down home just loved the way he did it to them!"

Longarm whistled softly and asked, "Then you suspect he was a Mormon, after all, Miss Trixie?"

She said, "He swore he wasn't when I accused him of that. He said he followed another good book that mentioned Moses and Lord Jesus but not one word about any Angel Moroni, and he said Joseph Smith didn't know what he was talking about, save for the part about it being all right for a natural man to have more than one wife as long as he was kindly to them all."

Longarm grimaced and asked, "Are you sure you took this Ben O'Mar for a *Mexican,* Miss Trixie? I've yet to meet a Spanish-speaking Papist who holds with polygamy. I've always had the notion their church was against the notion."

She said, "That's what I thought, growing up in California around a lot of Spics. But he gave me this fool book to prove his point. Only I can't read the scribble-scrabble printing at all. I got it in my . . . where did I put that fool book?"

She waved at a hatbox atop her dresser and said, " 'S in that box, I think, and whass in this drink?"

Longarm set his own tumbler aside and rose to cross over and pop the lid of her hatbox. A frilly sunbonnet that matched her summer outfit sat atop a modest-sized book with gold-edged pages, bound in maroon shagreen. When Longarm lifted it out to hold it up to the light he couldn't make out the scribble-scrabble either, but since he read more than most West-by-God-Virginia boys his age, Longarm was able to guess at what the unreadable pages between the fancy covers added up to.

Turning back to the gal on the bed, who now lay flat on her back with an adoring smile at the pressed tin ceiling, Longarm said, "This here seems to be a copy of that Arabian Koran, and you say this Ben O'Mar gave it to you?"

When she murmured, "I think I'm falling in love." Longarm nodded to himself and said, "Well, sure, his name was *Ben Omar*, or mayhaps *Bin* Omar if I've read Mr. Richard Burton's travel books right! Your romantic freight-hauling ranchero out of Yuma must be one of them Turks leftover from the U.S. Camel Corps!"

She said, "I've been so lonely, all those nights on the desert as I dreamed of my handsome Ben O'Mar and all the way north to Provo with another wagon train no faster than a jackass can walk!"

Longarm said, "There's one such Turkish old-timer down along the Colorado who left the Camel Corps to marry up with an American gal and do right well in the freight-hauling beeswax. His name was Haj Ali as a Turk. His wife makes him spell it Hi Jolly and, far as I know, old Hi Jolly's become at least a lukewarm Christian with only that one wife."

"Kiss me, you fool!" replied the woman on the bed as she raised her knees to spread them under the ruffles of shantung.

Longarm put her copy of the Koran back in her hatbox, under her hat, since it was hers and he knew she'd say yes to most anything he asked of her at the moment.

He knew he was likely to regret it, but being he didn't steal pennies from blind news dealers or shoot fish in a barrel, Longarm quietly let himself and what was left of the Maryland rye on out, and she never seemed to notice, playing with herself like that.

In his own room, alone in his own bed, Longarm read about this Oriental mountain kingdom where the womenfolk owned all the property and got to marry up with as many sheepherding men as they felt like. The travel writer never explained who'd had that revelation.

Longarm had long since decided men and women deserved something better than one another. For no matter how they worked things out, they always seemed ready for a new revelation.

He finally fell asleep. It wasn't easy with a hard-on and so much on his mind. Then at last it was morning, and he took his time getting cleaned up and dressed to face what was shaping up to be one long, long day.

Having breakfast in the hotel dining room, Longarm was joined by the now sober and repentant Trixie Mondale. Sitting down across from him without asking, her being a woman and him not being a border Mex, Trixie said, "I'm sorry. You must think I'm an awful slut."

He soberly replied, "I don't recall either of us doing anything we need to feel ashamed of, Miss Trixie."

She fluttered her lashes and said, "I expected you to take advantage of my hasty nature, having read about you in the papers."

Longarm cocked a brow to ask, "Some newspaper reporters have accused this child of rolling drunks? No offense . . ."

She flustered, "Not in so many words but . . . Never mind. Your advice about Ben O'Mar or whatever his name might be would be to thank my lucky stars I didn't wind up in some Turkish hayride and head on home?"

He said, "I suspect *harem* is the word you're groping for, and such notions are against the law in Arizona Territory, and come to study on it, this territory as well. Though it ain't easy to enforce laws against polygamy when at least one

76

sheriff I know had five wives, last time I counted."

He sipped some buttermilk, wishing it was coffee, to add, "Bin Omar likely figured he could shop for multiple housekeeping in Saint George near the Arizona, Utah, Nevada borders. I'll mention this on my way on through such parts. As to anyone arresting him, you said all he did was kiss you, and you'd have to go back to Saint George for the hearing."

She said, "I'd rather be on my way home. But what if he tries that same nasty trick on some other poor Christian girl?"

Longarm could only answer, "Up to her, not us, to press charges. The law's a lot like the warning signs posted for thin ice. Nobody gets in trouble skating on thin ice before they bust through."

She politely declined his offer of some buttermilk and allowed she had to go upstairs and pack up, unless he wanted to question her some more. He said he had other rows to hoe that morning. So they parted on tensely friendly terms.

He went first to the Western Union. Billy Vail had wired back they were already working those angles he'd suggested and warned him not to ever make such suggestions again at a nickel a word, collect. Vail being a Scotch name.

Back at Provo Police Headquarters, a uniformed lieutenant came out to shake Longarm's hand, ask how come he'd only talked to a desk sergeant the night before, and advise him that of course he was free to ride on after only doing what he had to when a murderous horse thief resisted arrest. So Longarm suspected his pals in Ogden had been on the wire a tad early that morning.

After shaking hands all around, Longarm returned to his hotel, checked himself and his borrowed mules out, and headed south some more at a mile-eating trot in the cool of a greenup morning.

But even as he rode, he couldn't help wondering, "Which fork in the road ahead do we take when we get to, say, Panguitch? West along the Old Spanish Trail or south for Arizona and advertising A-rabs somewhere along the South Smith Trail? Bin Omar or somebody like him could surely account for a mail-order bride or more never making it far as Ogden!"

Chapter 12

With the weather holding cooler than it was fixing to get, as he traveled light, Longarm pushed his saddle mules harder than he might have pushed ponies across sage flats and made it to the Mormon settlement of Nephi by dark. They'd named the handy trail stop in the middle of nowhere much after yet another Mormon prophet Longarm neither knew nor cared a whole lot about. Being the only serious place to stop for miles as well as the seat of Juab County, Nephi catered to the needs of travelers of all persuasions, and if some Saints found that scandalous, others went along with Brother Brannan, Sam Brannan, the first Mormon millionaire, who'd had a revelation during the gold rush of '49 that seeing he couldn't stop all those pesky Gentiles passing through the proposed state of Deseret, and seeing they seemed just bound and determined to seek tobacco and whiskey and other forbidden stimulants, it was no skin off his immortal soul if he only *sold* the same without partaking of it.

Like-minded Saints had set up, or allowed to be set up, one saloon and a couple of beaneries serving coffee in Nephi for their transient trade. As Mormon pals had explained about similar arrangements right in Salt Lake City, they'd been instructed that artificial stimulants were just plain bad for you. A Mormon sipping tea wasn't as much out of line as say a hungry cuss of the Hebrew persuasion eating cheese off the same plate as roast beef. A heap of Mormon customs seemed to have been handed down more as fatherly advice than revelations from on high. Old Brigham Young, himself, had once brushed off accusations of sophistication by declaiming with a sheepish grin, "Don't do as I do. Do as I say!"

So an upright piano was playing against a back wall as Longarm bellied up to the bar after seeing to his mules and booking a room at one of the few places in town with rooms to let.

Their barmaid with light brown hair was a Mormon gal they all called Miss Tabitha. She must have been instructed it was all right to pour as long as she never tasted. The customers on Longarm's side of the rough pine bar were riders and teamsters bound one way or the other along the trail across the sage flats all around. Nephi did brag on a usually dry wash that seemed to offer the local bore wells a boost during rainy spells.

Longarm ordered their draft, a mistake, he realized, as soon as he tasted what a Mormon brewer forbidden to taste his own product could wind up with. But what the hell, it was wet and tasted more like beer than buttermilk.

Longarm kept his mouth shut and his ears open until a crusty-looking but friendly enough teamster suddenly asked, "Are you a married man, pilgrim?"

When Longarm allowed he'd managed to duck in time, the older man said, "Story I just heard would be funnier to you if you was married up, like me. You want me to try it on you, anyways?"

Longarm told him to shoot, and the old-timer shot a sly glance at Miss Tabitha, who seemed to pay no attention as the teamster began, "Seems like, back when old Adam was all alone in that Garden of Eden, the Lord looked down from Heaven to catch him jerking off. So the Lord said, 'Cut that out, Adam! Do you want to wind up with pimples?' But old Adam said, 'Can't help it, Lord! Seems all the other critters you made down this way get to rut all they want, whilst all you gave me to rut with was this hand!'"

The old-timer asked how Longarm liked it so far. Longarm told him to get to the funny parts. Old Adam jerking off all alone in that garden sounded more pathetic than comical.

The teamster continued, "Lord tells Adam, 'Funny you should mention that, old son. I've been studying on a proper mate for thee.' They talk like so in the Good Book. So Adam tells the Lord he's been wishing for someone to rut with in his own image, save for being softer and way better-looking.

He asks the Lord if he can have a wife with cameo features and a perfect figure. One she'll get to keep no matter how many kids she has. So the Lord says, 'That's a tall order, but I am God, so I reckon we can manage that. Anything else before I whip her up for thee?' So Adam says there surely is. He wants his beautiful bride to like rutting much as he does, ever ready to service him when he wants some, but willing to just get up and serve him breakfast in bed when he says he's had enough. You ever run into a gal like that, pilgrim?"

Longarm sighed and said, "On occasion. It's tough to get the really good-looking ones to spoil you like so."

The teamster said, "Old Adam wasn't done, as long as he had the ear of the Lord. He said he wanted this perfect bed partner to be a swell cook who'd never pester him with small talk about such matters. He said he wanted her willing to listen with interest to any small talk he had to offer and to laugh at all his jokes, sincere, no matter how often he repeated 'em."

Longarm smiled crookedly and interjected, "In sum, the perfect woman we've all been searching for in vain."

The old-timer said, "You know it. I said I was married up. Adam asks for a few more favors, such as his beautiful bride being unable to nag him no matter what he might forget to do and turning a blind eye should he ever want to rut with other critters. So the Lord rumbles thunder and lighting overhead and allows he can do it, but it's going to cost old Adam an arm and a leg. You know what old Adam says next, pilgrim?"

Longarm nodded and replied, "That's a mite steep, Lord. What can you let me have for a rib?"

The teamster said, "You should have told me you'd heard it. I'd be Fingus Fuller, bound for Provo with all sorts of shit from the San Pedro docks. Even got some silk and rice paper from Canton in one of the wagons. You?"

Longarm told him who he was and explained he was out to overtake Esau Skaggs's southbound train.

Fuller said, "Met them earlier today, near the bend of the Sevier. What are you chasing them with?"

Longarm told him. The man who knew the trail opined,

"You'll catch up this side of Gunnison at the rate they were moving. I know that old Mormon cuss, Esau, of old. Some wagon masters push harder at first and wind up with weary teams by the time they get to the hard country. Esau Skaggs would rather stop short at a good campsite than make just a few more miles and bed down poorly."

Longarm asked if Fingus Fuller knew Caleb Nugent or an Arizona cuss calling himself Ben O'Mar.

Fuller said, "Caleb Nugent's another Mormon, but he's all right. I don't recall no Ben O'Mar hauling back or forth in these parts, and it ain't the sort of name one forgets. You sure it was Ben O'Mar?"

Longarm said, "Nope. He seems to have changed it from Bin Omar for business reasons. One of them Turks riding with the U.S. Camel Corps out this way, before the war?"

The old-timer said, "Oh, them? Heard most of 'em went back home when the 'speriment failed. Heard tell of one doing right well down along the Colorado under the American name of Jolly."

Longarm nodded and said, "Haj Ali. Everbody's heard of him and his sons hauling freight down yonder. Ben O'Mar or Bin Omar seems to be a new sport in the game, and that's sort of hard to figure, because those Turks who didn't ask to be dealt in, back in the late fifties, should be driving camels in other parts by this late in the game!"

Fuller sipped some suds and said, "Can't say I met all that many driving nothing, nowheres. They get to marry up with lots of gals, the same as Mormons, right?"

Longarm said, "I understand the famous Haj Ali only got one American gal to marry up with him. Know of any others, hauling freight this far north and mayhaps in the market for matrimony, Fingus?"

Fuller said, "Not hardly. Hi Jolly is the only Turkish wagon master I ever heard of, and he hauls up and down the lower Colorado or east and west along the Gila. Never heard of such outlandish furriners up here in Utah."

The brown-haired Tabitha chimed in from her side of the zinc-topped bar, "I have. We've been warned not to marry up with anybody with more than one wife. LDS or Islamic.

Elders say it stands in the way of our statehood, and there are times one has to make sacrifices."

The two Gentiles exchanged glances. Longarm asked, "You say you have been advised against marrying up Islamic, Miss Tabitha?"

She said, "We have. Seems some such gents have been sending mash notes to Christian gals, there being so few Turkish ladies in these parts. Subject came up at a recent Sunday-go-to-meeting-on-the-green. Seems like any LDS gal who marries up Islamic is expected to forswear the Book of Mormon in favor of another book called the Coroner."

Longarm nodded and said, "Close enough. You know any ladies of your own persuasion who've recieved one of them romantic letters, ma'am?"

She replied, "Not personal. But you know what they say. Where you see smoke there's got to be fire. Why would they be warning us to be careful about sweet-talking Turks if there were none around?"

Longarm didn't pursue it further. He'd learned the hard way that trying to trace such gossip back along the grapevine to where it had commenced was as tedious and rewarding as trying to square the circle or decide how far up, up went.

He encouraged others to join in by telling a mildly dirty story about Indians shooting pool and got to question a traveling windmill salesman as well.

The portly gent who sold and helped install wind-powered bore wells told Longarm there were a few scattered Quakers settled south of Provo, but he failed to recall any Turks, single or presiding over harems.

Tabitha said, "Quakers are Christians, almost. I used to spark with a Quaker boy until his own kin made him stop. I bet they thought I was out to seduce him!"

Longarm figured that was no bet. Mormon gals on average were neither more nor less passionate than average. But it jarred folk who knew they felt so strong about stimulants to discover they liked other sorts of stimulating fine. Some of them stole stock and held up trains while abstaining, too. Folk were everywhere different and everywhere much the same, as many a Hindu, Turk, or medicine man could no doubt tell you.

When some of his new pals wondered aloud why a famous lawman was suddenly so interested in Turks, Longarm allowed, "I didn't know I was until recent. I can't say for certain I am as yet. Have any of you gents spent much time in Saint George on the Virgin?"

Those who'd been through at all opined it was a tad out of the way for hauling back and forth from California. Fingus Fuller explained, "Too many creeks to ford that far south. Best to follow the general route of the Old Spanish Trail west of the Cedar Breaks. It ain't as if there's a paved road. You gets your choice of ruts north or south of the bumps too high to roll over. I generally trend south of the Breaks, follow Kolob Canyon through the Hurricane Cliffs, and make for Pine Valley and Mountain Meadows, same as that Fancher party. The LDS killed that bunch to keep such a swell route secret a spell longer."

The Mormon barmaid blazed, "That's a big fib! Everybody knows Horse Utes killed those invading Gentiles over to Mountain Meadows!"

Fuller shrugged and said, "I heard it was Paiute and, either way, Captain Fancher was leading his train *out* of Mormon territory when he and over a hundred and twenty others were butchered like hogs under a flag of truce!"

Longarm saw Tabitha was fixing to cloud up and rain all over them. So he suggested, "Let's talk about the Haun's Hill Massacre, seeing the records on that one are less disputed."

Fingus Fuller marveled, "Mormons massacred folk at a place called Haun's Hill, too?"

Longarm said, "Not exactly. An inspired Fundamentalist Christian called Nehemiah Comstock led a mob of two hundred like-minded Bible thumpers in an unprovoked attack on a Mormon wagon train in Missouri. Slaughtered the men and women. Threw the children down a well, alive, 'til they drowned down yonder, slow and dirty. Then they looted the camp and marched home, singing the praises of *their* religion. Governor of Missouri said he was proud of Comstock and his raiders. Pardoned one and all, called out the Missouri Militia to finish the job. But by then the surviving Saints had retreated to Illinois."

He drained his stein, put it back on the bar, and nodded at Tabitha as he quietly continued, "That's where another mob of good Christians murdered Joseph Smith and his brother, Hiram, after they'd come in as demanded to the county jail at Carthage, Illinois. That's the way men can get, arguing about religion."

As the brown-haired Tabitha refilled his stein for him, free, with a mighty friendly smile, Longarm observed, "I try not to have me such arguments. Used to try and get the Lord to talk to me when I was little and alone and scared in bed. Ain't saying nobody's up there. But if He wanted me to kill folk for him when I grew up, he never said so."

He sipped some suds and added, "Seems to me an all-powerful God would feel insulted if I allowed He wasn't powerful enough to thunder-ghast His own sinners or, seeing He can do anything, convince sinners not to annoy Him so!"

Nobody argued. Longarm finished the near beer and was sorry he had, as it came to him the stuff inspired more desire to piss than anything else. He naturally never declared his intentions in mixed company. He just set his stein on the zinc and went outside to find someplace in the dark to take a leak.

Before he did, the brown-haired Tabitha caught up with him to ask, "You're not leaving for the night, are you?"

It was a good question. He needed to piss really bad. He told her he didn't want to disturb the fellow where he was rooming by getting in too late.

Tabitha said, "Don't go. We've only just met. Stay 'til I get off in just another hour. That won't be so late, and we can talk, and if you think it's too late to go back to your rooming house we . . . might be able to work something out."

Longarm said he wanted to check on his mules, but that he'd come back in as soon as he had.

He didn't know her well enough to piss in front of her yet.

Chapter 13

Longarm walked Tabitha home through the silvery light and inky shadows of a midnight moon with a wary eye on said shadows, even as he idly wondered why. Mormon settlements tended to be safer, even for an outsider, than most others, and walking a gal of any faith home was as proper or improper as the lady chose. But one of the reasons the westward travails of Tabitha's kind had been so wild was that horses and most folk tended to spook at unexpected surprises, and Mormons and Gentiles were always surprising one another.

To begin with, members of the LDS looked and acted like the Know Nothing Party's picture of an ideal Anglo-Saxon American, and that of course could lead to foot-in-mouth surprises. For while you expected a stranger dressed like a Scotchman, a Pennsylvania Dutchman, or a Hopi to have different notions, Mormons had no peculiar outward trimmings to warn others of some peculiar notions, as others saw 'em.

Mormon men dressed to fit their station in life, be it plowing a field or presiding over a courtroom. Some wore beards. Some were smooth shaven. Mormon women were as fashion conscious as any others of whatever class they fit into in late Victorian times. So it hardly showed that none of them were smokers until a stranger lit up around them.

Longarm had read the Good Book of his own folk more than once and had a few stabs at the Book of Mormon. So he knew that despite raving fanatics who'd throw Mormon children down a well, there was little in the Book of Mormon that went against the original King James edition of the Old or New Testament. They wouldn't have called their new faith the Church of Jesus Christ of Latter-day Saints if they hadn't believed in Jesus of Nazareth lock, stock, and barrel. Their Prophet Joseph had written, or translated, how Jesus had done even *more* than the Bible of everyone else had recorded. The Book of Mormon related how the Indians of the Americas were the lost tribes of Israel mentioned in the Old Testament and told how, during some times of His youth left unwritten about in the New Testament, Lord Jesus had spent some time in America where, Old Zion being occupied at the time by Roman troops, He decreed a New Zion to be founded by His disciples somewhere in the American West, which had been most anywhere west of Palmyra, New York, at the time the Book of Mormon was being set in type.

Other notions the Smith brothers and their fellow prophets had come up with on their argumentative westard wendings had never, when others studied on it, gone against anything Abraham, Moses, or Jesus had said because they just weren't on record as being for or against later revelations about coffee, tea, or polygamy, save for that one sticking point about wine at the wedding in Cana or the Last Supper.

Another Mormon gal Longarm had asked about that said nit-picking got one nowhere, and didn't other Christians eat pork on the grounds a Jewish Lord had never said anything against pork in the New Testament? Lord Jesus had never said anybody *had* to drink His wine, and everybody knew alcohol, caffeine, and nicotine were bad for them.

Tabitha dwelt alone in a modest one-room cabin, and Longarm was neither delighted nor disgusted by the fair-to-middling housekeeping of a working gal with other chores to tend.

She sat him on her sofa across from the coyly draped bed and said she'd brew them some forbidden tea while they talked. Before this time, Longarm had gotten the distinct impression Tabitha hadn't been brought up to strict LDS standards or, if she had, they hadn't taken.

As she lit an oil-fired burner under her copper teakettle and got out some marble cake to slice, Longarm brought her up to date on his mission and questioned her more about those rumors of lovesick gents of the Moslem persuasion. When she sniffed that the Coroner was a crazy heathen tome,

Longarm sighed and said, "I must be missing a lot. Having read translations of the scriptures followed by all sorts of folk, I just can't fathom where *any* of them command us to kill each other in the name of a Lord who loves us all. Christians, Hebrews, and Moslems all subscribe to the very same Ten Commandments recieved from on high by Moses on Sinai. They all agree 'Thou shalt not kill,' and so we've been killing one another ever since to prove we believe more in the word of God."

Tabitha poured his tea. It tasted like hot water. Her Mormon mama hadn't told her how you brewed tea or mayhaps she was in a hurry. One Mormon custom outsiders could find a sudden surprise was their custom of wearing peculiar union suits under their outter duds. Tabitha had nothing on under her summer frock. She'd made sure he'd notice by unbuttoning her bodice to air the cleft betwixt her firm and somehow upthrust breasts. He confirmed she had a whalebone corset on when he somehow wound up with his arm around her waist, once she was sitting on his lap, uninvited.

Not that he nor any other natural man would have minded, of course. The parts of her coming out the other end of that corset were soft as marshmallow, and she smelled all over of lilac water.

But before they ever got around to kissing, as no doubt she'd been planning, Tabitha asked how he felt about carrying her along with him to California in the morning.

The effect on his dawning desires was as effective as an ice water surprise. But he tried not to let it show as he said, "I can't think of a thing I'd rather do, Miss Tabitha. But we wouldn't be alone on the trail, once we caught up. So there'd be bound to be some talk."

She wriggled her derriere as if to prove it was his for the asking as she replied, "Pooh, what do I care what strangers I'll never see again say about me, once I get to splash and splash all I want in the great Pacific Ocean?"

He said, "Some of the party ahead are members of your own LDS, and I got to go all the way back with everybody by way of Sacramento!"

He saw how she worried about the troubles of others when she pouted. "If you really liked me, you wouldn't *care* what anybody else thought. We'd have *weeks* of sweet love under the desert stars before you had to worry about what your friends back home might ever say, Custis!"

Knowing Billy Vail would expect him to probe the witness in more depth, Longarm hugged her some as he suggested, "Let's talk about *your* feelings. I can see how it might be tougher for a restless young thing to get shed of dull surroundings when they surrounded her in the middle of Mormon country. Is it safe to assume I ain't the first wayfaring stranger you've had this conversation with?"

She said, "Don't talk dirty. You're the very first Gentile I ever offered to go to Californee with. That Quaker boy I mentioned told me all about Californee 'cause he'd been there and back. And when he kissed me, he called me a thee, but then he said we'd never square things with his kith and kin 'cause I didn't quake their way."

She made herself out a liar by mentioning the Irishman who'd allowed she'd have to learn more about brewing tea and give up meat on Friday if she ever meant to get very far with him.

Longarm steered the conversation to other local gals with a similar lack of interest in Mormon underwear, and Tabitha confirmed his suspicion that there were restless young gals everywhere.

He said, "Met this French actress who started out Hebrew, ran off to become a Papist nun, and when that didn't take decided she was Church of England with a grain of salt. I understand men a long ways from home do advertise in the papers for gals who'd like to start all over in other parts. Might you have heard anything along those lines?"

She said, "I told you so. Lovesick Turks have been advertising for mail-order brides. Other gents as well, I hear tell. Papers published with the approval of the Salt Lake Temple don't carry such advertising, and we can't get the *Tribune* or *Rocky Mountain News* in this one-horse town. If you'll take me with you to Californee, I'll let you indulge in crimes against nature on my person!"

He said, "We were talking about other avenues of escape. Have any Mormon gals you know of responded to such offers in the forbidden out-of-town papers?"

She shrugged and said, "Couple from around here, I guess. Rachel North grew weary of milking cows for a strict father who discouraged gentlemen callers, and I understand Martha Thornbury left her husband when he brought home a bride she'd never liked. I don't know the names of the others."

"Then there've been others?" Longarm asked.

She said, "Sure. Lots. The older folk take the Book more seriously than many of my generation. I mean, what's the point of going on and on about westward ho when you were *born* out our way? Deseret's all right, I guess. But there's a whole big world outside, with all sorts of new sights and sounds and smells and . . . Take me to Californee with you, Custis! I'll let you tie me up and beat me black and blue if that's your pleasure! I'll be your love slave forever, until we get on out to Californee!"

It wouldn't have been kind to tell her he didn't even feel tempted. So he said, "It's getting late. Why don't we both think about it for now and mayhaps talk about it some more in the cold gray dawn?"

As he perforce set her to one side on her sofa to get back to his feet, she gleeped, "Wait! Don't go! I don't want you to go! Stay here with me tonight, and I'll give you a free sample of all I have to offer for the chance to get the fuck *out* of here!"

Tabitha was, of course, named for that lady in the New Testament who had risen from the dead like Lazarus. This one rose to blow out that candle, and if she grabbed for Longarm in the dark, she missed. For he was out the door and striding off as she wept from her doorstep for him to come back and take his beating like a man.

He'd told a white lie, himself, about not wanting to wake anybody at his rooming house. The Mormon landlady had shown him to a room for hire in their carriage house, above his mules and their own stock. So he spent the rest of the night comfortable but restless in a featherbed, and when an old Shanghai rooster cut loose before sunrise, Longarm rose to water the mules, saddle up, and ride on, telling his morning hard-on to behave itself.

Forging south across the sage flats, Longarm confided to

his mount, "I don't know if I'm getting old or growing up. That's two easy lays in a row this child has passed on, and it's commencing to hurt!"

The mules never answered. Longarm didn't care. He knew how dumb it would have been to stray from his mission with either the hard-eyed Trixie or the softer-fleshed but hard-hearted Tabitha. He'd forgotten the name of that kindly old philosopher who'd warned, naturally in French, about swapping hours of worry for minutes of pleasure.

He explained to the mule, "It ain't as if I felt too high and mighty for old Trixie, and she'd just said she'd spent weeks alone on the trail. There was something about her . . . desperation, I reckon, that warned me not to skate no closer."

The mules just kept plodding on up the trail, kicking up enough dust to make Longarm bless the April breezes.

He said, "It ain't as if I've never kissed a Mormon gal, and Lord knows old Tabitha back yonder was above the age of consent and hardly pure. I reckon what put me off about her was her mixed-up mind. On the one hand she got all warm-eyed at me for sticking up for her church, but not long after that, she was telling me how awful the LDS was as she offered to be my love slave to get shed of kith and kin!"

He looked around and, seeing he was alone in the middle of a sage flat, he fished out a three-for-a-nickel cheroot and lit up.

Enjoying the first drag even more than he'd expected, Longarm told the mules, "I'd have doubtless enjoyed Tabitha more than usual after passing on Trixie and spending a night alone, wondering why. Since we ain't about to overtake our wagon train anytime in the near future, if then, this child is purely going to regret that outburst of purity in Nephi by the time we catch up, and even when and if we catch up, who's left, now that old Cass has hauled her friendly ass back East?"

In a latter-day reenactment of Zeno's Paradox, Longarm was riding faster than the wheels of Esau Skaggs were rolling. But by the time Longarm made it to the westward bend of the Sevier River, the wagons had been rolling south over forty-eight hours, if Fingus Fuller's word was good, and another night was coming on.

Nobody with a lick of sense spread his bedroll where other folk and their livestock had been milling about and shitting overnight. So he rode on up the river in the cool shades of evening, knowing he could bed down most anywhere with water handy for the taking, now.

As the gloaming light was giving way to the gathering dusk, Longarm spied a grassy swale forming a shallow saddle between clumps of willow with the shallows of the Sevier at high water lapping at their roots. He announced, "This is the place," and reined in. But before he could dismount, he spied a mighty low star or a lamp in a window, not all that far up the riverside trail.

He rode down to the shallows and let his mules water themselves as he announced, "Change of plans, Lord willing and they don't put the dogs on us. For even *I* can see the three of us might be more comforted for the coming night at yonder homestead."

Mules made up for going longer without water than horses by drinking more like camels when they got the chance. Longarm finally told them they'd had enough and insisted they move on.

It wasn't easy. Mules had less tender jaws than horses and didn't seem to feel it when you kicked their ribs without spurs on your boots.

But being Longarm was strong of wrist as well as will, he rode into the dooryard of the dark, rambling soddy with one lamp in one window a few minutes later, braced for the usual baying of their yard dog.

They didn't seem to keep one chained out front. He called out, "Hello the house! Deputy U.S. Marshal Custis Long, here, and I've come in peace, hear?"

There came what sounded like the scurry of giggling mice inside the soddy. Then the front door opened, and a friendly she-male voice called out to him, "Come in, *Saltu ka Taibo!* We have been expecting you!"

As Longarm dismounted with a grin, two gals came out to help him with his mules. He couldn't see just what they looked like with the moon so low in the east at that hour, but *Saltu ka Taibo* meant something translating in the sense of "Colored man who ain't a Nigger" or "Mexican who ain't a fucking greaser," and so that seemed to be what some Paiute had decided to call him. Others called him *Saltu ka Saltu* or "Stranger who is no stranger." He'd arrested some crooked Indian agents in his time, and word had gotten around, it seemed.

He didn't ask how Paiute settled near the campsite of his own wagon party might have wound up expecting him. He just allowed the two gals to shower him with praise, and as one led his mules around back, Longarm followed the other into the house.

By the soft light of that one oil lamp, Longarm saw his hostess was short in stature while long of hair, dressed in a Mother Hubbard of calico print. It wasn't until she turned to smile up at him adoringly that he saw she was just plain no-shit beautiful.

Chapter 14

She said her Paiute momma had named her Pui-esi, but her Dutch dad had called her Pussy. It was easy to see why. Her eyes were indeed gray while her likely quarter-breed fixture of features had wound up sort of feline. Pussy sat him on their *norinadi,* which combined the funcions of divan and bed, to rustle up some grub for him. His coffee-starved nose had already detected the smell of *tupai,* and he was afraid he knew what she was fixing to serve him. But what the hell, it was past his usual suppertime, and if the Digger Indian mush they called *koatzap* had next to no taste, at least it was filling and didn't taste awful.

As she worked, Pussy explained their late dad had been a back-and-forth teamster born a Dutch Lutheran but convinced by the life he'd led that all *puha* or medicine was *posa* or crazy. Their momma had been another outcast he'd naturally taken up with. She'd been the daughter of a mountain man who'd civilized her just enough to make the life of a Digger *wahyipi* distasteful to her, but not civilized enough for your average white man to take home to meet the family.

The occasional white man of the house had filed a homestead claim out there between Mormon settlements or claims in order to raise the daughters Pui-esi and Totsiyama or Pussy and Topsy.

Topsy came in from tending to the mules as Pussy handed Longarm a tin cup of Arbuckle brand *tupai,* and she was more Indian-looking but, if anything, even prettier.

Pussy brought Topsy up to date on the conversation and went on to tell Longarm how, trading with both passing wagon trains in English and Digger kin in Ho, or Uto-Aztec as the professors had the common lingo of the wandering nations originating in the Great Basin from a common, simple food-gathering culture. Passing travelers tended to have brought along more manufactured shit than they really needed out under wide-open skies, while the local Indians often had more pine nuts, jerked antelope, and rabbit meat or swell baskets than they needed. The Diggers never having invented pottery they'd have found awkward to tote if they had, and having little use for clothing as they wandered far and dusty, they'd learned to make basketry so tightly woven it would hold water. Albeit he noticed Pussy was heating up that Digger mush in an iron pot over the coals of a cast-iron Franklin stove somebody must have gotten tired of hauling to California.

Sipping the *tupai* a heap of Utah folk didn't approve of, Longarm idly wondered if his quarter-breed hostesses even knew how their grandmother had started out making mush or hot soup in a waterproof straw basket by dropping red-hot rocks in the water to bring it to a boil.

Longarm had been surprised, earlier, by how few changes of red-hot rocks it took. It paid to pay attention to the despised Digger Indians instead of using them as target practice. Greenhorns were still winding up dead in a murdersome wilderness bitty Indian kids played tag in.

Longarm knew that unlike all too many forty-niners, the Mormons had tried to get along with the long-lost tribes of

Israel, and so they had in turn gotten sound advice on a land unlike old or New England indeed.

Snuggling comfortably on their *norinadi* with him in her own loose calico Mother Hubbard, Topsy explained how they'd heard from Esau Skaggs that the famous Longarm would be coming up the river, and of course they'd heard about him earlier from their less-civilized kin.

It sure beat all how an occasional act of common decency could get around in Indian circles. Longarm knew he was far from the only white man admired and trusted by Indians. But Indians seemed to find them so few in number they traded stories about them, the way whites traded the names and personal quirks of famous baseball players.

The runty Kit Carson, an Indian fighter you didn't want to mess with, had been known far and wide as the firm but fair "Rope Thrower" after he'd shown Indians who wanted to get along how to twirl a Mex reata.

The artistic George Catlin, after delighting his Indian hosts with his realistic sketches, had wandered freely through territory decribed as hostile by the War Department and visited the sacred pipestone quarries guarded by the truculent and original Minnesota Sioux. *Minnesota* meaning "milky water" in their lingo and *Sioux* meaning "throat-cutting miserable bastards" in the lingo of their Ojibwa enemies. George Catlin had even gotten on with Blackfoot, described by early mountain men as impossible to befriend. But then old George had been content to sketch their likenesses without stealing their pelts or fucking their wives without permission.

The folk called Apache, or "throat-cutting miserable bastards" by their Pueblo enemies called a superintendent of the Overland Mail Depot in Tucson *Taglito* or "Red Beard" and left his mail coaches be while at war with the U.S. Cavalry in the same Chiricahua Mountains. Not because he'd been some sort of saintly figure to them but because he'd bothered to learn their ways, some of their lingo, and cut a simple live-and-let-live deal with the occasionaly murderous Cochise.

John Clum, the current publisher of the *Tombstone Epitaph*, had been a rare white eyes the same nation had admired for sticking up for them and then resigning in protest as their

Indian agent during the crackdown of '77, when all Indians were expected to do penance for Little Big Horn.

Indian pals had explained to Longarm they admired a man willing to stand up to them when he had to, while willing to smoke with anyone who wasn't spoiling for a fight. For that was the code real men were supposed to follow and, save for crazy people under the protection of the medicine beings, mealymouthed sissies who preached about real men loving one another were just made for the scalping knife.

Since they'd been told *Saltu ka Saltu* or *Piirapiaprey* was a white man to be treated with extreme respect, Pussy had made the usually way blander *koatzap* with bacon bits stirred into the corn mush, and it sure beat all how a little flavoring could turn *koatzap* into a rib-sticking repast.

Their *tupai* hit the spot as well after going without his customary black coffee for a spell. He'd warned Pussy when she'd been pouring he liked his *tupai* neat. But as the three of them sort of snuggled on their one substantial piece of furniture, he saw the part-Paiute sisters didn't share the almost universal Indian custom of stirring white flour instead of sugar into trade coffee. They both seemed to prefer it with brown sugar. A lot of brown sugar.

Topsy explained they'd heard something about Longarm's mission from his fellow lawman, Captain Burbank, when they'd visited the wagon ring with fresh eggs from out back and pine nuts of most any age, since pine nuts kept and were kept indefinitely by wandering Paiute.

He told the sisters the little more he'd found out since parting company with Burbank and the other lawmen. He didn't talk down to them as if they were children he had to humor. Even full-bloods who spoke less English were grown-ups with brains keen enough to feed themselves and their families in country that didn't lightly suffer fools, and he knew that breeds who dwelt by the side of the trail to be on friendly terms with most who passed by knew as much or more than he did about those missing white women.

All but one, that was. Longarm explained, "One of the chagrined gents who sent away for a bride that was never delivered would seem to be an Oriental of means who owns a Chinee laundry in Fort Collins. So I suspect his missing bride might be Oriental as well."

Pussy asked in an impish tone whether it was true what they said about Chinese women.

Longarm said he was in no position to say.

This was not true. Thanks to some firm but fair law enforcement during the nasty anti-Chinese riots of recent memory, Longarm was more popular among the sons and daughters of Han than most round eyes and could have assured the curious quarter breeds a daughter of Han had a *taina* much like their own. But he didn't know them that well, and unless he was fixing to know them better, talking dirty late at night on a *norinadi* between two eyelash-fluttering gals could wind up pure and simple cruelty to dumb animals. His old organ grinder having a mind of its own but no brains worth mention after two nights alone in bed.

His right friendly hostess gals were certain they'd recall any Oriental gals passing by outside and assured him they got a good look at most every party moving up or down the trail.

He asked, "Most? Not all?"

Topsy shrugged and said, "Sometimes riders, almost never wagons, pass without stopping for at least a howdy. We don't see much of the ones riding by at night. I can't remember any such parties with any rider sitting sidesaddle. You, Pui-esi?"

The one called Pussy shook her head and said, "No. I don't remember any Turks, either. But on the other hand, what might a Turk look like?"

It was a smart question.

Longarm said, "I read in this library book how the old-time Turks started out as a Mongol tribe but intermarried with the best-looking white gals they could find when they swept into the Middle East to take over. They took up the Moslem religion and ways of those good-looking white gals they admired until in the end they wound up looking and acting much like other A-rab gents, save for getting to lord it over everybody, of course. They wear these funny red fez hats and go about by day in a sort of long nightgown. But of course, if any Turk put on a Carlsbad Stetson, a hickory shirt, and jeans, he'd look like any other good old boy of, say, Eye-talian or even Black Irish persuasion."

He set his empty tin cup aside as he added, "I'm glad you drew that picture in my head just now, Miss Pussy. Now that I study on it, the famous Hi Jolly and his American sons hauling freight down Yuma way would hardly be traipsing about in fez hats and nightgowns at this late date. So this Ben O'Mar or Bin Omar might pass for a Mormon or a Gentile from across the road, and I'll need to find somebody who can tell me what he *looks* like before I can ask him what he knows about courting gals at a distance in the newspapers!"

When he added he was anxious to catch up with his own wagon train, Topsy suggested he'd start fresher in the morning if he got to sleep early. Then she took his hat off for him as her sister trimmed that one lamp and one or the other seemed to be unbuttoning his fly for him in the dark.

He started to ask what in thunder she thought she was up to, and then his old organ grinder was all the way up, and whoever that was down yonder was sucking on it, as the one at his other end shoved him on his back across their *norinadi* to kiss him French as she got to work on his shirt buttons.

He didn't want her popping any, so he mumbled into her open mouth he could take his own damned duds off, and she proceeded to shuck her Mother Hubbard the hard way, hauling her naked flesh out the top as they went on kissing mighty friendly. It still wasn't clear which of the two she might be.

The one kissing him even more warmly down below managed to haul his boots and jeans off by the time he rolled his lips free to warn her he was fixing to come in her mouth.

That was when he learned she'd peeled off her own Mother Hubbard the hard way. She was stark naked as she slithered up him like a passionate crocodile coming ashore to elbow whoever had been kissing him out of her way and kiss his lips, herself, as she impaled herself warmly on what he suspected they called his *gweehaw*.

Since the dirty words were the first words one learned in any new lingo, Longarm knew they called a cunt a *taina* while tits and ass were *pitzi* and *pawohtoc*. He rolled whichever one he was enjoying his *kamakiri* with on her back to finish right with an elbow hooked under each widespread knee as she laughed and yelled, *"Ha! Ha! Gweehawma pia! Kobi ueto mana-kkwa!"* To which the other replied, as far as Longarm could follow, it was her turn to take a big dong deep as a wild pony could shove it, now.

So whoever might have said virtue was its own reward must have had in mind going without for a couple of nights before meeting up with such warm-natured and sharing sisters. He'd have never managed half so well had he taken either Trixie or Tabitha up on those earlier offers.

Pretending he didn't follow the drift of the baby-talk Paiute they were using to use and abuse him, Longarm let them wrestle atop him in the dark as he got his breath back, and that felt swell, too.

Then, whoever he'd started out swapping French spit with had taken the place of the one who'd been sucking him, sucking almost as hard with her warm wet innards as she kissed him some more in a somewhat more familiar fashion. He had to allow that whoever she might be, she kissed best with both ends as her sister bounced on the mattress beside them, urging them to to hurry up and come so's she could have another go at it.

Longarm and whoever that was on top came almost together and, as if in silent conspiracy, just lay still as she milked his virility with internal spasms until her sister literally shoved her off, protesting she was being a mean old *muviporoo.*

Longarm had just decided that meant something like "selfish pig," when she was hogging his semierection with her own renewed interest, and damned if that didn't feel interesting, too!

So a good time was had by all as Longarm took turns with the mighty sharing sisters, changing his mind in the dark from time to time as he tried to match husky voices offering unfamilar endearments with their curvacious but different soft or firm spots.

He knew that if he really put his mind to it, or simply asked, he'd know for certain which was the best kisser, which had the deepest throat or the tighter twat. But he wasn't sure he wanted to know for certain, so he never asked, and later, as he'd hoped, once he'd kissed them both in the dark and ridden on right after cockcrow, he knew he'd always get to picure either pretty face in most any of those wild positions back there, leaving him with twice the pleasant memories of a very pleasant stay indeed!

Chapter 15

Zeno's Paradox had been whipped up by an old-time Greek, working with bead counters, to prove that once somebody had a lead on you, it was impossible to catch up, no matter how fast you rode. Zeno figured that by the time you got to where the cuss you were chasing was, he'd have moved on a ways. So you had to get to yonder, only to find he was farther on, and so forth, until you were trying in vain to make up less than in inch before he could move on a hairsbreadth.

Since anyone with a lick of sense could see this was bullshit no matter what Zeno's arithmetic said, more sensible mathematicians had come up with trigonometry to prove what Longarm needed no arithmetic to figure out.

The wagons led south by Easau Skaggs had gone another twenty-odd miles south while he'd ridden twenty-odd back to Provo. So once he was done in Provo, starting after his pals with a late start, they'd had a forty-odd-mile lead on him. Since he could make thirty-odd a day, it meant he had to overtake the southbound wagons in four days, and that was how it worked out, Zeno be damned.

He caught up as they were making camp after that last hard day's drive to the junction of the main stream and the substantial East Fork running north from Bryce Canyon. They were still forming up a wagon ring as Longarm rode in through the long shadows and orange cow dust of a Great

Basin sunset. As he dismounted off to one side, the ash-blond Dawn Atwell came tearing over to throw herself in Longarm's arms, sobbing she'd been so worried about him.

She felt a lot more willowsome than the last quarter-breed sister he'd hugged like so, whichever that one had been.

Aware of the picture they presented as others came out through the swirling cow dust to greet him, Longarm gently but firmly disentangled himself from the literally clinging blonde to answer the questions he knew they'd be piling on.

Their peerless leader in no-longer-white deerskin, the still overweight Hudson Livermore, demanded to know where Longarm had been all that time.

Longarm said, "Trying to do my job. Don't push me on that, Mr. Livermore. For openers, I not only sent and recieved more raw data by wire but stumbled across a lead none of us knew beans about the last this expedition saw Provo."

He nodded at Wagon Master Skaggs to add, "Evening, Esau. These mules you lent me were better than you promised. Can I just hand 'em back to you and your hands or do you want me to rub 'em down and such?"

The older man said, "Got kids on my payroll with such chores in mind, Longarm. Come on over to the grub line with us so's we can hear about your adventures as we sup."

That made more sense than anything their peerless leader had said since Longarm had ever laid eyes on the obvious political apointee.

Eastern reporters, including some with the party before they'd been with the party a spell, wrote about quaint chuck wagon crews serving biscuits and gravy for breakfast or flapjacks for supper. On the trail with a chuck wagon you saw how biscuits could bake slow overnight in a dutch oven over a campfire laid at sunset after a long haul with no fires lit at all. The dutch oven was put on the coals late, as a crew was finishing up for the night. Flapjacks could be flapped within minutes of making camp from batter that had ridden a spell to stir itself in a rolling chuck wagon. Their Mormon cookie mixed a mighty fine batter during the noonday trail stop while his hands were serving cold canned beans with tomato preserves. Longarm admired the sweet butter and honey served on the warm flapjacks, but he was sorely missing that *tupai* served hot with quarter-breed kissing to match.

As he had to be a sport about his supper while relating more detail to the investigating committee, reporters, lawmen, and Mormons gathered 'round, Longarm was trying to figure which of them Dawn was with when she wasn't throwing herself up against him. Young Brett Garwood, the assistant Dawn took shorthand off, seemed to be seated on a wagon tongue right friendly with Miss Cindy Lou, another stenograph gal with wavier hair a more dishwater shade of blond. The one called Mary Jane seemed to need help with her flapjacks from that cub reporter, Hovak, from the *Denver Post*. It wasn't as clear who Dawn or the auburn-haired Miss Rose Ann were supping with.

The deerskin-clad Hudson Livermore seemed annoyed at Longarm for the unwelcome news that at least one mail-order bride claimed to have been ordered by a leftover camel drover from the prewar failure of that U.S. Camel Corps.

Longarm said, "I wired the War Department about Bin Omar before I left Provo. Them assimilated Paiute breeds you might remember from your campsite by the bend of the Sevier said they've never seen Turk one or that missing Chinee lady. By the way, what happened to the Paiute you had scouting ahead for you all?"

Captain Burbank said, "They're scouting ahead, of course. We'll be moving through natural ambush country in a few days, and we had a talk about that."

The Mormon lawman looked uncomfortable as he added, "We're just about agreed none of those Gentile women were abducted here in the delta for the simple reason they never made it to the delta. So somebody grabbed them farther along, where others have run into trouble in the past."

"He's talking about Mountain Meadows," one of the reporters murmured to another.

Longarm said, "He's talking about farther along, where we'll know more about it, as it goes in that old church song. We've way farther along to go before we get to Mountain Meadows, and there've been robberies and a lot worse, closer. As you'll see once we leave this open river valley, we'll be passing rimrock and thick groves of pinyon and cedar, which is what they call juniper trees in these parts, over a bounding main of dusty hill and dale. So let's not worry about what might or might not have happened in one small stretch of still-unsettled country a generation ago. Let's hope our Digger scouts don't miss anybody newer to these parts atop a rimrock with a telescoped Springfield .45-70!"

Captain Burbank mulled those words over with his own flapjacks before he said, "Saint George is a day out of our way, and what about the women coming up out of the Mojave the *regular* way? Might we not miss a clue or more, digressing down the Virgin far as Saint George?"

Turning to the older Esau Skaggs, the Utah lawman asked how often a wagon train bound for Provo and points beyond took a detour down to Saint George.

Skaggs said, "They don't, unless Saint George is their destination. As I hope you've all noticed, these wagons don't wiggle-waggle off to the right or left that much as we make such progress as we can each day. Saint George exists mostly as a winter resort at lower altitude near the Grand Canyon. By this late in the greenup, most folk with real money have left for the summer. Those caretakers and such left to carry on will soon see why. Gets up to a hundred and twenty in the shade with no shade when you summer in Saint George. That Turk you mentioned can't be living there if he can afford to send away for wives."

Longarm said, "That Miss Trixie I mentioned said she met him there in Saint George, so she must have taken what, a detour off to the side of the more trodden trail? She said she got that far traveling with a wagon master called Caleb Nugent. Your turn."

Skaggs said, "I know Brother Caleb. He's an honest man. If he hauled in to Saint George with that lady, he had some good reason. He must have been delivering freight somebody ordered. Swinging that far south this late in the year ain't customary. How did that Gentile lady meet up with you, well north of here, if Caleb Nugent let her off down in Saint George?"

Longarm replied, "Said she traveled north from Saint George with a smaller party. Make sense to you?"

Skaggs said, "Sure. Like I told you, everybody who can manage wants to get out of Saint George before it warms up.

I was talking about that Turk who says he lives there. If he can afford anywhere else, he don't live year round in Saint George."

Captain Burbank asked, "What if, like Hi Jolly, he hauls freight up the Colorado River Trail out of Yuma?"

Skaggs shrugged and said, "Everybody has to come from somewheres. I heard of Hi Jolly farther down the Colorado. Ain't never heard of nobody called Ben O'Mar, Bin Omar, or Suleiman the Magnificent in these parts. What if he's some sort Greek or Spaniard, jealous of our LDS marriage customs and just pretending to be a Moslem?"

Longarm didn't join in the laughter. He nodded soberly and observed, "Men have told stranger stories to turn the head of a maiden fair. But to his dubious credit, the Miss Trixie I told you all about said he finally took no for an answer and never threatened or abducted her when she declared her independence there in Saint George."

"Then why are we wasting time in talk about this mysterious Turk?" demanded their peerless leader petulantly.

Longarm told Livermore, "The gal's Arabesque tale establishes that at least *she* wasn't lured up the regular trail by proposals through the U.S. mails. Others might have responded to similar notions, and we have to make certian none of them ran into a more persistent Turk, Greek, Spaniard, or whatever."

Captain Burbank asked, "Why? None of those missing persons reports were filed by anyone in Saint George or by anyone anywhere in Utah Territory! Those *missing* women were bound for Ogden and the South Pass by rail!"

"Unless some of them got sidetracked," Longarm pointed out, adding, "Met this other lady in Nephi, anxious to see the world. So anxious she said she was willing to go most anywhere and do most anything with most anybody."

Dawn Atwell, seated nearby, gasped, "Custis! You didn't!"

Longarm smiled down at her to reply, "She ain't here with me this evening, is she? My point is that any number of California gals ready and willing to pull up stakes and go join a man they never met, just to get out of where they were, might have wanted to get out of there a heap, so how

103

big a carrot might it take to lure a hungry mare into, say, a greener-looking pasture, see?"

One of the Mormon teamsters did. He volunteered, "Now that you've brung up mysterious habits, Longarm, I did hear gossip, last time I was down in Moab, about some canyon stronghold infested by sinister Gentiles with no visible means of support, somewheres farther south in Arizona Territory."

Captain Burbank snorted. "I didn't, and I'm the law in *Utah* Territory!" He turned to Longarm to protest, "Don't you see where this line of guesswork can lead us? Why stop at Saint George? Why stop way farther off at Moab? Why not search for those missing women at the top of Jack's beanstalk? Dosen't *that* fairy tale make mention of a secret castle somewhere'a up yonder?"

Longarm nodded but asked Esau Skaggs if he had a map of southwest Utah Territory handy.

The wagon master said, "Not handy. Ain't certain I can find you one at all, seeing I usually follow the same route to Californee and back. I'll root around in my possibles by daylight, come morning, and do I find one, it's yours."

Burbank repeated his plaint that they didn't have the time or the manpower to chase after will-o'-the-wisp rumors about mysterious Moslems in canyon hideouts. Longarm suggested they all sleep on it, more than once, adding, "There's no other direction to worry about but south as we haul on up the Sevier, Captain."

There came a general murmur of agreement. One of the dudes asked a dumb question about the troubles of the trail ahead, and the conversation drifted off in directions Longarm wasn't worried about as it got ever darker.

After star bright but earlier than most usually turned in, Brett Garwood made a great show of yawning, and when he declared his intent to catch up on his sleep and tottered off, it wasn't Dawn Atwell who tottered after him after a studied interval that didn't fool anybody. It was the dishwater-blond Cindy Lou.

When their peerless leader whose Ojibwa beadwork advertised for a brave man to take care of him declared his own intent to turn in early and take care of his youth, one of the reporters wondered aloud after he'd left, "Wonder why Livermore didn't invite his youth to sup with us."

Longarm had to laugh alone. Some few of the teamsters might not have gotten it; the three stenographer gals didn't let on they had.

After nobody had said anything to him for a spell, Longarm rose to gather up his saddle and Winchester to tote them upwind and uphill, away from the wagon ring and pent-up draft critters.

Above the junction the west fork of the Sevier ran less water but swifter, because its valley had been rising slowly but surely higher to the south, and Longarm was able to find a wide swath of still-green short grass to spread his bedding across.

He did so by unlashing his bedroll before he turned the saddle upside down to dry with its crotch to the wind and the stars. He leaned his Winchester on the overturned saddle and spread his roll so's he'd have an easy grab for the same in the dark. He put his six-gun in his overturned Stetson to be as handy grabbing the other way.

He unrolled his bedding and sat on the same to haul off his boots. So that was the position Dawn Atwell found him in when she came his way in the dark, softly calling out for him.

Longarm said, "Over here, ma'am. Be advised I'm half undressed."

She appeared a paler patch of darkness as she moved in to flop down on his bedding beside him and shyly confess, "I'm afraid you're going to think me wicked, Custis. But I've always been getting in trouble by acting on impulses and, well, now I really need some help I fear only you can offer!"

He said, "That's mighty flattering, ma'am," as he took her in his arms, glad he'd spent the night before alone on the trail after all.

Chapter 16

They started out natural. Dawn shuddered closer and kissed him back, French, moaning deep and low as the two of them reclined across his bedding. His roaming free hand soon established she was indeed more willowy than either Pussy or Topsy of fond recent memory. Then Dawn proved that old saw about big tits stuck to the front of a lean and hungry torso when she twisted her lips from his to protest, "Oh, no! Not below my *waist,* darling!"

Longarm left his questing hand where she'd stopped it, inches from where he'd felt sure it was headed, to soberly reply, "You seem to have the advantage on me, Miss Dawn. I thought I just heard you say you were in need of a helping hand."

She confided, "I am! More than one fresh boy in our bunch seemed out to spark with me. So I let it slip, on purpose, that you and I had this . . . understanding."

Longarm rolled his eyes up at the stars to sigh, "Why me, Lord?" as she snuggled closer to ask, "You're not cross with me for fibbing just a little about you and me, are you? Tell me you're not cross, darling!"

Longarm held her politely but far less firmly as he told her, "I ain't cross, exactly. But let's spell out some ground rules, here, Miss Dawn. To begin with, I ain't nobody's darling when confined above her waist."

She giggled and said, "You're awful! Reporter Hovak was telling us what his boss, Reporter Crawford, told him about you and wilder girls. Did you really take Calamity Jane away from Wild Bill Hickok that time?"

Longarm snorted, "His name was James Butler Hickok, and he had his faults, but Calamity Jane wasn't one of them.

He'd just married up with a circus trick rider named Agnes, Agnes Lake, after courting her four or five years, shortly before he was murdered in Deadwood's Number Ten Saloon. Miss Martha Jane Cannary, better known as Calamity Jane, was not in Deadwood at the time. She drifted in drunk, and ugly, too, only after he lay cold and dead, proclaimed that they'd been lovers. To my misfortune, I have met up with Calamity Jane and so now she claims me as a lover, too. There's no evidence as would stand up in court that old Jim Hickok ever knew her, and I've warned Reporter Crawford to go easy on that hogwash about the two of us narrowly avoiding a walkdown when Jim Hickok up and conceded it was up to the lady to choose betwixt us."

Dawn snuggled and said, "I'm so happy for you both. I've seen recent photographs of Calamity Jane Cannary . . . and where do you think that naughty hand is going, Custis?"

He said, "Sorry. Force of habit. This just ain't going to work, no offense. If Calamity Jane has the right to tell reporters I'm in love with her but devoted to my higher mission, I reckon you have the right to intimate we're . . . flirtatious, as long as I don't have to sign any papers. But I want you to get up and go back to your own bedding, now, Miss Dawn, and comes the cold gray dawn, I don't want you rubbing your pretty self against me like a tabby cat or calling me your anything."

She pouted. "How are we to appear to be lovers if we don't act sort of, you know, intimate?"

Longarm honestly replied, "I ain't certain. This play is usually staged with the roles reversed. When the lovers appear in public with their duds on after some slap-and-tickle, they assure everybody they're just friends. What if we just told everybody we were just friends and let their dirty minds supply the words betwixt the lines?"

She pouted. "I have to *feel* like your girl if I'm to play the part of your girl." But when he tried to feel her up, she grabbed his wrist in both hands and placed his hand upon one considerable breast.

She confided, "I don't mind a boy's hand *here*. It's sort of exciting. But every time a boy puts his hand on my . . .

107

you know, it makes me feel hot and wet and awfully queer down there!"

He said he hadn't heard *that* feeling described as queer and asked how often she entertained such feelings.

She said she'd been engaged to this congressional page a couple of years back when she'd first shown up in Washington. She said they'd broken up when she'd insisted he quit making her feel so queer.

Longarm muttered, "I was afraid of that. But such things are possible, even in Washington. So I ain't out to go any further, Miss Dawn. It ain't that you ain't adorable, you understand. I just don't care to assume the responsibility."

She studied on that some before she confessed, "That's what another older man said, just last winter after he took me home after an office New Year's party. I'm not sure I understand what either of you meant."

He said, "If you understood, the responsibilty might not seem too awesome, Miss Dawn. I sure wish you'd let go my crotch, now, ma'am."

She rubbed his denim-covered balls some more as she asked, "Don't you like it? That boy I was engaged to liked it when I petted him like this, and I said I wouldn't mind him petting me the same way if only he wouldn't run his naughty hand inside my pantaloons and . . . put his finger in me."

Longarm sighed. "A *finger* is likely to be the least of our worries if we don't cut this kid game out! I really mean that, Miss Dawn. It's your pure fortune I *am* a man full grown instead of a horny kid. For you are a woman grown, not a helpless child, and this childish charade is downright painful, even to a veteran of this battle betwixt species who sees through you!"

She said, "That's what the congressman who carried me home from that office party said, and Rollo, the page I told you about, accused me of causing him pain, too. What does it feel like to you boys? Do you get hot and wet when we cuddle this warmly?"

He said, "Hot and *hard* might describe the feeling better, and I meant what I just said, Miss Dawn! We got to quit this shit, pardon my French, before I lose control of this dumb situation!"

She slid her hand up his fly to feel his raging erection under the denim and marvel, "Heavens! You're not made at all, down here, like that sculpture of a young King David I've seen in picture books!"

Longarm decided, "Well, if the mountain won't leave Muhammad alone, I reckon Muhammad will have to leave the mountain alone."

"Where are you going?" Dawn gasped as he sat up to pull his boots on. He said, "Down to the night fire. You're welcome to come along and hear the idle talk of grown-ups, if you like."

She was still calling him a big silly as he rose with his Winchester and .44-40 to get shed of the little prick teaser. She was welcome to tease his hat if she was of a mind to.

With his eyes on the distant night fire nigh the wagon ring, Longarm was downright spooked by the soft and low warning of, "Watch your step, you big moose!"

Her warning had come too late. Longarm had already tripped over yet another bedroll spread across the short-grass, and so it was all he could do to fall mostly on the far side instead of smack atop whoever he was tripping over.

Thus he was on the ground himself, not outlined by the distant fire, as Dawn rose from his nearby bedding to call out, "Yoo-hoo, Custis . . . ? Where are you, dear?"

Longarm didn't answer. He didn't even breathe. The gal his booted shins lay across lay just as still while Dawn passed perilously near, calling out to him like a lost prick-teasing lamb.

As she bleated out of easy earshot, Longarm rolled all the way off the other gal to say, "I thank you kindly, ma'am. Whomesover you may be! I thought I was a goner, there!"

She answered in a knowing, husky tone, "Rose Ann Farber, here. I know how you must feel, Custis. I couldn't help overhearing every word just now. Try not to judge our Dawn too harshly, her folk were well-off, and beautiful girls never get to exercise their brains, growing up, unless they grow up poor."

Longarm sat up in the grass to lay his weaponry aside as

he gallantly decided, "I'm sorry you grew up poor, then, Miss Rose Ann. For any fool around the fire, earlier, could have seen how pretty you are, and I have just commenced to notice you have a brain."

She said, "Thank you, I guess. I prefer to think I just have common sense. I warned Dawn, earlier, not to weave a tangled web of romantic fibs when all you have to say to a man you're not interested in is that you're not interested in him."

Longarm sighed and said, "If only more ladies saw things that way, Miss Rose Ann. I fear Miss Dawn ain't the first . . . disinterested gal who ever rejected my flowers, books, and candy by implying she was the one true love of Buffalo Bill."

They both laughed at the picture. He liked the way she laughed. He hesitated, then suggested, "Well, I can see you came up here to catch some sleep, and seeing you've saved me from a fate worse than death, I reckon I'd best be going."

She asked, "Why? It's early yet, and I'll never get to sleep now, thanks to a bug that silly Dawn Atwell just put in my ear!"

He asked what sort of bee they might be talking about. She patted the bedding at her side as she replied, "Marble. But let's talk about you, Custis. I guess you know a lot of us Washington girls were all agog when you and that notorious blond cowgirl out of Texas were asked to the White House for supper. Is it true what they say about Lemonade Lucy serving fruit juice cocktails but playing footsie under the table with her better-looking guests?"

Longarm moved his butt from the grass to her canvas tarp as he told her, truthfully, "The First Lady acted like a lady around this child the one meal I set across from her. I suspicion such spiteful tales grew like Topsy from Mrs. Hayes being a still right handsome woman who must have been earth-shattering in her younger days. The younger Texas gal of whom we're gossiping never played footsie with President Hayes as we supped with them, unless I was missing something. Miss Starbuck and me were invited to the White House after we'd prevented the theft of a diplomatic gift from Queen Victoria, and I just can't say whether all that dirty talk about Queen Victoria and her hired help might be true or not. Why are we talking dirty about other ladies, Miss Rose Ann?"

She said, "I guess it just comes natural. We were never raised to entertain pure thoughts about anyone at all attractive. That well may be why we can't help it. Would you like to hear something dirty about me, Custis?"

He shrugged and said, "Depends on whether you're confessing or bragging, I reckon."

She sighed and said, "I wish I knew. My wedding night and just a few disasters since have left me so confused."

He didn't answer.

She said, "Unlike our tee-hee-above-the-waist Dawn Atwell, I was married before I left my Ohio home for Washington and a new life. I married the boy next door. We went to New York State on our honeymoon, and on our wedding night I discovered for the first time he was, indeed, built very much like that famous statue of young David."

Longarm nodded soberly and allowed a thing like that could leave some brides of more natural proportions feeling a mite let down.

She suppressed a sob and said, "It wasn't his fault. He surely must have been as disappointed, and he was very gallant about it, if not too swift to agree when I suggested an annulment."

Longarm whistled silently and marveled, "The poor boy had been *that* shortchanged by Dame Nature?"

She quietly replied, "He was far from a raging satyr, but I guess he could have managed to satisfy . . . smaller girls. To be fair, I was as much or more a freak of nature in my own way. I wasn't sure before I . . . tried again with someone in Washington who might have *tried* to be more understanding. It *hurts* when a man in bed with you laughs out loud and asks how you ever survived such an awful accident with an ax, Custis!"

He took her in his arms and soothed, "Some folk talk cruel to cover up when they feel they ain't up to a job, Miss Rose Ann. Like you said, our . . . physical proportions ain't nobody's fault. All of us are just . . . the way we are."

Rose Ann said, "I was lying here laughing to myself as the two of you were fumbling at one another like teenagers

111

in the dark, and then she put that bug in my ear by announcing to the world around how much better you were hung than . . . that famous statue."

As they lay side by side with her top tarp between them, Longarm said, "Aw, that ain't saying much, no offense to the real King David. Seeing that statue of him was to go on public display, Mr. Michelangelo gave him just enough to show he was a boy. So if that was Miss Dawn's notion of a grown man's old organ grinder, it's small wonder she seemed surprised when she clutched at mine."

As he felt her hand slide out from under the tarp. He added with a weary sigh, "Miss Rose Ann, I'd be proud to show it hard if I thought you really wanted some. But to tell the pure truth, this groping for my privates in the dark is commencing to try my patience."

She calmly replied, "Mine, too. So why don't you get undressed, get under these covers with me, and I'll show you, if you'll show me!"

He laughed like hell at the little-girl lilt she threw in at the end of that kids-in-the-woodshed invitation, even as he was shucking his own duds to take her up on it.

He wasn't surprised, under the tarp and top flannel blanket, to find the auburn-haired Rose Ann slept naked as a jay and as ever, praise the pagan gods in charge of such matters, taking a strange new naked body in his arms felt as if he'd just discovered something new and wondrous: the law of gravity or the source of the Nile.

She reached down between them to make her own discovery as they kissed with stored-up desire, and then he forked a leg between hers to follow willingly where she was leading him by hand and, Jesus H. Christ, she sure had an echo canyon between her smooth, shapely, and widespread thighs, didn't she!

But on a scale of one to ten between too tight to get it in and too loose to bother, he figured he could give her an eight or nine, and as she got her hand out of the way so's he could give her all he had to offer, he asked politely, with his lips brushing hers, if he was in too deep.

To which she replied with a thrust of her wide hips, "That

will be the day, but oh my stars and garters if this dosen't feel just the way I always imagined it was supposed to and ... yes ... yes ... give it to me, Custis! For at long last I know what it feels like to fuck!"

Chapter 17

Thus it came to pass a healthy young couple built larger than life enjoyed the novel experience, to them, of the average fit most couples experienced most every time and, since Rose Ann was fairer of face and form than most, and moved what she had to offer with more built-up frustration than experience, neither had any complaints, and she said it was lovely and she wanted to do it again, on top, and then some more, dog style, as Longarm warned her she was carrying on loud enough to be heard down around the night fire.

She enjoyed giggling sneaky in the dark, too. They almost fell asleep in each other's arms. But Longarm was wiser in the ways of a cross-country wagon drive, and so they were each alone in their bedrolls by the dawn's early light as the night pickets circled farther out.

Having the added advantage that they were both full grown, Longarm and Miss Rose Ann were able to keep others from noticing their friendly public behavior might be anything more. She'd confided in the dark to him, dog style, she'd meant to behave and didn't want folk back in Washington gossiping about her once she got back.

Another long day on the dusty trail got them as far as the combined Indian agency and Mormon settlement of Panguitch. Like many a Mormon settlement, Panguitch had a longer-settled atmosphere than heaps of smaller Western towns. A sawmill served by wooded slopes to the west and nearby clay quarries added up to substantial brick construction in the peculiar self-taught classical style of Utah Territory.

The settlement thriving at the junction of north-south and east-west wagon traces, the most important Mormon settlement they'd see for a spell, enjoyed cool summer weather and heavy snow in winter. So the weather was about right and getting warmer in Panguitch, even as it was about right but fixing to get unbearably hot in the way lower Saint George, out of their way to the southwest, according to Jubal Burbank and Esau Skaggs, who said they knew.

Longarm wasn't as certain, seeing they were stuck in Panguitch by the mysterious failure of their Digger guides to report back from the high, uncertainly mapped or named jumble of canyons and snow-topped peaks to the west. So, old Skaggs having failed to find the survey map for him earlier, Longarm spent some time in their small, neat, red-brick public library, poring over maps a motherly Mormon lady seemed proud to show him. She said her daddy had laid out some of those very trails back in the fifties so converts from Europe could avoid persecution farther east by coming 'round the Horn and following the Joshua trees across the uncontested desert from San Diego or San Pedro. Longarm was pleased to see that his own mental map of the Four Corners canyon country wasn't too far off. He asked the friendly old gal for some blank paper and outlined a map for himself in pencil before he thanked her for her help and they parted friendly.

Back at the wagon circle, formed up east of the Sevier on the Bryce Canyon Trail, Longarm drew Captain Burbank and the other lawmen to one side, outlined the situation as they knew it so far, and went on, "That tale about lovesick Turks courting Californee gals may be a will-o'-the-wisp, but we're going to wish somebody had chased it if we get all the way to Pueblo de Los Angeles without cutting better sign. So one of us has to eliminate that possible bullshit."

Captain Burbank said, "Saint George is thirty miles out of our way. Sixty miles or three more days on the trail with the weather getting drier when you count going down the Virgin and hauling back up the same!"

Longarm said, "I know. It gets worse if I get to Saint

George and they offer me a mailing address for Bin Omar in, say, Mount Carmel or Kanab near the Arizona line."

Burbank gasped. "Worse? It gets impossible. Kanab's another sixty miles east of Saint George, adding a hundred-and-sixty-mile round trip to the sixty I just mentioned, adding up to—"

"I've been doing the arithmetic," Longarm cut in, adding, "You are right as rain about doing it that way. Whilst I was round-tripping two hundred and twenty miles, the rest of you would roll clean through Nevada down to the Mojave by the time I got back to where we parted company. So there has to be a better way."

He broke out his penciled map to explain, "Mount Carmel and then Kanab and the Arizona line lie due south of where we are *right now!* Do I take four mules, two to carry me and a pack saddle with another two spares to spell with, I could make Kanab in two hard days whilst the rest of you made it west to, say, Cedar City."

Burbank said, "Esau likes to swing south of Cedar City and avoid fences."

Longarm said, "Whatever. My point is that by the time you all get that far west, I'll have cut sign or drawn a blank in Kanab. So then I can forge west along the South Smith Trail, gaining ten miles or more a day on the westward lead you all have on me. I figure I can make it to Saint George, following up on Miss Trixie's story bass-ackwards, and whether I find anything or not, I'll be forging on west farther south, and I figure I ought to overtake you by the time you're fixing to pull out of Las Vegas."

"What if you can't?" asked another lawman.

Longarm said, "I'll have to chase after you all across the damned Mojave, gaining slow but sure and, what the hell, we know none of those missing women are being held against their will or honeymooning, for that matter, in the middle of the damned Mojave!"

Another Washington man asked, "What if some fiend murdered them out on the desert and buried them there?"

Longarm said, "What if the dog hadn't stopped to shit? Wouldn't it have caught the rabbit? Those missing women *could* be anyplace. All we can do is look every sensible place we can think of. Nobody's told us shit about sex fiends out on the open desert. At least one witness has at least one unknown quality trying to lure Christian gals to something that surely sounds like Alamut."

He saw he was confusing some of them and added, "Secret canyon hideout of the original old man of the mountains, speaking of mysterious characters. He and his original Alamut ain't there no more, I hope. But others have picked up the notion since. There used to be such hideouts along the Rhine and up in the Transylvanian hills and, more recent, let us not forget Robbers' Roost and the Hole in the Wall out our way. Only take one such latter-day Alamut in the canyon lands to the southeast to hide any number of absconded brides, dead or alive."

Captain Burbank decided, "You'll never catch up and, either way, you could be riding into trouble. You'd best take at least two of these old boys with you."

Longarm shook his head and said, "He travels faster, like they say, riding alone. If I run into too big a boo to handle, the rest of you will know it when I never catch up with you at all. So you'll be able to backtrack me in force to where I went under and, like you keep harping, we can't afford to waste time, and I'm likely chasing a red herring. Miss Trixie said she was able to fight this Ben Omar off, bare-handed. I doubt he'll hurt me worse when and if I catch up with him."

"Then why in thunder do you need to catch up with him?" one of the Washington deputies demanded.

Longarm said, "To eliminate him. We're talking in circles, and I have to talk to old Esau or mayhaps the livery here in town about the four legged-up saddle mules I'll need."

He felt no call to mention parting proper with Rose Ann, who'd been looking forward all day, in sly asides, to some luxurious fornication behind locked doors aboard a hotel mattress.

Esau Skaggs put up less of an argument than Captain Burbank had. He was proud of his mules. He said there was no need and there'd be less trouble returning property if Longarm trusted him to just pick out four fast trotters and have 'em ready, come sunrise. His arithmetic agreed with

Longarm's if nothing held the procedure up in Mount Carmel, Kanab, or Saint George. They could both see much shilly-shally could result in Longarm crossing some of the worst of the Mojave alone.

Thanks to the LDS church being far less old-timey stuffy than some thought, there was more than one hotel in Panguitch catering to the heavy wagon traffic without concern for the religious notions of the guests. So Longarm and Rose Ann registered seperate, and nobody worried whether they stayed in their own small rooms or not. Folk who solved unbalanced sexual ratios in their congregations by allowing more than one wife under the same roof were less inclined than, say, the Pentecostal Holy Rollers to worry about such matters. The LDS held the prohibitions on alcohol, caffeine, and nicotine were inspired by practical concerns for health as well. They tended to just feel sorry for outsiders who abused themselves and didn't fuss at them that much.

Alone again at last, she panted, Rose Ann was anxious to try out some notions that had come to her riding sidesaddle all day and damned if she *couldn't* get a way tighter grip on a man with her legs straight and stiff down between his, once he was all the way in her.

Longarm agreed she felt tight as average in that position, and then he educated her with a few more positions from that under-the-counter Hindu sex manual, the *Kama Sutra*, and managed to try out some positions he'd never managed with gals of more average proportions. It wouldn't have been polite to surmise out loud how the Hindu artists depicting or making up some of those positions had likely been working with a double-jointed model with an awesome twat.

In any case, the results felt tight as well right sassy when they tried them, and Rose Ann laughed like hell and said, "Oh, dear Lord, I can see you going in and out of me in this position, and it looks so wicked and it makes me so hot!"

Of course, as was usually the case when one experimented with the *Kama Sutra*, they wound up old-fashioned, or in this case her version of old-fashioned, with her thighs pressed tight against the roots of his ebbing virility, and the grand thing about treating good old Rose Ann with consideration turned out to be her attitude about the future.

117

All too many gals a man neglected to beat with a big black whip seemed to think they were soul mates fated to fornicate down through the ages ahead until the great-getting-up-morning of Gabriel's trumpet and tended to cloud up and rain all over a man with a tumbleweed job and a taste for novelty when it came time to part. But even as he was shoving it to her languidly while nibbling an earlobe, she declared triumphantly she could hardly wait to get back to Washington and invite a certain congressional aide to a home-cooked meal. For he was young and pretty, too, and now she had a ring-dang-doo that would never again let her or any man down. Giving Longarm's love-slicked shaft an affectionate squeeze, and damned if she wasn't getting better at that by the hour, Rose Ann said, "Size dosen't matter all that much once a girl knows how to grab hold of the dear little things. Thanks to you, and I will never forget this, I see where I went wrong on my honeymoon with that advice about total surrender! Both parties have to *work* at fucking to make it work right!"

He came in her, as most men would have at such times, and allowed she really had it just about right. She sighed and said she wished she could ride with him down to Kanab in the morning, adding, "Think of the nights we'd have alone on the trail, naked beneath the stars!"

"Don't be cruel to dumb animals," he replied, adding, "Got to ride alone. Ain't sure that *I* will be able to keep up with me, at the pace I have to set. Unless I average better than ten miles more a day than you all with the wagons, I'll never catch up this side of Barstow, and we know more than one of them missing women wired from Barstow they'd made it that far."

"From where?" she asked casually as they let him soak inside her.

He said, "Hard to say before the common bottleneck at San Berdoo, as they call San Bernardino at the southwest entrance to the Mojave. That's where the Old Spanish Trail cuts through mountains of the same name that cut the rain clouds of the Pacific off from the Mojave. So the town of San Berdoo can be said to be the final commitment to that particular desert trail. You can pass through San Berdoo from west to east, of course, if you'd rather get lost in the *Colorado* Desert."

She perked up to ask, "Colorado, due east of Pueblo de Los Angeles?"

He said, "Colorado River, not Colorado State. The state is named for the bodacious river that forms up on the west slope of its Rockies and runs south from there through parts of Utah, Arizona, and California to Mexico and its Sea of Cortez. The tedious acres of greasewood they call the Colorado *Desert* lie betwixt the coastal ranges of southern Californee and the Colorado River, see?"

She said, "I think so. Would you care to take it out now? I'd like to dry off and cool off a bit."

As they parted friendly, she asked, "What would happen to one or more mail-order bride who took the wrong turn at this San Berdoo and wound up crossing the wrong desert, dear?"

He said, "She'd wind up in Yuma, Arizona Territory, where there's a telegraph office. Them other lawmen and me have been over that way out. Unless a confused traveler got lost in the desert total, crossing the wide-open expanses to Yuma, she'd wind up along the more settled stretch of Arizona's Gila River, which meets up with the Colorado at Yuma. No way a body could stay lost and out of touch with her intended once she found herself as far east as Yuma."

As Rose Ann delicately wiped her crotch with a corner of the sheet, she demurely asked, "What if she met somebody she liked as well or better in Arizona, after a dull, dry trip across that Colorado Desert? Why would she ever bother to get in touch with some other boyfriend way up north? Might she not feel that would be needless expense and cruelty? Haven't you ever simply lost touch with someone you had no further use for and . . . quit while you were ahead?"

Longarm sighed. "I wish you hadn't said that, Miss Rose Ann. It makes too much sense. Even though it's less likely *all* those missing gals did as you say, *some* of 'em may have, and as Captain Burbank keeps saying, it just ain't possible for the hounds to bay after every possible stink in the bushes!"

Rose Ann said, "Goody. Stay with the rest of us, and

about this time tomorrow night we'll be up in those wooded mountains where a girl may not get as sweaty raising her sweet young boy!"

Longarm didn't answer. He knew he'd get her hopes up if he told her she'd never know how tempting that last suggestion had been! He just knew he wasn't going to find any latter-day Alamut in the canyon lands to the south. Just as he knew he had to what-the-hell make certain.

Chapter 18

That Scotch poet's warning about the best laid plans of mice and men going to hell in a hack was proven right the next morning when Longarm went to fetch those mules and found everybody all het up as they jawed with those Digger scouts.

The Paiute had come back overnight to report a big gang of what they described as *taibo totzo,* translating in the meaning of bronco Apache as applied to white men, holed up in the Cedar Breaks over to the west and lobbing long-range shots at Indians uppity enough to walk the same earth with them, it would seem.

Esau Skaggs allowed he wasn't planning on risking any axles driving directly through the Cedar Breaks but agreed any outlaws holed up in the same would be within easy raiding range, downhill, through timber cover.

Captain Burbank declared that as Utah lawmen he and his own boys meant to see what the strange riders were up to and, if was against the law, make them stop. He admitted he had no authority over Longarm and the four federal men out of Washington.

Longarm said, "You're wrong, Captain. I'm with you, and these other federal men are with me, I hope I can assume?"

The Washington lawmen replied as one that they were in.

Lawmen tended to get awesomely bored with riding day after day with nobody to fuss with.

The bearded captain almost smiled. He caught himself in the nick of time and sternly ordered Esau Skaggs to hold the wagon circle where it was with his own crew while the Paiutes led the three Mormon and five Gentile lawmen along a back trail through the hills that owlhoot riders from other parts might not know.

As they saddled up, they told volunteers from the congressional fact-finding committee to stay put and guard the women and other livestock with the circled wagons and their lives.

But as they rode out, Cub Reporter Hovak from the *Post* and an eager squirt from the *Kansas City Star* called Onderdonk galloped after them. It was easier to let them tag along and learn the hard way than it was to tie them both to trees. But Captain Burbank warned them sternly it would be on their own heads if they couldn't keep up or disobeyed one order under fire.

The wiry bare-ass Paiute, after jogging any number of miles through the night, jogged ahead of Captain Burbank in the lead at the same pace as his trotting mule. Sticking tight to Longarm, as he'd been advised to back in Denver, Miles Hovak panted, "How do those Indians do it? I could never jog ten miles if my life depended on it. I tried to run a marathon in college, and less than halfway along I ran into this big glass wall."

Longarm replied, "Few white men can run a mile. Some white men can run twenty-one, or they couldn't hold marathon races. It's all in what you're used to. Paitute are used to outrunning the Horse Ute, who chase them for sport. They run where horses find the going rough, across the salt pans, alkali flats, and outcrops of wind-polished slickrock. The so-called Diggers can't keep riding stock where Horse Ute can't go. So they grow up high-speed pedestrians. Really high-speed pedestrians. A Paiute can run an antelope down in open country if he puts his mind to it."

Hovak snorted. "You're trying to green me! A pronghorn antelope can run sixty miles an hour! They've been timed at that speed from a moving train!"

Longarm said, "Forty, for no more than a mile or so, going all out. Paiute knows this. So he keeps jogging after old antelope, mile after mile, as each burst of all-out gets shorter and carries the fleeing antelope less far. Sooner or later the confounded critter just can't run anymore, and the Paiutes have antelope for supper."

Hovak stared into the dust kicked up by those out ahead as he gasped, "I believe you, I guess, but wouldn't our Indian guides move ever so much faster riding instead of running?"

Longarm shook his head and replied, "Nope. To begin with, they'd have to worry about controlling their mounts instead of staring down for sign in the direction they were jogging. Riders who look down on Paiute as mere Diggers miss a lot of sign a scout on foot can pick up on the fly. Paitue can spy a rabbit turd ahead and judge how long it's been there and which way the rabbit likely went by the time he's jogged on by. That's likely why Captain Burbank asked those old bare-ass boys up ahead to scout for us. You don't ask old boys to scout for you if you don't think they know what they're doing."

Neither spoke for a time as the trail took a steeper grade through thick pinyon. The local Saints tended to dismiss pin-yon as *pine* on their local maps. That was fair as calling juniper cedar, but unlike the ponderosa and lodgepole pine at higher altitudes, the squat, knobby pinyon sported its long pine needles and edible seed cones on a sort of crab apple framework. So Longarm stiff-armed a gnarled limb higher and called back, "Low bridge!" before he let it go to ride on.

The springy pinyon limb nearly knocked the cub reporter off his mule as it whapped him while he was saying, "Beg your pardon?"

Longarm called back, "Sorry, old son. I can see you ain't done much riding in high chaparral."

The cub reporter from coal country confessed he hadn't done much riding at all and sighed, "I fear I grabbed the horn, just now. That's not allowed, right?"

Longarm asked, "Not allowed by whom? The horn of your roping saddle was intended for roping cows. But you show me a rider who's never had to grab the horn, and I'll show you a man who's never done much serious riding."

122

Miles Hovak laughed and said he'd still as soon keep it a secret.

Longarm didn't bother to say he didn't give a shit either way. They weren't headed for the Cedar Breaks to offer riding lessons to tagalong kids for God's sake.

The Cedar Breaks lay about thirty miles southwest of Panguitch, with the easy approach most of the way up the valley of Panguitch Creek. But of course their guides chose a ridge-running route less likely to be spotted early on by a lookout. Ridge running on their own, the legged-up Paiute might have set a steadier pace. If Captain Burbank had never ridden with the U.S. Cav, the Nauvoo Legion of the LDS rode to the same drill. For Burbank held them to the cross-country pace of a cavalry company, figuring to move on on the Cedar Breaks in the gathering dusk of the coming night.

They'd trot a spell and walk a spell, trail breaking for ten minutes once an hour until along about noon, Burbank called a twenty-minute halt for cold grub from their saddlebags.

Longarm was washing down his canned pork and beans with canned tomato preserves when Miles Hovak and that other kid reporter, Onderdonk, came to join him. Onderdonk was the one most confused by ridge running in timbered country. He asked, "Won't those outlaws know about this trail we're following and have it covered?"

Longarm said, "It ain't a trail. It's the way things are along mountain ridges. The ridges are the ribs of the bedrock underneath, where the topsoil's most shallow and the winter winds lash seedlings harder. Wild game, following a sort of natural hair part so's they can watch out for trouble down either slope, scrape the ridgetops barer with their hooves. Anybody else up in these hills ought to know this, of course. But you can't watch every ridge all around unless you have so many riders you don't need to post lookouts."

He pointed with his jaw through a gap in the pinyon and juniper at a barely visible section of the valley to their southeast as he added, "They'll have enough on their plate watching more sensible approaches to the Cedar Breaks."

Miles Hovak asked hesitantly, "What's a cedar break?"

Longarm didn't laugh. He explained, "It's what the Mormons named a freak of erosion run wild. What looks like a jumble of mountains all around is called in general the Mar-kagunt by the Indians who discovered it first. When all the low country east and west was sea bottom a whole lot of years ago, this Markagunt was an island, whipped by wind, pounded by waves, and sliced by running rainwater down through its red sandstone bedrock in places. The Cedar Breaks, carved from higher ground by more years of rough weather than a mortal cares to think about, is a swamping amphitheater bigger than all those the Romans built if you put them together, surrounded by eroded spires of yellow, orange, red, purple, or brown rock."

He let that sink in while he thought back on having been this way before with Mormon guides before he added, "In spite of all the mineral stain, prospectors failed to find paying quantities of iron or manganese and Lord knows nobody wants to be at that elevation year 'round. So the Cedar Breaks, themselves, were never settled, and the wagon traces avoid 'em with good reason. The onliest reason anyone ever visits them is to wonder at the view. Mayhaps someday when this territory is a lot more settled, tourists will be taken out from, say, Cedar City to take pictures of such a hole in the ground. But at present that's about all there is to the Cedar Breaks."

Miles started to ask a dumb question. Then he nodded and said, "Makes a handy hideout, overlooking the more beaten path, right?"

Longarm didn't answer. Captain Burbank had called an end to their noon break, and it was time to mount up and ride on.

It got less certain where they were riding as the Paiute led on foot through thicker and less certain woods. Like the more famous Adirondacks of New York State, what appeared a jumble of mountains between the headwaters of the north-flowing Sevier and the south-flowing Virgin was one swamping plateau diced every way by erosion so that many of the ridges widened out to flat-topped mesas, and even an Indian who didn't know the Markagunt could get seriously lost atop it.

By now they were riding too high for pinyon and juniper between tall ponderosa and brooding spruce over carpets of needle duff that tended to muffle hoofbeats to where the jingle of spurs and bits or the slaps of quirts or rein ends made more noise in the clammy shade. It never got really hot atop the Markagunt, and that early in the year the smell of Jack Frost still lingered where the shade lay deeper. So in contrast to the usual riding customs of the Southwest, Captain Burbank tried to call trail breaks in the sunny open patches or mountain meadows.

It was during such a break that Onderdonk asked where they were now, in relation to the infamous Cedar City.

Longarm pointed west-southwest to say, "Yonder. About twenty miles, if I'm right about how far we've ridden today. But it ain't all that notorious. Cedar City's just a larger southwest Mormon outpost. If you're talking about that massacre, Cedar City had no part in it. The Fancher party surrendered their weapons to Brother Lee when he *told* them they were under arrest and he was taking them back to Cedar City to turn them over to his superiors. The particular mountain meadows the murders took place in are north of the Veyo warm springs a good forty miles on past Cedar City."

Miles Hovak squinted at his somewhat better mental map of the West and mused, "Then those California-bound Gentiles had passed clean through Mormon territory and were headed out the back door when those Indians . . . What did I say, Longarm? Why are you looking so disgusted?"

Longarm said, "What Indians? Captain Charlie Fancher was leading a party of some hundred and forty, at least a third of them armed men and boys. Paiute Diggers might have approached them with caution, to trade for sugar or tobacco. Aplogists for Brother Lee agree they were *friendlies,* mayhaps Horse Utes if they were mounted up, themselves. I call 'em as I see 'em. That self-styled nineteenth wife of Brigham Young was a big fibber. But so are the Mormons who can't accept the sad truth that Mountain Meadows was a darker chapter in their history."

One of the other riders coming out of the woods from a squat-and-drop strode into view just in time to hear enough to shout, "A lot you know, you persistent dweller in darkness! Were you *there* when all those hostile Gentiles threatened to burn Salt Lake City to the ground?"

Longarm said, "Nope. Neither were you. But to the everlasting credit of Lee's Mormon Militia, they didn't have it in them to finish off the smaller children from the Fancher wagon train. After they butchered the men, women, and elder children under a flag of truce, that's in black and white in the transcript of the court-martial. There might not have ever been a court-martial if Lee and his riders hadn't taken pity on seventeen terrified little kids, too young, they figured, to testify in court against anybody."

The Mormon just glared. Onderdonk asked whatever might have happened to those seventeen little Gentile kids.

Longarm said, "This and that, and then they all grew up. So seventeen years after they'd seen their parents and elder siblings killed in cold blood, all seventeen survivors, questioned seperately as responsible adults by army investigators, told the same story."

Smiling thinly at the Utah rider who prefered another version, Longarm said, "At his trial, the late John Lee, in honest atonement or to cover the mistakes of those higher up, confessed in full to mass murder and allowed he'd acted alone during a fit of pique. He said Captain Fancher had made nasty remarks about sharp trading practices of some Saints or, hell, let's say he was an ornery cuss and made wild threats. It ain't nice to murder a hundred and twenty–odd men, women, and children. So the army treated Brother Lee to a buckboard ride out to Mountain Meadows, seated on his coffin, then shot him and buried him in the same, where some of the scattered bones of his victims still bleach to this day."

"Are you quite done with your dissertation, Deputy Long?" a colder new voice cut in from behind him.

Longarm turned to say, "Howdy, Captain Burbank. You fixing to ride on some more?"

The older and never too cheerful Mormon said they were. As everyone got to their feet, Burbank called Longarm aside, glanced about to make certain it was a private conversation, and asked, "Can't you people ever give it a rest? That Fancher incident still leads to fistfights among our own kind, and it was over twenty years ago during tenser times out our way!"

Longarm said, "I never brought it up. I'll go along with

126

letting a sleeping dog lie, but dead dogs stink worse when you try to cover 'em over with fibs. Indians say how much farther we have to go to uncover whatever that stink might be in the Cedar Breaks?"

Burbank said, "I'm trying to time it so's we have just enough of the gloaming to scout what the Diggers describe as a big camp. While we're on the suject, watch your own back in the possibly confusing times ahead. That Saint you were just setting the record straight for is the son of a man who rode with John Lee at Mountain Meadows, and on top of that, he's a Danite, or that is, he used to be, before the LDS gave up such notions a few short summers ago!"

Chapter 19

After a long, hard day in the saddle, Longarm, Captain Burbank, and his Indian scouts were standing amid twisted timber at the base of a fairy-tale castle of varicolored sandstone, adazzle with the sunset's glow on its west side but inky black against a red sky from down in the main crater of the Cedar Breaks.

The Indian, Tzenayuup, said, "Hear me. It is not hard, even for a *tai . . . saltu* to climb this *tetzaya* on the sunny side they cannot see. When you get near the top, your heads will be small as *ekapusya* against the glare of *tabettuhkati*. But if you do not start now, the darkness will catch you up there, and you will never get down. I have spoken."

Anyone could see the old Digger made sense. So the two lawmen set their rifles down and each found a crevice to follow skyward. It was easy at first and only got ass puckering once they were too far up to survive a slip.

After that it was still more a matter of slithering up vertical clefts between needles of gritty rock. So they both made it high enough, still at easy conversational range, to see way the hell down into the mostly shaded amphitheater where, sure enough, a party of about two dozen were bedded down around a campfire near a rainwater pool within easy handling of one hell of a remuda.

Longarm counted in his head, with both hands clinging to rock, and decided, "I make that over fifty ponies, at least some of 'em shod and all groomed within the year. So those ain't wild mustangs, and they ain't muststangers, down yonder."

Captain Burbank muttered someting under his breath and replied, "Horse thieves. Some of them our own kind, alas. I recognize that white Texas sombrero and red-checked shirt on Frank Waters out of Circleville and that skinny squirt in the Mexican hat and shotgun chaps has to be Lester Pratt from Salina Creek."

Longarm thought and said, "We're talking about range to the north of here, and I told you about those horse thieves I brushed with up in Provo, didn't I?"

Burbank said, "You did. I wish you'd shot the ones down there, may the Lord forgive me for speaking the simple truth. For anyone can see some of our not-too-saintly Saints mean to worry that stolen herd down to Arizona Territory and out of my jurisdiction by the time I can hope to finish our more important mission."

Longarm suggested, "Why don't we just arrest 'em now, then? Couldn't we run them and that stolen stock over to, say, Cedar City and turn them over to your lawmen yonder?"

Burbank grinned like a kid contemplating an apple orchard over some old maid's garden wall with sunset coming on, but asked, "Are you sure you and those other federal deputies have jurisdiction? Don't they have to run stolen stock across a state or territorial line to make it a federal offense?"

Longarm said, "They do, and you just *said* they were headed for Arizona. After that, Utah horse thieves are surely under *your* jurisdiction, and ain't we pals?"

Jubal Burbank laughed out loud for the first time since they'd met and said, "I wish you'd let me make up my mind whether I can stand you or not. Let's get down whilst the getting is good. And then what? We circle in after dark and try to take out their sentries before we rush the camp?"

Longarm said, "No offense, but gunfights in the dark can take as much as fifty years off a man's life, and didn't you say you recognized at least two of them, Captain?"

Burbank said, "Frank Waters and Lester Pratt for certain, probably Mike Cassidy as well, seeing Waters hails from Circleville when he's not stealing stock."

Longarm said, "Mike Cassidy was up Provo way when I shot it out with his horse-thieving pal, the federal want, Sandy Desmond. I am commencing to see a pattern here. So here's what I suggest . . ."

And so it came to pass that an hour later, as the stars were winking down in ever greater numbers and it was black as a bitch all around the campfire down by that rainwater pool, a firm but fair voice rang out from the darkness to the north, "Hello the camp! Captain Burbank of the Utah Territorial Police and LDS, here! I know who you boys are, and so even if you get away, you'll never be able to go home again."

From the darkness to the south, Longarm called out, "Mike Cassidy up Provo way wanted me to tell his pals, Frank Waters and Lester Pratt, how Sandy Desmond got shot in Provo as things went to hell in a hack."

That Mormon son of a Danite who'd ridden under John Lee called out from the darkness to the west, "You see how it is, or for all I care, you don't, and we get to save your parents the shame of your public trials as skunks who'd raid their own henhouse! I see you there with your sick coyote grin, David Bowman! Go for your gun and save your poor old mother in Beaver the trouble of going your bail!"

Captain Burbank called out, "I wish you hadn't said that, Sergeant! I wanted these scoundrels to contemplate jail time all the way to the magistrate in Cedar City!"

It worked. A cautious voice called out, "What do you reckon they'll knock off our sentences if you tell 'em we came in voluntary, meek as lambs beside still waters?"

Burbank answered gruffly, "Not for me to say. Come quiet, and I'll say that much for you. Make a fight of it here and, well, Cedar City is a long ways over rough trails if you're lucky enough to need any doctoring when we cease fire."

So the leader of the bunch, a not-too-observant Saint called Slim Bolton, allowed they had a deal and came out to Captain Burbank to shake on it.

Having done so, the outlaws invited the lawmen they'd surrendered to, to sup with them. Captain Burbank cautiously allowed his followers, including Longarm, to sashay in by the fire by twos and hunker down for some mulligan made with brung-along spuds and carrots with fresh venison and wild camus bulbs.

It was served without coffee, of course. They were horse thieves, not atheists.

The two sides were on tolerably good terms by turn-in, and Captain Burbank estimated roughly, at dawn, no more than two or three of them had slipped away in the dark.

The outlaws were of course disarmed but allowed to ride free so as to herd the stolen horseflesh over to Cedar City as evidence against them.

Cedar City being half as far from the Cedar Breaks as their circled wagons back on the Sevier, Longarm lit out alone at daybreak in hopes of making it down to Kanab by the time Burbank and the rest made it back to Panguitch. If he timed his detour lucky, Longarm hoped to be headed west from about the same longitude as the fact-finding committee took the higher road over the Markagunt and Tushars farther west. If he found nothing to bog him down in Kanab, he'd be hitting Saint George about the time the wagons were circled by the Veyo hot springs and, what the hell, they might meet up just past the Nevada line, Lord willing and his luck held up.

The ride back to Panguitch took him all day, of course, so Rose Ann sent him off the next morning walking sort of stiff while Easau Skaggs sent him on up the Sevier riding one spanking saddle mule with three others in tow, only one of them packing the trail supplies he'd need past Assay Creek, where the riding got drier.

He figured that even as he was riding due south, Captain Burbank and the others would be pushing east back to the main party. Unless he ran into a snag, he'd make it in and out of Kanab before the wagons stirred from Panguitch.

The morning air was downright crisp for April at that altitude, and he was glad he'd packed a sweater to wear under his denim jacket as they trotted upstream to the south.

Saddle mules, like horses, trotted way faster than a man afoot, unless he was a Paiute. So they were averaging six or eight miles and hour, and he only had to swap saddles once before they'd made it to the dinky settlement of Hatch, where the Assay and the misnamed Mammoth Creeks joined forces to form the Sevier.

Being about the end of upstream, Hatch had a one-room shed post office, a smithy, and sold food and fodder but nothing stronger for man nor beast.

Having been on the trail a spell with the day warming up, Longarm ran the mules into their public corral and bet the Indian hostler two bits he couldn't water the mules and feed 'em some cracked corn without bloating 'em.

Then he took off that sweater, put it away with the jacket, and after some consideration, put his federal badge on. There came times and places it was best to let them know right off what you were doing in their tight, clannish community.

Hoping he wouldn't spook any women or make any horses faint, he ducked through the low dooorway into the wayside stop near the post office advertising warm meals and sandwiches to go. A motherly, gray-haired woman behind the counter seemed pleased as punch to see him. The stocky thirteeen- or fourteen-year-old in raggedy jeans, a torn shirt, and scuffed boots didn't, albeit he tried to smile gamely as he took in Longarm's badge, considerable size, and .44-40.

When Longarm allowed he could sure go for some of that shepherd's pie they offered out front, she told him to sit right down and she'd be proud to fetch him some from her kitchen. Longarm took a stool at her counter. As she bustled into the kitchen, the stocky kid who'd been working on some apple pie sighed and said, "I was halfway sure someone would peach on me to get in good with you lawmen. But then I figured they'd steer you north to Circleville after me and . . . how did you do it, ah, Marshal? I never told anybody I'd head south toward Arizona instead of running for home!"

Longarm said, "Trade secret. I'd be just a Deputy Marshal Custis Long and you'd be . . ."

"Parker, Robert Leroy, and you knew that. There's no need to play cat and mouse with me, Deputy . . . Great Caesar's Ghost! Are you the one they call Longarm?"

To which Longarm could only reply with a modest shrug, "I reckon." He wasn't ready to confide he wasn't sure what the kid was talking about. A picture was emerging from the mists.

Young Parker gushed, "Hot dawg! Wait 'til my pals hear I was tracked down by Longarm in the flesh! That'll learn 'em to call me a tagalong punk! But you can see I ain't armed, and I'm willing to come quiet and cop a plea if you'll do me one little favor."

The motherly older woman came back to the counter with the shepherd's pie. Longarm thanked her with a nod and asked, "What did you have in mind, Leroy?"

The kid scowled, "I don't let my pals call me that. My momma hailed from quality in the old country and thought Leroy sounded elegant. But it sounds sissy if you ask me. So my friends all call me Butch."

Longarm nodded and said, "You did some pretty hard riding down from the Cedar Breaks, Butch. Where might your mount be now? Didn't see anything on four legs in that corral that looked that hard ridden."

Butch Parker said, "Never rode her that far. Had to turn her loose to fend for herself when she broke down on me a dozen miles from here."

Longarm nodded soberly and said, "That explains the boots and the missing hat. You say you were headed for Arizona by way of Kanab, Butch?"

The kid shot a sheepish look at their motherly hostess and replied, "Thought I was. See I ain't. Would you mind booking me under a name less well-known to the LDS? My mom and dad hail from England and Scotland, where things are run more formal. So they and all but two of us ten little Saints brush our teeth and say our prayers as the Parker family."

Longarm said, "That sounds reasonable. What can you tell me about less properly brung up folk in Kanab, Butch?"

Young Parker shrugged and said, "Heard tell life might

be a lot . . . looser down along the Arizona line, cut off from the rest of . . . us as it is."

Their hostess wasn't smiling at him as he went on with a defensive toss of his head, "It ain't that I want to do anything against Mom and Dad, you understand. They're good Saints, and they were good to all of us. But me and mayhaps my brother Dave ain't certain we *want* to just go on and on and on until somebody pats our saintly faces flat with a shovel after long dull lives of . . . just living, day after day after day."

The older woman behind the counter said, "Don't you worry about that, young sir! Speaking from experience, I can tell you that you'll surely be hoping for one more day after day by the time you've made it through as many days after days as I have!"

Longarm said, "What this lady just told you is on the money, Butch. But seeing nobody your age ever takes any advice from anybody old as twenty, you said you had a favor to ask?"

The kid said, "I don't want you to take me in as Robert Leroy Parker. My mom would have a fit. Could you sign me in under another name? Say as . . . how about Cassidy?"

Longarm said, "I met your pal, Mike Cassidy, up Provo way, running with another lost soul called Sandy Desmond. You really *admire* such a poor excuse for a horse thief, Butch?"

The kid said, "Old Mike's the best! He taught my brother Dave and me to rope and throw, and nicker a mare out of her paddock at night as slick as a whistle. So can I go to jail as a Cassidy instead of my real name, Parker?"

Longarm smiled at the bemused older woman as he shook his head and murmured, "Kids today, he thinks I have nothing better to do with my federal badge if I could *prove* he was a horse thief."

"You ain't arresting me?" the burly youth marveled.

Longarm said, "I'd like to. I can't. You just ain't important enough, no offense. But allow me to add some advice to what this kindly lady just now told you, Butch. Them sugarplum outlaw dream Mike Cassidy spun for you kids takes you nowhere but a long way from home and pays off

with a lonely end to a life not half as fine as your average
cowhand averages."

As the kid rose from his stool with a look of sheer relief,
Longarm said, "Quit whilst you're ahead. Go home and behave your fool self, Butch Cassidy. For lawmen you meet
up with in the future may have more time to bother with you,
hear?"

Chapter 20

The riding got ever rougher as Longarm followed the trail
Esau Skaggs had aimed him along like a careless bowler
sending his ball down a gopher hole. Leaving the dubious
headwaters of the Sevier, the trail wound 'round a lonesome
crag dubbed Mount Carmel by inspired Saints to the sometimes waters of the southward-flowing Kanab Creek. The
creek ran almost due south to cross the Arizona line to carve
its way down to a mile-deep side branch of the Grand
Canyon miles from nowhere. The tiny town named after the
creek lay roughly five miles north of the Arizona line on the
east bank of the creek. Kanab was the end of the trail and
the end of civilization as far as their church cared. Longarm
had been warned by Mormons that the folk he'd find there
might strike him as tough to get along with.

There'd have been no point in his visit to Kanab if it had
really been the end of the trail. But he knew that whatever
it might be to the LDS, there was that east-west seldom used
but practical desert trail that meandered more or less along
the Arizona-Utah line, with Kanab at the east-west crossing
of the often dry and sometimes rampaging creek.

Mormons were far from the only sort that could go overboard in out-of-the-way places when it came to religious notions, as fifty-odd unfortunate women of Salem Village,

Massachusetts, had discovered and, while nary a Pope had ever recommended it, according to observant Papists Longarm knew, there were villages in the Sangre de Cristos where folk were still nailed alive to crosses as a favor to their souls.

So Longarm knew polygamy was only the tip of an autocratic iceberg in parts where the Salt Lake Temple had only nominal control, albeit the recent attempts to soft-pedal multiple marriages had supplied a lot of ammunition to prophets of ever-newer revelations.

There was, in point of fact, some argument whether the Prophet Joseph or his disciple, Brigham Young, had revealed the pragmatic joys of the now-discouraged practice. For there was a rival Church of Jesus Christ of Latter-day Saints back East that claimed they'd read no such thing in *their* Book of Mormon. But whatever the angel Moroni had said, Brigham Young had married at least fifty-seven women all told, while never living with more than twenty-seven at a time and only leaving seventeen widows. So younger elders with some catching up to do tended to take revelations to the contrary with a grain of salt and, more ominously, feel they had the same rights as the pragmatic, usually good-humored but sometimes ruthless President Young to lay down the law on other matters and back his fatherly instructions with downright scary means. Official government investigations into night riders described as Avenging Angels, Danites, or the quasimilitary Nauvoo Legion had ended with President Young's unexpected death in '77, along with the execution of the mysterious John Lee. President Rutherford B. Hayes had chosen to believe, and Longarm had no call to disagree, the more progressive younger leadership in Salt Lake City was best fit to tidy up such sinister notions.

Longarm knew enough rational Mormons to buy their embarrassed, red-faced repudiations of the occasional fanatics he ran into from time to time out their way. The Salt Lake Temple hadn't even known that wild bunch out on the Great Salt Desert was *there* before they'd almost got him that time.

So Longarm was braced for more of the same as he rode into Kanab after one hell of a day in the saddle with the sunset gilding the German-silver badge on the front of his salty shirt.

His shirt was salty instead of wet because your salty sweat dried as fast as it came out as you rode lower into the canyon lands south of the Sevier.

You didn't have to ride into a tight-knit Mormon settlement as a stranger to get that collective stare. A Protestant in a Black Irish village or a Papist in an Orange Irish neighborhood could feel about as welcome a long way from home with night coming on.

Surrounded as it was by sage and chaparral, Kanab served as a market town and post office drop for the stock grazers all around. Trying to grow a cash crop or enough truck to be worth hauling anywhere would have been an exercise in self-abuse.

Kanab had only been settled three years before Brigham Young died, by zealots who'd found the night life of big cities like Provo way too wicked for their sterner tastes.

So the very few business establishments of Kanab catered to local needs of a close congregation dwelling all about with private kitchens in their private homes. There was nothing in the way of a hotel or even a restaurant in Kanab. The most impressive structure in the tiny four-square town was what they likely called their tabernacle because it looked more like a circus tent made out of timber than what what the LDS called a temple. Tabernacles in the Good Book had been real tents. The Mormon Tabernacle up in Salt Lake City stood solid as a rock under a swamping timber roof fitted together without one nail. The nearby Mormon Temple looked like a stone cathedral designed by a boomtown carpenter.

Kanab did have a crossroads smithy with a corral out back. Longarm dismounted there, and when a muscular troll wearing no shirt under his leather apron came out, hammer in hand, Longarm declared who he was and asked if he could water and fodder his four mules.

The Mormon smith said, "You'll find yourself and your critters more welcome at the Kaibab Indian Agency ten or twelve miles on."

Longarm said, "I thought Kanab was the end of this trail."

The surly smith said, "It is, for us Saints. You better mount up if you don't want to be caught on the trail south by starbright."

Longarm glanced up at the flamingo belly desert sky to opine, "That aint a friendly warning, it's an unfriendly gloat, friend."

The Mormon shrugged and said, "I got to get to work. You can go . . . wherever you've a mind to."

Then things seemed to be getting worse. There was no water in Kanab Creek, he'd hung two sacks of cracked corn across the pack saddle, and it didn't look like rain. Then he saw four men in black advancing his way, spread out and abreast with their long shadows preceding them across the sunset-gilded dust.

Knowing they could see him better in the tricky light, which might have been why they'd circled to have the sunset at their backs, Longarm said, "Evening, gents. I'd be Deputy U.S. Marshal Custis Long, riding with the knowlege and approval of your Salt Lake Temple on a matter we don't suspect any Saints are involved in. Might I be adressing your mayor, your bishop, or whatever?"

They stopped, all in a row, close enough for Longarm to see the firm jaw and beetle brows of the one who answered, "Close enough. They call me Brother Bram, and I'll be the judge of . . . Say, might you be the same Deputy Long who offered those amusing views of Sister Ann Eliza in that Gentile newspaper?"

When Longarm modestly confessed he'd offered some educated guesses on that so-called nineteenth wife, the Mormon elder replied to him with a knowing smile, "We laughed as much at your wild guesses about us. But your heart was in the right place, and you'll be spending the night with my family and me, seeing you have no other choice in these parts."

Calling out to the blacksmith in the nearby doorway, Brother Bram said, "Brother Hiram, I'd take it kindly if you'd see to the riding stock of our guest, here."

Knowing how it might be taken if he brought along his Winchester and saddlebags, Longarm trusted them to the honesty of a town that likely saw little in the way of crime.

The other three men in black parted friendly to have their own sit-downs as Brother Bram led the way to his rambling home spread on the outskirts of town. As they chased their ever-lengthening shadows up the street, the Mormon elder explained, "You were right about her being no better than she should have been, but for the record, Brigham Young took Sister Ann Eliza as his nineteenth wife in what may have been a moment of premature senility. She was young and pretty, too, and you know how that rowdy cowboy song goes from there."

Longarm didn't think this was the time to sing out loud, "Oh she was young and pretty, too, and had what you call a ring-dang-doo!"

The Mormon Elder said, "Your interview was on the money about any woman being forced to flee for her life across the salt flats after being forced into marriage with a dirty old man. Sister Ann Eliza set her cap for the most important man she could sink her pretty kitten claws into. As you observed in your interview, any lady who marries a rich and powerful older man has to expect him to want to kiss her now and again. Her protestations she divorced him still a virgin with the wedding unconsummated were, as you said, hard to understand. You were on the money when you speculated on why any frightened young thing in fear for her life with any number of Avenging Angels stalking her would be sort of dumb to appear in public on the vaudeville stage, pushing the sales of her tell-all book. Have you ever read her notorious ghost-written *Wife No. 19*, by the way?"

Longarm said, "Tried to. Couldn't get through it. Your notion it was writ by some hack writer unfamilar with your church or the Utah Territory excuses me from figuring young Ann Eliza Young was somebody she just made up. I figured your Danites left her alone rather than dignify her whoppers with martyrdom."

Brother Bram said sternly, "If President Young ever directed any Danites who might or might not have existed to pay informal calls on anybody, he'd have never sent them out on a personal matter. Others went over the books when he was taken from us by surprise. Say what one might about him dying right well off, there was no evidence he ever took a penny from the temple tithes!"

Longarm said they hadn't sent him out that way to examine the books of the LDS. He explained the case he and those Mormon lawmen were working together. By the time he was up to parting company with Burbank, leaving out his meeting with young Robert Leroy Parker, the two of them were crossing the dooryard as a schoolroom of kids exploded out the door to run at them laughing and cutting up to greet their pappy.

Introductions on the front veranda and inside were more confounding. As near as Longarm ever figured out, since some of the younger Mormon beauties seemed to be teen-aged daughters of the older wives, Brother Bram was presiding, happily, it seemed, over a houshold consisting of eight wives and thirty-seven children of all ages. That was four more wives than the Koran allowed a true believer, but Mormons seldom read the Koran, so what the hey.

To manage that many kids from teenagers to toddlers, a man had to get an early start and just keep taking young and fertile brides. If the older wives felt sore about that, it didn't show. Feeding that many folk in shifts took some doing, but with so many helping hands working together, with one of the elder women making a sensible suggestion from time to time, things went smoother than during a train stop at a Harvey House.

Seated at the head of the table, if it wasn't the foot, between two relly pretty wives if they weren't daughters, Longarm got to tell his story over, and the Mormon gals assembled were all agog about the notion somebody in Utah Territory could be raiding wagon trains like Indians for the fair white bodies of even Gentile gals.

Longarm explained there was no evidence any of the abductions had taken place in Mormon country and told them how Trixie Mondale had fought off that lovesick Turk in Saint George. He thought it best to describe Trixie as a Theresa and leave out her tarted-up hair.

As the conversation went on, first at the table and later out on the veranda where it felt cooler, Longarm was struck more than once by how *natural* the unnatural domestic arrangements of Brother Bram seemed as one got used to them. Brother Bram and the eight or ten wives or older daughters lounging 'round, since only a limited number could tidy up inside and see the smaller kids off to bed, were followers of a faith a lot of Longarm's other friends found downright spooky. Had this been a mainstream Christian or even Hebrew household at this same hour, they'd have been smoking or sipping coffee out on the veranda, in smaller numbers. Longarm suspected the friendly folk gathered around had that funny Mormon underwear on under their natural-looking country dress, too. Yet the conversation was as relaxed and sensible as you might hear anywhere, with some of the women offering suggestions about Longarm's mission and nobody telling anybody else she was full of it.

In the case of this old-time Mormon family, at least, it seemed true that women who'd accepted the revelations about polygamy could welcome another wife under her roof or, in some cases where the first wife was a lot older, under her wing, and . . . then what? Did they all form a big pile of flesh? Did they take turns with Brother Bram playing a game of musical beds? Were some of the older wives glad enough to get out of having to pleasure any man? Was it anybody's beeswax but their own?

For as he sat amid friendly folk in the gathering dusk, it came to Longarm how *every* married-up couple you might have supper with did *something* alone and in private that might look shocking or silly to a houseguest who hadn't understood the visit was over.

Brother Bram's multiple marriage seemed a happy marriage. So just as in the case of other marriages, the other Mormons all around were doubtless married-up happy, not so happy, and miserable. A thoughtful cuss who was a good provider could make a good husband for any number of women, while a drunken brute could make more than one miserable at the same time. As to the lurid details stirred up more by the notion of two women at once than anything a man might *do* with two that he couldn't do with one, *everybody* tended to get silly at such times and for all her airs, old Queen Victoria in her day had likely experimented with some officious crimes against nature with her stuffy Albert.

The facts of Mormon life Longarm found more important to his mission were that kids *raised* LDS like that restless barmaid, Tabitha, or that horse-thieving, self-styled Butch Cassidy, felt free to think for themselves and just ride. As he glanced around at the contented womenfolk of Brother Bram, Longarm found it hard to buy some holdout member of the LDS trying to hold a kicking and fussing Gentile gal of the more adventurous persuasion against her own free will.

Chapter 21

Regardless of the sleeping habits of Brother Bram's happy family, Longarm was led off to a guest room by candlelight at around ten, the candlestick held by their Elsbeth Mae in a manner to light up her honey-blond hair and fine young features. Longarm never asked if she was a mighty young wife or a sort of mature daughter. As Elsbeth Mae showed him into a plain but neatly furnished bedchamber, she set the candlestick on a bed table to matter-of-factly inform him of the chamber pot under the bed and tell him how to find the nearest water pump just outside. When he politely declined her offer to fetch water from the kitchen, Elsbeth Mae said, "In that case, let me thank you for a right interestting evening, Deputy Long. You're the first . . . outsider I've ever talked to about the . . . differences of our ways. I was surprised and pleased to see you didn't believe some of the awful things they write about us in the outside papers. How did you get so educated about religious matters, you being a lawman and all?"

Longarm said, "Aw, I ain't all that educated, Miss Elsbeth Mae. They gave a war in my honor, and I was invited to come before I graduated from school back in West-by-God-Virginia, but I like to think I grew up with common sense, and a lawman who gets around learns that when you're in Rome, it's best not to kick up a fuss."

She didn't seem to follow his drift, never having been around much.

He explained, "Back at our little country church in the hollow, they expected you to take off your hat during the services, and they had no holy water font. But since then I've learned to doubt it could imperil my immortal soul to leave my hat on at a Hebrew wedding or dip my fingers in clean water and make the sign of the cross down Mexico way. I've gone quite a spell without my usual black coffee, and I've been out to cut down on my smoking for some time, anyhow. It's no big deal. It's common sense: just eat what's on your plate when you're invited to sup in Rome, see?"

She sighed and said, "That's so sweet, ah, Custis. Would a girl such as I be expected to drink and smoke if ever she found herself out in . . . the wider world?"

Longarm said, "Not if she didn't want to. Lots of Gentile gals I know don't smoke, and there's a whole posse of Gentile ladies wrecking saloons under the banner of the Women's Christian Temperance Union."

She said, "The outside world sounds sort of scary as well as awfully mixed-up. How do you Romans keep track of how to act around one another with everybody allowed to act different?"

He said, "It ain't easy. A lot of folk can't manage. That's how come they hire men like me to carry badges."

She said it was different in her more ordered world of Deseret.

He said, "Begging your pardon, ma'am, close to a score of women and still counting seem to be missing somewhere along the wagon route from Pueblo de Los Angeles to Ogden."

She flared, "But you said before you didn't suspect LDS polygamists!"

He said, "I did. I still don't. My point is that those other women never made it up to Ogden through your theocratic Utopia, and so who's to say how safe anyone may be in any quarter of this imperfect world?"

She somehow seemed to be standing closer as she murmured she hadn't meant to fuss. He said he knew that, and after a long, awkward silence, Elsbeth Mae said, "Well, if there's nothing else I can do for you, I suppose it's time to say . . . good night?"

He said, "Good night, Miss Elsbeth Mae," and she turned 'round to sort of bolt from the room. So he shut the door, shot the lock, and sat down to haul off his boots, wondering whether she'd been a bored younger wife or a restless older daughter and in either case, out for the real deal or no more than a flirty kiss.

He knew he'd never know. As he unbuttoned his shirt, he decided it hurt less to assume she'd just been an awkward country gal, no more than reluctant to say good night to an interesting diversion.

He swore under his breath and muttered half aloud, "What difference does it make? Innocent kid or hot and heavy adulteress, we're under the roof of a trusting host and a real man dosen't betray the trust of his host or hostess come hell, high water, or a hard-on!"

Having settled accounts with his fool organ grinder, Longarm turned in, slept like a log in such a swell bed after such a long day in the saddle, and awoke at dawn to the sound of children laughing outside.

There were less pleasant morning sounds to wake up to.

After an early hearty breakfast of biscuits and gravy with fried eggs one of the little girls said she'd found for him, Longarm bade a fond farewell to Brother Bram and his brood and then, since the sun was low in the east now, chased his long shadows along the same unpaved street to the center of the tiny town.

There he found the formerly surly smith or his apprentices had gone and groomed the four mules sleek and shiny and the smith refused to be paid for replacing one loose shoe. There was no way to offer a Mormon a three-for-a-nickel cheroot, so they could only shake and part friendly.

There was no telegraph office in Kanab, so Longarm couldn't wire his home office that he'd eliminated it. But he felt sure he had if everybody there knew everybody else and the biggest frog in the little puddle said he hadn't heard beans about those missing gals.

By the same reasoning, wasting half a day down at that Indian agency across the Arizona line made no sense. The Kaibab Nation didn't raid wagon trains for women or any other kind of riding stock, and if they had recently changed their habits, driving captives afoot with their digging sticks, the Mormon stockmen spread out all around Kanab would have noticed.

The only way to that agency from the south involved a long haul out of the Grand Canyon up its Kanab side canyon, and none of those women had vanished from an Arizona wagon train.

Riding west with the sun at his back and the desert breezes cooler than they'd be by June, Longarm went back over that long, rambling, and likely open discussion of conservative Mormon customs with a friendly bunch of conservative Mormons. Longarm was friendly enough and open-minded enough to see how old-timey folk living remote under Western skies, whether red, white, or those runaway Cimarrons, felt they had the right, as long as they weren't hurting anybody, to live their own ways, outlandish as their ways might seem to the others they weren't hurting.

But the Great White Father had forbidden the sun dance and rites of passage involving the theft of horses, along with customs, red and white, of paying no federal taxes and having more than one wife at a time. So the Salt Lake Temple, trying to seem more progressive with Utah statehood tempting it from courses set by earlier revelations, was already discouraging such *big* happy families as that of Brother Bram and trying to get up the nerve, and the votes, to outlaw multiple marriage entire. Longarm figured ten more years at the latest. He had no personal stake in that fuss and didn't see how it could be a whole lot worse to live openly with more than one woman than it was to marry one and visit a parlor house with your pals every payday night if you didn't keep a mistress or more on the side. But as he kept trying to advise others in his travels, the times were forever changing, and what was open range now would be fenced-in farmlands then. The buffalo were about gone, and no amount of ghost dancing was ever going to bring 'em back the way they'd once been. It made more sense to settle down and learn to grow your food than it did to chase after rabbits and grub roots in ever-shrinking hunting grounds. So the younger kids back there at Brother Bram's were fixing to grow up

Mormons neither Joseph Smith nor Brigham Young would feel comfortable with.

That was fair, Longarm decided, seeing that future Mormons were likely to be sort of uncomfortable about some of the notions of Joseph Smith and Brigham Young. All churches, like all critters, tended to evolve over time the way Professor Darwin said. Longarm had read in this big-words book from the Denver Public Library how none of the religions of his day would be recognized by the prophets who'd started them and, what the hey, it seemed doubtful those missing women had been abducted by Hebrews or Holy Rollers, either.

He trotted some, walked some, and rested some as the sunny but not too sultry morn gave way to a warmer afternoon. He knew they were making way better time than their pals with Esau Skaggs, even if the wagons were already rolling west, way to their north. They followed some long-established wagon traces and game trails cut through the cardboard-crisp desert pavement of grit cemented by mineral salts and lichens too tiny to see without a microscope, between bodacious boulders and spires of mostly rusty red sandstone 'til they were crossing a sea of coral pink dunes that seemed to go on forever and slowed the mules down considerably. But by sundown they'd made it to the headwaters of Pierce's Creek running west to joint the Virgin just downstream from Saint George and, praise the Lord, telegraph connections.

They had to make it through the coming night first, and Longarm was more pleased than surprised to see that, sure enough, somebody had settled a desert spread where desert springs fed the canyon creek to the west.

He rode past a ferociously barking but well-chained yard dog to dismount out front as a tall, plain woman in a tall, plain Mother Hubbard came out on her front veranda with a duck-choked double-barrel twelve-gauge cradled like a child, politely, in her bare arms. There was still enough light for her to see the badge Longarm had left on the front of his jacket. She said, "Be my guest and read the brands out back if you care to, Mr. Law. I'd be the Widow Wade. My friends used to call me Maggy when I still had friends. Nobody out

145

this way but coyotes, snakes, and Mormons. You want to spend the night here, it'll cost you four bits with coffee for you and fodder for your mules included. Anything else is extra, and that don't include my fair white body. You riding on or coming in?"

Longarm said he hadn't had coffee for a coon's age and bet her an extra two bits she didn't allow smoking.

Maggy Wade said, "You lose. I used to be a Mormon. I threw the old rascal out when he brung home a younger gal and declared her my sister under God and cowife. I get by here alone with Paiute help."

She proved that by yelling, loud and shrill, "Ueyahcoro! Get your lazy red ass out here and tend to this man's damn mules!"

As a shy little Indian gal in a flour sack smock came around the red freestone corner of the sprawl, the tall and plain Maggy Wade told Longarm, "Come on in. Bring your rifle and saddlebags if you don't trust my Digger help."

Longarm smiled down at the thirteen- or fourteen-year-old to say, "I reckon my possibles will be safe with Miss Butterfly, here."

Both women looked startled. As he followed her inside the rustic but clean-smelling interior, illuminated by the desert version of a reed light, with the tallow-soaked reed a dried cactus rib in this case, she asked him where he'd learned to speak Paiute.

He modestly replied, "I don't. It ain't possible for our kind to get all their tricky grammar right. But it pays to be able to baby talk your way out of a needless fight with spooked Indians of any nation."

Waving him to a seat on the horsehide-covered sofa facing her big baronial fireplace, the lady of the house said, "Make yourself to home and light up, for all I care, whilst I rustle up some coffee and cake. I suspect I know who you must be. I've heard my help talking about a white lawman they can turn to in times of trouble."

Longarm didn't answer. He saved a fraction of a cent by leaning foreward to shove a sliver of sun-cured tinder into the glowing coals of her night fire to light his cheroot. It sure felt swell to lean back comfortable with a smoke under a roof for a change.

By the time Maggy Wade rejoined him with that promised coffee and some tolerable corn cake sweetened with wild honey, Longarm had shed his denim jacket, Stetson hat, and gun belt. When his hostess sniffed and said his tobacco brought back memories, he offered her a cheroot, and she took it. But she said she'd smoke it later, mayhaps alone in bed.

She added with a chuckle, "I've indulged in all sort of bad habits since I left the LDS, and they all feel good. I've goat's cream and this crystallized honey for your coffee, if you like."

Longarm said he took his black coffee like a man and asked if she'd been born a Mormon or converted when she married one.

She said, "I reckon you could call it either way. I can't say what the mother who bore me might have been. She died on the way west back in '49. My dad, if he was my dad, left me with Aunt Iris, one of the wives of Elisha Wade. Nobody ever came back for me. I was raised a Wade of the LDS persuasion. There are worse ways to grow up. I never went to bed hungry, even when I'd been wicked, and as you can see, my bones grew long and strong on plain but plentiful farm produce. I was taught to fear no evil nor shirk my chores and to tell the truth. You do have chores when a tenth of all you produce on irrigated desert is contributed to the Salt Lake Temple."

Longarm said, "I have heard your elders do dig into the temple funds in times of trouble."

Maggy sipped her own black coffee, strong and bitter, and conceded, "During that combined great drought and financial depression of the early seventies not one Mormon child went to bed hungry. So church tithes are all right, I reckon, if you get to decide yourself. When my husband and me came out this way from Saint George because the fool was so sure there'd be a town here someday, I was willing to work harder to send a tenth of the little we could produce up to Salt Lake. But since I threw the rascal and his play-pretty out, I've been keeping it all myself, such as it is. Now and again some self-styled missionary comes by with LDS tracts to invite me back into the faith. I guess you know what I tell them they can do with the Book of Mormon!"

Longarm said, "I reckon I can. But let me get this straight, Miss Maggy. You say you settled this spread with a paid-up Saint and then you threw him off his own claim?"

She sniffed, "Half of it was mine. I'd done more than half the work whilst he was praying and chasing skirts over to Saint George. Was I the one who came home with a handsome young boy to tell Elisha to move over in bed?"

Longarm had to chuckle at the picture. Then all of a sudden the plain and tall Maggy Wade had snuffed out her rush light and seemed to be all over him in the dark as she gasped in his ear, "Oh, no! They're back!"

To which he could only reply, "Who might be back, Miss Maggy?"

She said, "Danites. Night riding Avenging Angels. Elisha said they might get really ugly if I refused to heed their first warning!"

Chapter 22

By the faint ruby light from the glowing coals of her fireplace, he could see she looked really scared. He murmured, "Don't hear your yard dog barking, Miss Maggy. Didn't hear nothing earlier, no offense."

She whispered, "Be still! Elisha must be with them. That's why the hound he raised from a pup hasn't barked at them. My ears are keen, and you get to notice changes in the night noises, living out here in the desert amidst critters who *belong* here!"

He said, "If you'd care to let me up and lend me that

twelve-gauge, I'll strap on my six-gun and have a look around outside."

She gasped, "No! They'll have you outlined in the moonlight by my stone walls and they'll shoot you down like a dog! I've barred all the ways in here. Elisha laid these thick stone walls out with any possible Indian attacks in mind. So he knows better than any of them that they can't get at us if we just sit tight in here with our own guns!"

He asked her, "Then what? What about your Indian help, outside this inner sanctum, Miss Maggy?"

She said, "Night must fall and day must break, sooner or later. My Diggers are safe enough. This is not their fight, and the LDS tries to get along with friendly Indians. My Indians are likely hugging and kissing that pesky Elisha this very minute!"

He didn't argue that. He said, "I meant what happens after daybreak? Nobody riding all the way out this way from Saint George will feel any call to just turn around and ride back a good forty miles because the sun shines down on all this empty, wide-open space, Miss Maggy!"

She started to cry.

He said, "Aw, mush, let me up, and I'll see what I can do about a mighty dumb situation."

She sobbed, "They'll kill you!" as Longarm rose to his considerable height, strapped his side arm back around his hips, and picked up her shotgun, muttering to himself about sore losers.

Not liking to get shot in doorways any more than your average well-trained gunfighter, Longarm moved over to one of the narrow combined windows and loopholes through the thick stone walls to call out into the night, "Hello, Brother Elisha Wade out yonder. This is Deputy U.S. Marshal Custis Long, and I've written down your name and left it where it will be found by friends of mine who know my methods better. I have heard your sad story, and I'll allow you may have good reason to feel a a mite cross with a woman who was tougher than you. But the beef is betwixt you and the wife you couldn't lord it over. It's not betwixt a woman who considers herself your grass widow and the Church of Jesus Christ of Latter-day Saints!"

He let that sink in before he added, "I want any of the same out there in the dark like kids playing Halloween pranks to listen tight to what comes next. What comes next is that I am down this way with the permit and full knowlege of your Salt Lake Temple. I spent last night under the roof of a Mormon elder I choose not to name, save for warning you he's likely to fill in some blanks for your own territorial police as soon as they notice I'm missing down this way. So what say you just go on about more important beeswax and leave this domestic dispute to a henpecked sissy without the hair on his chest to fight one woman without a gang of night riders to back his spineless play?"

There came no answer. Longarm hadn't expected any. Turning away from the slot, he rejoined the beseiged grass widow on her sofa in the dark to say, "They'll argue about it out yonder for a spell. Then, unless they drink more than the Book of Mormon allows, they'll see the simple logic of my words and tell old Elisha he's on his own out here. Do you reckon he has the hair on his chest to rush us alone?"

Maggy laughed bitterly and said, "He hasn't enough hair *anywhere* to impress anybody. If they back down, he'll back down with them. I expect they will. You sure have a way with words and a deep, stern voice to say them with, Custis."

He smiled thinly and confessed, "We practice. Like an army drill master, a lawman with a mousy voice encourages more trouble than his job is worth. Any Danite leader outside likely practices just as hard to sound authoritative. But he'll see I wasn't bluffing, once he studies on my words some. Night riders by definition ain't pussyfooting around in the dark because they want to be caught, and when you get right down to your night riding, there's nothing out this way worth such a serious risk."

She murmured, "Thank you. Aunt Iris always assured me men admire plain girls with good hearts. Aunt Iris thought the Paiute were Jews, too."

Longarm soothed, "I meant there was no sensible way to repossess this property without a proper court order in the face of a federal lawman, Miss Maggy. I never meant to imply you weren't woman enough to tempt a roving band of sex maniacs."

She moved closer in the dark to murmur, "Oh."

He expanded, "For all the stern things said about them by outsiders, the irregulars left over from the disbanded Nauvoo Legion have never behaved as common criminals. Religious fanatics with a Book of Mormon in one fist and a .45 Dragoon in the other ain't inclined to looting and raping in the dark of the night. But I feel sure your average band of Apache or border bandidos would be proud to rape you, ma'am."

She laughed in surprise and decided, "That's about the sweetest compliment I've ever had, Custis! But compliments won't change the way the mealymouth I gave my all to scorned me for someone younger and prettier!"

She added bitterly, "She was only younger because I was born and discarded way earlier. She didn't lift a finger to grow up prettier than me, either. It just up and happened. Why do such things happen? If there's a Lord God up yonder who loves us all, down to the fallen sparrow, how come some of his creations get it all whilst others keep getting the short end of the stick?"

Longarm said, "At another little country church in a hollow they sang a song that allowed we'd all understand it better, farther along someday by and by. I suspect, for now, that if every one of us grew up just as good-looking, smart, and rich, there'd be nothing for any of us to feel better about. Clams and trees all grow up as pretty, if that makes them feel happier than us. You ain't that old and ugly, Miss Maggy. Speaking as another worthless man, he likely married that other gal because his church allowed it and because she was a woman. Men are like that when it comes to women. No matter how swell the woman we have may be, we always want another. It ain't nobody's fault. It's the nature of the beast. I suspect that angel, Moroni, must have been of the male persuasion. A she-male angel might have revealed things different."

She sniffed and confided, "A lot you know. Us girls have feelings as well! How often at night, alone out here in the middle of nowhere with no man of my own, have I been tortured by the wicked yearnings of any woman alone! If I

151

confessed half the shocking secret sins I've dreamed up, wide-awake, you'd run screaming out the door!"

He draped an arm around her, since that seemed less awkward after she'd wriggled up under one armpit like so, and said, "Everbody on earth has wicked thoughts in the dark of the night. They go with having human feelings. They don't count unless we *act* on them at the expense of others or our own physical safety."

She gasped, "You, too? What's the dirtiest thing you ever wanted to do, Custis?"

He thought before he honestly replied, "Hard to say. When I was young and in my teens, I racked my brains piling dirty atop dirty in my head, thinking it would be better if I ever got down and dirty with anyone or anything."

He started to fish out another smoke, thought better of it, and then confessed, "Lucky for me and doubtless a heap of girls I was to meet up with farther along, I met before I'd done any lasting damage with a kindly old philosopheress I'll ever be grateful to. She let me play with her ring-dang-doo and got me to slow down and strum guitar instead of banjo as she explained a fact of life that Mr. de Sade and those Hindu artists who fashioned the *Kama Sutra* never managed to grasp."

She eagerly asked, "What secrets of depravity did that older woman teach you, my poor innocent child?"

He said, "That there ain't no secret. Nine out of ten total strangers are swell in bed, at least at first, whilst that unusual tenth one is an interesting novelty. It don't matter all that much how you go about what comes natural to dumb animals as long as the one you're doing it with is *friendly*. As most folk notice by the time they've busted up with somebody, it don't matter *what* you do in which position with somebody you don't like no more. They call it making love with good reason. With somebody you like it's lovely. With somebody you don't it ain't. Degenerates like de Sade, who didn't *like* the poor gals he was messing with, tried in vain to enjoy the experience by piling one nasty notion atop the other until the sheer work alone must have made him wonder why he was bothering."

152

Somewhere in the night a pony nickered. Maggy said, "One of mine. Name's Nancy. I know her voice. Tell me some more about that awful Marquis de Sade! Is it true he died insane? I've tried ever so hard to find a copy of his wicked book about the depraved Justine! I understand there's nothing nastier in the English language! Have you ever read it?"

Longarm soberly replied, "Yep. Miss Justine gets right nasty before the end. That's my point. In the most depraved passage in the dirty book, whilst an inexperienced moon calf might abuse himself over the depravity, or a dirty old man who's forgotten the real thing might drool, natural men and women who still enjoy the real thing tend to wonder what on earth Miss Justine thinks she's getting out of such carryings on, aside from going, 'Tee-hee-hee, look at me, and ain't I awful?' "

Maggy snuggled closer to ask, "What's she doing in that awful book, Custis? I've heard tell it was mighty shocking!"

He shrugged and said, "I reckon shock for the sake of shocking was what de Sade had in mind when he made such a scene up. I dasn't repeat what he wrote in front of a respectable woman, Miss Maggy."

She put a hand on his jeans as she confided, "Aw, I ain't so respectable. A woman alone out here in the desert gets to coming up with some awfully wicked wishes if she ever finds Aladdin's lamp out back. What dirty deeds does Justine do in that dirty book? I really want to know, in case I run out of lonesome daydreams!"

He shook his head and said, "Sorry. I'd feel red-faced repeating it to ladies I know better, in the biblical sense. Regular slap and tickle is one thing. What Miss Justine does to her own kin in de Sade's sick story is too filthy for us to share."

She said they'd see about that, and Longarm got some sense of what Elisha Wade had experienced at her strong hands when she commenced to haul his duds off, panting like a she wolf in heat as he ran her open lips back and forth across his face. So, seeing she wanted to hear about Miss Justine's dirty doings that badly, Longarm grabbed hold to kiss her right as they helped each other undress in the dark.

Once they had, they wound up on the Navaho rug between the sofa and the hearth and by such ruby light as there was, Longarm could see as he braced himself above her, stiff-armed, that while plain and tall, she was built like one of the slimmer marble statues of Greek goddess gals.

As she bumped and ground her open groin under him with her heels planted firmly on the rammed clay floor, Maggy moaned, "Oh, my land, you *do* forget what it's really like, making up dirty notions for your hand to play with! I see what you mean! We're not doing anything crazy, yet it feels so swell! That is what you mean, isn't it, and whatever your answer, don't stop! Don't ever stop until you come in me a hundred times and I just have to throw this fool rug away!"

Longarm was willing to try. But of course even Maggy had to stop for breath after she claimed they'd beaten all honeymoon records her married-up chums had ever claimed.

After a cautious midnight stroll around outside, bare ass but armed and dangerous, the both of them, Longarm and Maggy Wade, wound up in her four-poster behind the additional barrier of her barred bedchamber door.

Maggy giggled as their night-chilled, naked flesh resumed contact. He felt as inspired, and they hadn't tried it dog style yet.

So it was as he was thrusting lazy in that best of all positions for bedroom conversations that Maggy insisted she'd paid her dues to be in on the dirtier doings of Justine.

Longarm got a good grip on either hip bone, with his bare feet widespread on the rug as he thrust slow but deeply, saying, "Once upon a time there was this sassy French gal, Miss Justine, brung up proper but determined to be the baddest gal she'd ever known. So she recruited her a gang of like-minded sinners from all walks of life, high and low, then screwed them all high and low until they took to making up dirtier ways to come, too dumb to see that once your passions cool past useful function, it's time to just do something *else* 'til such spirits move you some more."

Maggy purred, "Move it in me some more!"

Longarm complied as he continued, "Miss Justine and her gang staged one depraved orgy after another 'til they got past nasty to criminal. So in that one scene everybody remembers,

154

Justine has her cohorts kidnap her own mother and bring the poor scared woman to this spooky den of depravity. They strip the respectable mother naked. Justine shucks her own duds, straps on a big fake dick, and proceeds to rape her poor old weeping and wailing mother, going 'Tee-hee-hee, look at me, the nasty lesbian, committing incest and rape at the same time and ain't I awful?' "

Maggy arched her spine to take him deeper as she asked in a puzzled tone, "What was Justine getting out of it, aside from being awesomely disrespectful to her mother?"

Longarm said, "Welcome to the club of grown-up fornication. For all his wild notions, poor de Sade was too busy acting shocking to enjoy much coming and . . . speaking of coming . . ."

Maggy moaned, "Me, too, and I'm so glad I never tried to talk you into some of the naughty shit I was planning if ever you came my way, and can we come this way some more?"

Longarm allowed he'd try as he gazed fondly down on the view of her lean but shapely ass, idly wondering what it would be like if he could just step sideways and shove it to another gal and then another, dog style in the Mormon fashion.

Maggy gasped, "Oh, Custis, you're such a natural man!"

To which he could only reply in a modest tone, "A lot you knew about *imagining* this sort of action, Mr. de Sade!"

Chapter 23

Next morning just at sunrise, Longarm felt sincere as he assured his gracious hostess he'd be proud to stay on a spell if he had the time. He said, "With any luck, I'm even or a tad ahead of the wagon train way to the north. But I figure to lose time in Saint George as I canvass some for sinister Turks. The less likely I am to find any, the longer I'm likely to be stuck there and . . . Aw, don't cloud up on me like that, honey! I want to remember you *smiling* every time I think of you in times to come."

She smiled gamely, threw in a kiss, and they tore off a quickie with their duds half on after breakfast.

Gathering up his mules—the Indian help had already saddled up for him—Longarm rode out a ways to circle Maggy's spread a furlong out as the sun's low rays etched every pebble of the desert pavement sharply.

He cut no sign. He wasn't surprised. He hadn't heard shit, the yard dog hadn't barked, and there was nothing wrong with his own ears.

"Perfidy, thy name is woman!" he announced to his mules as they all headed west. But after lighting up and studying on her motives a spell, Longarm decided, "Oh, well, she lied in a good cause, and as long as I was fixing to stay the night back there in any case . . . but ain't it a caution how they lead us poor boys astray with fluttery eyelashes and total bullshit?"

The mules, being sterile, had no suggestions to offer.

As he rode along, Longarm decided, "Thinking back over this detour, I'd say we about eliminated the LDS. The more progressive Mormons in Salt Lake City have assigned their own lawmen to investigate, and Jubal Burbank is one hell of an actor or acting in good faith."

He took a drag on his cheroot and opined, "For all the sinister tales about less-progressive old-timey Mormons, we've met up with some rebellious youngsters and a defiant Mormon backslider any Danites left seem to be leaving alone, in spite of old Maggy using them as an excuse to use and abuse us. None of the polygamist Saints we've met up with look as if they keep kidnapped brides chained to their bedposts. So what's left, and what if somebody has been kidnapping women in the *vicinity* of Mormons, hoping Mormons will be suspected of their crime?"

The sun was warmer on his back now, for they were on lower and thus hotter desert this far south, albeit they were

156

still a mile above sea level because nothing in northern Arizona nor any of Utah ever went any lower.

Breaking trail to remove his riding and pack saddles from sweaty backs to fork 'em over fresh, dry hides, Longarm let all four critters browse some rabbit brush by the side of the trail before riding on. They called the tough weed rabbit brush for the obvious reason that it stayed juicy and green long after all the meager desert forbs and grass had gone dormant and mummified.

As they browsed, he hunkered in the dappled shade of a creekside cottonwood, considering the motives for kidnapping mail-order brides no better than they should have been. The sort of gal who'd marry up with a man she'd never met for a roof overhead and three square meals a day, with bedroom privileges thrown in, was skating perilously close to premeditated prostitution. So it hardly seemed likely somebody was picking cherries for dirty old men with expensive tastes. For a few dollars more, gals like Miss Trixie Mondale would doubtless agree to just be "engaged" for the time being. So what was the son of a bitching *motive* for grabbing gals on their way through Mormon country and blaming it on the Mormons?

As Longarm rose to gather up his riding stock and take it on down the trail, he muttered, "Hold that thought. Where in the U.S. Constitution does it say anyone's been kidnapped anywheres particular betwixt, say, Barstow or even San Berdoo and . . . Right, Ogden. Burbank said Utah terrirorials have determined none of those missing women got aboard any trains Out of Ogden."

Mounting up, he added, "He says none of them have ever been seen for certain in any Mormon settlement. But didn't we meet Miss Trixie in a Mormon town after she said she'd wrestled a mail-order courting man in Saint George up ahead?"

Riding another furlong or more as he gnawed that bone, Longarm shook his head and said, "Miss Trixie wasn't missing when we met up with her in Provo. So she wasn't kidnapped in any Mormon settlement she'd been through, and we chalk that elimination up to Burbank, bless his defensive attitude!"

But fair was fair, and Longarm could see how Mormons felt about a lot of nonsense they were accused of. Folk who didn't act all that odd were forever being accused of shit. That Japanese proverb about the nail sticking out the most being the next one hammered made a grim heap of sense. Longarm had once had a swell argument, only ended by an offer to bet real money, with his pal Sergeant Nolan of the Denver P.D. over that Russian police bulletin about the Hebrew elders of Zion making that mawkish bread, which came out pure white, with the blood of Christian children, which wouldn't.

The silliest part of the sober-sided Russian warning about fiendish Hebrew bakers, to anybody who knew the folk in Denver's Little Palestine, was how shy such folk were about blood, any sort of blood. They refused to eat meat or poultry unless the critters had been ritually bled to where some less fussy eaters turned up their noses at the drier taste of the Kosher brand. His offer to bet Nolan a month's wages there was no blood of any kind in mawkish bread had put the burly Black Irishman to *thinking* about that Russian bulletin and of course, once you thought about it, there was no way to bake bread white if the flour had been mixed with any kind of blood.

Mormons didn't blow on goats' horns or pray with little boxes tied to their foreheads, and while they didn't serve wine with dinner, they ate about the same as anybody else. Longarm doubted the sheer hatred of some fellow Christians had a heap to do with departures from the King James version of the Good Book. Nobody lynched Pentecostal preachers, even when they spoke in tongues and rolled in the aisles. The LDS was reviled on suspicion of sex mania and distrusted, even by the government in Washington, for having tighter control over its congregation than even the Church of Rome, or *appearing* to. Some nominal Mormons he'd met out this way had been neither under control nor all that scared of the Salt Lake Temple, and the anti-Mormon *Salt Lake Tribune* was put out by avowed Mormon haters an easy stroll from Temple Square.

"Danites out in the dark indeed!" Longarm laughed as he thought back to the way the love-starved Maggy had played him for a fool, to his eternal gratitude.

As he rode along, he asked his mule, "Why do I keep coming back to that circle around the mulberry bush, Mule? I thought we'd agreed it was hardly likely night riding Mormons have been carrying off Gentile women, and Maggy was hours ago! She surely beat sleeping alone, but not a thing she said or did pointed finger one at anybody. So why do I keep feeling it did?"

Longarm shoved that line of thinking to the back of the stove. He knew how, sometimes, when you let a puzzle simmer a spell, the taste and above all the smell tended to make more sense.

Not wanting to camp on the desert with Saint George just over the horizon, Longarm pushed his borrowed mules with more trotting and way shorter trail breaks than most ponies would have tolerated. They didn't cotton much to that, but, being mules, they could take it.

He ate his noon dinner in the saddle on the go, washing down his canned grub with the canteen of black coffee Maggy Wade had sent him off with, bless her backsliding Mormon heart.

He had to stop now and again to water and rest the four mules. But he drove 'em an hour and a half between trail breaks instead of the cavalry or cattle-drive hour. In sum, he drove 'em hard, and even so, the sun was setting some more when they made it into Saint George at a walk, hooves dragging.

Aside from having been the winter residence of the late Brigham Young, at lower altitude near the southwest limits of firm Mormon control, Saint George on the northwest bank of the Virgin was laid out in that same tediously four-square Mormon grid with Tabernacle the only street with a name instead of a three-digit number east and west, while Main was the only named street running north and south. The tabernacle rose more than anything else at Tabernacle and Main, but they had a temple, too, between 200 East and 300 East. Longarm wasn't too sure about the distinction and didn't care. How and where others might pray was their beeswax and none of his own.

The de facto main street of Saint George was 100 North Street, a block above Tabernacle, with nothing but that tabernacle facing the officious Main Street as darkness fell. He found a livery for the mules and a hotel flop for himself facing the open square at 100 North and Main. Saint George was more solidly LDS than Salt Lake City but not as thin-lipped as Kanab. Catering as it did to prosperous winter visitors and just now knuckling down to a hot and lonesome summer, the business center of Saint George seemed almost like a well-behaved cow town until you gazed all about for a tobacco stand or tea shop. To give the devil, or the angel Moroni, his due, towns tended to be more well-behaved when nobody out after dark was all that drunk. Saint George was big enough, and enough of a resort, for a man with a terrible thirst to indulge it. Mormons didn't smoke or drink, themselves, but Mormon lawmen didn't arrest those who chose to, unless they acted up.

Having seen to the comfort of his hard-driven mules and hired a room to store his possibles, Longarm scouted up the Western Union not far from old Brigham Young's winter home, fancy as his beehive house in Salt Lake City.

Getting off a progress report to his home office and sending out requests for more information on the prospective husbands of those missing mail-order brides, the saddle-sore Longarm strode out on the streets of Saint George for such action as there was to be found in a town with nary a saloon to its name.

He wasn't looking to get screwed, blewed, and tattooed. He was out to cut the trail of the love-starved Ben O'Mar, as they likely knew him if they knew him at all.

Spying bright lights and a swirling crowd not far off from President Young's mansion, Longarm drifted in to join the well-dressed bunch as he wished he was wearing his store-boughts back at his hotel. For the occasion was an opening night at the Saint George Opera House, with the opera that evening being Mr. Verdi's *Aida*, put on by a genuine French cast, according to the posters out front.

Longarm smiled fondly at memories of his bodyguarding tour with the National Treasure of France and that other French bunch backing the play of Miss Sarah Bernhardt. They hadn't toured Saint George. But passing through other parts of Utah Territory, Miss Sarah had expressed pleasant surprise at the swell theaters and opera houses, erected in that same distinctly Mormon version of Victorian eclectic.

The Saints assembled to enjoy the horrible death of Miss Aida could have passed for fashionable Denver folk attending the same show. Once you made it inside the Saint George city limits, it was hard to feel like you were out in the middle of some mighty remote desert.

None of the well-dressed and well-bred operagoers commented on Longarm's sun-faded and trail-dusty denim duds. Unless he stripped to his unholy underwear, they'd probably accept him as a country boy of the LDS persuasion. But Longarm didn't like sticking out like a sore thumb, and he'd already watched Miss Aida dying at the top of her lungs. So he headed back the other way, and as luck would have it, spied a barber shop open for the evening trade.

The well-traveled Longarm knew that next to a saloon, there was no better place than a barber shop for a stranger in town to get the feel of the local gossip. So he ambled in and, better yet, the place was crowded.

Longarm hung up his hat and sat down at one end of the lined-up Windsor chairs along one wall. The thickset, gray-haired barber had the best view of him as he sat there, poker faced. For the reasons he'd worn his badge in Kanab, he'd been wearing it ever since. When folk could see at a glance you were an outsider wearing a .44-40, it paid to let them see your badge.

Others perked up with interest all around as the barber observed, or declared, "Lawman, are we? You here for a haircut or am I in some sort of trouble?"

Longarm laughed as easily and said, "Haircut. I've been working with your Captain Burbank. He's with Esau Skaggs, up around Veyo if we've timed things right. I swung down this way, orders of your Utah territorials, to see if I could cut the trail of a material witness called either Ben O'Mar or Bin Omar, depending. I ain't out to arrest old Ben, you understand. Captain Burbank and me only want his statement on one incident and his opinion on some others."

One of the locals asked, "What sort of a name might Bin Omar be? It sounds *Oriental* if you ask me!"

Longarm said, "It is. Another witness told us he lives somewhere around Saint George."

There came a collective clucking. It sounded to Longarm as if a gopher snake had just slithered into a henhouse. After more than one year-round local had opined they had no use for Orientals there in Saint George, a plaintive voice piped up, "I know where there's a whole mess of Orientals. Down the Virgin, across the Arizona line at a place called Alamut."

Longarm sat bolt upright to demand, "Did you say *Alamut,* as in the remote stronghold of that old man of the mountains, friend?"

The Mormon said, "Never heard nothing about old men of any sort. I heard there was this Arizona mining camp, on higher ground across from where the Virgin joind the Colorado in Nevada Territory. Can't tell you much more about the place. Way I hear it, the few prospectors who've stumbled within rifle range of this Alamut have been fired on. It ain't certain everyone so fired upon made it out of there alive."

Another waiting customer whistled and decided, "Now that you mention it, I did hear something about a whole mess of Orientals up to something on that unsettled mesa country beyond the Colorado. What do you suppose all them Orientals might be guarding down that way, Will?"

Will said, "Don't know. Can't say. Whatever it might be, they sure are guarding it serious!"

Chapter 24

Longarm slept on the ominous tales of an unmapped Alamut, hoping against hope a better way would come to him.

In the morning none had, and the others with the wagons extended any lead they had on Longarm if he hoped to meet up with them in Las Vegas.

But he drew a blank with the county clerk and city directory, and none of the hotels he canvassed with his badge had registered any Ben O'Mar or Bin Omar in recorded history.

Consulting a large-scale survey map at the federal land office in Saint George only told Longarm what he'd already guessed. The northwest corner of Arizona Territory facing the Nevada juncture of the Virgin and the Colorado was only that summer being surveyed official by railroad builder Lewis Kingman. An Edward Beale had surveyed one narrow wagon route out of Fort Mojave on the Colorado, near the pointy southern nose of Nevada, back in '57, on *camel back* with Turkish camel drivers backing his play!

Other than those two detailed surveys, most everything between the sharp bend of the combined waters of the Virgin and the Colorado by way of Boulder Canyon and the Bill Williams River two hundred miles south was up for grabs and guesswork. There stood the scattered pinpoints of Chloride, Oatman, and Jerome, tiny desert mining camps, with Oatman too close to Fort Mojave on the Colorado to hide all that many abducted brides, while Chloride, a silver strike way out on the desert between the Colorado and the arid Music Mountains, was about the earliest silver strike in those parts and, God damn it to hell, not possible to eliminate from Saint George!

Prospected in the early sixties by one of those half-mad desert rats who wandered the barren wastes until they struck it rich or more often vanished entire from human ken, Chloride was now connected to the more-traveled Lower Colorado by wagon trace, and other prospectors still fanned out across the desert from there. Those Music Mountains a good ways east of Chloride, say, a hard day's ride across busted-up rimrock and dry lake beds, conspired with the notions of long-ago camel drivers to draw fanciful images of the real albeit long-lost Alamut where the old man of the mountains had ruled over an army of hashish-crazed assassins and a harem of peris or houris, depending on whether those lovely, willing gals had been hashish dream fairies or the real thing.

It all fell into place until you asked yourself how in thunder any gal on the Old Spanish Trail far to the north on the far side of the deep-cut Colorado was likely to meet up with

Camel Corps Turks in the barren Music Mountains east of Chloride, Ariz-dammit-zona. And after that, it was too far out of the way.

But did that eliminate it?

Muttering, "Shit-fuck-shit-fuck-shit-fuck!" every step of the way, Longarm trudged back to the Western Union to block out night letters to his home office and Captain Burbank, in care of their telegraph office in Barstow, California, seeing that was the first telegraph office Burbank and the others were ever going to get to after wondering whatever could have happened to Longarm for quite a spell.

Then he treated himself to a hearty sit-down meal of waffles with sausages, lacking only the morning coffee he craved, before he went shopping for more trail grub, including, dammit, a can of Arbuckle Brand coffee sold without comment, like a dirty book, by a grocer doing well while outfitting prospectors of all faiths.

He trudged his thirty-pound load to the livery and bet the stable hand four bits they couldn't distribute the extra weight scientific on his pack saddle in their tack room. He asked them to make sure of all sixteen hooves while they were at it and went to check out of the hotel with his McClellan and Winchester.

By nine A.M., they were headed down the Virgin, with only Longarm capable of cussing that dirty. It still seemed like a hell of a way to run a railroad, and whether he cut sign or not, there was no way in hell he was going to rejoin the others this side of Barstow, if not San Berdoo for God's sake!

But as the pony track along the Virgin followed the greenup-fed waters along their floodplain between ever-rising high-water terraces, he got to smoke, and it steadied his nerves further when he brewed a cow camp serving of Arbuckle Brand over a trailside Digger fire.

Cow camps across the West favored that brand, ground special with the tin can brewing of drinkable coffee in mind. Made right in a regular coffeepot, the joe could get downright delightful.

Digger fires were made small, as a fistful of dry desert shit could hold a steady flame. But as long as he had one going, he heated up a can of bully beef to melt the fat in it less tallowsome.

By the time he'd eaten dinner and remounted, Longarm was feeling better or at least more resigned to their two-pronged attack on the situation. As he'd advised young outlaws he'd arrested in the past, one of the main advantages the law had over the lawbreaker was that there were way more honest men than crooks, spread all over creation. When you added modern wonders such as the telegraph, allowing lawmen to keep in touch over otherwise impossible distances, most every fork of the owl-hoot trail led only into prison. For it didn't help an outlaw to be smarter than your average lawman, albeit a few of them were. There was always another lawman out ahead of you, alerted to watch out for you by wire and, sooner or later, they were sure to *gitcha!*

Letting his dinner tamp down inside him as he rode, Longarm could see how it really wouldn't matter if Jubal Burbank and those other lawmen with him cut the sign of those kidnappers. If the combined force of Utah and Washington lawmen couldn't handle the boo, one more gunhand wasn't likely to make much difference.

His own more lonesome quest was both simpler and less likely to pan out. He didn't have to determine where, when, or how any gals had been abducted from whatever. He only had to locate the source of those barbershop rumors of mysterious Alamut and see if any women were being held there against their will. If any were, they'd doubtless solve the mystery of their abductions for the law, once the law had set them free.

If he found no women there, or the women he found there had come willing, it hardly mattered how many mysterious Orientals were out there in the desert doing what. It was a free country. Where in the U.S. Constitution did it say left-over Camel Corps herders couldn't build fairy-tale castles in uncharted wilderness and play at being old-time Turks, Persians, whatever in hell the old man of the mountains had been, as long as they weren't bothering anybody?

If the place existed, it was more likely to be a more natural sort of mining camp, just named after the mysterious, faraway Alamut by a prospector who'd been dreaming a spell about his big strike and private town. Longarm suspected it would turn out to be a gold strike. A silver strike required more workers and supplies to wrest profit from the bedrock with pick and shovel and dynamite. Gold was where you found it in all sorts of deposits, many of which could be worked by a small crew or even solo. Longarm had heard the tales of that eccentric Dutchman down the other side of the Gila, said to have a secret one-man gold mine in the Superstition Mountains east of Phoenix. They called him Jake Walzer. He'd shown up around Prescott during the war years and worked a spell in the Vulture mine near Wickenburg with other Dutch hardrock miners as their straw boss until he up and quit in the winter of '73–'74 to trail into the Superstitions with a couple of burros and an Apache gal described as a looker or a crone, depending. Apache killed her in '74.

That might have been because she and Jake Walzer had just come out of their sacred Superstition Mountains with $70,000 in pure gold nuggets or mayhaps wire gold, either easy to grub up with no more than a garden spade and a poke.

Walzer had never filed a claim. He and a later male pard named Jake as well, Jacob Wisner instead of Walzer to confuse the legend if it wasn't all bullshit, had just vanished into the Superstitions now and again to reappear in Phoenix with more raw gold to bank. Sinister rumor had claim jumpers following the Dutchmen into the wild and craggy Superstitions, never to be seen again. More recently, Jake Walzer had reported his pal Jake Wisner murdered by Tonto Apache off among the brooding red peaks. If he'd ever existed, the Indians had burned his body all crisp and crumbly over his own campfire so's he was in no fit condition to bring home.

Others, of course, said Jake Walzer was no more than a high-grader raiding the nearby Vulture mine he'd worked in for that gold he said he'd found in *sandstone,* which was barely possible if it was a placer he said that Apache gal had led him to. Nobody else had found shit in the Superstition Mountains. Yet year after year, that Dutchman kept on coming out of them with pokes of nigh pure high grade. So what if the mysterious Alamut, somewhere between Chloride and the Music Mountains, turned out to be such a pocket of easy money, worked by no more than a handful of . . . what? All anyone had called them was Oriental, and what would a handful of sneaky gold miners want with . . . No more than a score of such miners sounded about right and about a score of women had been sidetracked off the Old Spanish Trail!

So that fit all too well. With wagon travel about to let up for the summer and all the women they needed already abducted, the abductions were likely to cease and desist before anybody caught the abducting sons of bitches!

Longarm didn't like the picture emerging from the mists as he told his mule, "More than a few dozen pards of any persuasion could *hold* a gold strike against claim jumpers. So they wouldn't need to act all that sneaky. They could file a claim, throw their town open to the whores and gamblers, and help themselves to the same quality of tail without risking a serious stretch down in Yuma Prison. But how in the hell do you drag a kidnap victim that far, even across wide-open desert, without others noticing and . . . fuck it, that won't matter, once we get there!"

Riding along, alone on the riverside trail, Longarm threw back his head to sing to his mules:

> Farther along, we'll know more about it.
> Farther along, we'll understand why.
> Cheer up, my brothers, walk in the sunshine.
> We'll understand it, all by and by.

And so his day went till he rode into the Mormon hamlet of Littlefield below the junction of the Virgin and Beaver Creek at sundown, still sporting his badge. It wouldn't have been polite to ask, but he knew that canyon outpost of Saint George was about as far down the Colorado as LDS writ ran. The atmosphere was like that at Kanab writ small. At ther inevitable smithy, Longarm patiently explained who he was and what he was doing in their corner of Utopia. Whether it was his polite smile or whether business was sure slow down their way, the Saints there made him welcome enough, albeit

167

he was instructed to spread his roll in the hayloft of their sky pilot's barn.

He got to eat with the Indian hands out back and didn't care. He knew local Indians, Hualapai in this case, knew the country ahead as well as anybody. But when he asked about a recent influx of Turks or a new settlement called Alamut, it seemed he had farther along to ride.

The next morning he did, sneaking smokes and coffee like a mean little kid all alone on the lonesome trail through the dappled shade of cottonwood and willow.

The next time the sun set, it set early to plunge what was now the serious Canyon of the Virgin in deep purple under a flame-red sky. So he camped alone on higher ground away from the river but not too close to the rock-shedding canyon wall.

Passing the side canyon of the Meadow Valley Wash the next morning, Longarm was tempted to turn up it to the Nevada settlements along the same. But he knew if he tried to cover every route leading away from the Old Spanish Trail, he could wind up riding in circles until he and all those missing women were old and gray, if any of 'em were still alive. So he rode on down and down some more to make another night camp between really serious canyon walls beside the purling rusty waters of the aptly named Colorado.

The floodplain between the bodacious walls of mostly shale and sandstone spread wide enough in places for occasional, small, informally claimed stock spreads. Mostly goats and sheep. Both got by on rougher browse than cows, and neither had to be driven to market up a canyon wall. The goats supplied meat and milk for their owners while bales of wool could be mule-trained or rafted on down to Yuma.

That gave Longarm a whole new notion as he supped with some right friendly breeds above the big bend of Boulder Canyon. He'd only meant to be polite when he'd casually asked about the bales of wool they were ammassing day by day atop a riverside raft of cottonwood logs.

When his Anglo-Mex-Indian host said there were no serious rapids their side of Fort Mojave, Longarm bet him five bucks they'd never be able to ferry him and his four mules seventy-odd miles downstream.

168

The breed sheep rancher laughed and said, "You're on! I'll give *you* five dollars if we can't get you there in less than than a day. It'll soon be too dark to run the river. But stay the night, and if we start at dawn, it'll still be daylight when you pay off the bet!"

So Longarm enjoyed a good night's sleep under a friendly roof to wake up at dawn to the sound of wood-chopping.

Out beside the river his host, Pancho Gray, was at work on their market raft with two full-blood hands and his fat but pretty-faced *mujer*, Miss Esperanza. As he drifted out to join them, Longarm saw how they'd piled wool waist high fore and aft with alder saplings running from pile to pile on either side to form a central pen near the raft's natural center of gravity. Longarm didn't ask why. Any fool could see there was no way to raft upstream against that swift, swirling current. So after they dropped him off, the Grays meant to raft on downstream with half their usual load, his five dollars, and all that cottonwood firewood to sell in Yuma before they went home by shank's mare.

Miss Esperanza insisted they had time for a hearty breakfast. It was easy to see how she'd gotten so fat as they feasted on her notion of a hearty breakfast.

Then, stuffed to the gills with goat cheese and bean enchiladas washed down with coffee strong enough to strip paint, they shoved off with Miss Esperanza at the stern sweep, Pancho forward with the front sweep, and Longarm with the mules in the middle.

Their downstream passage was comical as well as swift, with Longarm steadying the wild-eyed mules on their shifty footing while the lovebirds bow and stern screamed at each other like Spanish-speaking alley cats.

"*¡Pendejo, a la derecha! ¿Que coño te pasa? Me maravilla que todavia estoy vivo,*" the fat Esperanza was inclined to scream.

To which her husband would scream back, "*Coño, no me friegues. No mas eres que una pata en el culo,*" when they weren't exchanging more pungent observations than "Steer to the right, you asshole. It's a wonder I'm still alive!" or "Don't fuck with me, you total pain in the ass!"

And yet when they tied up to a streamside willow to enjoy

the picnic lunch she'd packed, Miss Esperanza and old Pancho seemed downright fond of each other, and Longarm suspected they'd have gone further if he hadn't been watching.

Some warm-natured women were like that, Longarm knew to his sorrow. He just wasn't up to having a gal calling him a worthless total shit for brains before she fucked him half unconscious.

So he found their bickering was wearing on him long before they got to a long stretch of pebble beach Pancho steered into, calling out, "Like the prophet proclaimed, Custis, this is the place!"

Longarm paid off his bet, and they helped him unload. Miss Esperanza wiped a tear from her fat cheek and kissed Longarm on his, sobbing she was surely going to miss him.

She likely enjoyed having company when she described her husband as a shit-eating dog with his head up his ass in Spanish.

As Longarm resaddled his mules, they were already on their way down the Colorado, screaming at each other like the puppets in a Punch and Judy show.

It was late in the day, and it was sultry down on the floodplains of a now wider and slower Colorado. Its channel got ever wider with less dramatic canyon walls as it wound its way down to the Sea of Cortez by way of its sprawling delta in Mexican territory. There where the Grays had let him off, the eastern wall rose more like the stairsteps of a mountain range, and some maps called the higher land to the east the Black Mountains.

Others held the Black Mountains were more a mesa, cut off from the flat desert to the east by the deep Detrital Wash, so called by survey men because it was so choked up by wind and waterborne grit you never saw the water running north in wet weather under all that shit.

Longarm led the four mules on foot, single file, up the winding path to the top that Pancho Gray had told him about. As they reached the summit, the sun was setting on the far side of the Colorado. Longarm stared at a wishing star or a night fire on the horizon as he confided to his mules, "If that's Chloride, yonder, it's still over twenty miles off across rough rimrocks and dry basins full of rock flour. So why don't we camp right here in these April breezes and make an easy day of it, come morning?"

He led the mules along the rise away from the trail across it to tether them to some Joshua, unsaddle them, and put their nose bags on. They'd already been well watered down along the river.

Wiping them all down with a feed sack, Longarm glanced about for firewood before he warned himself, "Forget it. Don't tell anyone you're coming. Let them guess. Thanks to Miss Esperanza, you have yet another canteen of cooled coffee and canned pork and beans taste no better warmed over windfall.

But a little later, as he washed his cold beans down with cold and bitter black coffee, Longarm dryly chuckled. "Ain't I something? How could anybody be expecting shit? I never told a living soul where I was headed when I rode out of Saint George. So nobody could know I've left!"

This was not true, but Longarm might have been amused had he known the consternation in certain criminal haunts occasioned by the wire from a sneak in Saint George that the dangerous Longarm had split off from that fact-finding committee, looking for facts on his own.

The scary part after this was that Longarm had indeed told nobody where he was headed from Saint George, and so the crooks he was after had no way of knowing for certain he had no idea who the hell or where they really were.

Chapter 25

Longarm rode into Chloride, Arizona Territory, the next afternoon. It wasn't easy. It would be tougher later in the year when the hellish rocky desert got even hotter.

Silver chloride was the most common ore of the same.

The ramshackle sprawl named after its only product was the oldest mining town in the territory, the strike having occurred in '61, with the details lost to history except it was agreed nobody sober would have been wandering more than twenty miles from the wild-enough Colorado. The maps had yet to agree on whether those mountains looming off to the northeast were the Musics or the Cerbats or something else. Their positions varied with each map, and prospectors were advised to stay the hell out of them because the Hualapai were really two-faced cocksuckers, by the standards of Mr. Lo, the poor Indian.

It was also said you needed a gold mine to run a silver mine, which was laying it on a tad, but it did take more work by more hands to win silver from its complex ores than it did for way more profitable gold.

The seeming paradox of silver being worth less than a tenth as much as gold lay in the abundance of both metals in the earth, by the ton, regardless of how much it wanted to come out of the ground for you. Gold was where you found it in rich pockets of often pure metal, ready to be pounded into jewelry. Silver chloride looked like ink-stained furnace ash, in more considerable quantity, and you had to haul a wagon load out of the desert for the same profit as a poke of gold.

So the silver strike at Chloride provided work for enough hard-rockers to support a row of boardinghouses, a longer row of whorehouses, two saloons, and of course a jail.

First things coming first, Longarm dismounted out front, tethered the four mules along the hitch rail, and mosied into the jail to pay the required courtesy call of an out-of-town lawman with his badge on his chest.

The town law, an older gent with rusty hair and a gimp leg, said he'd just been about to head on home for supper, there being not a customer in either dinky cell the guard room straddled on a workday evening. He said his name was Hagan, Rory Hagan, and Longarm was welcome to come along and have supper with him if he just had to talk some more about ghost towns in the Music Mountains for God's sake!

Longarm thanked old Hagan but allowed he'd take a rain

check on the generous invite, seeing he had jaded mules and other matters to tend to.

As they stepped outside together, Longarm asked if they had a telegraph office. Constable Hagan said they had a post office, served by a now-and-then mail ambulance down to Fort Mojave. But that was about it.

They parted friendly, with Longarm muttering, "Shit and shiny boots if life ain't getting complexicated. How am I supposed to update Billy Vail or Captain Burbank by wire where there ain't no wire?"

He found the only livery in town easy. There wasn't enough town to get lost in, the silver being dug from a rocky hillside a mile and a quarter off.

The livery hostler complimented Longarm on his swell stock and allowed he'd treat 'em as honored guests for two bits a day for the four of 'em. They shook on it, and Longarm was free to tote his saddlebags and Winchester up the dirt street to the boardinghouse Constable Hagan had recommended.

It was run by a once-pretty widow who'd been a schoolmarm in her salad days and still bossed grown men around like they were ten years old and lacking in proper manners. Her name was Mrs. Murdstone, and she told him he was just in time for supper if he got a move on.

She curtly ordered her parlor maid, a smoldering breed whose trim figure and delicate features hinted at some good-looking mountain men in her family tree, to show Longarm and his shit up to his own hired room. It was up under the roof with a gabled window facing east into the sunrise. It was going to be too hot for human habitation by July, but what the hell, it was still April.

Tipping the pretty but sort of sullen-faced breed a nickel for her trouble, Longarm locked up with the key she handed him and went back down to find another older Indian gal was already serving out the corned beef and mashed potatoes with fried onions.

As Longarm introduced himself and had a seat at the table, he found himself supping with a straw boss from the nearby silver strike, a pair of local merchants, and the only

173

lawyer in town. Rory Hagan had intimated the Widow Murd-stone ran a quality boardinghouse.

The federal badge he still wore seemed to head off any questions about his faded, dusty, denim trail duds, in the unlikely event anybody with a lick of sense would expect a body to ride across over twenty miles of northwest Arizona in a three-piece suit with a flower in his buttonhole like that fool lawyer wore.

As Longarm dug in, it was naturally the prissy lawyer who asked what a federal lawman might be doing in Chloride. The Good Book said that as ye gave so should ye receive, so Longarm openly and honestly told his fellow borders as much as he knew, assuring them he wasn't likely to arrest anybody there in Chloride, passing through to wherever that mysterious settlement of Alamut might be.

One of the merchants who outfitted desert rats allowed he'd heard tell of such a place. He couldn't place it on the map for Longarm but said a prospector he served had come in from the Music Mountains with a bullet hole in one water bag.

The water had stopped and preserved the bullet before it leaked out the hole. So they knew he'd been fired on by a high-powered Springfield .45-70, the single-shot but awesomely deadly rifle the Indian Fighting Army still issued to dust off Mr. Lo at ranges he couldn't hope to match with his trading post repeaters.

The mining man opined, "Must be a gold strike, worked by no more than a handful who aim to keep their diggings all to themselves. A larger crew wouldn't be afaid of lone prospectors. They're working a placer or no more than one rich vein."

The gent who outfitted desert rats demurred, "Formations such as the Musics tend to run to copper, silver, lead, and such, don't they?"

The man who dug such for a living insisted, "Gold is where you find it. The stuff never oxidizes, and it's carried hither and yon by wind and water. What kind of a name might Alamut be? Ain't a sensible name for any sort of mine, if you ask me."

Longarm explained, "I suspicion it's named after another Alamut in the Persian hills. Hideout for some mighty unfriendly Moslems."

He washed down some grub with Mrs. Murdstone's swell coffee, with a sudden perspective on how it likely felt to be a Mormon kid just out of Utah, and added, "I doubt the owners of the Alhambra Saloon in Dodge are Moors, and I know the Denver Parthenton ain't owned and operated by ancient Greeks. But I am looking for a mysterious Moslem, and mysterious Alamut has a Moslem name. So, seeing I have to start somewheres . . ."

A hitherto silent minority at the far end piped up, "Hi Jolly might know, him being a Turk and all."

Longarm cocked a brow to ask, "Might we be talking about the famous Haji Ali, hauling out of Yuma?"

The local at the far end said, "Quartzite. Hi Jolly lives in Quartzite, hundred miles north of Yuma. Hauls silver ore out of here every other week or so."

The mine straw boss said, "I know the freighter you're talking about. I took him for a Greek. I don't recall whether it's Hi Jolly or Nick Pantages camped over by the diggings this evening. Whoever it is will be there come morning. Takes two or three days to fill all them twenty-mule-team ore wagons, and old Nick or Hi Jolly just got here."

Longarm said in that case, he'd stay for dessert.

So it was getting dark again when he strolled into the wagon camp out by the open pit operation. Half those big ore wagons were filled with silver chloride, so a warily agreeable young cuss, holding a ten-gauge Greener polite, naturally asked what Longarm wanted out yonder.

When Longarm told him he was looking for the famous Hi Jolly, it turned out the kid was guarding the wagons of the less-famous Nick Pantages.

Longarm allowed he hadn't thought the world could be as small as all that and asked if he could talk to the other wagon master.

He could. Nick Pantages was a less-than-ancient Greek of about sixty with a friendly, gold-toothed smile and a firm handshake. He led Longarm inside the wagon circle for some sit-down Greek coffee and honey cakes as he explained how he and three other freighters alternated hauling ore out of Chloride. He said his pal Hi Jolly was due in the week after next and asked how come Longarm was looking for him.

175

Longarm said he wasn't. He was looking for another Turk entire.

Pantages said, "Hi Jolly's not a Turk. We could never be such friends if he was. Early on, when we first met, he explained how, though Allah be more merciful, he'd been born a Turkish subject to Syrian parents. Since it seemed his folk hated Turks as much or more than my folk, we saw we had a lot in common."

He sipped some of his own coffee, bitter as bile and thick as black bean soup, and went on, "We met prospecting out this way, during the war back East. Fought Apache together. Hi Jolly learned how to fight Apache riding out of Fort Mojave with that Army Camel Corps. Neither ever struck it rich. Both learned you can make nearly as much hauling color than digging it up. Steady work beats boom or bust. What's the tale on this Turk you're after? What has he done?"

Longarm said, "Ain't sure he's done anything I can charge him with in a federal court. Some other lawmen and me have been trying to cut the trail of somebody running off into the desert with brides pledged to others. One such gal who got away says she fought off this Turk called Ben O'Mar or Bin Omar, up in Saint George, Utah Territory. Haven't been able to find him. Another witness suggested I search for him in that mysterious Alamut, somewhere over in them Music Mountains."

Pantages lookd surprised and said, "I've heard Hi Jolly mention a Haji Bin Omar. Haji ain't exactly a first name. All Moslems who've ever been to Mecca call themselves a haji. Our two hajis don't like each other all that much. Hi Jolly, or Haji Ali, says Bin Omar *is* a Turk, and a crazy one to boot. Crazy and *rich,* too. Had better luck prospecting down the other side of the Gila. Sold his gold strike and used his newfound wealth to found some new sort of Moslem mosque. That's what they call their churches, mosques. Hi Jolly says Bin Omar's crazy. Hi Jolly married up with a Christian gal, a pretty one, and hasn't been bowing five times a day to Mecca for some time. But he says he recalls enough of that Koran to know Bin Omar is full of it."

Longarm mused, "Hasin bin Sabah, the old-time Moslem who founded an assassin sect based in the original Alamut, was said to have some right unusual views on the Koran. I've often wondered if that might not be the reason so many great religions seem to have sprung up from wide-open spaces under big old empty desert skies."

Pantages looked up at the cloudless bloodred dome above them as he wrinkled his nose and said, "You do get to speculating on the meaning of it all out here in a land of little rain where it seems you can see forever into infinity. Men who worry more than the rest of us about the meaning of it all think *bigger* out under such big skies. Rattle shakers populating the dark of the night in tropical jungles or northern black forests wind up with cozier gods and demons, closer in and smaller than than the no-bull thunderbolt-throwing God of the Bible or Koran. I don't know enough about Islam to say why Hi Jolly thinks Bin Omar's God is crazy. I think Hi Jolly said something about his Koran saying it was better to set folk free than it was to turn them into slaves."

Longarm whistled softly and said, "I'm with Hi Jolly and his version of their Good Book! Do you think Hi Jolly might know where Bin Omar or his new Alamut might be found?"

The Greek-American said, "I can't speak for Hi Jolly, understand, but I don't see how. We meet up often, hauling for the same outfits. I've heard rumors of secret Gardens of Eden up remote desert canyons and lost mines as well. But I've never hauled in freight or wagon loads of ore from Erewon or Atlantis, either. Are you sure this woman who got away fought Bin Omar off in Utah, Longarm? I've never heard anything about any of those Camel Corps veterans across the Colorado."

Longarm shrugged and said, "I was across the Colorado a few short days ago, and she said he called himself Ben O'Mar. If it wasn't him, he can tell me so, once I catch up with him. Your turn."

Panatages answered simply, "My heart bleeds for you, but I just can't reach you. I'd show you the way to Alamut if only I knew the way. But I don't. So I can't."

Longarm allowed that sounded reasonable, thanked the Greek for such help as he'd managed, and excused himself to head back to his boardinghouse as the sky above went from red to star-spangled purple velvet.

He'd had a hard day in the saddle, Nick Pantages probably knew more about Bin Omar than anyone he was likely to meet in a whorehouse or a saloon, so he decided to turn on in.

The Widow Murdstone was knitting on her porch swing and nodded at Longarm in an approving manner as he passed on by. He went on upstairs, reaching for the key in his pants.

Before he could stick it in the lock of his hired door, Longarm saw the match stem he'd wedged under the bottom hinge now lay on the floor.

Longarm shifted the key to his left hand and drew his .44-40 with the right. He gingerly slid the key in the lock but silently turned the knob before he turned the key. The door wasn't locked. Longarm popped it open to chase the muzzle of his six-gun into the candlelight beyond.

The figure seated on his hired bed had saved herself a shot in the head or at the least a pistol-whipping in the dark by lighting that candle. As she gazed calmly up at him, expressionless as a tabby cat, Longarm saw it was that pretty breed servant gal who'd shown him up there earlier.

Closing the door behind him, Longarm holstered his six-gun as he asked to what he might owe the pleasure.

The pretty breed said, "Hear me. I am called Elizabeth in your tongue and Esihabiiti in mine. I know who you are. I know the way to the place you are looking for. I can show you the way, if you want to do something for me."

Chapter 26

Longarm said, "You jut made a deal if it's within my power. What do you want for showing me the way to Alamut, Miss Elizabeth?"

She said, "Hear me. I want to go home. I thought I would

be happier among my grandfather's people. Back home along the singing waters some joked about my Taibo looks. But nobody expected me to work, work, work from can't see to can't see! My grandfather's people never joke about me. My grandfather's people never see me! To my grandfather's people, I am a little brown . . . thing, to work, work, work like one of their . . . *kutsiwobi?*"

He said, *"Burro* is the word you're groping for. I follow your drift. You want to go home. Where's home? What is your nation?"

She answered simply, "Papago. My people hunt and gather on the wider lands on the other side of the Music Mountains. I know the way. It would take me no more than three, maybe four days to walk there on foot if there was nobody in the way. But there are those cruel men over in the Music Mountains. The ones you are looking for, I think. Most of you Taibo are bad enough. Some of you, some, shoot our men for no good reason and kill our women when you are done with them. But most of you don't pay that much attention to us. The Taibo over in those mountains are some other kind of Taibo. They have features more like ours, but their skin is pale and jaundiced, as if they have had what the *Yuutaibo* call *el vomito negro.*"

He nodded and said, "We call it yellow jack. Sounds as if you might be describing Chinee, Miss Elizabeth."

She said, "Their leader, or master, is what the Yuutaibo call a *Moro.* I don't know why. He and some of those guarding his spring-fed canyon in the Music Mountains look more like the rest of you, but wear funny red hats and every once in a while one of them yells down from a stone tower and everybody in the canyon gets down on all fours like a . . . *piarabo?*"

Longarm said, "Jackrabbit's close enough. I get the picture. You're willing to lead me there before I carry you home to your agency along, say, the Williams River, right?"

She said, "Wrong. I know some say you are not like other strangers. Myabe you are not. But I did not think the prospector who got me to run away from my people with him would sell me as a servant after he fucked me more than once. First I will show you through a pass those *Moros* do not know about. Then you will see me safely across the rim-rocks beyond to within sound of the singing river. There we will part, and you will be in a much, much better position to approach that canyon called Alamut from a direction they won't expect as much trouble from. None of my people have gone anywhere near the Music Mountains since some of them were fired upon. We Papago are a happy people. We would rather laugh and run away than stand and die on foot with our digging sticks. The *Moros* you want to kill will be expecting trouble from the southwest, not the east."

Longarm said, "I ain't out to kill nobody, and how am I supposed to find the place from any direction after we part company on open desert?"

She soothed, "Don't frown like that. Once we are on the far side, I will point out the twin peaks, like two *pitzi wayippe* you must pass between, on foot or, better yet, crawling. From up there, high above that hidden canyon, you will be able to see down into it as you decide how to kill everybody."

He smiled crookedly and again said he wasn't out to kill anybody. Esihabiiti of the peaceable Papago Nation smiled like Miss Mona Lisa and said, "You will kill them. They are bad *Taibo,* and you are a good *Saltu.* It will seem as natural to you, when the time comes, as the strike of brother *wih-kitzutzu* at a nasty *pahsoweyo!* They are very bad, and crazy."

Longarm asked if her folk knew of any women dwelling willing or unwilling over in Bin Omar's latter-day Alamut.

She said she didn't know. She only knew the place from description by her own kind.

Longarm repeated they had a deal and asked when she'd be ready to go.

She said, "When the *yaketi* crows before dawn. Get up as if nothing is going on. Get your mules and ride into the sunrise as if to go hunting. I shall be waiting out in the chaparral. I am already laughing to think of the woman who bought me like a . . . burro, wondering where I could be."

He agreed that sounded comical. As she got to her feet, he didn't know whether he was supposed to shake her hand or kiss her. He just stood there, and she stepped around him to let herself out, sneaky, after dousing that candle.

Once she'd gone, Longarm relit it. He was wide awake, now. He got out his watch to see it was for Chrisske not even ten yet. The action would be peaking in your average mining town saloon and—

"Forget it!" Longarm sternly warned himself, sitting down on the bed and lighting a cheroot from the candle.

He wasn't going to pick up a better lead, and at the same time, the more folk knew he was in those parts, the more likely it was for Bin Omar to hear about it. There was no way to operate whatever he thought he was operating out there in the nearby hills without sneaky outside help. Whether he was operating a secret gold claim or living like some Arabian Nights prince on the proceeds of one he'd found earlier, he had be be smuggling supplies in across the desert. Abducted brides could be hauled in across open desert. The stores right there in Chloride would be best for discreet amounts of coffee, tobacco, sugar, and such. They'd have already been hauled across the desert most of the way. Who was likely to notice "prospectors" drifting out during working hours with their burros loaded heavy?

He rose to open the window and exclaimed to the resulting cool smell, "You know, of course, we're as likely whupping up a complexicated conspiracy out of whole cloth, don't you? What if Bin Omar don't have any pals here in Chloride? What if he ain't there at all, and a homestick Indian kid is feeding you a pile of shit?"

The answer to both questions was the same. It was better to be safe than sorry. It was like old Pascal's wager with the atheist. The sardonic French philosopher had said that if there was no God, or secret pals of Bin Omar, it didn't hurt to speak respectful of what wasn't there while, at the same time, it was taking an awful chance to disrespect God, or Bin Omar, if somebody with that much power was really there in the sweet by and by!

So Longarm could see his best bet would be to buy Elizabeth's deal until he caught her lying to him, alone in the desert where he could turn her over his knee. He had a rundown alarm clock in one of those saddlebags draped over the foot rail of the bed. He could set it and wind it up for, say, five and . . . that would be smart. Wake up a whole boardinghouse at five in the morning and try to pussyfoot out without anyone noticing?

He took a drag on his cheroot, blew a thoughtful smoke ring, and told it, "Cockcrow's a good eight hours off, and when was the last time we lay slugabed more than eight hours? We'll wake up in plenty of time if we stop trying to set ourselves on fire in bed and try for some shut-eye!"

He finished the cheroot, snubbed what was left of it out, and took off his duds to hang and air by the open dormer window. He was about to snuff the candle when there came soft tapping on the door.

Wrapping his shirt around his waist but drawing that .44-40 just in case, he moved over to the door to open it, hoping the loosely knotted arms of his shirt would keep him decent as they freed both hands.

They didn't. As he opened the door to see Mrs. Murdstone there with a tray, the damned shirt slipped, and the widow woman got an eyeful by the time Longarm could grab for and recover some modesty.

She said, "I was on my own way to bed with this bedside snack when I saw the light under your door and wondered if you'd like to share with me, ah, Custis?"

He almost said no, polite, to get rid of her, before he thought of all those questions he had for her and said, "That's mighty thoughtful of you, ma'am. I fear I owe you an apology for my state of dishabille, but I wasn't expecting company."

She said with a smile she'd noticed as she brought the tray in to kick the door shut behind her. The coffee and marble cake were tempting. She wasn't bad, herself, when you recalled what old Ben Franklin had observed about trees wilting from the head down, with the juicy roots lasting longer than most men thought.

After that, as the boss his Indian guide accused of buying her off a desert rat, Mrs. Murdstone was in better position than most to offer an opinion or so of her own.

Putting his gun away and knotting the arms of his shirt more firmly, Longarm sat on the bed with his gracious hostess, the German-silver tray on the covers between them, and said nothing about her having headed for her own room with two cups and two slices of marble cake on as many saucers.

She'd been smiling at him that way all evening, or she suspected something was up with him and her serving wench. As an opening gambit, Longarm casually said he'd have expected that Indian gal, what's her name, to serve him a late snack.

The widow woman said, "I told you, I prepared this tray myself in the kitchen. Elizabeth's been in bed for hours, poor little thing. I keep telling her to slow down, but she seems to like to work, work, work as she puts it. She ran away from the reservation to learn our ways, and sometimes I fear she's still afraid of us. Some of our own can be needlessly cruel to the harmless Diggers, you know, and you can call me Pru for Prudence, Custis."

He had to laugh. He assured her he was laughing at her bewildered servant gal, adding, "Lots of misundertandings betwixt what both sides think they're looking at can lead to jangled nerves. She likely feels that since you bought her—"

It was too late. Taking back such a slip would only make it worse. Once you farted in church, you could only hope nobody noticed.

Pru Murdstone asked in an unsuspicious tone, "Whatever gave you the idea anyone bought or sold the pretty little thing? Chattel slavery has been against the law of the land since the Union won!"

He chawed some cake to give hs brain time to catch up and decided. "Never meant she'd been bought and sold like she hailed from Africa. I had in mind the less formal but more pervasive peonage customs of the hitherto Hispanic southwest. Leftover Mex *peónes* and local Indians converted to their customs tend to *act* like the property of their *patron,* whatever the legal ramifications. Your runaway Digger gal may just *think* she's your property, see?"

Pru sounded sincere as she replied, "I'll have to have a talk with her. Poor little thing. I took her in as a half-naked waif when the white boy she'd run off with deserted her here in Chloride. I feared if I didn't take her in, those awful women along Red Light Row would take advantage of her simple ways."

Longarm allowed that had been mighty white of her, feeling a pang of conscience as he looked forward to Esihabiiti of the Papago Nation running off with another white man in the near future.

By this time, they'd put away the two slices of cake. Pru Murdstone suggested pouring more coffee. You got the feeling she wasn't anxious to leave.

He said, "Lord love you, that's really good coffee, and I just got here from Mormon country, Miss Pru. But as keyed up as I already am, I won't sleep a wink if I have a second cup, and I got me some riding to do in the cold gray dawn."

"Oh, are you leaving so soon, Custis?"

He said, "For just a spell. I'll have to come back through Chloride no matter what I find out yonder. We talked downstairs about my being a lawman, remember?"

She almost sobbed, "It hardly seems fair! You just got here, and we barely know one another, but I had this feeling we sort of *liked* one another and . . . Oh, shit, what can you do or say at times like these?"

Longarm reached out to snuff the candle with his fingers. Pru put the tray aside, even as she asked breathlessly in the dark, "Oh, dear me, this can't be proper! I was planning on you staying here with us a few days, first, and what are you *doing,* you naughty boy? Whatever gave you the notion I was that sort of girl and, oh, yessss! I *like* being that sort of girl!"

Once he'd made her come the first time, on top of her bare ass, her with her housedress up around her bare hips and protesting it made her feel like a wicked schoolgirl, they both got undressed and under the covers with the help of that open dormer window. Desert nights got cold, no matter the season.

The same could not be said for the Widow Murdstone. For a change and for a wonder, old Pru was one of those rare women who could fuck really fine without offering a rundown on every other man they'd ever fucked. Some seemed to feel anyone in bed with them wanted to know.

The advantages of a widow willing to just up and do it, over say a divorced *grass* widow, was that the real thing had often gotten good at it during a happy marriage, while you knew up front with a woman with a husband still above the grass that she hadn't enjoyed it much with at least one other gent.

By the time they'd warmed up enough for that open window not to matter as they did it dog style, Longarm felt sure she'd had a happy marriage indeed, and she'd somehow gotten pretty as that princess of Wales or the sultry young Eleanora Duse in the *Police Gazette*. The cynic who'd said all cats were gray in the dark hadn't had much imagination. Every woman in the world was a raving beauty in the dark when they knew how to wiggle like *that!*

But as all things good and bad must end, not long after midnight Pru Murdstone sighed and said she had to sneak back to her own room lest she fall asleep in his arms and be caught sneaking out in the morning by her work, work, working Elizabeth.

Longarm didn't try to stop her. He'd been wondering how he'd ever get out there to meet Elizabeth with her boss lady clinging to him like a love-starved vine.

Chapter 27

Longarm and the four mules were well out of town, and he'd started wondering whether he'd been played for a fool, when all of a sudden the pretty little thing was just there in waist-high greasewood, looking even prettier because she had hardly any clothes on. As Longarm got close enough to howdy her, the restored Esihabiiti of the Papago Nation turned to dogtrot ahead of him toward the Music Mountains, and that made a pretty picture, too. He'd already surmised she had a swell ass before she'd barely covered it with that breechclout of rabbit fur. He knew where they were going, he hoped, and had no call to ask a born Digger why she preferred jogging to riding. She sure jogged pretty at the same mile-eating pace

185

as his current mount. He was the one who had to call a halt in the bottom of a dry wash across their route, partly to rest his only-human mules but more so because he'd spotted sign.

Esihabiiti—he'd decided to call her Betty—came back to join him as he hunkered over a scattering of well-dried but distinctively equine droppings. The hoofprints along the sandy wash were too blurry to read as mule or pony, wild or shod. Betty asked, "Why have you stopped here? We have far to go. Far. Those bad Taibo over in the mountains cross the desert along these sunken washes. Didn't you know they would?"

He said, "Do now. Must be packing supplies in and high grade out by mule train. Which way's that Alamut canyon from here, Betty?"

She said, "I will show you after you see me safely to my own people. Look at me! I am only a woman alone with no weapons, and men always want to fuck me!"

Longarm allowed he could see how she might have got that impression. A gal raised to roam the desert naked before she sprouted tits doubtless had a loose grasp of Victorian dress codes.

He asked if she'd care to share some beans and tomato preserves with him, or a least a swallow of canteen water. When she said the day was young and they still had a ways to go, he told her he aimed to water the mules anyhow, adding in a dry tone, "Mules are such sissies."

She soberly replied, "I know. That is why my people have always run on our own feet. We run good. Or we die young. When a Papago child is too big to carry, its mother puts it on the ground to trot beside her. If it can not keep up, it is left behind. The Bureau of Indian Affairs forbids this tradition and tells us we are being cruel. They have never had to run, run, run from Navajo."

As Longarm broke out the nose bags from the pack saddle, she mused aloud, standing by, "The Apache you people have so much trouble with seldom chase us like the Navajo do. I have heard it said Apache feel it is no honor to kill or rape what you call Digger Indians? Could you tell me if this is true, and why?"

As he watered the mules, Longarm said Apache had odd

notions. It might have hurt her feelings to hear her nation described as weak and harmless with nothing worth taking.

In their shining times, as recorded by mountain men and gold rushers, the far-ranging Papago, who might have been a nomadic offshoot of their distant Hopi Pueblo cousins, had roamed and thrived all over the Arizona cactus country. Now they were confined to scattered reserves across parched lands nobody else had much use for, worth nothing save as scenery.

In their shining times, a nation dismissed as harmless Diggers had been good folk to know and bad folk to cross. It was suspected Papago had killed more than one forty-niner with nothing better to do than mess with such seemingly helpless folk.

Papago had taught the Apache branch of the NaDéné folk a famous lesson in neighborly manners when a band of White Mountain Apache had thought to hone their raiding skills on a Digger band.

The Papago, on foot, had followed the Apache all the way back to the White Mountains to whittle away at them from cover with their cactus-rib arrows until they'd wiped out every last one of the raiding party and a good many more before the proud Apache had paid them to go home for Pete's sake.

But in the end, the the proud but poorly armed pedestrian Papago had of course been whittled way down to little more than government wards playing at hunting and gathering as they lived for the most part on handouts from the Bureau of Indian Affairs.

Having seen to the mules with vulcanized water, Longarm drank from a canteen and offered some to the nigh-naked Betty. She shook her head and said she was not a fat Taibo woman who couldn't run because of all that food and water sloshing around inside her.

He told her to suit herself. Lots of poor whites who'd grown up not owning shit were proud they were used to going without. They said Uncle John Chisum, about the biggest cattle baron in New Mexico Territory, was inclined to stretch out on his Persian carpet for the night when he just

187

couldn't fall asleep between laundered sheets in his four-poster featherbed.

As he hunkered in the strip of shade along the northeast wall of the desert wash, Betty remained standing, shifting her weight from one bare foot to the other. He felt sure it was impatience. She likely had no idea of the effect her perky naked tits might have on a natural man, nipples bobbing back and forth like so. She repeated her observation about the eating and drinking habits of Taibo.

He said, "I know. Your folk can outlast a mounted Navajo on foot out on open desert. Navajo have told me so. Nobody, nowhere, gets by on less than you original human beings. This museum collecting lady I know has told me you Ho-speaking Papago, Paiute, Shivwits, and such are still living, or trying to live, in what she called the Old Stone Age. The rest of us, including other Indians, have gone on to invent notions as prissy as tents, footwear, bows and arrows, and such. But, hey, long as you want to remain noble savages on government handouts, you may as well feel savage as all get out with empty guts."

She coldly replied, "I want to go home. If you will only try to move faster, I will fuck you when we reach the Music Mountains."

Longarm had been fixing to rise and gather up the mules. He leaned back against the sandy wall and fished out a cheroot as he calmly told her, "Hear me. I am about to relate a tradional tale of my own nation."

Betty said, "I don't want to hear any more stories about walking on water or waking up dead people."

He went on, "This one is about two longhorn bulls that could talk like human beings, or that snake in the Garden of Eden. There's a moral to the story, whether you believe in talking critters or not."

She said, "I have heard Old Man Coyote can talk to people. How else would he ask women to fuck him? But I have never heard of cows talking. What do cows talk about?"

He said, "What do any critters talk about? These bulls were *he* cows, an old bull and a young bull. They were walking along when down in a fenced-in meadow vale they spotted a herd of heifers or *she* cows. So the young bull suggests

188

they bust down the fence, tear down the slope, and fuck some of those cows. You've heard this one, right?"

She said, "No. Did they rip out the fence with their horns, charge down into that herd, and fuck some of those she cows?"

Longarm said, "Nope. The older bull had a better notion. They *walked* on to the gate, *walked* over to those she cows, and fucked 'em *all.*"

She didn't even smile. She stared owl-eyed and asked what the moral of the story was.

He sighed and said, "Forget it. I'm sorry I tried. We are what we are, and it ain't your fault nor mine that we'll never see things the same way."

She said she didn't understand.

He said, "I know. You were never taught to try. You might have just as well been born the czar of all the Russians, and fate might have cast me as a South Sea island hula dancer. We wound up a bitterly resentful kid caught betwixt two worlds she's never tried to understand and a well-meaning West-by-God-Virginia boy with nothing to apologize about to your nation."

She stamped a bare foot in the dust and snapped, "Hear me! Once we hunted and gathered as far north as the Harcuvar Mountains! Once we strode clean and free under endless sky because we could walk away from our own shit and ashes. Now we live like, like *muviporo* in our own shit and ashes, day after day in the same campsites near the supply dumps of your BIA. The blue sleeves from Fort Mojave herded us there as if we were . . . *birii!*"

Longarm lit his smoke, shook out the waterproof Mex match, and told her, "I wasn't there. I've never done toad squat to your nation. Nobody asked this child whether he wanted you living like pigs or herded like sheep. If you find it a hard row to hoe, consider this full-blood Arapaho family running a thriving bakery in Denver, or a Cherokee publishing a newspaper for white folk to advertise in, out Californee way. When first we met, just yesterday, you had a solid roof over your head and a tolerable job with a boss who kept telling you to take it easy. If you'd rather run barefoot back to what you yourself describe as a pigsty, so be it. It's a free country."

She went into a tirade about white folk looking down on her, even though one grandfather had been white.

Longarm took a drag, snorted smoke out his nostrils like a pissed-off bull, but answered not unkindly, "Speaking of breeds, did I fail to mention poor old mixed-up Quanah Parker, half white and raised by his Comanche kin? After fighting his mom's kin like a demon and making all the usual speeches about us killing all their women and raping all their buffalo, Chief Quanah saw that was just getting Comanche killed. So these days he's collecting two-bits-a-head grazing fees off the Texas trail herders crossing the good-sized Comanche reserve they now hold legal title to."

He shook his head wearily and added with a tolerant smile, "That old Quanah is sure something else. Does business, sharp, like a white man, whilst living Comanche with four young wives. In a house. Eating three or more square meals a day, even if some of it's store-bought instead of tracked down noble in rain or shine."

Betty said, "You are right. We will never understand one another. Your words buzz around my ears like *animui*. I am going on. Do you want to follow, or do you want to sit there like a pile of shit?"

You had to know when to hold 'em and when to fold 'em. He took his time getting up. But he got up, and she was already scampering off as he was putting the nose bags away. She was almost—but only *almost*—out of sight through the low chaparral by the time Longarm had remounted to trail after her. The higher sun shone pretty on her bare, brown, bobbing ass. Bare ass didn't get slick with sweat on the dry desert. That same museum gal had said they suspected humankind had evolved in dry open desert or savannah because such country was where sweating worked best. It dried and cooled the skin as it came out in country like Arizona Territory. Made cotton shirts itchy as the evaporating sweat left its salts behind, though.

The Music Mountains being visible on the horizon from Chloride, it only took them the rest of the day to reach a tiny Eden Betty knew of in the foothills of the Musics.

A spring-fed pool nested in a blind canyon, shaded and kept cool by surrounding cottonwoods. Betty grudgingly agreed it made sense to camp there and rest up overnight. She wasn't about to admit she might need rest after jogging thirty or forty miles under a cloudless sky. As he watered the mules from the pool, she said she'd run the same distance under an *August* sun in drier country.

Longarm said he hadn't asked.

Once he'd let the mules swill their fill, mules being smarter than ponies about such matters, he poured cracked corn in their nose bags as he soothed, "I'll take them bags off, water you again, and leave you tethered where you can browse greenup cottonwood leaves, pards. Right now I got to feed a pouty brat."

He did. It wasn't easy. Even as she ate bully beef a Lakota might have killed for, with sweeter pork and beans than Mexicans could have served her, washed down with Arbuckle Brand coffee, with sugar if she wanted it or, hell, white flour if she insisted on being so Indian, Betty bitched she missed the unsalted rabbit meat, pinyon nuts, and grubbed-up desert roots her momma had served her on the run, way back when, before they'd had to switch to government beef and white flour many Indians found sweet as sugar next to stone-ground grits.

As the first wishing star winked on above them in the deep purple, Longarm unlashed his bedroll from his McClellan, rolled it out near the small, dying fire, and peeled off the top tarp and a flannel sheet or thin blanket, depending on how one used it.

Betty asked how come he seemed intent on fashioning two seperate bedrolls. She asked, Aren't we going to sleep together?"

He answered dryly, "Correct me if I'm wrong, but haven't you been bitching and moaning about being used and abused by my kind ever since we left Chloride, Miss Betty?"

She didn't answer for a time. It was hard to read her expression in the gathering dusk. When she did speak, she sounded little-girl shy as she said, "I didn't mean *you*. I *never* meant *you!* My people sing of *Saltu ka Taibo* who is not like the rest of his bad-hearted people."

Longarm moved over to his own bedding to peel off his hat and gun belt as he told her, "Yes I am. It ain't no compliment to tell a man he's different than the rest of his shitty breed. A Denver gent I've played cards with told me one time how he felt about being assured he wasn't like other dirty, dishonest kikes. I am what I am. My folk are as you find 'em, some good, some bad, most just trying to get along. In other words, not too different from *your* folk, and we'd best try for a few winks, now, if we mean to rise with the sun."

Betty just stood there in the dark as Longarm sat down to shuck his boots. After waiting in vain for him to say more—she liked the sound of his voice—Esihabiiti of the Papago Nation shyly asked, "Don't you *want* to fuck me?"

To which Longarm could only reply, "What I want and what a man is are two different deals. So for all I care, you are purely welcome to just go fuck yourself, Miss Betty."

Chapter 28

Come sunrise Betty alternated between pensive and flirty as they broke fast and broke camp a heap slower than her kind was used to. In Stone Age times, glorified apes had only had to literally rise and shine.

Longarm was indulging some pensive thoughts as he followed her, at a walk, up canyon trails through a windswept pass she said not even their Navajo tormentors had ever tumbled to. Longarm wasn't feeling pensive about her tawny young ass; his mental map had him just about due south of the Utah-Nevada line after nigh a week's detour. So, even as he rode farther out of his way, Captain Burbank and the others would have made it past the Meadow Valley Wash if not Las Vegas by now. He had a hell of a lot of catching up to do if he didn't mean to catch up with them at a clambake on a Pacific beach!

Going downhill, Betty broke into a fanny-bobbing trot again, and the mules found the going easy as well. Longarm muttered, "Enjoy your fool selves. It's later than you think. Do I sell you at Fort Mojave so as to not lose old Esau's investment in you? I can likely raft on down to Yuma in forty-eight hours or so, catch a westbound Southern Pacific, and, sure, wait for them in San Berdoo with time to spare!"

Betty noticed his restored good humor during their next trail break. She demanded, "Are you laughing at me?"

When he confessed he hadn't been thinking about her that much, Betty started to cry. He let her. Crying was good for anyone born with her disadvantages.

To begin with, Esihabiiti of the Papago Nation had been born a beautiful, healthy baby. Beautiful gals growing up in good health felt no great call to use their brains, because they didn't have to. While their plainer playmates were forced to figure out how to get whatever they might want, the beauties had everything handed to them.

After that she'd been raised, or spoiled, by Indians with simple notions for Indians. So she'd bought all the legends true or false of her mom's dream singers without ever taking time to study on anything.

Deciding she'd have a sip of canteen water after all, Betty hunkered down beside Longarm as he sat on a trailside boulder to soberly ask him, "Why do you hate me? What have I done to you to make you hate me? Hear me, I have led you along this secret path of my people, as you wished. I offered to fuck you, and you didn't wish to! Every man I have ever met has wanted to fuck me! Do you have a looking glass in your saddlebags? I was not able to see anything wrong with my face in that pool at sunrise. But to you I must seem ugly, ugly!"

Longarm said, "You're very pretty. We both know this. You are not as pretty as you think you are, because no woman could be. I do like you. I wish you well. That is why I can't treat you the way other men have always treated you."

She said, "I don't understand. Since we broke camp at dawn, all this way along the trail, I have been thinking, thinking, thinking, and I still don't see why you don't want to fuck me!"

He said, "Keep it up. You're doing fine. How much farther before you point out those titty peaks to me, Betty?"

She said, "By noon we will come to the parting of our ways, and I want to know so many things about . . . us. Won't you tell me? Is it a *puha* secret?"

He soberly assured her, "My medicine ain't the matter before the house, Miss Betty. Your medicine keeps leading you up shit creek without a paddle and, like I said, I like you. We'd best move on."

She said, "We have time to fuck, here, if you really like me!"

He rose, gathered reins and leads, and mounted up as he asked her to pray continue.

He could have pointed out how, for all her sass, she'd been led astray by a no-account Taibo, given away like a used magazine, landed on her feet but sulked like a pouty twelve-year-old waiting for her Prince Charming to come and take her away from her wicked stepmother and so on into the fucked-up thinking of the beautiful but dumb. Whorehouses across the West were staffed with pretty dimwits led astray by flattery and selling their asses, cheap, as they dreamed of their own Prince Charmings or some rich old bird who'd take them to London town or New York City and make society ladies out of them.

He knew that at small sacrifice to himself, since Pru Murdstone had screwed him so much smarter, there was a chance—an outside chance—the pretty little breed might be shocked into thinking back, and back, as she wondered what the fuck had happened back there the night before.

He recalled what that real society gal had told him about romantic notions leading her to run off with a tinhorn gambler and how all the flattery and pussy-eating had seemed so swell until one night in yet another fleabag hotel she noticed the Lothario going down on her had lice, inspiring her to examine herself for the same and suddenly lose interest in living the Bohemian life.

That was what romantic society gals called running off with unwashed but artistic-talking tramps: Bohemian.

As he studied the tempting bobbing form down the trail ahead, Longarm idly wondered how BIA rations stretched out and augmented by such natural treats as grilled grasshoppers was likely to strike the fancy of those used to Pru Murdstone's hearty boardinghouse fare. For all her imagined slavery, she'd been sleeping between clean sheets on a mattress of late, too.

He didn't want to think of the next cuss she'd give her fair brown body to, likely one of the white wranglers at the Indian agency, now that he had her wondering how come every white man in the world wasn't drooling over her, after all.

The sun was nigh overhead when Betty called a halt, tears running down her brown cheeks, and pointed off to the northwest, along the trend of the Music Mountains.

Once pointed out to him, the twin peaks he'd been picturing a lot different were easier to make out. One peak was thrust out sideways from the main fault-block range. Betty said, "Hear me, there is a game trail running along those mountains, halfway up and hard to make out from north of the notch between those *pitzi*. From another pass leading southwest toward that Alamut you seek, at a sharp angle, the notch you will pass through between those *pitzi* look like nothing you need to watch. I think you should tether your mules this side of that notch near sunset and move in the rest of the way on foot. Some of our own boys have crept close enough to see down into this Alamut. It is green all summer. There are mud-walled houses with red tile roofs, made in the Yuutaibo ways. Our boys did not creep near enough to steal anything as a trophy. There are many guards with many rifles. They are very bad men, even for Taibo. Won't you even *kiss* me, *Saltu ka Taibo?*"

He gallantly swept off his hat and bent low in the saddle to kiss her upturned face as she stood on tiptoe. As she ran off sobbing with her hands to her face, he sighed and said, *"Vaya con Dios,* and later on this evening I'm going to feel I was just as foolish as you, Betty. But a man has to look at hisself in the mirror when he shaves, and somebody had to break the chain!"

Aware anyone up on the ridges of the Musics had a swell,

field-glass-panning view of the open desert he and the mules were out on, Longarm beelined directly for the nearest slopes and forged on up to the game trail Betty had mentioned, winding level along a contour line.

He hadn't ridden it far before he commenced to wonder what it was doing there. Many Indians, like many uneducated country whites who couldn't be bothered with book learning, tended to jump to conclusions based on traditional lore that might or might not make a lick of sense. Having been trained as a military scout a spell back, Longarm knew game trails tended to run along ridges while man-made trails were inclined to run along contour lines, avoiding up-and downhill ridge running. Betty had said nobody in the mysterious depths of the Music Mountains would know this trail he was on was there. Betty could be right if nobody in the mysterious new settlement of Alamut cared to explore their immediate surroundings.

Following the trail around a bend at a cautious walk, Longarm told the mule he was riding, "Read this amusing article about country lore in the the Sunday papers a spell back. Seems they put a whole lot of country kids and a whole lot of city kids to the same written test on natural history. The city kids, whose experience with Mother Nature was at best a few field trips through botanical gardens and zoos, along with what they'd read in schoolbooks, beat the country kids all hollow."

The lop-eared mule just kept plodding along.

Longarm insisted, "It's true. Won a bar bet on it. The country kids naturally knew way more about pitching hay, gathering eggs, and milking goats and such. But their pure country minds were all cluttered up with tall tales of herb-gathering grannies and field hands out to top one one another's tall tales of raccons mating with housecats, red-tailed hawks carrying babies off, rattlers never crawling over rope or being avenged by their mates, years later."

He spotted something ahead, even as he was saying, "The city kids had never heard such bullshit. So they tended to get the answers to that test right by just recalling something they'd read about the object of the question and that ain't a

196

deer turd nor an antelope turd. That's a horse turd. Not more than a few days old!"

He reined in and dismounted to hunker down and poke at the sun-dried horse apple with a twig, muttering, "Folk who ought to know better buy Indian snake oil as a sure cure for most anything, mixed in a hotel sink from all that swell shit the Mandan used to save themselves that time from the smallpox that wiped them out. Some old boy's been on this mountain trail since day before yesterday, tops. Going toward Alamut or patrolling out from Alamut, and won't that be fine if we've a return patrol on our ass?"

Remounting, he heeled his mule foreward, promising, "We'll tether you boys to whatever comes handy, say, three furlongs from that notch ahead, and Mr. Winchester and me will go on from there afoot."

The mule never answered. The mule never got to take another step. As it trod the buried infernal device with one hoof, said hoof and foreleg high as the elbow evaporated in a cloud of bloody froth, and what was left did a double back flip.

Longarm knew as he hit the ground on his back he'd suffered one of those bad falls every rider figures on no more than once in a whole lot of whiles. One where you just lie there admiring all those stars buzzing over you like flies over a pile of shit while you try and try to take a breath and nothing happens.

Longarm had lived through such falls before in his time. He was glad it hadn't been too many times. He tried to tell himself he'd get his wind back sooner if he just lay still, staring up at the sky.

Then he was staring up into two grinning faces. One white. The other some sort of breed. The white man said, "He's still alive. We can soon fix that."

The darker one said, "Such matters are not for us to decide. Since Allah has spared him the full effects of our land mine, let us take him to the Haji and let the Haji decide his *kismet.*"

Longarm weakly tried in vain to lift a damned finger as the white one hunkered down to roughly disarm him, ripping Longarm's badge off as an additional trophy.

Finding the handcuffs hooked to the rear of the gun belt, the gunslick gloated, "Well, see what I have here."

He rolled Longarm on his face in the blood-flecked trail dust to cuff his wrists behind him, muttering, "Ought to be a key here somewheres. If there ain't, fuck him, he can just go on wearing his own infernal handcuffs. Help me get him to his fucking feet!"

The Turk or whatever did. When Longarm's knees buckled, it was the Turk who slapped him across the face to state in a matter-of-fact tone, "You must try to do better. You are too big to carry. Please not to think I am softhearted, you uncircumcised infidel trespasser. When I said it was up to the Haji whether you lived or died, I never meant I had fallen in love with you!"

The American confided, "He'll fuck you in the ass if you don't watch out."

Between them, with Longarm managing some of his weight on his wobbly knees, they got him to a stunned but still functional mule and helped him aboard to ride bareback, backwards, with his hands cuffed behind his back.

Hence it wasn't hard to see what everyone was grinning about an hour later as they rode him into a village square in a sure-enough village built in the Moro-Hispanic style. He didn't see any kids. The few women peering out of keyhole windows at him were covered total in sort of Ku Klux Klan robes without the hoods being peaked. But then Longarm had his breath back and could grip his mount better with his legs, for all the good it was doing him.

His captors reined up out front of an ornate doorway of nailhead-studded oak, outlined by an archway of fancy Arabesque tiles.

Longarm fell to one knee as they hauled him roughly off his mount.

He was the only one there who didn't think that was funny.

They hauled him back to his feet and frog-marched him inside. As his eyes adjusted to the darker light, he saw they had him facing a long divan along the far wall, covered with Oriental carpeting and plump pillows with Arabesque lettering and fancy trimmings embroidered in gold thread. A fat

198

man sat like a jade Buddha atop the divan with his legs crossed. He was wearing silk pajamas and a red felt fez as he toyed with the business end of an Oriental water pipe. The half-dressed woman seated beside him on the divan looked like she belonged more in some Chinatown chop suey joint. But after that she was right good-looking, and Longarm suspected she'd noticed.

The big shot between her and the pleasures of his water pipe smiled pleasantly enough at Longarm and said, "Welcome to New Alamut. I am the Haji Bin Omar. Would you care for some fresh mint tea or perhaps a glass of pomegranate juice before you die?"

Chapter 29

Longarm said, "Nice place you got here. I'd be Deputy U.S. Marshal Long. I ain't the only outsider who knows what you got here and where it can be found. I was guided here by somebody awaiting my return out where you can't get at 'em. I understand you used to work for the same U.S. government out of Fort Mojave. Mr. Ben O'Mar?"

The Turk smiled wistfully and said, "Many years ago, patrolling a land so like my own with the U.S. Camel Corps. Both the lieutenant and all four of his noncoms, though Allah be more merciful, were killed in the great war that broke out soon after. Had they lived, I would have had business partners. The six of us who knew what we had stumbled over here agreed to return later, as civilians, and file a joint claim. The ignorant troopers with us, of course, thought all gold ore looked like it had gold in it."

Longarm whistled and said, "Gold chloride, eh? Makes sense in these parts. Same chlorinated hot springs as leave bigger veins of silver chloride tend to froth gold chloride earlier. You ever hear how they thought Leadville was a gold strike, then a silver strike, then a lead strike? Chemistry sure can get interesting. But we were talking about how many others know I'm here and what them more modern troops out of your old army post might do when I'm reported missing, with the map coordinates supplied."

"I think you may be bluffing," Bin Omar said pleasantly.

Longarm said, "Anything's possible. You ever hear tell of Pascal's wager, pard?"

Bin Omar snorted, "of course I know of Pascal's wager. Do I look like an unread bedouin? I am a haji! I have been to Mecca and circled the Kaaba seven times! I know everything there is to know about the one and only God. I have read everything written on the subject. What has Blaise Pascal's inane speculation about the existence of God have to do with our disposal of an unwelcome guest?"

Longarm said, "It's the same bet. If I'm bluffing and nobody knows I'm here in your power, you're no worse off if you take time to look before you leap. If you kill me before you've made certain, and this *ain't* a bluff, you could be in a hell of a mess." He nodded at the exotic gal on the divan and added, "Pardon my French, ma'am."

She never let on she'd noticed he was standing there.

The Turk at her side smiled. It was not a pretty smile as he decided. "It might be more amusing to give you, as you infidels say, enough rope. Should your threatened army column arrive, we shall naturally tell them we've been holding you, an intruder with an unlikely story, hoping to turn you over to the law as soon as we could."

He took a puff on his water pipe—it sounded like somebody's guts were rumbling—and promised, "If nobody comes after a day or so, we have a custom you might find amusing when we deal with Christians who have dared to enter our holy shrine. We crucify them so they can know how it felt to their own Jesus."

Longarm just stood there, smiling lopsided.

The Haji Bin Omar shifted uncertainly and said, "I know, I know, The Prophet revered Moses and Jesus as earlier men of God whose devotees distorted their teachings. We're still going to crucify you by the end of the week if nobody comes for you!"

Longarm tried not to let it show as he shrugged and said, "In that case, I got nothing to worry about. What are you going to tell the troops from Fort Mojave about all those women you're holding here as well?"

Bin Omar frowned and asked, "What are you talking about? Nobody is here against their will but *you!*"

Longarm asked, "Didn't you advertise for a wife or more in the newspapers, and didn't you try and fail to get Miss Theresa Mondale to come down here with you as you wrestled up in Saint George a spell back?"

Bin Omar snorted, "I don't know what you are talking about. I have never wrestled with any woman named Theresa. What did she look like?"

Longarm shot a glance at the really lovely gal the Haji seemed to have at his full disposal and decided, "She might have had another Bin Omar in mind. Or somebody's saying he's you. Why don't we talk about that?"

The Turk said, "You fatigue me with your sophistry. You shall be shown to comfortable but secure quarters, for now. If you have the key to those handcuffs on you, my people will remove them once they have you securely locked up."

Longarm sighed and said, "I sure wish somebody would. I got the key in this left breast pocket."

The Turk nodded curtly. The darker rider who'd brought Longarm in reached in his empty breast pocket and shook his head.

Longarm said, "Aw, hell. Sorry, ma'am. This Anglo rascal must have spilled it in the dust when he helped hisself to my watch!"

Bin Omar cocked a brow and murmured, "A watch, my beloved Baja?"

The Anglo called Baja replied defensively, "He had his derringer on the other end of the watch chain. I disremember any keys in that pocket."

"Search his other pockets." the Turk suggested, nodding at Longarm to murmur, "Pascal's wager."

Baja failed to find any keys as he helped himself to the few items he hadn't already.

Bin Omar shrugged and said, "Take him to the north tower. That storeroom under the dovecote should do nicely."

"What about these handcuffs?" Longarm protested.

Bin Omar replied, "What about them indeed? It won't hurt you to be spoon-fed like a baby or go just a few days without masturbation. You are bluffing or you are not bluffing. Either way, your troubles will be over by the end of the week."

Baja and the darker cuss who answered to Hakim led Longarm outside and just up the plaza to another adobe building with one corner rising to a beehive-shaped dovecote atop a sort of silo. They prodded him up a spiral staircase of rough lumber. At the top, Longarm found himself in a low-ceilinged chamber with the floor plan of half a pumpkin pie. A narrow window cut through the curved wall offered light and a view down the canyon but no escape for anybody built as broad as Longarm.

The flat wall facing the stairwell was knotty pine with a solid door in the center of it. Baja pointed at the bare plank floor and suggested, "Make yourself comfortable, Lawman. I'm quartered just below you. If you need anything, call out, and I'll come up and kick the shit out of you."

Then they left him up there to his own devices.

There wasn't much to study in the semicircular cell. He'd already figured the flutters and coos coming down through the ceiling beams came from the doomed doves above. Spanish-speaking folk were more likely than most to raise awsome flocks of *palomas* or eating doves the color of those better known palomino ponies. Better known to Anglos, leastways, "La Paloma" had been the favorite song of the late Emperor Maximilian. The Juaristas had played it for him as they marched him out to be shot. The Emperor Maximillian had been such a sap.

Longarm ignored the soft, romantic coos above his head in favor of the one window. The afternoon sun was lower now, going on suppertime in an Anglo settlement. Mexicans ate after dark. He had no idea what time Turks ate.

Whenever they did, some barefoot, bareheaded men in blue denim or white canvas pajamas were loading a train of burros with balanced open-topped panniers of what looked from up where he was like railroad ballast. Anyone could see the gold flecks in the "blossom rock" self-taught prospectors looked for, most often in vain. Gold chloride was sneakier. Metallic gold was immune to most acids. That was why it could stay pure through hell and high water for millions of years in the ground. But a devil's brew of sulfuric and hydrochloric acid, known as *aqua regia* in an alchemist's stinky chambers, disolved gold like it was sugar, and it turned to a salt instead of metal in the pores of any country rock it soaked into. Bin Omar, or more likely those army men he discovered this canyon with, had known his rocks.

As Longarm watched, he decided from the way they moved and by the long pigtails hanging down their backs, those workers down below had to be Chinese. That fit the rumors about "Orientals" down this way.

Why they were working a secret gold mine was no mystery. President Hayes had just vetoed that Chinese Exclusion Act forbidding more of the unwelcome same from immigrating.

They'd been more welcome in the West before the wedding of the rails back in '69. Up until then, steamboating across the Pacific had been way cheaper than around the horn or cross-country by coach or covered wagon. So a thriving trade between ports like Frisco and San Diego, Canton and Shanghai had been going strong when imported coolie labor had fucked things up by helping to build the Western Pacific half of the transcontinental railroad.

Once it was cheap and easy, the West had seemed a land of opportunity to the crowded East, and it was, where cheaper help from Canton wasn't encouraging low wages for everybody.

It was a pisser. More complicated than either the rabble-rousing labor agitators or the do-gooders who didn't have to meet a payroll were prone to put it. So Longarm had done his duty as he saw it during the recent race riots of the seventies, cracking heads and saving asses for both sides. He got along better with the sons of Han than Anglos who called them fucking Chinks. He'd had to crack down on some of those hatchet men enforcing the dictates of the sometimes ruthless Tongs, as well.

As a result, Longarm felt he knew their customs to some extent. So he was surprised when all of a sudden somebody he couldn't see commenced to yell about "Allah akbaaaaar!" from somewhere high, and all but one of the Chinese down yonder fell to the their hands and knees to bang on the ground with their foreheads.

The one who hadn't prostrated himself to the east looked young and excited as he waved his skinny arms about and yelled at everyone in Cantonese. It looked to Longarm as if he didn't approve of his countrymen akbaring Allah. It must have looked like that to a swarthy cuss with a red fez and a Spencer '52 repeater as well, for he strode over to the complaining Chinese, never said one word, and shot him down like a dog.

None of the others bowing to Mecca seemed to notice. They went on bowing, with their asses in the air, while the Turk finished his one infidel off with a second shot.

"Cocksucker!" Longarm gasped as the gunsmoke cleared to reveal what a good job that second round full in the kid's face had done. Longarm could see why the Turk had done it. The murderous bastard held strict notions on his religion. But the Chinese Longarm knew were inclined to go by a curious mixture of three different religions they managed to blend without getting all that excited.

Most if not all those sons of Han with their asses in the air to Allah lit josh sticks to Lord Buddha, a whole raft of older dieties such as the sweetly serene Kuan Yin, or took the practical advice of their Confucius, who sounded more like Ben Franklin than an average prophet.

The unseen voice praising Allah yelled new instructions, and as everybody got back to their feet, the Turk who'd murdered one of them instructed some of them to carry the body away while the others got back to work.

"That can't be right," Longarm growled, trying to make sense out what he'd just seen.

By the time he'd run it all through his mind a few more times, eliminating this and that, Longarm had come up with the only answer that worked.

Those coolie laborers, like himself, were *prisoners* of the Haji Bin Omar and his gang. It was no wonder the murderous assholes were ready to kill to keep this verdant canyon with its gold mine such a secret. They were operating without a claim, paying no taxes, with slave labor, paying no wages.

That was why they were assholes. An incorporated mining company, working a federally filed claim, got to do so openly, at profit, with skilled hardrock miners willing to work for three dollars a shift or no more than thrice what you paid a trail herder.

As he stared down at the murderous Turk waving that Spencer around, Longarm sneered, "Them hardcase gunslicks are running you more than it would cost to have half a dozen honest men on your payroll, you stupid bastard!"

Then he shrugged and sighed, "Oh, well, if there weren't so many stupid bastards in this imperfect world, I'd be out of a job, and they'd have me herding cows again!"

Chapter 30

Somebody running New Alamut had been reading the Marquis de Sade. Longarm was hopping from one foot to the other with his hands cuffed behind his back and no place to piss if he could have gotten it out when the door suddenly popped open and a pretty little señorita came in with a platter of tortillas and beans in one hand and a chamber pot in the other. She said, "I am called Rosalinda. La Señora Fong Yu say for me to bring you something for to eat and see if you have for make the *aguas menores*. But for how are you to eat or make the *aguas menores* with *las manos* behind your back, eh?"

It was a good question. He said, "In my saddlebags, the right one, I have a ring of keys in a brown paper envelope. One is the spare for the key Baja lost on me. Do you know where my saddle might be?"

She said, "Sí, in the, how you say, tack room of the one big stable. Only Don Haji and his bodyguard are allowed for to ride, here in Alamut. You say the saddlebag *a la derecha*?"

He groaned, "Sí, sí, *toda prisa!* My back teeth are floating!"

She said, "I do not know I can get there and back in time. Better I give you the helping *mano,* no?"

He wasn't about to say no, silly as it felt, as she set the grub and chamber pot down to unbutton his fly and haul out his old organ grinder, which might have sprung to fuller attention if he hadn't had to piss so bad.

It sure beat all, but he still had trouble letting it out while a pretty stranger wearing a flirty, low-cut cotton blouse had hold of a man like so. She asked what was wrong, shaking it like a puppy's paw. He told her not to do that and, as she held it still, he shut his eyes and tried to recall the ugliest old sawbones who'd ever fooled with his privates.

It still wasn't easy, but with old doc Dunbar, the surgeon at Fort Dodge, assuring he didn't have the clap after all, Longarm was able to let fly as Rosalinda aimed it for him with the chamber pot in her other hand.

You had to wonder where and when, with whom, when a gal shook the the dew off the lily once he'd stopped. But he just thanked her gravely.

She demurely replied, "*Por nada,* do you wish for me to put it back in your *pantalones,* now?"

He started to nod, smiled sheepishly, and decided. "Might as well leave it waving in the breeze, seeing it ain't no secret anymore. How am I supposed to eat if you don't fetch me a spare key, Rosalinda?"

She said, "Let us sit upon the floor. I shall feed you with my own fingers, eh?"

He figured, what the hell, that had been his dick she'd been holding in her dainty hand. He slid down the wall to manage a cross-legged seat on the gritty wooden floor. Rosalinda scooped up beans with some all-purpose tortilla, the combined bread and eating utensil of Mexico.

As she fed him, Rosalinda bragged on being almost pure Spanish and hailing from old Mexico south of Yuma, where the rusty waters of the Colorado met the azure Sea of Cortez.

206

She said she'd come on up the Colorado with other Mexicans, delivering a gaggle of *los Chinos*.

He made mention of that recent execution he'd witnessed from the window and asked what all those Chinese were doing up this way to start with.

She explained, "They are from China, here for to find work. Is not enough work in China, and they do not feel *bienvenido* in *puertos* such as San Pedro or San Diego. So they land in Mexico at Rio Colorado. But of course is no work for *anyone* there. La Señora Fung Yu was one who had *inspiración* for to bring them up here to Nuevo Alamut with same burro trains El Haji uses for to send his *oro* to how you say, *fundirra*?"

He said, "Smelter's close enough. You know where it's at?"

She tucked another morsel in his mouth as she said, "Near Yuma, I think. Maybe closer. They tell us nothing. *La* Señora Fung Yu does not tell *los Chinos* this, of course, but once they are here, they must do as they are told, as if they were *esclavos*. Five times a day, I do not know for why, everyone is told for to bow down to the east on their hands and knees. When anyone refuses . . . You say you saw, no?"

Longarm growled, "Ain't no *almost* slaves about it, Miss Rosalinda. When you think you have the power of life and death over folk working for you, they're in worse shape than slaves in old Dixie. Slaveholders under rules of the peculiar institution needed a better excuse than religious differences to blow a man's face off with a Spencer! Might this be a dumb question, or am I guessing correct about the day wages of those smuggled-in Orientals?"

Rosalinda said, "Nobody but the men with guns are paid *dinero* here in Alamut. El Haji says the rest of us should be grateful to him for saving their souls. I do not know what this means. When I go outside now, I have to cover myself head to toe in a big black thing they call a *chadir*. I do not know for why. If Allah did not like the way all of us look, for why did he make us to look this way? What sort of a god needs el Haji to manage such small matters for him? When people do not pray enough to please *our* God in *my* country our God takes care of them Himself! Was a *brujo* in our village who burned black candles and cut the throats of chickens for *el Diablo*. None of my people did anything to him. They were afraid to go near him. So one day after the smell got bad, our *alcalde* sent some *muchachos* in for to see what was dead. They found the *brujo* was dead in front of his altar with ants all over him and a look of fear on his purple face. *Our* God takes care of those who insult Him, Himself! You sure you have no way of taking off those handcuffs, or at least getting them around to the front of you?"

Longarm made a wry face and asked, "Don't you think I've tried? If I was a tad skinnier, I could slip my chained wrists down across my rump and sort of climb out of the loop. What difference would it make? I'd still be handcuffed, wouldn't I?"

She said, *"Sí, pero* you could feed yourself and take your own *piton* out for to make the *aguas, menores, El Brazo Largo."*

Longarm had to study on those three Spanish words before he answered. Since Rosalinda had *bragged* on hailing from the Colorado delta, it was no great mystery how she'd come by tales of a *Yanqui* lawman in bad with the current Mex administration down yonder.

Longarm thought of himself as a live-and-let-live cuss just doing his job. It had been the grand notion of certain Mex *rurales*, their answer to the Texas Rangers, to start up with him when he'd only been out to pick up an owl-hoot rider wanted, federal, north of the border.

But from the way some Mexicans carried on about him only defending his fool self, you'd think he was another famous Mex rebel called *El Brazo Largo,* meaning the long arm.

He chewed and swallowed the wad of tortilla and beans she'd shoved in his face before he cautiously asked where she'd gotten the notion he was somebody wanted by the law in her old country.

Rosalinda said, "You were pointed out to us when you passed through our village, running from *los rurales.* I thought the *muchacha* who told us about you was lying about the size of your *piton.* Now I see she only told the truth."

Longarm didn't tumble to the possible ruse. He said, "No

offense, but these refried beans are drier than usual, and tortillas always mind me some of blotting paper. Could you drop off some *agua,* next time you get up this way?"

She gasped, "*Ay, que estupida* of me! I shall fetch some for you at once! Would you care to piss some more before I empty this *orinal* for you?"

He allowed he could last until she brought it back empty. So she shoved the last of the tortilla and beans in his face and rose with platter and potty as Longarm just sat there staring at the dust motes in the beam of bright light cast by the low afternoon sun. Too late he saw Rosalinda had left with both hands full, meaning that door had been unlocked and unlatched all the time!

He grunted himself back to his feet. It wasn't easy, and he moved over to the door with his dick hanging out of his fly. He turned to gingerly try the latch. The fucker was locked. It appeared she'd left a spring bolt half sprung to let herself out, but slammed it all the way shut, bless her heart, on her way out.

Out on the spiral staircase, the Anglo gunslick called Baja asked her, "Well?"

Rosalinda shrugged and replied, "You were listening outside the door. Do you still think he could have a secret key or another way for to slip off those *esposas?* He was so red in the face when I had for to help him make the *aguas menores!*"

Baja grinned wickedly at the picture and asked, "What was that shit about him being *El Brazo Largo?*"

She asked, "You have *heard* of El Brazo Largo, Baja?"

The border ruffian sneered, "Have I heard about El Presidente Díaz and the king's ransom he's put out on Longarm's head? Why did you think they called me *Baja,* because I'd been recruited in Canada? You're damned right I was listening at the door, and I cottoned to the way you skated across his natural suspicions on blades of truth that hardly mattered. You knew he knew our beloved leader shoots folk who remain on their feet during those asshole calls to prayer. Telling him the simple truth about those poor Chinks was smart. He'd already guessed the half of it. So here's what I want you to do next."

He glanced about as if to be certain they were alone on the stairs before he said, "When you take his water up to him, I want you to take along a couple of them chatters the Haji makes you women wear. You got spare chatters, right?"

She said, "More than I ever wish for to see again, and they are called chadors, not chatters."

Baja said, "Whatever. Find the biggest one you can for him to slip into with his dick hanging out and his hands cuffed behind him. Who's to know? Tell him you're another greaser gal in love with *El Brazo Largo*, and so you're just dying to help him escape, see?"

Rosalinda said, *"Pero no,* I thought El Haji ordered us for to see if he was bluffing about those *soldados.* Nothing was said about helping him escape."

Baja said, "I know. This grand notion is all mine. Once you have the big moose disguised as a gal—he can manage a *tall* gal if only he bends some at the knees inside that chatter—the two of you will walk across the plaza like Moslem ladies taking an evening stroll. None of the fucking Turks will say anything to you. Allah don't allow a man to talk to a strange woman in public."

Rosalinda laughed and said, *"Es verdad* a *mujer* could go naked with a rose sticking out her *culo* inside her chador and no man would ever know it. Is a most *estupido fey,* no? *A donde* you wish for me to take my *amiga muy grosa* in her her most tight chador?"

Baja said, "Tack room, down the far end of the stable. Tell him the two of you are going there to get his saddle, his guns, that key he needs to get them cuffs off. Tell him anything. Just get him there."

"Where will you be?" Rosalinda asked uncertainly.

Baja said, "Waiting for you in the tack room, after dark, of course. With him handcuffed helpless, I'll be able to finish him off without making any noise. Once I have, you're welcome to tag along and keep my bedroll warm as I head down to old Mexico to collect the bounty on a cuss they want real bad."

Rosalinda demurred, "You mean for to carry a body that size all the way to my country with the desert warming more each dawn?"

Baja shook his head and said, "His badge, his gun with its tailored grips, and his head will do us. Didn't Captain Love collect the bounty on Joaquin Murieta on his pickled head alone?"

She gagged and said, "Some Californios have told me those bounty hunters collected on the head of an innocent young *vaquero*. But will not El Haji be cross with us for, how you say, going into business for ourselves?"

Baja curtly answered, "Fuck him, or better yet, look out for our own selves for a change. When the tight-fisted Turk recruited us, he said we'd be sharing the bounty of his table in the paradise of Alamut. So far, all I've seen is crumbs in a kingdom of less than a quarter section. Stick with me, Rosalinda, and you'll be dressed in red silk fandango skirts instead of black sackcloth. Stick with me while I stick it to *El Brazo Largo,* and El Haji can shove all his ore up his ass."

They kissed on the stairs to seal the bargain, and Rosalinda went on down to dump Longarm's piss in the latrine and swish it fresh with a well pump. She dropped the dirty platter off at the kitchen door with curt orders to the younger Mexican scullery maid.

Then she crossed the inner patio to enter her own quarters, set the the chamber pot aside, and rustle chadors out of her wardrobe, holding one after the other up as she judged the sizes and finally decided to just slit one up the back and another up the front. If the big man she meant to betray put them both on with the slits on opposite sides, he'd look modest enough for Allah in a ragged chador no Moslem man would dare to ask about.

She draped three chadors over her arm and took both the cleaned chamber pot and a clay water olla up the stairs to unlock that door with the key hung around her neck inside her flirty blouse. As she rejoined Longarm in the semicircular chamber, it was already getting dark inside. Such sky as one could see through the slitty window was lavender at the top and peach near the bottom.

Rosalinda shut the door, gave Longarm a drink of water, and kissed him before she showed him how the three black chadors might get them all the way to the stables, where his

211

guns and possibles waited along with a whole lot of horseflesh.

Longarm frowned down at her to ask, "Are you saying
the two of us can just walk across that plaza in plain sight,
with nobody trying to stop us?"

She said, "*Sí*, is forbidden for men to ask strange women
anything under rules of their Koran."

Longarm laughed and said, "Let's get me into that outlandish outfit then. Who are we to argue with any Good
Book?"

Chapter 31

Longarm saw what Rosalinda meant about feeling exposed
under the stuffy folds of a Moslem woman's chador as the
two of them stepped out into the open in the tricky light of
the gloaming. But his confidence grew as they walked right
past a rifle-toting Turk, Longarm's knees bent to discomfort,
and the Turk looked away.

Crossing what felt like acres and acres of open plaza with
her, he marveled, "This works good as that cloak of invisi-
bility that goddess gave that Greek hero!"

They'd almost made it to the stable when a third chador-
wearing and and even shorter figure fell in beside Rosalinda
to murmur in Spanish that she was in.

In the same lingo, Rosalinda whispered, "In what? Who
are you? What do you think you're doing?"

The mystery was resolved when the third entry identified
herself as Lolita from the kitchen and added, "I have been
paying attention to the unexpected guest you ordered us to
feed. I have not enjoyed my captivity here any more than
you have, Rosalinda. So now both of us are on our way out
of this insane asylum with *El Brazo Largo*, no?"

Rosalinda said no. But Longarm murmured, in passable border Spanish, "She is in. We have no choice, Rosalinda. You can't break out of jail and leave a sobbing cell mate behind! Keep going, both of you. We are almost to the darkness of that stable door now!"

The three properly dressed young things entered the stable, and if any paid-up Moslem wondered why, he never asked them.

Longarm was braced for passing stable hands on bended knee, but there was nobody at work along the gravel-paved passage between the equine rumps to either side. Rosalinda said the tack room lay just ahead and ordered Lolita, "Wait out here with the horses for to warn us if anyone comes!"

Then she led Longarm on in, where it was even darker. As Longarm gazed about for the familiar lines of his own army saddle, the familiar figure of Baja popped up like a jack-in-the-box and stepped around one end of a saddle rack with his six-gun in its holster and a wrought-iron stove poker in his hand, grinning like a mean little kid as he said, "Evening, Longarm. Sorry you won't be with us longer."

But Longarm moved faster, grabbing Baja's wrist with his left hand and planting a gut-busting sucker punch with his big right fist.

As Baja sank to his knees to stare owlishly up, his breathless lips formed a silent question.

Longarm said, "Magic," and drop-kicked Baja's head for a field goal. Or he would have, had not said head been connected to the rest of the husky Baja by a neck that snapped as loudly as if he'd hit the end of a hangman's rope.

Whirling on Rosalinda with both dukes up, Longarm didn't see her at first. Then he glanced down at the feet of the black blur of Lolita, standing there with a hay fork, to see what was left of Rosalinda in a heap on the floor.

All four tines of the hay fork shone red with Rosalinda's blood. But Lolita sounded unconcerned as she asked, "How did you do that? I thought your wrists were chained behind your back, *El Brazo Largo!*"

He said, "My friends call me Custis. I had a spare key hidden in my pants, and I lied when I said I couldn't get my hands around to the front of my big behind. I see you were full of surprises, too. Ain't it a wonder how you can surprise folk just by not letting them know you are on to them?"

She asked, "What now . . . Custis? Is too early for to mount up and make the break for it?"

He said, "You can likely get out of this canyon with my help around ten or so, when things have settled down and I only have to take out a perimeter picket or so. I can't leave just yet. Is there somewheres more private we can hole up a spell, after I hide these bodies up in the hayloft and gather up some stuff?"

She said, "I have my own garret room in the building you just broke out of. I never expected to see it again, but . . . Why not? I shall help you, here. How long do you think their bodies may remain hidden above the stalls?"

He shrugged inside his two chadors and said, "Overnight, I hope. By then it might not matter."

Fumbling his arms free of the wispy black muslin again, Longarm hunkered to pat the body of Baja down. When he found his own badge, he snorted, "Must have thought he'd carry this about like a rabbit's foot or to show to his pals."

Lolita said, "He was planning for to collect the bounty on you down in my old country. Did you not know this before you killed him?"

Longarm shrugged and said, "Didn't know *what* might be going on until they tipped their mitt. But, no offense, I've had pretty señoritas ask me home by way of unfamiliar necks of their woods before. So I figured I'd play my cards close to my vest."

Tucking his own badge, wallet ID, watch, and derringer inside the chadors with the rest of him, Longarm rose with Baja's Schofield .45, gun belt and all, to hand it to Lolita along with Baja's wallet, saying, "Put these away. You do know how to use a gun, don't you?"

She tossed aside her bloody hay fork to accept even more lethal weaponry and her reward for a job well done with a nod of thanks. It was hard to tell whether a gal was smiling or what she even *looked* like in that outfit.

The two of them dragged the bodies by the heels out to the stable. Baja was heavy, and it was a bitch getting him up to the hayloft with Lolita pushing from the bottom. Once he had, Longarm found the body of the young Chinese stable hand already sprawled in the hay. He muttered, "Great minds run in the same channel. Sorry about that, pard."

Rosalinda was way easier to lift. Leaving the three cadavers hidden well enough for now, Longarm scouted the tack room for his own saddle, found it with his six-gun rig stuffed in an open saddlebag, and put it on under his girlish disguise. Then he stuffed two boxes of S&W .44-40 slugs in his jacket pockets, hauled the Winchester '73 from its boot, and found it as easy to hide that inside the floppy black folds just by holding it down at his side.

Glancing about he said, *"Bueno,* show me to that private chamber you just mentioned, and we'll hang tight a spell. Like I said, it ought to be safe for you to blue-streak for Chloride after midnight."

She asked, "Will you not be riding with me, Custis?"

He said, "Can't. I'm a lawman, and thse birds have been bending the law all out of shape in these parts. Most of the folk here in New Alamut are unwilling guests or let's just call them slaves. So once I figure how to separate the sheep from the goats, I mean to make me some arrests, or failing that, settle on just doing my duty when they *resist* arrest."

She replied, "Brrr! I just saw Baja resisting arrest! Is true, the things they say abut *El Brazo Largo,* one who is most simpatico until you cross him!"

Longarm said, "Aw, mush. Let's get out of here."

They did, feeling more vulnerable than they likely were as the two of them moved like dark shadows no man was supposed to notice all the way back to the building Longarm had just escaped from.

Lolita led him up to her tiny room below the roof tiles. He could see why she'd been anxious to escape with them. As the summer warmed up, you'd be able to bake bread on the floorboards. It was cooling down to bearable with both windows open after an April sunset.

Once she'd barred the door, Lolita shucked her chador before she lit a candle stub by her cot. The rest of her spartan furniture consisted of the usual trunks and chest of drawers you saw in working-class Mex quarters, minus the usual cross on the wall above the bed.

Without her spooky black coverall, Lolita turned out different than he'd expected. She was around eighteeen or less with unbound, shoulder-length hair, wearing a one-piece cotton smock barely covering her knees as she stood there in her rope-soled sandals. She had green eyes, chocolate hair, and that peach complexion peculiar to some parts of Spain and Spain alone. He'd never yet met a white woman with hide that color who hadn't been Spanish. Purer Spanish than the late Rosalinda, for all her brag about being so *sangre azul.*

Lolita took a seat on her cot and patted the covers beside her, there being no place else to sit down up in her room. So Longarm shed his own disguise, sat down, and started to reach for a smoke before he saw how dumb that would be. Nice girls living alone didn't smoke three-for-a-nickel cheroots.

Lolita seemed pleasantly surprised at his appearance as well, after picturing *El Brazo Largo* as a fire-snorting whale of destruction up until then.

She shyly asked if it was true he and the notorious Mex rebel, El Gato, had once wiped out a *federale* field artillery train.

He answered, "Had to. They were out to wipe *us* out. Let's speak of here and now. How many armed thugs would you say Haji Bin Omar has on tap up here in this cuckoo's nest?"

Lolita pursed her pretty lips and decided, "No more than twenty or so with a larger number of guns guarding that burro train he just sent out with all that *oro. Pero* the twenty or more still here are his most loyal and *ferocidad* fighters. Most of them *Moros,* like himself. He has perhaps a dozen such as Baja, *Anglo y la raza,* but uses them mostly to guard his *oro* trains. *Moros* encountered on the Arizona desert by a prospector are more apt to be remembered, no?"

Longarm said, "Some of his Chinee staggering up from the Sea of Cortez on foot in winter weather must have been spotted, hazy as the gossip wound up. I suspect as in that case of them burros just leaving, they travel wide of others at night and hole up in draws by day. But as long as I take out Bin Omar, his leaderless underlings won't enslave no

216

more folk up this way. They won't want to come back."

She asked how he meant to get El Haji.

It was a good question.

He said, "Reckon I'll have to start by looking for him. Pussyfooting around as a harem gal going to or coming from the outhouse. How many gals might he have in his harem, by the way?"

She shook her brown curls and said, "He has no harem. El Haji is most straight of laces for a *Moro*. Or perhaps that *imperioso* Fung Yu is enough for any man his age. No?"

Longarm frowned thoughtfully and decided, "Somebody else must have the same name. There'd be no sense in pretending to be a mad Turk, and this other lady I met up in Provo said she'd had a wrestling match with an amorous Turk calling himself . . . How would a gal get away from such a high-and-mighty cuss if he really wanted her? Bin Omar never said he wanted me, that way, and he still had me served to him on a platter."

It took a while, even speaking tersely and leaving out the small details, but he brought Lolita up to his meeting with Trixie Mondale, and the Mex gal decided, "Someone else is pretending to be El Haji for to lure women astray or perhaps to make you look for them in the wrong place after he has lured them somewhere else?"

Longarm sighed and said, "He sure as shooting succeeded! I'd have never in this world wound up here in New Alamut if I hadn't met up with Trixie Mondale first and . . . What if some other Turk, knowing what old Bin Omar was up to, here, and aiming to put a stop to it . . . Naw, that eliminates. Miss Trixie says she responded to a newspaper proposal long before I was assigned to another case entire, and there was no way either could have anticipated my meeting up with Miss Trixie days after their kid-stuff wrestling match! I'm back with your notion some lovesick loon with the same name led me astray through sheer . . . serendipity. That's what you call it when you go to the store for a sack of beans and discover they're having a sale on sugar: serendipity. Bin Omar's chattel slavery and first-degree murders over this way add up to more serious crimes than the murder of all those missing brides I just told you about, if that's what's happened to them!"

She said, "Oh, that is terrible! What sort of a fiend would murder one young woman after another?"

He said, "Sex fiend, or some other sort of maniac. Bad enough. But not as bad as this little bit of the Ottoman Empire here in Arizona. I read about them Ottoman Turks in the Denver library. I read some when I'm low on pocket jingle. The Good Book folk in the Holy Lands had bond servants. When you read *servant* in the King James Bible, it means what we'd call a slave. But the Ottoman Turks, starting out as herdsmen on the the Siberian plains, were masters at rounding up and domesticating livestock. So as they carved out that empire, that was how they treated their new subjects. Like stock to be broken to the bit and saddle. They wound up with army divisions of born Christians. They called 'em Januaries or something like that. The point is that a third or more were killed, brutal, in front of the other Januaries until the ones left were about as wild and crazy Turkish troops as you'd never want to tangle with."

Something was going on outside. Longarm snuffed the candle and rose from Lolita's bed as he added, "Old Haji must read a lot, too. But this pipe dream in the desert has to cease and desist."

He moved over to the window. It was hard to make out details now, but the plaza down below was astir with swirling and shouting blurs.

Lolita asked what was up. He said, "Looks like somebody noticed I ain't up in the tower. With any luck, they'll chase me out across the desert in the dark."

He warned her not to talk anymore, seeing she was supposed to be up there alone. He relit the candle by her bed to make her servant's quarters less mysterious with light showing under her door. As he did so, he whispered, "Anyone not knowing what was up would be up, wondering what was up."

She nodded silently, her green eyes wide.

They got wider a few minutes later when there came a loud pounding on her door. Lolita called out in Spanish, "Who is it? I am undressed in bed!"

A rough male voice speaking Spanish with an accent gruffly called back, "Though Allah be more merciful, it can't be helped. The Haji Bin Omar has ordered a room-to-room search of every building, and we must insist you open this door and open it *now!*"

Chapter 32

So Lolita opened her door with a defiant smile and nothing on her from head to toe but candlelight. The younger of the two armed Turks gasped in his own lingo and turned away. The older Turk was made of sterner stuff and had his orders. He tried not to look at the candlelit curves of naked, peachy flesh as his eyes swept the interior of her tiny room. He could see at a glance there were no closet doors, and the cot was too low to the floor, or was it?

Shoving Lolita aside without looking at her, the Turk dropped to his knees as if bowing to Mecca, but he was more interested in the space under that cot until he saw there was nothing there.

He cursed in Turkish as he got back to his feet with a contemptuous glance at the bedcovers piled against the adobe wall and snapped, "Go back to bed and keep this door locked. The big American they had up under the dovecote has broken out, killing three people, may his tribe be accursed unto the seventh generation!"

Lolita said, "My God, you have to catch him before he kills us all!"

The Turk stepped outside, muttering to himself. Lolita shut the door and barred it before she turned to whisper, "I heard them on the stairs. I think I fooled them!"

Longarm flung off the loosely piled covers she'd tossed on him as he scrootched against her wall with his six-gun on

219

his hip and Winchester lined up along the wall. He smiled up at her to marvel, "You would have fooled me had I been searching in his place. Your unfair sex has the drop on us more easily distracted humans."

She smiled down at him knowingly and said, "That is for why I just answered the door without my *blusa* on. Do you wish for me to put it back on now?"

He said, "Not if you don't want to."

So she rejoined him on the bed by perching her bare behind in his lap with her arms around him. He just as naturally hugged her back, and when they kissed, he sensed she hadn't been getting any lately.

But they soon fixed that, and he had to warn her to keep it down as she moaned and twisted under him in time to his thrusts with her trim, peachy arms and legs around him.

She whispered, "I know. I am trying for not to rage with you like a cat of the alley. But I have not gone mad with a man like this all the time I have been here!"

He didn't ask how come until they'd both come more than once. Then, dying for a smoke as they got their second wind side by side on her narrow cot, he listened to her personal tale of woe.

Nothing she said surprised him all that much. That imperious Fung Yu had hired Lolita and other Mex servant girls down in the Mex seaport of Rio Colorado. She'd told them they'd be working in the land of opportunity without mentioning Haj Bin Omar's peculiar views on labor relations. Once in New Alamut, it had only taken a few sharp slaps in her pretty face to convince Lolita it might be best not to mention the subjects of wages or the U.S. Constitution. She said she'd read about the Thirteenth Amendment down Mexico way and been right disappointed in the way New Alamut was governed, as a sort of glorified dollhouse owned and operated by a really mean rich kid.

He kissed her and soothed, "It was too bad to last. If it hadn't been me, some other lawman would have stumbled over it. For in spite of Mr. Buntline's dime novels, it's only wild out here like our climate is. We do get some gully washers, but they always blow over. Lightning and hailstones don't add up to a way of life. Bin Omar reminds me of

220

another fool named Henry Plummer. Got himself elected sheriff up Montana way and thought that meant he could abuse everyone else indefinite. But he was strung up by vigilantes in the same year he was elected. Range wars they write so much about blow over as sudden. The DeWitt County War in Texas smoldered on and off the longest, with months of laying low from the law betwixt outbursts. The wild and wooly Lincoln County War ended in less than six months when they heard about it in Washington and sent a new governor with hair on his chest to lay down the law. Bin Omar's dream was impractical from the first. It just ain't true there's no law west of the Pecos. It may take longer to catch up because things are so spread out."

She nestled her warm flesh against his to purr she was glad it had been him and not some other Americano who'd cut the sign of el Haji.

He got a better grip on her and said, "Me, too. Even though all this eliminating's put me way out of my way. I got to clean things up and get it on down the road, pronto, if I'm to ever catch up with the mission they *sent* me on!"

She commenced to nibble his collarbone and, with one nibble leading to another, he was back in the saddle, having too nice a ride to study on how the hell he'd wound up in such an odd position.

He was just about to come in her again when they were frozen in midstroke by a soft but insistant tapping on Lolita's door.

She called out, "*¿Quien es?*" with Longarm in her.

A familiar raspy voice replied from out in the dark hallway, "Lolita? Open the door and see what I have for you, my ripe little pomegranate!"

It was that older Turk. He hadn't been as oblivious to Lolita's bare tits and ass as he'd let on.

Lolita and Longarm made a great team. As they moved into position in the dark, she called out in a worried voice, "Are you alone? El Haji may be cross, and Fung Yu may beat me if I let you in."

He insted with the urgency of the hard up, "Nobody will ever know. I made certain none of my comrades had any idea what I had planned for us tonight!"

Lolita hesitated, then shyly asked, "You will be gentle, won't you? You are handsome, it is true, but so muscular and strong!"

"By the beard of the prophet, I shall treat you as if you were the very shadow of a sweet little nightingale!" He sort of groaned. So, seeing he wanted to come in that badly, Lolita let him in, and it ended badly for him.

Hunkering nude by the man he'd smashed flat with the stock of his Winchester while Lolita shut and barred the door, Longarm felt the Turk's throat for a pulse, and when he didn't find one, all he could say was, "Aw, you're no fun. How was I to know you wouldn't be wearing a dish towel around your soft skull?"

She asked, "How badly is he hurt? Let us be off!"

Longarm asked, "How come? Didn't he just say none of his pals knew he was up here? Is there someplace up here under the roof tiles where we could store him, though? He'll be oozing half the night, and there's no sense stinking up your room."

She gasped, "Custis! We can't stay here! Even as we speak, they are searching for you!"

He said, "No they ain't. It's been quiet out for some time. So they figure I'm long gone. This fool wouldn't have been wandering about all alone in the dark if he'd thought I was out there *in* it! Where do I put him, *querida?*"

She thought and said, "Is an empty storeroom down at the far end. Is nothing there for anyone to be searching for, now that they have searched this building from top to bottom."

Longarm said, *"Bueno.* We'd best slip on them black chadors again lest somebody spot our bare asses."

Lolita giggled that it made her feel most naked to have nothing on under a head-to-toe black envelope of loose muslin, save for her sandals.

Longarm didn't bother with his boots but strapped his six-gun on around his naked hips before he disguised himself as a very large daughter of the faithful.

Then, with Lolita leading, barely visible in the dark corridor ahead of him, Longarm dragged her dead would-be lover after her to deposit him in a far corner of the empty chamber, where the slanted roof met the dusty plank flooring.

They went back to her chamber and tore off another piece to give the pot more time to boil. It was midnight in the dark of the moon, albeit under stars so bright they looked as if you could sweep 'em out of the clear black desert sky with your hat, when Longarm moved down the stairs in his raggedy black disguise.

He'd told Lolita to stay put in her room and just look innocent 'til he got back. He added, "If I don't get back, you're still in the clear. You don't know nothing about night-crawling lovers who never said where they were going."

He put his low-heeled boots and duds back on, of course, wadding up his Stetson to ride against the small of his back under his gun belt and holding the Winchester down at his side.

Thanks to the way Bin Omar liked to hold court as he taunted his subjects and prisoners, he kept late hours. Longarm strode along one side of the plaza, like three little maids on their way to school in one chador, until he spotted an infernal guard posted by that ornate entrance.

After that it seemed safe to bet a door being guarded might just be opened, and if there'd been a guardroom on the other side of the nail-studded oak, there'd have been no point in that one lonesome Turk to be standing there. They were more a desert band than any military unit. So they were allowed to do things the sensible way.

The lone Turk spotted Longarm mincing toward him in as feminine a walk as he could manage with feet his size in cavalry stovepipes. As Longarm had hoped, it was tougher to gauge the size of objects moving along in tricky light. So, by the way the guard looked away, Longarm saw he'd been seen as a woman he wasn't allowed to talk to in public.

Knowing "she" wasn't supposed to talk to him, the guard assumed he was avoiding the temptations of a woman with a coal sack over her head by not looking at her as she passed on by to wherever in the name of Allah she was going at this hour.

So he never knew what hit him. Longarm didn't mess around when he hit an armed man with a rifle butt. Holding the Winchester in one hand and the scruff of the downed

Turk's shirt in the other, Longarm hauled the limp form around the far corner into the dark slot between the palace of the Haji and the barracks beyond.

Moving back to the doorway, he picked up the fallen Turk's own rifle, along with his red fez. The rifle was another Spencer. Only seven shots, but they were .52-50 buffalo busters. Better yet, the Spencer repeater had a canvas sling.

Slinging it over his left shoulder under the chador and holding the Winchester in his right hand, Longarm tried the latch with his left hand. It opened. It was black as a bitch inside. He was glad.

Feeling his way by memory to the half-assed throne room, Longarm risked striking a wax-stemmed Mex match, seeing he had to be alone in there.

He lit a lone candle near one end of that long divan. It cast a meager light in the cavernous audience chamber. Longarm saw no other ways in or out. He figured there had to be. He stepped up on the divan, kicking fancy pillows out of the way as he explored behind the hanging wall rugs and, sure enough, there was nothing but a hole in the wall behind one near that fancy water pipe.

He moved along the dark corridor and around a bend, to see light under a door down at the end. He nodded and moved along on the balls of his feet to where he could make out a delirious moaning, coming at him from the lamplit chamber beyond.

Longarm took a deep breath with the muzzles of the Spencer and the Winchester sticking out the front of his sloppy chador. Then he took three running steps at the door and kicked it high, hard as he could.

The door flew off its hinges to reveal a scene from an Arabesque hashish fantasy. Haji Bin Omar reclined in a sensuous sprawl in a big nest of silken pillows of every shade. He lay naked as a jay. Fong Yu was stark naked, too. Only she was on her hands and knees with her really swell ass pointed at the doorway so she could suck the self-styled holy man on her hands and knees.

Such action ceased, of course, as what must have seemed a spooky black bogeyman snapped, "Freeze or die! I ain't fixing to say that again!"

But Fong Yu rolled over on her back to instinctively spread her shapely legs as the still hard Bin Omar hauled a swamping Le Mat from its hidey-hole amid those pillows.

So Longarm fired both rifles. The Spencer did the most damage as both rounds smashed through the Turk's skull. Sobbing in fear amid the swirling gunsmoke, the exotic Fong Yu wailed, "Don't kill me! Please don't kill me! I will suck your cock while I fuck your dog if only you won't kill me!"

Longarm levered fresh rounds into both rifles by practiced flips of their weight on stationary arming levers and said, "Shut up and listen tight. We ain't got time for you to fuck my dog. You heard me tell him what I wanted. So I hope we've established I get what I want when I'm covering anyone with two guns?"

She sobbed, "Anything, anything, anything, in any hole you choose!"

He said, "I'm particular where I shove mine. So here's what I want you to do instead."

Thus it came to pass, though Allah be more merciful, that when the palace guard burst into the still smoky chamber with their own guns loaded and locked, the imperious naked infidel houri stood shamelessly in all her glory beside a serving woman in a proper chador. There was no sign of their Haji. His known love toy pointed at the shattered door and said, "After them. Two Cantonese dogs just broke in here as if to steal something. Your master is chasing them with his big revolver as we speak! Can't you smell the smoke?"

So they all went tear-assing off into the night, and if they ever caught up with anybody, Longarm never heard about it. Because around two A.M. he and the two women had made it out of New Alamut on those last three mules belonging to Esau Skaggs.

He never fucked Fong Yu and let her go, as he'd promised, once they made it safely to Chloride. Lolita rode with him all the way to Fort Mojave, where they parted friendly, after fucking at most every trail stop along the way.

He sent Lolita on her way with a Schofield, a Le Mat, and the contents of Baja's wallet. Haji Bin Omar hadn't had anything on him when they were hiding him under those pillows.

Chapter 33

Longarm had sent Lolita down the river ahead of him because she'd been in a hurry to get home, they'd have only parted in Yuma in any case, and because he knew he'd be in a savage mood until he could tidy up and get the hell on out of Fort Mojave.

The cavalry post had been built to keep an eye on the Indian nation of the same name. The Mojave were a tad more advanced and a whole lot meaner than their Hualapai cousins and inclined to shoot them just for the hell of it, too.

The Indians raising hell that year were the Apache cousins of the Navajo. The troops at Fort Mojave were on the alert but being held in reserve for trouble. The bored junior officers Longarm reported the situation at New Alamut to were all for saddling up to go rescue those unfortunate sons of Han.

The major in charge of operations was enough of a sport to invite their civilian guest to the officers' club for supper, but over coffee and cigars, pushed back from the table with Longarm and other field-grade officers, he opined that every dead Chink was a net gain for Manifest Destiny.

He pointed out, "Nobody invited those Cantonese coolies to come all the way across the Pacific to compete for jobs with bad-enough Irish Catholics. As for the Turks and for that matter the blasted Russians, this world will be a kinder, gentler place once the Manchu Empire, the Ottoman Empire, and the czar of all the Russians fall of their own rotten weight to be replaced by something else!"

Longarm asked what the major had in mind for the Manchu, Ottoman, and Russian Empires.

The major shrugged and said, "Anything has to be an

improvement. All three are feared and hated by their subjects. It's too late in history for autocratic empires. Mark my words, they'll fall just like the French monarchy, and things will be more peaceful!"

Longarm felt no call to lecture an older man with a college education on the Reign of Terror and Napoleonic Wars the world had barely recovered from. He'd thrown a considerable cramp in the slave-holding operation up in New Alamut and reported what he'd found and done there to the nearest important federal authorities. If they didn't care to mop up, it was no skin off his ass. They'd never sent him out into the field to put an end to Haji Bin Omar's hashish dreams. As bad as he'd been, the crazy cuss hadn't been holding any of those missing mail-order brides, against or of her own free will. The whole adventure had been shit-house luck for those unwilling workers and likely a serious danger to the mission he'd been *sent* on.

He stayed on overnight as a guest of the army and next moring took the mules over to the nearby Indian agency, the army remount officer having said cruel things about the teeth of three good old time-tested mules.

That was what the remount officer had complained about. The army remount tried to replace perfectly good horses before they were eight. Well cared for in a livery stable, a horse might still offer a spunky ride at twenty, while a mule could wear out a plowboy at the age of forty. But the three Longarm had borrowed off Esau Skaggs were too old for the army at, say, eighteen or twenty.

Longarm was sore tempted to throw caution to the winds, cross the Colorado down by Needles, on the California side, and strike out across the damned desert to see if he might intersect the wagon train he'd lost track of long ago and far away.

He didn't because he knew that would be dumb. If he couldn't sell 'em, he couldn't sell 'em, and he already owed Esau for that one mule they'd lost to that infernal machine that Baja, Hakim, or some other son of a bitch had laid for it.

But he had better luck at the Indian agency. He could only hope the Mojave had admired the three fine saddle mules for their Arab lines on their dam's side. He never asked. But he felt pretty sure it was the Apache who considered mule meat almost as sweet as burro.

He got forty and change for the three of them, throwing in that pack saddle but hanging on to his McClellan. Then he dickered himself and his possibles aboard yet another market raft bound down the rusty, foaming Colorado.

The river was still high, and they made good time, scaring the shit out of themselves from time to time where they couldn't call it white water because it was liquid mud. This raft was carrying hides, tallow, and firewood down to Yuma, manned by the powerful Widow Pulver and her four grown sons. So even though the stout, middle-aged skipper somehow got better-looking every time they tied up to the banks for a meal, and even though she got to batting her lashes some, any romance was doomed from the start.

You tied up for meals and to rest now and again because there was a way to let go the sweeps as tore with the current down a river in high water.

The run down to Yuma from Fort Mojave took the better part of two days and felt like forever to Longarm as they went lickety-split ever farther apart from the others with the wagon train. But there was of course method in his madness. Parting friendly with the Pulvers where they tied up below the Southern Pacific's trestle, Longarm toted his saddle and possibles to the depot of the same on Second Street and checked them in for San Bernardino as soon as he had a ticket. The next westbound wasn't due for nigh three hours. He legged it to the Western Union and got off a mighty long wire Billy Vail was going to piss and moan over signing for, even though it was going at night letter rates. Hoping he knew what he was doing, Longarm added his office could likely reply in care of Western Union, San Bernardino.

Then with just his saddlebags over one arm, he scouted up a public bath, followed by a change of shirt and underwear and a sit-down shave with bay rum lest the other passengers aboard his train take him for an escaped convict from the nearby notorious territorial prison.

The east-west Fourth Avenue was the main or market street of Yuma. Facing five or more hours aboard that train, he treated himself to the first decent meal he'd had since he boarded that raft up the river. He dined on chicken enchiladas, beef tamales, and frijoles, topped off by tuna pie and black coffee. He figured they'd be pushing sandwiches and beer aboard the train.

Strolling back to the depot, he had time to stock up on smokes and an edition of the *Illustrated Police Gazette* he hadn't read yet. He was a tad too keyed up to sit, so he paced the platform until at last the damned train showed up to perform miracles.

Finding a coach seat on the north, shady, side in a smoking car, he cussed Mr. C. S. Huntington of the Southern Pacific Line until at long last they were under way, rattling along the trestle built on Yuma Crossing, the wide, shallow ford the Indians had discovered in the first place.

There were no such things as Yuma Indians, exactly. The term had been applied collectively to the Cocopah, Mojave, and Quechan, who shared a common dialect as well as that popular crossing.

The military Fort Yuma and Indian Reserve lay south of the tracks on the California side of the Colorado. Longarm didn't care. He knew what they looked like because he'd ridden this line before, and as ever he felt amazed by the wonders of a rapidly changing world.

Longarm was barely in his prime, and yet he could remember when a six-gun had to be loaded with loose powder, a cap, and ball. He'd just come down the river on a log raft those ancient cavemen could have understood and been taught to steer, after one hell of ride across the desert averaging less than five miles an hour. And yet here he sat, at his ease on green plush like a rich gent smoking in his club as he tore along doing better than thirty miles an hour, nonstop, hour after hour, to move west in one afternoon as far as his pals with the wagons had in all that time since he'd parted with them up in Utah Territory.

After that, they had time to move south as far or farther. Barring side trips and delays such as he'd just suffered, they could have made it to San Bernardino and then some, damn those rolling wagons.

But there was no sense rolling on west before he made

certain as the bottleneck they had to or might have already passed through. That wire he was hoping for from Denver wasn't going to be waiting for him there. He'd had to send his progress report at night letter rates because he'd known Billy Vail would never accept any message that long at a nickel a word straight wire. Vail was a Scotch name.

It wasn't easy, but he managed to quit trying to heel the train to run faster. He was out ahead of that wagon train or he wasn't. If they hadn't made it that far yet, he had nothing to worry about as he just waited for them to catch up in San Bernardino. If they'd already passed on through, he wasn't going to be able to do shit about it before old Billy Vail got back in touch with him to give him what for.

Longarm wasn't ashamed of the results of his side issues, so far. He'd busted up a gang of horse thieves and ended the vicious madness of a bunch more dangerous than anybody who at worst had murdered no more than a score of—

"Cut that out!" he warned himself, chagrined at how easy it was to dismiss fellow human beings as little loss to the world.

For it was true not much could be said for the pride or the brains of drabs like old Trixie Mondale, willing to drop whatever life they had to travel a thousand miles to marry up with a total stranger in the hopes that might be some improvement. But he warned himself not grab for easy answers, as it was getting closer to May Day than April Fools', and somebody was still out there, likely doing something awful to the serving wenches, hotel maids, and, sure, downright whores responding to those long-distance proposals.

As in the case of those illiterate Cantonese coolies back there in New Alamut, all human beings who hadn't murdered anyone had the God-given right not to be murdered, and what *else* could have happened to all those missing gals?

As he stared out at the passing scenery, the Colorado Desert being about the dullest scenery on the North American continent unless you admired mile after mile of dead-flat former sea bottom covered with a uniform fuzzy gray blanket of knee-deep greasewood, Longarm reflected on how tough it might be to get away with murdering and hiding anybody out in the middle of a desert. They'd about eliminated the notion any of the missing gals had been headed up to the cross-country rails by way of this Colorado Desert. He'd just proven how tough it would be to go up the Colorado to Utah Territory. Those unfortunate sons of Han enticed to a desert paradise from Mexican ports of call had had a tough enough time legging it less than half the distance at gunpoint.

The Mojave, Nevada, and Utah wildrenesses those missing gals had never made it across offered more varied hiding places. But hiding a dead body was not the question before the house. Converting anybody traveling with a wagon train into a dead body without anybody else *noticing* was the question before the house. You couldn't fall off a wagon train the way you could a ship at sea, and even when you fell overboard at sea, somebody usually noticed you weren't there anymore by the time your ship put in somewhere.

"Inside job!" Longarm muttered half aloud as he stared out at the tedious scenery, mighty glad he was crossing it so comfortable and so sudden with his heavy tote in the baggage car ahead.

The gal seated just ahead, smoking a cigarette in her fancy holder, turned with arched brow to ask him if he'd been talking to her.

Longarm smiled sheepish and started to confess he'd gotten into bad habits riding slower, alone. Then he noticed she was a still-handsome natural redhead not much older than himself in a summer-weight travel duster she filled right nice under a perky straw boater with a half veil of fly netting, so he said, "Not directly, ma'am. I was asking in general if anybody knew how much farther San Berdoo might be."

She pointed with her lit cigarette to the now not far distant brown hills on the horizon to say, "A little over an hour, now. Those are the eastern or little San Bernardino Mountains, one of the transverse ranges dividing this Colorado Desert from the Mojave. You'll see as we go on how these tracks and those mountains converge. The town you have dismissed as San Berdoo dominates the meeting of the old with the new. The north-south desert wagon routes crossing the San Bernardino Pass to the Mojave meet this east-west railroad there and, as I said, we'll arrive in a little over an hour."

231

Longarm said, "We're making better time than I thought, or I've been thinking so hard I've lost track. Would you do me the honor of sharing some refreshings in the club car with me, ma'am? Seeing we still got the time and you've been so helpsome?"

Aware others were listening, he added, "I'd be Deputy U.S. Marshal Custis Long, traveling on government business, ma'am."

She half turned to prop one elbow up on the seat back between them, took a puff on her cigarette, and said, "In that case I'm Carmen Culhane on her way to San Bernardino, but after that, I am on my way to wed a swain who spoke up first."

Longarm laughed like a good sport and said, "Just my luck. But I'd still be proud to take you back to the club car, with pure intentions, Miss Carmen. I've been looking for somebody who can tell me about San Berdoo or, sorry, San Bernardino."

She hesitated, took another drag on her cigarette, and decided, "Let us not and say we did, ah, Custis. I can see you're an experienced ... traveler. So am I, and there's no sense crying over spilled resolutions. But I'm really on my way to get married, and I know myself well enough to arrive alone!"

Longarm smiled sincrely and said, "In that case, allow me to offer my congratulations to the lucky cuss. Will he be waiting at the station up ahead?"

The natural redhead laughed in a natural way and said, "I wouldn't have turned down some harmless flirting in the club car if my life was that simple. I fear my journey will have barely started when we arrive in San Bernardino. I'm on my way to meet my intended in Montana by way of the Old Spanish Trail!"

Longarm frowned thoughtfully and marveled, "Your intended has gone on ahead of you, ma'am?"

To which she replied, "I've never met him. It's a long story, and I fear you'd never understand."

Chapter 34

Carmen Culhane's amber eyes slowly but surely went from know-it-all worldly to lost-child scared by the time Longarm had filled her in on his mission.

She said, "My God! Are you suggesting I've been courting by mail with some sort of monster?"

Longarm shook his head and said, "Don't even know for certain you're in any danger, Miss Carmen. Lots of gals get lots of love letters, and we'd be in a real fix if half of them were sent by fiends."

She gulped and stammered, "But you just said all those other girls on their way to wed men they met by mail never got there!"

He soothed, "We'd have never recieved complaints about mail-order brides who got there, Miss Carmen. We know heaps of she-male travelers have arrived safe and sound by wagon along the Old Spanish Trail since the first complaints came in. Falling in with you like this might have been no more than a coincidence, with nobody out to harm a hair on your head, see?"

She said, "I see falling in with you might have just saved my life! I feel as if somebody just sloshed a bucket of cold water in my face! What could I have been thinking to sell my shop in Yuma after agreeing to marry a man I've yet to meet!"

He suggested, "Maybe we'd best study on that, ma'am. Shall we go on back to the club car, now?"

She slid from her seat as Longarm rose from his. Across the way a little old lady got up to say, "I want to come, too! I can't wait to hear how this turns out!"

Longarm started to shake his head, laughed, and said, "Sure, come on in. The water's fine."

In an aside to the younger redhead he observed, "With your permit, Miss Carmen. This other lady's only going to turn a busted jar of olives into a wagon load of watermelon hit by a train, unless you got something personal to tell you don't want told, of course."

Carmen smiled, held out her hand to the little old lady, and told her, "I'm Carmen Culhane of Yuma, and you may know my hat shop over on Fourth Street?"

The little old lady said she was a Mabel Flagg from Tucson, on her way to a family funeral in San Fernando. Longarm herded the two of 'em ahead of him to the club car, where they found a table, and the ladies both ordered gin and tonics, bless their refined hearts.

Longarm ordered a needled beer. By the time the colored car attendant brought their drinks from the bar, the older gal had agreed with Carmen that she'd been out of her mind to sell a going hat shop and take such a flying leap into the unknown, no matter how many assay offices any man in Montana might claim he owned and operated, lonesome.

The redhead stared down at her untasted drink to murmur, "I felt I knew all too well what he meant about working alone in the back after closing hours. He said he was a recent widower. My man's been dead two years now."

Old Mabel sniffed and said, "I don't know what's got into you women today. You don't know how to quit when you're ahead and . . . say, was that your hat shop at Fourth and Sixth? The one with those French bonnets on sale? They were adorable! I'd have come in and bought one if they hadn't looked too young for this old face and I'd had more time in Yuma!"

Carmen said, "Thank you. I made them myself, alone in the back. Alone a lot in the back. It wouldn't have done me any good if you had bought one of those hats in the window. I sold my shop and all its stock over a week ago, before I sold my house and all its furnishings."

The older woman sniffed and said, "Someday you'll regret it, even if your assay man up Montana way dosen't murder you or keep other women on the side. When you get to my age, you'll have seen all marriages end as tragedies or dirty jokes! I had to marry up three times before I found a

234

man that was right for me. He was a loving man and a good provider, and we never fussed. So then he up and died on me. They all do, sooner or later, unless you die first. Having a husband is a lot like having any other pet. You just get attached to 'em and they up and die on you. I live alone and tend my house plants now. Dosen't hurt as much when a fern gives up the ghost on you. You just toss it on the mulch pile and get on with more important things."

Longarm said, "Ladies, could we get on with more recent events now? We're running low on time, here!"

The little old lady dimpled and allowed she'd gotten to be a chatterbox, tending ferns since she'd buried that last husband.

Carmen nodded and said, "Let's do!"

He got out his notebook and a pencil stub as she went over her own tale of woe. He'd heard the part about her husband dying and leaving her feeling lonesome as she made hats. The bird she'd written a coy reply to, followed by ever more serious letters until, as she said, she'd lost touch with reality, was named Norman MacLean, said he was a smoking but nondrinking Scotch Presbyterian who liked children and dogs but wasn't sure about cats. He'd written he'd started out Canadian on Prince Edward Island, but he'd become an American citizen just after he'd enlisted in the Union Army in '64 as a man who just couldn't abide slavery after talking to colored folk who'd escaped to Canada. If he was telling the truth, old Norm now had his own thriving business up in Helena, alone and lonesome after a long, happy, but childless marriage had ended badly, with him waiting hand and foot on a still-lovely woman dying slow and dirty of the consumption.

Old Mabel said, "You see? What did I tell you? If she hadn't died on the poor man, he'd have caught her in bed with his best friend. A dirty joke or a tragedy! That story can have but two endings!"

Longarm said, "Old Norm sounds like a nice, simple soul. Couple of wires ought to establish whether he's a monster or not. How were you planning on joining him, Miss Carmen?"

She said, "Norman wrote me to wait in San Bernardino

until a crusty but trustworthy freight hauler called Buckskin Jacobs gets there. He hauls back and forth between San Bernardino and Ogden along some old Spanish and Mormon trails. I've never met him, of course. I've never been to San Bernardino."

Longarm cocked a brow and observed, "I'd got the impression you had when you corrected my calling it San Berdoo."

She smiled wanly and said, "I'd have chided you for calling Pueblo de Los Angeles L.A., or San Diego Dago. I was born and raised what we now call a Native Daughter. Calling San Franciso Frisco gives us the same shudders as fingernails on a slate blackboard."

Old Mabel smiled impishly and interjected, "I thought it was the Native *Sons* who shot you for saying Frisco." She struck a pose to recite, "The miners came in forty-nine. / The whores in fifty-one / Then they got together / And produced the Native Son!"

Carmen flushed and said, "Really . . . !"

The salty old woman shrugged and said, "When you get to be my age, you'll use worse words than *whore*. I call 'em as I see 'em, and these old eyes have seen a lot!"

Longarm asked Carmen when she'd married up and moved to Arizona.

She said her huband had died in California and she'd moved over to Yuma more recently when she'd heard that hat shop was for sale. Mabel sniffed and observed Carmen should have given her business longer, no matter how lonesome it was to make hats. She added, "I saw your hats. You should have made more of them!"

The sweet old thing was getting on Longarm's nerves with her dumb, distracting observations. But he'd invited her to have a drink with them, so what the hell.

He asked Carmen how she was supposed to go about meeting up with that famous Buckskin Jacobs, adding that a Mormon lawman he knew had vouched for the wagon master.

She told him her Norman had written she was to simply go west to San Bernardino by rail, check into any hotel of her choice, and spread the word at the freight depot she was in the market for a wagon trip up to Ogden, the Union Pacific, and the eagerly waiting Norman MacLean.

He put his notebook away for the time being, allowing they ought to consider moving back to their coach seats if they meant to get off with their baggage.

The two women walking ahead of him talked back and forth all the way. When they reached the smoking car, Carmen turned to Longarm to tell him, "I've decided not to get off in San Bernardino, after all. I'm going on with dear Mabel to attend that family funeral with her in San Fernando before we both go back to Arizona together!"

Longarm asked, "What about old Norm? What about your *baggage?*"

She started to say something about Norman having to understand, and then she blanched and gasped, "Oh, you're right! I have to see the conductor lest they drop all my baggage off in San Bernardino!"

As she started to turn away, she favored him with a grateful smile and said she'd never forget him, or how he might have saved her from something just awful.

It was a free country, and even if it hadn't been, Longarm felt he had no right to use a good-looking human being as bait. Buckskin Jacobs wasn't likely to show his hand right there in San Berdoo in any case, if he was up to something.

As Longarm resumed his seat with neither of the two women in sight, he reflected on how gals had apparently vanished from the wagon trains of others, and how Captain Burbank had vouched for Buckskin Jacobs. The odds on the easy answer were sort of slim. So was the notion that good- or at least fair-looking women were just popping like soap bubbles to be seen no more along the Old Spanish Trail.

A short time later, the Southern Pacific dropped Longarm and his shit off at San Bernardino with niether ceremony nor a proper railroad platform. As he strode up the side of the tracks to where his heavily laden saddle squatted on the dusty ballast like a turtle fixing to lay eggs, a squirt perched on a nearby buckboard asked if he'd like a ride to the Arrow Head Hotel. Longarm said he guessed and, once he'd tossed his load in the back and joined the squirt on the sprung seat, they were headed for the now impressive San Bernardinos behind a mule whose heart just wasn't in it for a trot.

The town ahead, between a headwaters creek of the Santa Ana and the only pass through those mountains for miles, had commenced as a small outpost of the larger Spanish mission to the Cahuilla Indians at San Gabriel before it had been settled by Mormons in the fifties as the gateway to the Mojave and beyond. There wasn't much other point in having a town there. Its nearby rival, Riverside, on the main stream of the Santa Ana, had been growing oranges in ever-increasing numbers since the early seventies. But San Bernardino was still little more than a train town.

With unusual imagination for Mormons, the streets of San Bernardino were named numerical east and west or alphabetical north to south. The center of the business district was Fourth and D Streets. The Arrow Head Hotel, named with as much ingenuity as everything else, was over on Sixth and D. All sorts of things were named Arrow Head in San Bernardino because there was an unexplained bald spot on the wooded slopes to the northeast that was shaped like a seven-acre arrowhead. Some said the Indians had done that. The Indians said they'd done no such thing. So nobody seemed to be able to drop the topic. They'd even named a whole lake farther up in the mountains Lake Arrowhead for no better reason.

First things coming first, the squirt having already told him Esau Skaggs hadn't beaten him to town, Longarm checked into the hotel, put his saddle and possibles away, and double-checked at the freight yards before he strode over to the Western Union to report in to Denver via night letter rates. He wasn't surprised to find there were no wires waiting there for him. Out on the walk he lit a cheroot, shook out the match, and chuckled, "Hot doggies, we beat them here after all and, for all its memories of the great Mormon migration, this ain't exactly a Mormon town no more!"

San Bernardino was notorious from the Colorado River to the great Pacific Ocean for its wall-to-wall whorehouses along D Street to the south of Fourth, putting his hotel somewhere amid the same, albeit, gazing about, he didn't see any naked women waving from windows as the legend would have it.

Since that wasn't his style in any case, Longarm ambled over to E Street to wet his whistle, stuff his gut, and see if he could pick up anything new from other early drinking gents.

In the Arrow Head Saloon, across the way from the Arrowhead Saloon, he found they served a fair free lunch with the beer on tap still cool that early in the year.

As he nibbled and sipped with his ears open, he heard nothing about missing women. The regulars were agog over a silver strike out in the Mojave to the north, about ten miles from Barstow; and to think how you could have bought a lot on Barstow's Main Street for a song just yesterday!

Longarm idly tried to fit a spanking-new silver strike into women going missing for some time. He wasn't able to. Desert rats were always finding something in the desert or saying they had. That was why they kept wandering around out yonder.

The Arrow Head Saloon, as distinct from the Arrowhead Saloon across the way, had its swinging batwing doors facing west across E Street. Thus, seeing it was now late afternoon, the lowering sun was shining so as to present the tall figure coming through said batwings as a black silhouette outlined in gilded fuzz.

Longarm didn't care, having a clear conscience and not expecting any trouble before the rest of his party caught up with him, there in that remote wide spot along the trail.

So Longarm was not only surprised but unsure of who the fuzzy black shadow meant as it broke stride, dropped into a gunfighting crouch, and gasped, "You? Here in Berdoo? What in the fuck are you doing here in Berdoo?"

Then they were both slapping leather. So Longarm never got to tell his would-be assassin shit.

Chapter 35

Longarm's .44-40 barked first and thrice. Whatever he'd shot flew backwards through the batwings to land faceup, illuminated better, in the sunlit dust of E Street.

Longarm had put his badge away in Yuma. He put it back on before he started to reload, staying put inside the saloon until, sure enough, a brace of town lawmen responded to the sound of gunplay with a whole lot of noise from their pie holes.

As one hunkered down over the dead man in the street, the other came inside, waving his own six-gun as he demanded some answers then and there, dad blast it.

The barkeep said, "It's all right, Jeff! This last man standing just put on a badge. Before that, the one in the street out yonder yelled at him and went for his own gun."

A regular who'd witnessed the shoot-out opined, "That was sure dumb of him. You should see how quick on the draw this lawman moves! Cuss who lost never got his own gun out!"

Longarm modestly confessed, "He'd have had me cold like a big-ass bird if he hadn't made the mistake of announcing his intentions so far in advance. I'd be Deputy U.S. Marshal Custis Long of the Denver District Court. I still don't know who I just shot it out with."

The San Bernardino deputy holstered his own six-gun as he said, "We've heard tell of you out this way, Longarm. What are you doing so far out of your own jurisdiction?"

Longarm answered easily, "Interstate case involving a possible sex fiend or white slavers. Working with other lawmen, federal and Utah Territory. Waiting for them here. Ain't certain where they are at the moment. Mind if I have a look at that body in your street?"

The San Bernardino lawman led the way as Longarm trailed after, putting his reloaded side arm back in its cross-draw holster on his left hip.

Out in the sunlight, the other town lawman looked up from the corpse to ask, "You want to see some neat shooting, Jeff? All three just over the heart, and you could cover them with one playing card!"

Longarm shrugged and said, "That's how come I pack a double action. When anybody slaps leather on you, it's a good idea to make sure you kill the fucker."

The one on his feet stared down to decide, "I've seen this bird in town before. Think that was him asking for work at the Lazy Nines out by the pass. Don't think they hired him, though."

Having gotten his first good look at the man he'd just shot, Longarm said, "I know who he was, now. His real name was Albert Lindstrom. He preferred to be known as Lightning Al along the owl-hoot trail. He must have thought I'd tracked him here. That happens to me a heap. I never. But he was wanted serious by the Pinkertons for stopping Uncle Pete's trains, more than once."

As others were slowly edging in within earshot, Longarm quickly added, "Lucky for you boys you recognized him, and it's his misfortune he resisted arrest two to one. The Pinks have a thousand-dollar bounty posted on his wayward hide, and that's five hundred apiece, right?"

The younger of the two started to ask an awfully dumb question in front of witnesses. The more experienced local lawmen, knowing federal deputies were not supposed to apply for bounties on the outlaws they dealt with, cut his junior off with a jovial laugh and said, "Hell, you distracted him for us, and we'll be proud to write you up for an assist, Longarm!"

Longarm said, "I wish you wouldn't. Soon as my pards get in, I may have to ride on sudden, and I'd as soon have no red tape slowing things down, if you follow my drift."

The older San Bernardino lawman said, "Consider yourself free to soar as a cactus wren with turpentine on its little asshole, pard. But can I buy you a drink once we get this fresh meat on ice?"

Longarm told them where they might find him if ever he was wanted desperate by San Bernardino. Then he went back inside to settle up with the barkeep for his needled beer and deviled eggs wrapped in sliced ham.

The barkeep said, "On the house. We're going to be spilling out onto the walk this evening, once word gets around we have a historical shooting to sort out, here in the Arrow Head. I mean to frame the front page of the *San Bernardino County Advertiser* as soon as they run . . . the shoot-out betwixt Lightning Al and our local boys. Aim to take down that framed photograph of Madame Modjeska dressed as Miss Rosalind in *As You Like It* and replace it with something that took place here in this very saloon!"

Longarm allowed that sounded reasonable, seeing they had all those pictures of the late James Butler Hickok in Deadwood's Number Ten Saloon where he died. He thought it best not to mention the saloon in Bodie, up by Mono Lake, where they had the actual skull of the desert rat the town was named after above the bar. It was a long story, and he didn't want to inspire any ghoulish notions about the late Lightning Al.

Longarm went back to the Western Union to get off a more accurate if coded report on the shooting of Lightning Al than Billy Vail was fixing to read in any newspapers. Longarm could only hope his busting up of a horse-thieving operation, the nipping of a potentially dangerous New Alamut in the bud, and this latest wrap on a lesser federal warrant might mitigate his failing to cut the trail of even one of those mail-order brides who'd never made it to the church on time.

He hadn't mentioned the federal warrant to the local authorities for the simple reason he'd meant what he'd said about red tape, and what the hell, the Pinks and Uncle Pete *had* posted a thousand-dollar reward in the wake of those mail car robberies.

Heading back to his hotel as the sun was setting in hopes of letting things die down, Longarm was treated to a better grasp on how they ran things in a town that had started out a religious institution.

The trail town's notorious D Street appeared to be the only street in San Bernardino where whores were allowed to operate openly, and even then with some modesty. No ladies of the evening were out of doors or even lounging in doorways as Longarm walked along D Street to his own hotel. None of them was hanging out her window with her tits perched on the sill like melons for sale. The whores of D Street were discreet.

As the sun was setting, they naturally had every right to light lamps in their own rooms, and where in the U.S. Constitution did it say any free citizen or citizeness had to hang curtains or blinds on a balmy desert evening in the privacy of their own quarters, or, as soon as you studied on it, where did it say folk had to wear *clothes* in private as long as they were just innocently reading a book or indulging in some needlework?

The effect grew more obvious as by the minute it got darker out. The sun set sudden and for keeps when the sky to the west was so clear, and one spectatcular blonde with bodacious bare tits was tempting, even to a romantic like Longarm, as she sat there reading her Bible in the cool of the evening near her open window.

Some cowhands dismounted just up the way to whoop their way up six steps to a green door and pound with the big brass knocker. Longarm was in earshot as the door opened and a discreet male voice called out more gently, "Welcome to the party, good sirs. But please don't . . . ah, disturb the neighbors."

One of the waddies gave a whoop, turned to shoot some holes in the sky, but thought better of it when he spotted Longarm's badge.

He gulped, said, "Evening, Sheriff!" and holstered his gun to go in and take his beating like a man.

Longarm chuckled softly as he strode on, breaking out his wallet as he unpinned the badge. He put it back in place with his wallet ID lest he put a crimp in D Street. It was none of his beeswax how they ran their dinky town, and he'd been in towns run less tidy.

There was no way to stop young sports away from home with pocket jingle to go easy on their drinking, gambling, and whoring around. But Dodge had its deadline, and in Tombstone, Marshal White kept the whores east of Sixth Street and allowed no soliciting out of doors. But there were other towns like Bodie where the whores ran down Main Street in their underwear with results any professional lawman could see coming. It was said Bodie ate a man a day for breakfast, and on one memorable weekend when not a soul had been killed, the local newspapers crowed how a "New Christian Spirit" seemed to be settling in.

San Bernardino seemed to have been tamed about right. Old hands still talked about how Abilene, Kansas, had put itself out of business as a trail town by taming itself down tedious.

There was more to being a lawman than just being a spoil-sport.

As he approached his hotel, he saw that same young squirt with the buckboard loading the same with baggage as two ladies stood by on the walk. You could see by the lamplight spilling out across the same they both had tolerable faces. You couldn't say one way or the other about what might or might not lie hidden inside a loose, dark travel duster. Long-arm didn't ask if they were headed down to the tracks to catch a train. It was none of his beeswax, and if it had been, there'd have been no better place for ladies coming out of a transient hotel to be headed at that hour.

The squirt nodded at Longarm as he approached. When the tall lawman was within easy conversing range, the squirt asked, "Say, might a lady with red hair have gotten off that westbound SP with you, earlier today, mister?"

Longarm shook his head and replied, "You were there. I got off alone."

The squirt said, "That's what I thought. That's what I told 'em."

Longarm asked, "Told who? A redhead you say they were looking for?"

The squirt said, "That's how they descripted the lady they had been expecting. Redhead, wearing a travel duster like these here ladies and, oh, yeah, a straw hat with a half veil."

Longarm nodded and said, "There was such a lady on that train with me. She never got off here because she went on to San Fernando, as I recall. You say there were two gents waiting for her at the flag stop this afternoon?"

The squirt said, "Not exactly. Older lady in a Berlin carriage and a Mex driver about my age. They'd been waiting in the shade of a live oak in a vacant lot near the tracks. Reckon they just set there, sort of puzzled, 'til I got back and they could ask me if I'd seen anybody else but you get off. The older lady sounded dumbfounded. The Mex kid just sat there looking dumb. I got the feeling his boss lady suspected I was holding out on her. I mean, you were there, mister! Did you see me hit a redheaded lady over the head and throw her aboard my open-to-the-sky buckboard bed with your saddle this afternoon?"

Longarm smiled thinly and said, "Not hardly. But I suspect I know what must have happened. You wouldn't know how I might get in touch with the worried lady in the Berlin, would you?"

The squirt said, "Sure I would. Ask at the Arrow Head Livery. I never saw her before, but that's surely where she hired that Berlin and a Mex to drive it."

One of the ladies with a train to catch called out to ask the squirt what the problem was. Longarm ticked his hat brim to them, allowed he was sorry, and walked around them so's they could get out of town, the lucky gals.

He went on in and asked the room clerk for directions to the Arrow Head Livery. The clerk said it was over on F Street, down the block from the Arrowhead Livery, closer to Fifth Street. Longarm thanked him and, seeing the night was still young, headed over that way as he got out his badge and pinned it on again.

Once he had himself looking more official, he took himself to the Arrow Head Livery Stable and Corral to see that, sure enough, they had a Berlin along with three shays, a surrey, and four station wagons out back. He wasn't surprised when the night manager was able to produce a young driver named Ramon who backed every word that buckboard squirt had said.

Ramon said he often met trains with la Señora Ellison

who ran a boardinghouse for young ladies over on the far side of the freight yards, which in San Bernardino were the dusty expanse where freight wagons, not railroad cars, rolled in or out to load up or unload by the tracks.

Longarm handed out three-for-a-nickel cheroots and headed that way after consulting his watch. It wasn't too late to be calling on a place of business on a government matter, and if a landlady running a boardinghouse wanted to say it was, he'd be no worse off than if he had turned in to toss and turn without checking it out.

The wagon freight yards would have been confusing by daylight. As he picked his way through the swirling confusion of live and rolling stock, in motion or not, with night fires lit hither and yon, Longarm asked teamsters he passed whether they'd seen Esau Skaggs or Buckskin Jacobs of late.

Nobody he talked to that evening had. He made his way out the far end, studied the address he'd written in his notebook under a streetlamp, and found the boardinghouse he was looking for.

It was a tile-roofed two-story adobe structure built around a swell-smelling patio where a fountain pissed in the dark. You had to figure this out through a wrought-iron gate, because the street entrance with a lantern lit above it stood off to one side of the tempting glimpse into the mysterious depths where night-blooming jasmine was beating back the barnyard smells of the nearby freight wagon yards.

Seeing the welcoming lantern and a bell pull by the oaken door, Longarm gave it a yank. It took a spell, but then the door opened, and a vision in old Spanish lace opened the same to smile and greet him with, *"Bienvenido, El Brazo Largo.* Come in. We have been expecting you."

Chapter 36

Longarm had long since decided things had been mighty odd in old Spain before anyone had started writing history. The willowy green brunette said she was the housekeeper, Inez Robles Verdugo Montez y Montoya, and she only looked green when you weren't looking right at her. As in the case of the ripe peach complexion of Lolita, there were parts of Spain and Spain alone where the pale brunettes looked as if an oddly green light was shining on them. Folk who'd never met such Spanish folk before found them sort of spooky. But they just grew that shade natural in some parts of old Spain.

When you looked right at Inez, she just looked ivory pale in her black Spanish lace. She led him back through what smelled more like a church than any boardinghouse and ushered him in where an older lady who looked as Spanish, albeit not as green around the gills, said she was Anna Maria Ellison, and that explained her Spanish ways. She was dressed in black widow's weeds. Longarm felt no call to ask how come she'd married an Anglo. Anyone could see the cuss had been rich.

She invited him to sit by her side on the sofa with a low rosewood coffee table in front of them already piled with nachos and a pitcher of sangria. The younger but just as severe-looking Inez stood near the doorway with her arms folded as Doña Anna Maria poured, explaining how they'd put two and two together as news of his being in town spread like spilled sangria across the tablecloth of San Bernardino's Hispanic population. She said, "We have been expecting *Tio* Sam to send the best, and when we heard of the shooting on E Street, we knew he had!"

Longarm modestly replied, "You just said news travels

fast here in San Berdoo, ma'am. How come you've been expecting me?"

She said, "Other lawmen were here weeks ago. Some women who roomed with us a while as they waited for transportation north across the Mojave never arrived at their destination. As I told those other lawmen when they showed me their lists, some of them, not all, but some, stayed here under different names than they gave the men who expected them at the end of their long trips. When we heard you were here in town, we wished to know whether you have any idea what it all means!"

He said, "That makes a heap of us, ma'am, starting with lonesome swains, or more Bluebeards than the odds of chance allow for. How many boarders have you got here tonight?"

She said, "Three. All working here in San Bernardino. We were expecting a guest from Yuma to arrive this afternoon. When she wrote to make her reservations, she explained she wasn't certain how long she might be here. She explained her intended had arranged for her to join a wagon train north from here. Her name was . . . Do you remember, Inez?"

The tall green brunette said, "Culhane, I think. I'm sure she gave Carmen as her first name."

Longarm asked, "Did this Miss Carmen say or ask for advice as to which wagon master she wanted to head north with?"

The Widow Ellison said, "Good heavens, I run a boardinghouse, not a travel agency. So ladies staying here come and go as they choose with whomever they choose. Not that I stand for any male guests in those rooms I let out, I hope you undrerstand!"

Longarm allowed he did and asked if those earlier lawmen might have established just how many of those missing mailorder brides had roomed or roomed and boarded there.

She sniffed and said, "I only offer room and board, or bed and a good breakfast if they only mean to stay the night. I seldom cater to such guests, of course. I ask for a week's room and board in advance. But now and then when they've

248

made their connections that way, they may leave in as little as an overnight stay."

"You have a hotel register, ma'am?" he asked.

Anna Maria Ellison laughed lightly and replied, "Surely you jest? I don't pretend this is a hotel, either. I simply took to offering room and board from time to time in this large, lonely house, and I guess word got around. I have those semipermanent working girls on monthly rates of course, and now I wish I'd never agreed to take in those . . . flighty out-of-town girls. When do you want to search my property, Marshal Long?"

Longarm replied, *"Deputy* Marshal, and why would I want to search your property on you, Miss Anna Maria?"

She sniffed and said, "To make certain Inez and me never posioned them at the dining tabe or strangled them in their beds, of course. I know we're under suspicion of murder or worse, here!"

Longarm sipped some sangria to gather his thoughts before he assured her with a smile, "One or more of those missing women wired ahead well north of here, ma'am. That latest vanishment is easier to explain. I met up with Carmen Culhane on that same train from Yuma. Soon as she heard about trouble on the Old Spanish Trail, she decided to go on to a funeral in San Fernando instead."

Anna Maria looked relieved and said, "Oh, thank you for telling us! We've been so worried! But she never said anything in her letter about having kin in San Fernando."

Longarm said, "She don't. It seems she's sort of impulsive. You'd have taken her for less flighty, had you met her, Miss Anna Maria, but to hear her tell it, one day she sells a going business to run off to Montana, and the next thing you know, she's on her way to San Fernando."

The two Spanish-American women exchanged knowing looks. The older one said, "Those other lawmen said some of our recent boarders have been . . . impulsive indeed. But none of them ever made mention of being mail-order brides when they wrote they'd be here in San Bernardino indefinitely. I'm not sure I'd want to be mixed up with women that . . . flighty."

Inez sniffed and opined, "If a woman is ready to exchange

wedding vows with a man she's never laid eyes on, think what a handsome young stranger might talk her into on a hayride!"

The three of them smiled knowingly at the picture. Longarm rephrased his questions to establish more certainly that neither of them could say which missing bride had gone over the pass into the great beyond with a particular party. Some of the names he reeled off sounded sort of half familiar to them. But when Anna Maria Ellison said they never offered room and board to teamsters, he believed her.

As he sipped more sangria, a Spanish summer drink whipped up from ice, fruit punch, and red wine, the word translated as *bloody*, old Anna Maria said, "I insist you swear out a search warrant and go over this propery from top to bottom! You know you suspect those girls are being waylaid by someone they trust. If not Inez and me, then surely by the people they've been traveling through uninhabited wilderness with!"

"The thought had crossed my mind," Longarm admitted, adding, "Then I run into too much eliminating."

"You what?" they asked as one.

He explained, "You just now said you have regular boarders here all the time, and it'll be easier for me to find out if they'd be working gals or wild and crazy ax murderesses. So, no offense, you other two ladies would have a hard row to hoe, bumping off and disposing of mail-order brides on these premises."

Anna Maria inisted, "I still want you to make certain they're not out in the patio or under the floor tiles. What about all those huge freight wagons? Those other lawmen said they couldn't buy a whole wagon train conspiring to bury dead bodies by the side of the Old Spanish Trail, but what if some fiend hid his victims in his overloaded wagon and waited until he had a chance to unload, long after the innocent ones lost track of the wagons at the end of the journey?"

Longarm started to say that notion was too disgusting to consider. Then he was glad he read so much when he ran low on drinking money by the end of the month. For he had read how, early in the century during the age of fighting sail, dead English sailors had been buried at sea or, leastways, fed to the crabs and hagfish on the bottom, while the French sailors who died at sea had been buried in the damp ballast sand to sort of marinate in bilgewater 'til their ship came in, sooner or later, and what was left could be planted in a proper Papist graveyard.

The history writer had figured the smell of death would be soaked up by the sand the body was packed in and so, what if you stuffed a dead body in a barrel with a lot of sand or, better yet, rock salt, to get rid of later, anytime later, up Ogden way?

Sipping sangria to wash the nasty taste from his mouth, Longarm told the two women, "I wish you hadn't given me such a sick notion to eliminate! Getting rid of a stinky barrel of salt would be even easier by the shores of the Great Salt Lake!"

He had to go on and tell them about French naval practices. Being of the same faith, neither found the notion of storing dead bodies in the hold of a ship or under the floor of your church as morbid as they might have around that little country church in the hollow.

That reminded him how often he'd found his views on other topics at odds with folk raised different. He'd learned in his travels it wasn't safe to assume others felt the same way about things just because they seemed to have as much common sense as yourself. There were no brass tacks scientific reasons why a Navajo would let his children starve to death before he'd serve them fresh-caught trout, or as far as that went, how white scouts could risk their scalps refusing a tasty offer of fresh-slaughtered puppy from a highly pissed Lakota host.

He asked the Spanish-American women, seeing they were women as well as followers of different ways, how they felt about this notion of mail-order courting at long distance.

Neither seemed to think much of the notion. The sultry Inez, who'd have no trouble getting most any man she set her sights on, thought a woman who'd agree to marry and bed a man she'd never laid eyes on was no better than a common prostitute.

She pontificated, "All they've negotiated by mail order is

251

the price. Those unfortunate women over on D Street will make love to a man they just met for a dollar. These missing mail-order brides everyone is so worried about expect a man they've yet to meet to agree he'll support them for the rest of their natural lives in exchange for *meeting* him! I've read those disgusting want ads, most requiring the poor, lonely sap to pay the way of a total stranger to where she can set down beside him and decide whether she even wants to hold his hand!"

The older Anna Maria sighed and said, "They all sound lost and lonely, if you ask me. We all feel lost and lonely, sometimes. But most of us have more common sense. When you get down to cases, isn't common sense, or the lack of it, all that distinguishes those mail-order brides from from the rest of us?"

"Not me!" flounced Inez, "I've never been able to walk down the street without some total stranger trying to undress me with his eyes. Can you see me writing love letters to some fool too awkward to just ask some girl in his very own town to have supper there in town at any nice restaurant?"

Longarm started to ask about awkward gents who didn't have the pocket jingle to treat local gals to sit-down suppers.

The question answered itself and raised another about miserly sex maniacs, as in . . .

> There was an old hermit named Dave
> Who kept a dead whore in his cave
> He said, I'll admit, she smells quite a
> bit,
> But consider the money I save!

Finishing his sangria and politely covering the glass with his palm when Anna Maria made as if to pour another, Longarm thanked the both of them for what they'd eliminated and the extra eliminating they'd stuck him with as he rose to leave.

The greenish but glamorous Inez showed him out to the street, intimating she wouldn't much mind if he wanted to come calling again. Her point that good-looking gals who wanted to meet men didn't need to get aboard a covered wagon had been well taken.

He just bade her a polite good night at the street entrance and got going, the night still being young but not so young he could afford to waste time flirting.

Not when his own wagon party, including the auburn-haired Rose Ann, who liked to get on top, would be arriving most any minute now!

He figured they'd been held up along the way, as he had, by side issues or detours. There was no way to get in touch with them before they got to San Bernardino, though. He figured they'd surely made it past Barstow in the middle of the Mojave to the north if they hadn't all been swallowed up by whatever ate mail-order brides out yonder! For the telegraph lines ran to Barstow, but there was no way to wire anybody on the trail those poles rose mile after mile beside.

Threading his way back through the freight wagon yards, where things had calmed down some by then, Longarm was stopped by a burly teamster who asked, "Might you be that lawman in search of that old mule thief of my heart, Buckskin Jacobs?"

Longarm allowed he was and introduced himself.

The teamster had heard of him. He stuck out a hamlike paw to say, "Put her there, Longarm! Then come over by our fire and tell us why you're after poor old Buckskin!"

As he followed the slightly shorter and way broader gent to a nearby fire where others sat waiting for the pot to boil, Longarm explained he had no federal charges against Buckskin Jacobs as yet.

Hunkering around their fire with rough-cut but amiable sorts who seemed to be friends of the well-known Jacobs, Longarm said he only wanted to compare notes with old Buckskin about one of the few missing mail-order brides they could tie to a particular wagon party.

Longarm said, "This one gal, I got her name here somewheres, wired her intended she was on her way with Buckskin Jabobs's wagons. After that, she never showed up."

He let that sink in before he said, "I just today met another mail-order bride who'd been *planning* on heading up to Ogden with that same Buckskin Jacobs. She changed her mind,

so we can eliminate her. I still want to talk to him about this
. . . lessee, Winnie Mae Waterman?"

The jovial teamster who'd stopped him said, "Old Buckskin came in last week with beeswax and other Mormon shit
from the Mormon delta. You just missed him. He headed
back north day before yesterday. Won't be back down here
until next spring."

Another teamster said, "Our next run north will be the
last for this year. Ain't nobody *starts* across all that sand
after May Day."

The one who'd stopped Longarm nodded and said, "Old
Buckskin must be halfways to Barstow by now. You might
still be able to catch up with him by wire. No way on earth
you'll ever overtake him in the flesh as of now!"

Chapter 37

The trig was simple. Barstow was eighty-odd miles out
across the Mojave with the noonday trail breaks getting
longer. Buckskin Jacobs and his heavy wagons would be
averaging twenty miles a day. Hence at the moment he'd be
camped on the desert a day short of Barstow and the telegraph station he might or might not have call to visit.

A railroad train, if they ever got around to that line across
the Mojave they kept jawing about, would get Longarm that
far in less than three hours. But there wasn't any railroad, so
that eliminated that.

Lighting out aboard legged-up saddle mules, he could
push no more than fifty in one day to be stuck halfway with
jaded stock. There had to be a better way.

There was. The Banning Stages were to southern California what the Wells Fargo Stages were to northern California. Owned and operated by the Anglo family that owned

Catalina Island, Banning Stages carried mail and passengers places no railroad did yet, at an average speed of nine miles an hour 'round the clock, or ten hours to Barstow if a Banning stage *ran* to Barstow.

They told him back at his hotel one did and, better yet, one left at midnight to roll into Barstow around noon after a cool run through the wee small and early morning hours.

Longarm had time to wire poor old Norm in Helena and save him and the taxpayers another wail about a missing mail-order bride before he hauled his saddle over to the San Bernardino Banning stop in case he had to play catch-up once they got him to Barstow.

Banning's San Bernardino stop near the railroad tracks was the usual team-swapping and passenger-watering adobe sprawl. Once he'd scouted up the night manager and paid his fare to Barstow, he toted his load to the waiting room, where another midnight passenger sat smoking on a long plank bench.

She was a brown-haired gal of around twenty-five, dressed up as if to put on a vaudeville skit about Calamity Jane, had Calamity Jane been pretty. This version was smoking a black stogie Billy Vail would have been proud of and introduced herself bold as brass as Miss Patty Crocker, who owned and operated her own livery in Barstow.

Longarm introduced himself and added, "I might want to hire riding stock off you if we get to Barstow too late."

She naturally wanted to know why. Telling her took halfway to the first stop-squat-and-drop at Hesperia on the Mojave side of the pass.

Tearing downhill behind a fresh team, they followed the general trend of the Mojave River, not as high as it had been, way higher than it was fixing to be in high summer, and in any case doomed to dry up and blow away off the sun-baked alkali flats in the dead heart of the desert, downstream from Barstow, praise the Lord.

They made good time to Victorville. The sun caught their coach like a cockroach crossing a kitchen floor just north of Oro Grande, and by the time it rose halfway to noon, the two of them were covered with dust and suffering mummified tongues.

Longarm had asked the crew as they were boarding, so along about ten, the shotgun messenger yelled down, "Wagons ho! Coming at us down the left side! We can slow enough for you to jump as I toss down your saddle. Yes or no?"

Longarm leaned out on that side to see what surely looked like old Captain Burbank, Esau Skaggs, and Hudson Livermore dressed like Buffalo Bill out ahead of the long train of wagons to their rear. There was no sign of those Paiute scouts. Longarm wasn't surprised.

He yelled up to the jehu, "Keep going!" and then as the three riders recognized who was waving at them from the oncoming coach, Longarm had time to yell, "Wait for me in Berdoo! Got to check something, up in Barstow!"

Then they were heading in opposite directions as Burbank, he thought, yelled something back at him.

Resuming his seat, Longarm told the Barstow gal he was riding with, "Yelling in air this dry takes a lot out of one. Am I allowed to belly flop in your Mojave River once we reach the end of this line?"

She croaked, "Only if you move over and make room for this sun-baked Patty. I know that ain't funny, but I'm too hot and thirsty to come up with anything better. Might a cold shower and bottled beer from an ice chest save you? I got both on sale at my livery."

He croaked, "You got a deal. How in thunder do you manage *ice* in a place like Barstow, Miss Patty?"

She wanly replied, "You couldn't *live* in a place like Barstow without ice. So a New England Yankee with a bore well sells nothing else in Barstow. I buy my ice from him and pay to have bottled beer hauled from the railroad back in San Berdoo."

He laughed and said he'd been told California gals insisted on calling it San Bernardino. She sniffed and said she didn't hold with them old Spanish airs affected by greasers and snobs, adding, "Sometimes they're the same thing out our way. Some of the hoity-toity landed families got so hoity-toity when tough Anglos married up with land grant heiresses and held more land than you could shake a stick at against all comers. So now poor whites who've never owned an acre

256

try to sound old Californio by pronouncing everything as in the San Joaquin–La Jolla joke."

Longarm had to confess he'd never heard that one.

Patty said, "Easterner talking to a stuck-up Californio in a Chicago saloon says he visited out yonder and thought the San Joaquin was a pretty valley whilst La Jolla was a pretty beach. Being a speaker of the English language, he pronounced the *J*s as in *Jack* until the stuck-up Californio corrects him, explaining *Joaquin* is pronounced *Wakeen* and *La Jolla* as *La Hoya*. Then he asks the dude when he was last out on the coast. So the dude says—"

"Woon and Hooligh." Longarm cut in with a chuckle, adding, "Reckon a lady I met aboard a train was putting on airs at that. Considering how high she must have really valued herself."

The mannishly dressed Patty impishly asked how well he'd gotten to know that hoity-toity aboard his train.

Longarm laughed and said, "If only. She wasn't bad-looking. But it seems she was spoken for, at least until she changed her mind at the last minute after insisting we were gettting off in San Bernardino."

"Wagons ho! On your left!" yelled the shotgun messenger.

This time they both leaned out but only waved at the southbound party since neither of them knew anybody in it.

Longarm explained about the lady on the train, and that got them back on the topic of his run up to Barstow. Patty said, "Lord knows I needed the company, Custis. But you sure have run yourself around Robin Hood's barn after those missing women the world will never really miss."

He shrugged and said, "Desperate wallflowers have the right to go on living, whether anybody wants to dance with them or not."

She coughed up dusty phlegm, spat it out the window, and said that was a mighty sweet thing to say, adding, "I was raised to be more charity-hearted. Things happen to a woman grown, and I reckon by the time she can take care of herself, she forgets what it felt like when she needed someone to take care of her."

The shotgun messenger yelled, "Wagons ho! Passing 'em to your right!"

So they leaned out that side and, sure enough, they were overtaking dusty freight wagons behind wearily walking teams. It was the changing teams every fifteen miles that allowed stagecoaches to roll at their steady trot.

So they were passing wagon after wagon at the relative speed of a swiftly striding man pacing past wagons parked along a curb. As they passed, Longarm yelled out, asking if they were the Buckskin Jacobs party. Some called something back. The clearest answer sounded like "Up yours, too!" and then they were out ahead of the wagon train. But the shotgun messenger yelled down, "That was Buckskin Jacobs out front on a gray mule! You want to jump out?"

Longarm yelled back, "I'll wait up for 'em in Barstow, wrapped around iced beer. How long are we talking about?"

The man more familiar with the run opined, "Us? Less'n two hours. Them? Three or four!"

So Longarm settled back with a dusty smile to say, "Like that old church song says, farther along, and it won't be all that much longer, now."

She said, "I can promise the beer. I'm not sure what you want from Buckskin Jacobs, though."

He said, "Winnie Mae Waterman. She wired her intended she was on her way across this desert with Buckskin Jacobs. She never arrived. I want to know what Buckskin Jacobs has to say about her."

Patty whistled and said, "I know old Buck, just to talk to, of course. Do you think he murders women when nobody's watching?"

Longarm said, "It's more likely he just lost track of one. Like the song says, farther along."

"We'll know more about it, amen," she finished for him with a sad little smile, adding, "Life seems so simple when we worried so much about going over the lines in our Sunday school coloring books. You say there's at least twenty of those poor desperate drabs missing, and I keep seeing all these ghastly visages staring up at the desert stars that just don't care. Have you ever come across a dead body left out on the desert, Custis?"

He soberly nodded.

She still said, "They don't rot away to dry bones. They don't preserve like Egyptian royalty. They turn into something awful, in between. You got to catch the son of a bitch, Custis!"

He said he aimed to try, and then she was in his arms like a mighty dusty rag doll, crying fit to bust as he did his best to comfort her.

As near as her sobs, sniffles, and expectorations made sense, she was a grass widow trying to run her small-town business alone after running a hard-drinking, skirt-chasing man out of said town with her dear old Dad's .36 Navy Colt. She swore she'd been trying to hit him and vowed she would the next time, having practiced some on tin cans since the last time she'd missed the no-good trash.

He had her calmed down and back in her own seat by the time their coach rolled into Barstow. At her invite, he carried his saddle and her gladstone up Main Street to her livery, where a couple of Mojave breeds still had her property and remuda of scrub stock secure as usual.

When Longarm asked who rode such pet food, no offense, it developed she'd been hiring out lots of rides at day rates to boomers interested in that new silver strike over in Wall Street Canyon in the multicolored Calico Mountains. They were still trying to prove the color up in that canyon. It would mean big things for Barstow if they struck it rich. Barstow would be no worse off if they never. That was life, out their way.

Dumping their loads as soon as they were back in the shade with the thermometer standing at 110° in the shade, they didn't go for any iced beer before they'd showered, together, platonic, rather than stand on ceremony just because she might be concave where he was convex. The water running over them from her roof tank was only slightly cooler than the hot, dry air all around. But by the time they were cooled down sane again, she was fluttering some about not being in the habit of showering with gents she'd never kissed for heaven's sake.

So he kissed her, hugging her soap-slicked, naked flesh against his own, and they might have done more than kiss, had there been time. But somewhere in the distance, a pistol or a teamster's whip was popping ever closer. So Longarm said he had to get dressed and go see about Winnie Mae Waterman.

Patty Crocker said she'd be waiting there with the iced beer.

Leaving his jacket off but strapping on his six-gun and pocketing the derringer, Longarm stepped back outside—it felt like opening a furnace door, and it wasn't *May Day* yet—to cover the short distance down Main Street, which was not only the main street but about the only street of any substance in the tiny desert town, to scout Buckskin Jacobs out from among the dusty teamsters trying to water man and beast at once from the one water pump they had to work with amid six or seven acres of dried dung and pulverized grit.

When he caught up with him, Buckskin Jacobs was wearing a thin cotton shirt. Buckskin Jacobs was no fool. He suggested they talk about missing mail-order brides in the nearby Mother Road Saloon if Uncle Sam was buying. As they entered the comparative coolness of shade above the temperature of a fatal fever, the crusty freight hauler said, "Before you pay for a drink, old son, I've had this conversation with others about that same fool Winnie Mae Waterman."

Longarm ordered two iced beers as they bellied up to the bar and allowed he'd like to hear it again.

The wagon master the missing woman had wired she was traveling with took a healthy swig of suds, gasped, "Oh, yeah, I'm coming! As for any Winnie Mae anything traveling far as here with me at any time, I still say she never. And no, I couldn't be mistaken, and no, I don't lose track of one case of goods or one human life entrusted to my care! What sort a wagon master would lose good-looking women in the desert as if they were loose change and he had a hole in his pocket? It ain't possible, and as I told those others, I keep lists of everybody traveling with me, and nobody named Winnie Mae Anything has ever been so listed. I don't care what she wired her infernal boyfriend from here in Barstow about me. If she said she was crossing the Mojave with this child, she was lying!"

Longarm frowned and said, "Lying or mixing you up with

another party she was really with. You're sort of famous, no offense, and a greenhorn hearing such a distinctive name bandied about . . . Yeah, that works, sort of."

Buckskin Jacobs said, "That's the first sensible word on the subject I've heard from you young jaspers. You're talking to the wrong man about a woman he knows nothing about. Sorry, sonny, but you chased us all this way for no good reason at all!"

And that was the way Longarm felt about it until he got back to the livery to find Patty had dismissed her help for the day and put more beer on ice, even as she'd been drying off without a stitch.

But in point of fact, they never got around to more than kissing before the damned sun went down so things could cool off outside and heat up inside, sort of sudden.

Chapter 38

As consenting adults who'd gotten to know each other a spell by the time they knew each other in the biblical sense, Longarm and Patty Crocker wound up in bed with some beer like old pals, and after that, since neither had approached the bed through a field of daisies with cupids plucking harps, they approached the subject as skilled riders out to give each other a good time.

So a good time was had by all as the desert air grew downright chilly, and you had to move fast to keep warm outside the bedcovers.

They had the covers up over them as they shared one of her cigars, after Patty had rejected his brand of cheroots as pointless puffing.

Fondling his old organ grinder under the cotton flannel as they let it rest a spell, Patty said, "You sure know how to pleasure a woman, Custis. How long do you reckon I'll be able to hold you here as my prisoner of love in my desert lair?"

He said, "I read that same book. I fear I won't be able to stay that long, Miss Patty. I'd like to. I want to. I can't. I got to catch up with those wagons we passed out on the desert. They'll in San Berdoo by now."

She suggested, "Fuck 'em. Let 'em find their own true loves. We know you're never going to solve the mystery of those missing women now that the desert crossings are ending for the year. None of them vanished as soon as you lawmen put your backs into looking for 'em. The killer or killers has quit killing. The bodies are scattered from hell to breakfast across hundreds of miles of wide-open spaces! Can't you see it ain't no use now?"

He snuggled her closer and put the stogie to her lips as he told her, "You're likely right. Unless Captain Burbank and the others now know something I don't know, we've been over the whole trail without cutting sign. It gets more hopeless down the other side of the San Bernardino Mountains. Them missing gals funneled into that one bottleneck from all over the Southwest. Backtracking any of them from San Berdoo to where they were sitting when they first decided to answer a proposal in a newspaper sounds sort of complicated."

She laughed, told him it was downright impossible, and snuffed the cigar to duck under the covers and puff on something bigger. So the next they knew, they were too excited to worry about tomorrow.

But of course tomorrow came, as it always did, to fuck up the poetry of François Villon and Omar Khayyám, with another Banning stage set to run for San Bernardino at sundown.

Since it was too hot by noon to even hold hands, Longarm took hot and stuffy advantage of their Western Union shed to get off all the wires he could think of, playing old Billy Vail's spider game of wire, wire, what can I feel out yonder on the wire?

The Western Union telegrapher rebelled by midafternoon

and went home to strip and balance some ice on his gut, he confided.

Longarm and Patty found it helped, albeit neither was up to getting really bawdy with the ice, as hot as it was. They just parted friendly before it got cool enough, again, and Patty said he'd always find her beer as cold and the rest of her as hot for him, if ever he came by again.

The coach ride back to San Bernardino was less fun, even half drunk on all that iced beer. He had nobody to talk to and so many questions on his mind.

By dawn he was starting to doze off, the way one did with a skinful after chasing the same questions around the mulberry bush a spell. To really get your back into a worry there had to be some possible answers to the sons of bitches. A man could worry swell about a coming showdown with a man or whether a gal you admired put out or not. But there were just no answers to such questions as how high was up, how long was forever, and what in tarnation had happened to all those mail-order brides!

The only advantage of the southbound run, and likely the reason they timed it that way, was that by the time the sun came up to catch them on steeper grades, they were at higher altitude, which meant more than latitude in the wide-open spaces of the great Southwest. Over an hour of the morning run was over the tree-shaded pass through the mountains, and then they were loping downhill into San Bernardino at last.

Captain Burbank was waiting alone at the Banning Station. When Longarm and his baggage got down to ask how come, Burbank explained that all the Washington jaspers, disgusted reporters, and those other Mormon lawmen had caught the Southern Pacific west in hopes of catching a northbound steamer due to leave San Pedro soon for Frisco Bay and cross-country rail connections.

Burbank said, "My boys were willing to stick it out here. I told them to go on home the easy way. They've been away from their homes and families long enough on this wild-goose chase. What did you find out back there in Barstow? We weren't able to find anything out. Nobody we talked to remembered one of those missing women."

He smiled wearily and added, "On the other hand, you'd hardly expect a woman passing through with a wagon train to run around telling the whole town she was a mail-order bride about to turn up missing!"

Longarm said, "Winnie Mae Waterman and two others on our list did send wires from Barstow. Their Western Union clerk said he'd never forgive me but dug out records he'd kept because the wires had been sent collect. Such records are held on to until the bills for that quarter have all been settled. The other gals who wired ahead they were coming were named Sally Sanchez and Myrtle Thalmann."

Burbank said, "Names sound Spanish and Dutch. You asked, of course?"

Longarm said, "I did. He said he couldn't remember either but knew they'd been by because their wires had gone in care of the poor saps waiting for them. Nobody there could pin down exactly which wagon party any of them were with. I believed Buckskin Jacobs when he swore Winnie Mae Waterman never went anywhere with him."

Burbank made a wry face and said, "We don't have as much as a wire along the way on any of the others. There've *been* no others since our full investigation was ordered. Whatever was going on has ceased and desisted. Open case with no likely wrap. It happens that way better than half the time. I only hung back in hopes you'd had some reason for your yelling at us like that in the middle of the infernal Mojave! I mean to send a wire to Salt Lake, asking permission to fold my hand and get up from the table. We don't hold with card games with strangers anyhow."

Longarm said, "You go on ahead, then. I mean to go over to my hotel to store this shit and treat myself to a tub bath and a change of duds before I decide my next move."

Burbank scowled and demanded, "What next move? It's *over,* Longarm! Like I said, it happens that way, and when it does, there's nothing you can do about it. We're never going to find out what happened to the princes in the Tower of London or the lost dauphin of France. Sometimes folk just vanish. Haven't you ever heard of that man who walked around those horses?"

Longarm replied, "You mean that diplomatic courier traveling by stagecoach across Europe? Every lawman's heard about that poser!"

The Utah lawman said, "Heard about it. Never solved it to this day. The other passengers saw the diplomat get out the far side of the coach at a rest stop and walk around the front of the team to go on into the inn with everybody."

"But he never made it." Longarm agreed. "They saw him walk around the horses and never saw him again, as if he'd vanished into thin air in the middle of the road. Ain't that a bitch? Those repeating the story are leaving out something everybody missed at the time, of course."

"Oh? And what might that've been?" the older lawman asked.

Longarm said, "Can't say. Wasn't there. Wasn't there when Winnie Mae Waterman, Sally Sanchez, or Myrtle Thalmann were last heard from in the middle of the Mojave Desert, neither. That's why I ain't ready to say what might have happened to them yet. All I know for certain is that something must have."

The morose Mormon said, "You weren't the only lawman scouting a town the size of Barstow for any sign of a score of women! Esau Skaggs had a fit when we held him there forty-eight hours. We had the manpower to canvass all around afoot or mounted up, and we did. As you must have noticed, you could throw a snowball from one end of Main Steet to the other if it ever snowed there and—"

"As a matter of fact, it *does* snow on the Mojave on occasion." Longarm cut in, conceding, "Not down here on the Colorado Desert, but do go on."

The older Mormon made a most unsaintly remark under his breath and said, "We talked to most everyone in a mighty small town. We rode over into the Calico canyons and had us some careful looks down abandoned try holes. It was as if none of those missing women had been anywhere near the infernal Mojave Desert!"

Longarm said, "Someone who lived out in the middle of it suggested how much of it there is to mummify a body behind a clump of greasswood fifty yards off the trail. What happened to those Digger scouts, by the way?"

The Utah rider shrugged and said, "Couldn't get them to

scout past Las Vegas. They said it was no longer their sort of country, and they didn't much care for the Diggers ahead. Same way of life but a whole different lingo and the wrong kind of medicine. They wouldn't have done us much good farther south, anyway."

Longarm didn't comment. He'd been raised to respect his elders, and some old boys took offense when you intimated they might have made a stupid move.

He just said, *"Bueno,* we'll have to take it on faith all those miles and miles and miles and miles betwixt Barstow and Las Vegas have been searched thorough as old fringy Hudson Livermore ordered. Everyone else in the party made it on over to the tracks with no complexications, I take it?"

Burbank smiled thinly and said, "The last I saw of them, your Miss Rose Ann with the auburn hair and quiet ways seemed mighty taken with that young reporter, Miles Hovak."

Longarm smiled gamely and said, "At least old Miles got something out of his long snipe hunt. I told him on occasion you really got to bag a snipe. But I reckon when he saw all the others giving up—"

"By this evening I'll know if I have permission to give up," the older lawman cut in, adding, "Unless they forbid me, I mean to catch the sunset run for San Pedro and board the next coastal steamer up to Frisco Bay. You?"

Longarm said, "Reckon I'll sit in another deal or more. Sunset, you say? If I ain't found anything new by then, I may come down to the flag stop to wave adios."

And that was about the way things happened. Back at his hotel, he wiped down his saddle with a damp rag before he hauled it upstairs. Then he unpacked fresh denim along with fresh underwear and toted it all down the hall to the *moderne* bath they advertised with genuine English indoor plumbing from the famous Crapper Firm in London town.

Once he'd locked himself in, he ran warm water over his Stetson and set his six-gun aside to rinse off his gun belt. He hung it up beside his clean, wet hat. Rinsed his boots off to set beside the big claw-foot tub and just dumped his trail-dusted duds on a clean towel from his hired room. He set his folded clean duds on the seat of the commode and pissed down the tub drain before he plugged it to run himself a serious bath. It took a change of water to get clean. But at last he was. So he got dressed, with his damp felt and leather already half dry in the thirsty desert air, and went on down feeling like a human being again.

He dropped his dirty duds off at a Cantonese laundry, ordering them to wash and fold the hotel's towel while they were at it.

His stage having arrived around noon, it was late for dinner but early for supper, so he sort of had both at a Mex joint he found on E Street, ordering *higado con ceballes* for dinner and a light supper of chicken enchiladas with his black coffee.

It was still early enough to check for wires at the Western Union. Answers to his earlier messages were piling up on him in San Bernardino, now. He stuck some of the less urgent ones in his hip pocket to read later. The one saying he was to come on home if he still hadn't cut any sign required an answer. So he sent one.

That left him time to canvass teamsters over in the freight yards some more. He wasn't surprised to see all new faces. Nobody wanted to fight with him, nobody could tell him toad squat about losing anybody from their wagon trains on open desert, and all agreed the season for wagon traffic across the same was winding down for the summer. Nobody he talked to expected to make a return trip that year.

He picked up a bag of cactus candy for Captain Burbank to nibble aboard his train, or throw out the window, the old sourpuss, and ambled down to the tracks to sure enough spy the long drink of Mormon by the tracks with the San Bernardino flagman and his red signal flag.

As Longarm joined them, Burbank explained they were waiting on an eastbound to pass through on the single track before his westbound came out of its siding to the east. Longarm agreed it was a hell of a way to run a railroad.

The flag man said, "A lot you know of economics, then. Have you any idea what double tracking costs?"

Longarm mildly suggested, "Twice as much?"

The flagman said, "You know it. But cheer up, I see that eastbound coming and . . . yep, she's fixing to stop here, too."

Hence they could only stand there as the train Burbank wasn't interested in hissed to a halt to disgorge some crates, a little baggage, and four passengers, both couples. Two women in travel dusters from the same catalogue escorted by two gents in matching summer-weight seersucker suits.

Longarm didn't laugh at anybody as he bent to give Burbank a hand with his brace of saddlebags and a valise. As he straightened up, his eyes met those of the henna redhead in the lead. She stared back at him as if she'd seen a ghost and made as if to just walk by. Longarm ticked his hat brim to her and said, "Well, howdy, Miss Trixie! What might you be doing here in San Berdoo?"

Trixie Mondale, the gal he'd met in Provo after her narrow escape from the late Haji Bin Omar, never answered Longarm.

With her eyes all ablaze with fear and hate, Trixie shouted at the top of her lungs, "Don't just *stand* there! Kill the fucking moose!"

Chapter 39

Caught flat-footed with a friendly smile on his face and Burbank's valise in his gun hand, Longarm knew he was only trying as he let go the baggage to go for his own gun, cross-draw, while the sport next to Trixie was already drawing his shoulder-holstered "Russian" S&W Schofield model 3, and then he wasn't, because Captain Burbank had fired over Longarm's shoulder to blow half the galoot's face away!

The second one got off a wild shot from behind Trixie as the other gal took off screaming. Longarm was the one who nailed that one to jackknife him with a round just below the belly button. So the second and third double-action rounds parted his hair and reamed out his spinal column for him as

Burbank yelled, "Halt right where you are, ma'am!" and when she just ran faster, he fired again.

He was later to say he'd aimed to hit the running woman in the legs. From the way her fashionable Paris hat went soaring, it was clear he'd nailed her with a spine shot. She hit the dust before her hat to never move another muscle.

Closer in, transfixed with shock amid the swirls of gunsmoke, the rusty-headed Trixie stared owl-eyed at Longarm as she stammered, "Oh, botheration! It wasn't supposed to turn out like this!"

Then she collapsed in a heap to lie just as still between the two male gunslicks.

In the smoky, stunned silence that suddenly set in, Captain Burbank numbly asked, "What happened?"

It was a good question.

The scared conductor had that eastbound moving out sudden. The local flagman was nowhere to be seen. But other figures were approaching, and Longarm broke out his badge before anyone could mistake which side of the law he might be on. Captain Burbank never put his Utah badge away.

Pointing his own gun muzzle at the dead rusty redhead at their feet, Longarm said, "Never laid eyes on the other three before. Met her up in Provo where she sold me a tale of woe. I see now it was meant to send me on a wild-goose chase. It did. Lucky for everyone but the late Haji Bin Omar and a few cohorts, I slipped in shit and came up smelling like roses."

"But why?" asked the Utah lawman. "If she was an enemy of that crazy Turk, who sent you after him to do what anyone would have expected you to do—"

"That wasn't the motive," Longarm cut in. "The motive was to have me looking somewhere else, anywhere else, for those missing mail-order brides. She implied she was one of them, who'd escaped from no such thing as a degenerate Turk, degenerate as Bin Omar was. She or more likely one of these armed pimps working with her and that other whore, had heard about Bin Omar and how loco he was. Instead of letting him play his madness out to its sure and certain end, they tried to sell me a tale of sex-starved Moslems kidnapping those women for their harems."

The Utah man wasn't slow. He gasped, "Just like they were trying sell the idea of fanatic Mormon elders forcing, let's face it, mighty desperate old maids!"

Longarm said, "You're learning. They were banking on the way outsiders assume the worst about gents with unsual views of love and marriage. A bunch of pool hall sports who'd wink at one of their members having an affair with a fourteen-year-old or fucking his best friend's wife are inclined to boil out of their cave with tar and feathers or worse when they hear some stable hand sucks cock. It ain't that you Saints get laid more often. Gents who brag about their weekly visits to the parlor house commence to run in circles after thier own tails when they hear of any man whose old woman don't weep and wail and slash her wrists when or if he beds another."

Starting to reload, he observed, "Same thing with Moslems. Some have sort of irritating habits to our way of thinking. Only the crazy ones go in for mass murder, so when you can't quite sell the notion of mad Mormon elders, a half-cracked Turk, sold on the notion of his own race being the master race, sure had me going for a while. But, for the record, Haji Bin Omar was a nasty son of a bitch content with only one woman. You had to have been there."

The same town lawman who'd responded to his saloon fight led the charge out across the dust toward the tracks. When he spied Longarm, he called out, "Things sure have gotten interesting since you showed up! Who did we just shoot it out with *this* time, pard?"

Longarm chuckled, introduced them to Burbank, and confessed, "I've only met the lady with the rusty hair before. Up in Provo. She gave her name as Theresa or Trixie Mondale. Can't say who shot her. There was a lot of that going around after she ordered the one with half a face to kill me."

Neither town lawman knew Trixie or the two men who who'd died along with her. But when one of the San Bernardino lawmen turned the other one over, he called, "I know this one. Works for Madame Dumont over on D Street. They called her French Lil on account her name was Lilie and she'd French you all the way for a slightly higher fee."

Captain Burbank said, "I thought they looked like fallen

women, but what does it all mean, Longarm?"

"I wish you hadn't asked that," his younger comrade at arms replied in a sincerely puzzled tone. For if that local lawman was right, and Longarm figured he ought to know the local whores, that dead denizen of their D Street turned over yet another wet rock crawling with new wriggles that made no sense.

Other townsmen were edging closer to get in on the fun. Longarm warned his fellow lawmen to mention no more names as he decided, "Miss rusty head, there, mistook my friendly surprise for my being on to her. That might mean the mystery ain't as mysterious as it seems. Have you ever mislaid, say, a key ring and hunted high and low, just missing it because it was in plain sight but not where you usually put it?"

They all agreed everyone knew that dumb feeling.

Longarm said, "Try this on for size. Knowing I was headed this way, and having heard I had a way with puzzles, they sent that rusty-headed sneak to head me off and hand me a bum steer. From here to Provo by wagon is one thing. What if she took a train from here to San Pedro, the steamer up to Frisco Bay, and beat me to Provo from the *north* by a slightly earlier train? What if she just handed me all that shit about coming up from here the hard way and meeting up with a mail-order groom who turned out to be a mad Turk, with an address they figured I'd be smart enough to locate?"

Captain Burbank nodded and said, "With results that didn't matter one way or the other to them, albeit things turned out well for those poor, unfortunate sons of Han. The motive was to split us up and keep us in the dark after they'd blown out the lights by simply leaving any other mail-order brides alone!"

"What's a mail-order bride?" a kid in the crowd asked.

An older townie hissed, "Shut up and listen. You might find out."

Another asked, "Say, ain't that French Lil over yonder oozing all that piss and blood?"

The older of the two town lawmen called out, "Sonny Davison, I'd be obliged if you'd run up to the square and tell Doc Silvers we need a deputy coroner down here right now. If I hear you've mentioned any of this to your sister working on D Street, I won't be obliged."

As the kid took off, the lawman who'd sent him running chuckled and told Longarm, "He ain't got no sisters, and his brother's a shop clerk."

Longarm was neither surprised nor optimistic about that. His earlier shoot-out up E Steet had made it over to Anna Maria's boardinghouse before he did. He wasn't expecting to surprise Madame Dumont with the news that one of her whores had been traveling in bad company.

He told Burbank, "If she headed north from Provo as I was chasing geese down Arizona way, she's had more than enough time to make it out to Sacramento by rail, to Frisco by river boat, or San Pedro by coastal steamer. Let's say she and these other unfortunates have been up to something over in Pueblo de Los Angeles they didn't think we ought to know about. Then let's say they came back here to San Berdoo, not expecting to see this child, got all flusterpated because Miss Trixie at the least thought I'd solved the mystery and, shit, how am I to solve it now, with all four of them dead?"

Burbank soothed, "We have solved *something*. We know, now, that this bottleneck through the mountains is the base, or close to the base of their whole sorry scheme!"

Longarm grunted. "That's what I was just saying. How am I to follow them on to their secret lair and mastermind, with them just laying there like that?"

Burbank suggested, "Let's go have a word with this Madame Dumont. She must know *something.*"

There came a lonesome whistle from the east. Longarm said, "Reckon I can ask. Ain't this your train coming in?"

The usually morose Mormon smiled boyishly and said, "Not now. I'm in, if that's the way we sporting bloods are supposed to say it."

Longarm allowed that was close enough, and they shook on it. As soon as they'd turned the mess over to the deputy coroner and toted the captain's baggage back to the hotel, they strode over to D Street and had no trouble finding Madame Dumont's house of ill repute. It had pale lilac siding with strawberry trim and an orange front door. Her picket fence was the same shade of strawberry, and her garden was a cactus collection it would be worth a burglar's very balls to pussyfoot across after dark.

The rest of the time, a fat Mex sat in a rocking chair on the porch with a Spencer .52 repeater and a benign expression.

He just shrugged when the two lawmen mounted the steps and declared their intentions of interviewing the madame.

The front door opened, and the colored maid in a fifi outfit, who'd surely been watching for them, invited them in, saying madame had been expecting them.

Madame Dumont was a surprise. She hadn't waited until she was too old and fat to serve her customers before she'd set up her own whorehouse to own and operate. She couldn't have been more than thirty, with a partly natural hourglass figure she flaunted in a bustier of flamingo satin and black lace. Her hair, piled atop her head as if on a lady of fashion, was the same strawberry shade as her fence out front, only silkier. One got the impression Madame Dumont had a love of bright colors.

Waving the two lawmen to plush seats with her long, German-silver cigarette holder, Madame Dumont planted her shapely bottom on another, crossed her exposed mesh stockings, and declared, "I knew no good would come of poor Lil's romantic shit. If I've told my girls once, I've told them a thousand times: there's nothing wrong with selling what all men want for what all women want, the good things in life. There's nothing wrong with falling in love. Everyone's entitled, even working girls. But you just can't mix giving your love and selling your ass. It's not natural. You can fuck a man and make him pay you. You can love a man and slave to send him through medical school. You can't love a man and expect him to pay you for loving him. It's a counter fiction of barns!"

Longarm suggested, "Contradiction in terms is what I suspect you mean, Madame Dumont. In any case, I follow your drift and agree with you. So this French Lil who . . . worked here fell in love with somebody?"

The lady of the whorehouse made a wry face and said, "She answered a newspaper proposal from some total nitwit seeking to order a wife by mail the way you send away for

273

ten easy ways to become rich and famous by some bird you never heard of, who's getting rich selling worthless advice to suckers. Lil wrote this bald old bird raising beef up Idaho way she was a recently widowed young woman of fashion, looking for a distinguished gent who could support her in the the manner to which she had become accustomed, serving teamsters all three ways for two dollars.

Longarm soberly observed, "Those are the chances a man takes when he sends away for anything sight unseen. Some of the women who responded to such offers seemed to have been sold a bill of goods by long distance as well."

Captian Burbank cleared his throat and awkwardly proposed, "Whether or not one approves or disapproves of a . . . woman with a past presenting herself as something a little more . . . acceptable, nobody has the right to waylay them on their way to delight or disappoint a lovelorn loon and blame it on the Church of Jesus Christ of Latter-day Saints or even Islam!"

Longarm said, "We've been over that. Pointing suspicion at others known to have unsual views on marriage was a ruse. Stage magicians call that sort of flimflam *misdirection.* Direct the chump to look somewheres you ain't doing nothing." Turning back to Madame Dumont, he asked if French Lil had return-addressed her love letters from a D Street house of . . . no offense.

Madame Dumonet laughed and said, "None taken. I run a nice clean whorehouse, and I'm not ashamed of it. Of course that two-faced Lil never sent or recieved mail with this address on it. She belonged to this lonely hearts club. A bunch of like-minded cunts with mighty high opinions on themselves."

Both lawmen perked up. Longarm asked if the madame knew how to get in touch with the late French Lil's fellow club members. Mayhaps to tell them she'd just died.

The brazen but sort of likable whore laughed and said, "They know. Everyone in town knows. You shot her on the fucking railroad tracks. But after that, I just can't tell you who Lil had forwarding and recieving those love letters for her. I know she got some, with money in 'em. She laughed like hell when she showed 'em to the other girls!"

The brassy strawberry blonde who sold ring-dang-doo for what she considered an honest living frowned like a little girl viewing a dead robin on the walk and added, "I thought that was mean. Not asking a man for money. Laughing at him when he sent you money. It didn't seem fair, somehow."

They thanked her for such help as she'd given, and all three rose to part friendly. As she held out her hand, Longarm took hold of it to raise it to his lips and kiss it. She blushed beet red all over and called him a sweet asshole.

Out on the walk. Longarm sheepishly told Burbank, "Don't ask. You wouldn't understand."

The stern-faced Mormon replied, "Don't have to ask. Do understand. She'd have made a greater lady than that beautiful but dumb princess of Wales if fate had dealt her as fair a hand. Where do we go from here?"

Longarm said, "There you go asking those tough questions again. I told 'em at the Western Union to send any messages coming in for me tonight to our hotel. Let's go see if I got any."

He had, along with a perfumed envelope with just his name on it and no return address. The perfume smelled like night-blooming jasmine.

He opened it, scanned the contents, and found he wasn't that surprised. The wire from Yuma said there had indeed been a hat shop run by Carmen Culhane at that address until she'd sold it in March. But the wire from Helena said they had no assay office there owned and operated by a Norman MacLean.

The one from Billy Vail said to get his ass on home if he hadn't cracked the case by the end of April Stop Deleted by Western Union.

Burbank aksed, "What's wrong? You don't look too cheerful."

Longarm shrugged and said, "Sure I do. We're fixing to be on our way home during the merry month of May, and I just got invited to a tryst."

"A what?" blinked the Utah man.

Longarm said, "I read too much. In romantical novels, a tryst is when you sneak off to meet a gal alone on a balcony, under a weepy willow tree, like Romeo met Juliet that time."

"Someone here in San Bernardino has invited you to a setup like that?"

Longarm shrugged and said, "I'm packing a six-gun and my sneaky old double derringer. That ought to give me an edge on young Romeo."

Chapter 40

They met of all places in the shaded churchyard of the local LDS church, about the last place gossips would expect a Spanish green brunette to tryst with an Anglo. The grass was still alive between the wide-spaced grave markers of a fairly young church. It was closed for the weekday night and heavily shaded by those California pepper trees that looked like willows but grew in drier soil. The pretty apple-green leaves smelled like black pepper when you crushed 'em. The whole yard smelled like a spice shop.

Inez Robles Verdugo Montez y Montoya was dressed in black Spanish lace indeed, with her pretty face half covered until he joined her, and she moved her mantilla out of the way of her radiant smile.

She said, "Custis, I was so worried when we heard what happened down by the railroad. That older one with the henna-rinsed hair, Theresa Mondale, she *stayed* with us back in February or early March! She said she was waiting for transportation, like those others! That's all we heard, or all *I* heard, at least! Have you been able to learn anything else about her since this afternoon?"

He steered her toward a marble bench in deeper shade as he replied, "We found out the woman with her was a denizen of D Street. You never met her, right?"

Inez repressed a shudder and confided, "That's what we

heard. And to think they almost killed you. Why do you think they were trying to kill you, Custis?"

He braced himself on the backless bench with one hand gripping cool marble behind her shapely derriere and said, "A fuzzy picture is commencing to emerge from the mists. There was a lot of mist floating around from the beginning. The three of us talked about those mail-order brides and how little trusting souls seemed to need to know before they ran blind down the tunnel of love. Just got two telegraph wires that make no sense at all until you study on 'em. You remember that lonesome Carmen Culhane I told you about, the one who sold her hat shop in Yuma to take a wagon train out of here with a final destination of Helena, Montana, in mind?"

She nodded, and he continued, "Call me suspicious natured, but I ran a check on her tale of woe. A Carmen Culhane did have such a hat shop in Yuma. She wasn't the one I met aboard the train. She was somebody else who knew a respectable lady by that name had sold out and left Yuma. So she chose to be her, on her way to marry up with good old Norm in Helena."

She didn't resist; she snuggled closer as Longarm's arm somehow wound up around her waist. She soberly said, "How awful for the poor man! She was a fortune hunter out to trap him by pretending to be this Carmen Culhane, right?"

He said, "Wrong. They made him up to fool me. She and another slick actress who had to be a slick actress if she'd thought hats in a shop that had been sold were adorable were waiting for me in Yuma. They met up with me aboard the train on purpose to feed me more red herrings. An earlier sneak had already tried to cast suspicion on a gruff but honest wagon master. The whole charade aboard that train was aimed at making me look closer at the poor old innocent cuss, or failing that, try to figure out who a missing mail-order bride had him mixed up with. They did pretty good. They got me to take the Banning Stage all the way up to Barstow."

He snuggled her closer, brushing her hair with his mustache as he said, "They should have quit whilst they were ahead. Running me all the way out to Barstow wasn't as uncomfortable a trip as they'd meant it to be on muleback. As I rode that way-swifter coach, it came to me how the one calling her lying self Winnie Mae Waterman appeared to disappear from that wagon train she wired she was traveling with."

Inez had one arm around Longarm's waist as she asked, "How did she manage that vanishing act?"

He said, "Aw, it wasn't all that slick. It just looked slick until I'd ridden out there and saw how easy it was. She never left here with those wagons. She rode out aboard the Banning Stage to wire she was there with them. It didn't matter whether they were in town at the time or not. Everyone knew they'd passed through Barstow by the time we got to looking for her. We had to look for her because she simply rode back to San Berdoo, aboard the same coach line, and vanished by train to wherever she went with all that travel money her sucker sent her."

Inez gasped. "I see what you're getting at! All those missing women had been sent *money* through the mails to pay their way to their true loves, and then you think someone robbed them? Is that the motive for all this mysterious business?"

He said, "Not hardly. Let's back up and study on just what's been going on."

She murmured, "Hold me closer, I'm frightened! Maybe you shouldn't be telling me all this, with no end of . . . killers still at large!"

He said, "All right. You want to go on over to E Street for some ice cream, or would you rather I just walk you home?"

She grabbed his thigh and held on as she protested, "Now you're out to tease me, Custis! You know I won't sleep a wink tonight unless I know at last what's been going on!"

He said, *"Bueno,* in the beginning there were all these fools of both sexes, carrying on like bashful teenagers through the U.S. mails."

She sniffed and opined, "Poor simps!"

He said, "Whatever. My point is that most of those poor simps were sincere. Most of the gals from all over heading all over to marry up and live to regret it or live happy ever after take the money, use it to get there, and that's all the law ever hears of them. But just as each and every card house attracts a number of cheats, this mail-order marriage stuff attracted less desperate and less honest crooks. It was easy to start a romance with a few fibbing letters. It was easy get the lovesick loners to send money, more than one, if one knew how to write convincing fiction. But of course, after you've milked a man dry and he hasn't had a kiss to show for it, he commences to ask questions and, knowing how using the mails to defraud is a federal crime, they didn't want anybody backtracking those begging love letters to their return addresses, so they very stupidly decided to let the mail-order brides start out for wherever and just vanish on their way to their weddings."

"Why was that more stupid?" she asked.

He said, "You're setting with it. Had the mail inspectors backtracked the begging letters to transient hotels or even post office boxes not being paid for anymore, they'd have put out a mail fraud alert and mayhaps the lonely loons would have noticed and maybe they wouldn't have. But whilst mail fraud is one thing, mass murder across state lines is taken serious. They noticed how serious once the papers commenced to write up that big, windy congressional investigation. Someone in the gang had heard of me by rep, and that's why Trixie fooled me before I up and scared her into tipping her mitt. The men escorting her and what I suspect was a former business associate will no doubt turn out to be the knock-around hairpins such ladies recruit as escorts cum bodyguards. Neither was good enough to be throwing down on trained lawmen. So tell me something. Whose grand notion was it to put that bee about corpses riding all over creation in wagons in that nice old lady's head?"

Inez gasped, "How should I know? I've never met this Buckskin Jacobs everyone was so supicious of. You surely don't think poor dear Anna Maria was mixed up in all this mail fraud, do you?"

He soberly replied, "Not hardly. She may be down on her luck in her declining years, but she's quality. Just can't see the respected widow of such a well-known and well-respected husband sinking low as writing begging love letters, or condoning it if she knew anyone under her roof was up to such . . . stuff. She may have been forced to let rooms in that proud old house. But I'd hazard a guess her only serious flaw is a trusting nature. When did I tell you one of the wagon masters we suspected was Buckskin Jacobs, Miss Inez?"

She stammered, "Didn't you? I must have heard Anna Maria mention him. When she was talking about dead bodies packed in wagon beds and all."

He said, "That must be it. That's how come you knew who I was talking about when I asked if you recalled that Carmen Culhane I'd talked about. Where might they be this evening, Miss Inez? I wired and wired all over the San Fernando valley, and nobody there could suggest a funeral for her and Miss Mabel to 'tend just now."

She snapped, "How am I supposed to know? I never laid eyes on the old bat!"

Longarm smiled gently and asked, "Did I *describe* Mabel Flagg as an old bat, or as anything at all? You're just digging yourself in deeper, honey. Fess up, and I might be able to put in a good word for you. And no way you're getting out of it. You have to be the mastermind who put it all together and complicated all our lives by piling lie upon lie up to where what started out a simple flimflam wound up a congressional investigation."

She leaned closer, threw both arms around him, and hooked a thigh over his as she husked, "How good a word for me, Custis? You yourself said it was over. We made our little score, and nobody's been hurt!"

He gently but firmly disengaged himself as he asked, "What do you call them bodies in your town morgue, fallen apples? If it hadn't been them, it would have been me! You gals play rough for this child, honey!"

She pleaded, "That wasn't my idea. I ordered Trixie to try to lead you astray, not to assassinate you! I'm glad you won! They had it coming and . . . speaking of coming . . ."

Longarm laughed and said, "You really do think men are made of putty, don't you? If I was cruel as women are always accusing, I'd take you up on your attempt to compromise your arresting officer. Some gal you were locked up with somewhere, sometime, told you no lawman can arrest a gal after he's fucked her, right?"

She gasped, "Custis, must you put it so crudely? I'll admit I've been taken by you since first we met, but—"

"But bullshit!" he snapped, kissing her hard, French, and enjoying it before he shook her like a wayward child and said, "I'm trying to be a gentleman. So listen tight you little slut! I've got you dead to rights. Even as we speak, wires are still coming in to tie up the loose ends. So I don't need you to help me wrap this up, but like I said, I'll say you did if and when you do. Neither fucking me nor sucking me will get you out of my arresting you. But we got time for some slap and tickle if you like. You ain't going to get laid again for some time."

She snapped, "Fuck you!"

He sighed and said, "If only I could, I'd no doubt fall in love with myself. Either way, you are under arrest, Inez Robles Verdugo Montez y Montoya, on the charges of using the mails to defraud, falsely reporting crimes and, shucks, we'll think of lots of stuff by the time you come to trial."

She snarled, not a pretty sound, and said, "A lot you know, you fool! Have you been listening to all this *mierda, mi muchacho?*"

When a gruff voice softly grunted, *"Sí,"* she snapped, "Then what are you *muchachos* waiting for? We've heard enough! Finish it!"

But nothing happened for a spell. Then Captain Burbank and a senior deputy of the San Bernardino force moved out into better light to join them, as Longarm asked, "How'd I do, pard?"

The normally morose Mormon was grinning as he replied, "Just the way you suggested you might. You ought to consider a career on the wicked stage if ever this gets tedious for you, Longarm."

Inez protested, "I don't understand! What is going on here? Where is Luis? Where is my Hernando?"

The town lawman, who knew her, said, "We carted them off to jail before you got here, Miss Inez. This federal man said he figured you meant to do to him what he just done to

281

you. Only you meant to kill him instead of arresting him, once he told you all he knew."

"Cocksucker!" she bayed like a she wolf.

So, seeing she had nothing nice to say, they frog-marched her off to jail, and while she hung tough, her young Mex toughs proved willing to testify against a wicked older woman who'd led them astray.

Within forty-eight hours, the Yuma law had picked up the self-styled Carmen Culhane and Mabel Flagg, living as mother and daughter under other names.

Longarm had figured they were Yuma residents when they weren't out on the owl-hoot trail because they'd known about the real Carmen Culhane selling her hat shop and moving away before they decided to be her and a Yuma visitor who'd back her story.

Lesser lights would be rounded up over the months to come as those arrested busted their guts trying to turn state's evidence.

In all, there would prove to be far less than the score of women who seemed to be missing. Like the professional deserters who joined up for the bounty to light off before anybody put them to work at anything, the ring of jaded whores, weary waitresses, and a couple of housewives who just wanted the extra money had doubled up, playing more than one sucker at a time and hence having to appear to vanish six or eight times in one case.

In the end, the attempt to cover up their petty, vicious confidence game was going to earn them far more jail time than it might have, had they known enough to just call it a night and go home as soon as things commenced to get messy.

The minor male members of the ring panned out as a pair of Mexican stock thieves and some pimps with delusions of grandeur.

After he'd gotten back to Denver the easy way, by steam instead of mule power, as the majority of real mail-order brides had traveled, he was watching the banjo clock on the wall of Billy Vail's office, wishing it would hurry up and be the old fart's suppertime, when Vail put his official report down at last to beam and say, "You did good, considering how little you did. Had not it been for those detours at the cost of way more dangerous crooks, your whole blamed mission would have been a waste of the taxpayers' money."

He reached in a drawer as he added, "Wiping out that Turk the Turks had no use for and freeing all them Chinee tickled the Chinee consulate pink as a baby's asshole. President Hayes just vetoed that Chinese Exclusion Act again. But we all know sooner or later Congress is going to pass it over any veto. So the dowager empress is on the prod about insults to any son of Han and pleased as punch whenever one of us long-nosed devils does right by any. So they've asked me to present you with this medal."

He handed it over. Longarm stared down in disbelief at what looked to be a gilt demitasse saucer embossed with funny lettering and a dragon.

He laughed and asked, "Where am I supposed to wear this? Down to the Jade Garden on Larimer Street?"

Vail said, "It's solid gold, at twenty dollars an ounce."

Longarm said, "In that case, I'd best accept, lest I insult her imperial majesty."

IN THIS GIANT-SIZED ADVENTURE, AN OUTLAW LEARNS THAT HE'S SAFER IN HIS GRAVE THAN FACING AN AVENGING ANGEL NAMED LONGARM.

0-515-13547-X